VOICES THROUGH THE WINDOW

WAYNE STOLT

THE GHOST PUBLISHING, LLC

Praise for Wayne Stolt

"If you care deeply about people and the American Dream, then put this book on your reading list. Stolt eloquently details a heartwarming story of a young Yemeni family's immigration, finding enlightenment and freedom through local Christian mission teams."

— Faten Fawaz- Award-winning Educator (Retired)

Voices through the Window is an exciting read that gives you an inside look at an Immigrant family's first months and years in America, the importance of relationships and community, and most importantly faith. I highly recommend this engaging story for anyone struggling with or thinking about how to welcome and engage those from different countries and faiths.

As Christians we are called to love the stranger and this amazing story gives great insights into how to do just that. As a Christ follower and professional religious worker for over 16 years I found this to be the perfect blend of a great read and helpful insights on our call to make disciples of all nations and to love the foreigner (Immigrants). I highly recommend this book to anyone wanting to understand the perspective and experiences of those coming to this country for the first time!

— Matt Hutch craft

Voices through the Window is a heartwarming and uplifting story of a Muslim family as they travel to America and their struggles as they find and follow Jesus as their Lord and Savior. As a Pastor and Missionary, I appreciate how he showed the dedication of the Christians that walked with them during their transformation into followers of Christ. I recommend this book as a must-read for every Christian as one pathway to befriend a Muslim, showing simplicity in the process and the success at the end.

— Ronald C. Epperson Pastor/Evangelist
President and Co-Founder Reaching and
Discipling, Inc. Detroit, Michigan

Wayne Stolt is a master storyteller. Intriguing in his method he gently weaves the life story of Arab immigrants Aisha and Abdul toward a wonderful conclusion. There is a great love that is inclusive if we only seek it. God doesn't see the divisions and restrictions we place on ourselves and our relationships. His is a love that reaches out to all.

— Ken Wasco - Retired Marketing Executive,
public speaker, doer

Wayne Stolt has done it again! In his excellent show of write-what-you-know, the author of *Voices Through the Window* lays out his message for Arab immigrants and local missionaries, (both of which he is very familiar) in an entertaining and informative way. Stolt skillfully weaves two timelines to tell the story of the geographical journey of a Yemeni family to the U.S. and the paralleling spiritual journey to the Promised Land of the Lord's church. The plot is superb, the story is inspiring, and the ending is worth your reading time!

— Wissam Al-Aethawi – Preacher

The novel *Voices through the Window* was a fascinating journey for me. It's an educational, inspirational, and motivational novel. Wayne Stolt is able to make readers understand how difficult it is for a Muslim to convert to Christianity. At the same time, Wayne emphasized that, the Holy Spirit can remove the obstacles and ease all our challenges.

— Adam Jamal Adam

© 2022

All rights are reserved as the sole property of the author. The author guarantees all content is original and does not infringe upon the legal rights of any other person or work. No part of this publication may be reproduced, stored in a retrieval system, or transmitted in any form or by any means, electronic, mechanical, photocopying, recording, or otherwise without the prior permission of the author or in accordance with the provisions of the Copyright, Designs, and Patents Act 1988, or under the terms of any license permitting limited copying issued by the Copyright Licensing Agency.

Unless otherwise identified, Scripture is taken from the New International Version, ©1998, 1989, 1990, 1991 by Tyndale House Publishers, Inc., Wheaton, IL, 60189. Published by Zondervan, Grand Rapids, Michigan, 49530. All rights reserved.

Author: Wayne Stolt

Editors: Eli Gonzalez and Christine James

Cover Design: Amanda Murray

Published by: The Ghost Publishing, LLC

Paperback ISBN-13 (Amazon): 979-8-9863992-6-3

Paperback ISBN-13 (Ingram): 978-1-0880-4987-7

Hardback ISBN-9798846393431

Will —
"A long time friend; God continue to bless you!"

This story is dedicated to the Arab immigrant who comes to America for more than a piece of the American Dream, but many of whom endeavor to embrace and acclimate to it.
Also, to the local mission teams in Dearborn that seek to find creative and innovative ways to share the Good News of Jesus.
Lastly, to my wife and friend, Patricia Stolt.

PROVERBS 26:3

God's peace in Christ's play, in God's Word

Voices Through the Window

The window is said to be a view into the soul.
How many windows does one have to reveal?
And how much does one open the window?
Maybe one would open with gusto, and freely for all to see and hear,
Or perhaps one would open only a bit for just a few voices to creep in,
Possibly partially open so a favored few may nimbly climb in.
If there is more than one window, and each is opened,
Then would there be chaos and a flurry of voices?
And does one cipher the caliber of truth among them?
Maybe a particular shrill demands attention,
While a trombone beats solemnly amid the shrill,
Or what is in the far corner, a still small voice I hear?

— Wayne Stolt

Chapter 1

Aisha

Dearborn Airport – DTW – Detroit, Michigan, U.S.A.

August 2003

This is so uncomfortable. Abdul, my husband, appears unfazed as I feel miserable, flying in the huge jet. Wedged into the narrow space provided, it was too small for both Aini and me, especially since I held her firmly in my lap. Despite the annoyed glances I'd endured from a man to my left, the cramped area I'd been allotted wasn't the main reason for my unease.

The captain's voice came over the tiny speaker above her head. He was making yet another announcement... something in English. I didn't understand part of it. It sounded like he was talking about the weather. Then he mentioned a word she recognized — "landing." I sighed and looked around in both relief and distress.

Our journey had begun in Yemen. Now, in just a few minutes, we would exit the plane and begin a new life in America. Abdul had insisted on this new life for our young family of four. I wasn't so certain. Fear gripped my heart. What if people treated us badly? What if they spat on us in the streets?

Aisha had worn her traditional Yemeni garb. There was barely enough room in the allotted space for their clothing, much less her and the child. Aisha's head was completely covered with a voluminous, red-print scarf; only her face was exposed. Her blouse covered her skin to her wrists, the skirt she wore extended to her ankles.

She knew her appearance would make her stand out among the Americans, who, if they were like the tourists she'd seen at home, typically wore baseball caps, shorts, and t-shirts. She was aware that many Americans behaved rudely toward anyone with Middle Eastern clothing and couldn't differentiate between countries. She'd been told that Americans assumed everyone from the Middle East was a terrorist and looked on them with fear and loathing.

The young mother of two sat next to her husband, who'd been still and silent throughout most of the plane ride. Earlier, they'd landed in Frankfurt, Germany, where some people left the plane and even more boarded. Now the plane was filled to capacity; many seemed to be either Europeans or Americans.

Again, she glanced at her husband, Abdul, for reassurance that they were minutes from landing, but he didn't meet her gaze. He busied himself by snapping his tray shut and then stuffing a magazine into the pocket of the seat. He was so intent on starting a new life for his family in America, but it was this new life that she was fearful of.

My mother had named me Aisha, which means a passionate woman who follows her heart. As of yet, especially in the early years of marriage, there had been little spontaneity in life—it was more like following my husband's heart. I sighed to myself, knowing what was expected of me: obedience, meekness, unending labor. Her husband, according to tradition, would always have the final word in any decision.

Abdul reached for the laptop his father had given him and held it to his chest in preparation for exiting the plane. Aisha patted his arm and he nodded but continued to stare at the seat in front of him.

Aini fussed. Aisha recognized the beginning of a crying episode. *Tired of being held. She wants freedom... so do I.*

The man on her left made an angry noise in his throat. Aisha quietly sang an old song her mother had taught her, hoping it would calm the baby girl.

The huge jet jerked about, then quickly dropped several feet. Aisha drew her breath in sharply. She noticed that a few women on the plane even shrieked. *So, I am not so different from these Americans.* The plane then settled down.

The pilot made another announcement. "Sorry folks, we've experienced a bit of turbulence… we'll be landing shortly."

I understood most of his words, but turbulence *was unknown. I'll try to remember the word and find out what it means.*

She bent, kissed her daughter's dark, wavy hair, and looked past the American to see out the window. The wingtips fluttered as the plane started its descent. She couldn't help but wonder, once again, if this was the best decision for their family. They'd been uprooted from home and her family, then flown halfway around the world to live among Abdul's family—people she didn't know.

Abdul was thirty years old and proud of the Ph.D. he had earned from a university. His family had sent him away for a good education in England. His name meant *servant of God*, but he was subtle in showing it. He refrained from making overt comments about his education versus her incomplete one, and he rarely mentioned that his family had more money than hers. His words were well chosen, and yet still showed he was the man in the marriage. He had made the decision for the family to go to Michigan. Aisha had merely been informed of his decision. He had connections—his uncle and cousin were in the United States.

Who do I know? Two children and a husband, of course, but then, who else? No one.

Her baby, Aini, cuddled in her arms, sobbed softly into her shoulder. *She needs a nap. I became distracted and stopped singing.* She patted Aini's back, soothing her. Ten-year-old Habib watched with wide eyes as the city appeared below. Aisha pulled her hijab closer, and with a shaky hand, tucked stray strands of hair back inside it.

In Yemen, when I had problems, I would talk to Mama and my aunts. They would listen and nod, and then I'd ask their advice on how to please Abdul. There were no simple answers from them.

Now I feared it wouldn't be any easier. Would life really be better here in America as Abdul said? The land of dreams was here, but all I'd had more restless nights thinking of it. Abdul impatiently tapped his fingers on his laptop, still held to his chest. The incessant strumming reminds me of Grandfather's gambus, a type of lute he played late at night.

Abdul stretched his neck to see out the window, trying to see the city. The beat of his fingers increased, going faster and faster as the ground seemed to rise to meet them. The plane shook again, and she started to shiver suddenly. Aisha could not seem to control her anxiety.

I have never been on a plane before, and I've heard of horrible crashes. My eyes closed tightly, and I waited for death to claim us.

A man in the next row whispered, "Safe and sound... see, Honey?" The wheels touched the pavement. They had landed. The older woman sighed loudly.

Abdul continued tapping. *Why hadn't he comforted her like the American husband had?* Aisha's shivering stopped and the baby quieted. She whispered a thankful prayer to Allah for their safe arrival, and that the baby was calm.

As the plane approached the gate, Aisha sat quietly looking around. The elderly couple in the seats ahead of them had looked back behind them a few times, and Aisha had caught the woman's eyes. Her eyes darted around the plane, but often landed on Aisha. When their eyes met, the woman quickly looked away. Aisha wondered why she stared so much. Waiting to be allowed to stand, Aisha gazed at the woman and contemplated her.

Had they not seen many Arab families before?

Finally, the line of people in front of them completed the retrieval of their bags. Her husband stood, roughly handled their two overhead bags, and set them on an empty seat. Under his breath, he mumbled an old saying about the importance of hurrying. People behind them waited, many of them talking on their cell phones. Abdul took a moment to brush a gentle hand over his daughter's mouth, trying to keep her from an outburst that might embarrass him.

"Habib, you are nearly a man. You should have been preparing to depart the plane." Abdul's voice was unnecessarily harsh when he spoke to the boy. "Gather your books. We leave."

Another family, a row behind them, now waited while Abdul organized his family and their belongings. The other toddler had cried frequently throughout the trip. Aisha thought of her daughter who'd barely fussed at all. She kissed the top of the girl's head, proud of her ability to cope at such a young age.

The other parents had chided their boy, cooed to him, fed him, and even read stories during the trip. None of it seemed to help. Now the toddler waved his arms, stretching forward, full of energy. The child's eyes sparkled when he reached forward to touch Aini's toes. She smiled at the young boy, but his mother pushed his hand away and spoke sharply to him. She pulled him closer to her chest, turned her body around, and gathered her bulky purse with her free hand.

She didn't look our way, but whispered, "Excuse me."

Her husband tapped her on the shoulder, hushing her. Then, the family moved toward the front of the plane.

Abdul glared at their backs while handing Aisha the bag for the baby. He pulled her purse down from above them and placed it in her hand.

They moved into the aisle and headed to the exit, not unlike a train of pack animals passing through a small town in Yemen. The young son burped with a sheepish grin, and the baby girl gurgled and spat up milk on her mama's shoulder.

"Our little train," Aisha said, only loud enough for her husband to hear. He responded by shaking his head and looking impatient. They moved past the rows of seats taking small steps. Aisha struggled to carry the baby along with her bags. Abdul focused on his laptop and his bag as he nudged their son up the aisle.

"You have a herdsman quality in your heritage. I see it in how you move our son along," Aisha said, then chuckled. *I wonder if I should have asked his mother more specific questions about their family tree.* He glanced back at her, and she stopped smiling. She looked away in embarrassment and pulled her hijab closer. *I should be more careful with what I think of Abdul. We were joined together, and I should show him the respect due him. It is what the Qur'an tells me to do, and Mama often said as much.*

The small caravan continued to bump into nearly every seat until they finally reached the front of the plane. The stewardess was very pleasant and professional. Her eyes lacked any judgment about them, and she smiled at each passenger. Her kindness showed when she bent down and handed the boy a small toy airplane. She patted Aisha on the shoulder and whispered a blessing for her from God. There was a small holdup, and it gave Aisha a moment to meet the woman's eyes.

"Thank you," Aisha said softly and smiled.

"We should go quickly, my love," Abdul said in Arabic as he shouldered his way around the airline stewardess.

The long ramp was quite a hike, made harder with leg muscles left stiff from hours of sitting. It didn't help that Aini cried louder.

Aisha said a silent prayer as Abdul tried to keep the family moving at a quick pace. They stopped upon entering the terminal. There was a crowd of people, both sitting and standing near their gate. People looked at the clock, most likely determining how long they must wait. They looked at Abdul and Aisha as if the immigrant family were to blame for the plane being late. They saw subtle, angry looks from people as they stood there.

"Is it the wait that bothers them or who we were when we all got off the plane?" Abdul asked, more to himself. "Where is my cousin? I thought he'd certainly be here to meet us."

He looked around. People who'd exited planes were moving as a large group down the corridor. No one hugged or greeted others. "Perhaps others are not allowed this far."

"I don't know, husband. I hope they are pleased with me and are happy we are here," Aisha said, then pointed at the travel-weary passengers. "They seem to know where they're going."

They followed the crowd, searching the faces for Abdul's cousin, Mohammed.

Aisha thought back to many years before. *Mohammed was much younger than Abdul and lived in a nearby village. He was loud and noisy as only a young boy could be. He irritated the girls by kicking the ball he always brought along. His endless chatter often frustrated Aisha. Could he not remain silent for one moment? Once, Mohammed jumped in her path while she was jumping rope with her friend. She gave him a verbal lashing. Would those memories create a barrier now?*

"Abdul! Abdul! Thank Allah you are here. It is so good to see you, my cousin!" Mohammed shouted through the crowd in Arabic. When they met, he laughed, and tears of joy ran down his cheeks. Mohammed and Abdul hugged each other fiercely.

Look at their strong bond. It is obvious their relationship had grown when Abdul worked here a year ago. He'd only been here three months, but they greeted each other like long, lost brothers.

After a few minutes, Abdul pulled away and pointed to Habib. "This is my son. He has asked about you quite a bit, Mohamed. Say 'hello' to Mohammed, my baba." Abdul squeezed their son's shoulder lightly as Mohammed bent over to look the boy in the eye.

"Hello, you strong looking young man! How are you?" Mohammed squatted next to the boy.

"Hello, Amo," Habib said. He tried to stand taller and broaden his shoulders. The worry of a new country in a large, uncomfortable airport seemed to slide down his back as he straightened up. He seemed to mature in a flash.

"I'm doing most excellent, Amo! Good, good, very good." Mohammed spoke rapidly.

After ten minutes of hurried walking, they all stopped when they saw a large sign above a long queue of passengers. Mohammed pointed at the sign, waved at the lines of people, and shook his head. Then he brought them all together in a circle for a meeting.

"Listen, I wasn't really supposed to meet you here." Mohammed laughed. "But I explained to the officials that you do not understand English, although Abdul understands it fairly well. I had to convince TSA that you depended on my translation at customs, and it was the only way I could meet you at the gate." He looked only at Aini for a moment, and then at each of them. His gaze stopped at Aisha. She knew her nervousness was evident in her eyes and immediately dropped her gaze.

"This will be no problem," he said, smiling broadly. "I have many friends who live near my home in Dearborn. They have not had any problems coming through immigration, nor were there any problems with the questions."

"Let's get in line over there." Mohammed pointed to a line of people under the sign that read "Immigration."

Mohammed talks with such confidence. Aisha looked around; her eyes wide. *What if they refuse us?*

Abdul pulled his family along to the line. At the front of the line stood a middle-aged man, continuously talking.

Abdul turned to Mohammed and spoke, his voice low. "What is he doing?"

Mohammed followed Abdul's gaze. "Oh, nothing. He just tells everyone to have their passports and paperwork ready, so it moves more quickly."

Abdul nodded. "I am ready. I have spent many hours preparing for this day."

Aisha saw her husband straighten to appear taller and was attempting to show confidence, but she saw his giveaway; he tapped one foot, a sure sign of nervousness she'd seen many times. As they waited, Aisha noticed a few families being taken out of line and down a hall. She tried to watch and see where they stopped.

As she watched, a door opened and a family—a couple with two children—filed out into the main room. The woman's head drooped with obvious disappointment. The man's fist kept opening and closing. *He is angry… like he wants to hit someone.* The woman began sobbing. Aisha heard the mother's heart-wrenching anguish even over the noise of so many people talking.

An official came through the door and steered the family in Aisha's direction.

The woman pulled her hijab tighter and gathered her children close to her while they walked.

They passed within a few feet of Aisha. She heard the official clear his throat. She guessed that he was rejecting their admission to America and was about to offer his final words.

"Sir, here are the documents we discussed. Again, it is unfortunate that your paperwork was not correct." The official, a gray-haired man, handed a file folder to the immigrant. "You can try to correct the insufficiencies and re-apply for entry."

"Yes. *Insha Allah*," the man mumbled.

"An officer will escort you to another room where they will review your next steps. You will be able to contact your family who are waiting elsewhere. The officer will also discuss the deportation steps." The lanky officer shifted from one foot to the other. "Ah, here he is."

Another uniformed man joined the group and the older official turned to walk away.

"This is not easy on families." The second official directed his words to the son of the group. "But we will help you work through this. Perhaps you may return when your papers are complete. Please follow me."

The children clung to their mother's skirts. She continued to sob, keeping her face averted from the official.

Aisha felt shaken to her bones. *This could be us. We could be turned away.* She continued to watch the family until they disappeared around a corner. Her group moved forward a few steps. She was sure that the disastrous outcome of the deported family was known throughout the line. *Anxiety threatens to overwhelm me. Are we doing the right thing?* She glanced toward Abdul, but his face maintained a constant resolve. *I'm afraid. Fear grips my heart like a fist squeezes it with an iron grip. Will my children even be safe here?*

"Hey, my friend. It will all be over in a little while," Mohammed said to her. "Don't let fear show in your face. There is nothing to be afraid of. You are here to join in the dream of America that so many people have come for. That is what you say to their questions."

Aisha nodded to him, but still lacked the certainty that he and Abdul obviously felt.

After twenty or thirty minutes, the family reached the area for immigration and were directed to a cubicle. Abdul handed the paperwork for the whole family to Mohammed, who then turned to the officer and smiled broadly. Mohammed handed each set of papers to the officer.

Habib, the son who has seemed to stand so tall before, had now lost his growth spurt. *He looks so small, and a little afraid.* Perhaps he had picked up on the fear in Aisha's eyes after watching the family be escorted away.

Mohammed spoke slowly, to interpret, as Abdul spoke rapidly to explain each document. The officer nodded and read through each document, one by one, after each explanation. Then he shuffled back to the first one and again to the second. This time he wore a frown on his face. He motioned to a nearby officer.

Aisha's worst fears were about to be realized. Her eyes darted around. *All these people will witness our shame.* They were escorted down the hall by a younger man. He smiled at all of them, patted the son on the head lightly, and winked at their daughter. She stared at him. His voice sounded calm, reassuring even. Was this how people were treated before they were refused entry into America?

The nice American officer led them down another hall. This hall had no doors or windows, only a tan-colored, blank wall. It looked bleak and unnerving, like the sandstorms that would occasionally stir up back home in their local village. She remembered hiding indoors from the incessant, swirling sand. *Will we have to get back on a plane and return home to our village? Will we all be placed in some detention facility while more paperwork is completed, or will they soon allow us to leave this airport and be driven to Dearborn with Mohammed?*

Finally, a door opened at the end of the hallway. There was a very small window at the top, just big enough for prisoners to see out. *Will that room be big enough to hold all of us? How long will we be detained?*

As the family neared the door, an authoritative man's voice could be heard asking questions over the phone. He asked them in a rapid-fire voice, like the men who practiced shooting in Aisha's home village. He might have said things like *food* or *lunch*, but Abdul, Mohammed, and Aisha looked at each other and shrugged.

Then the security agent held the door as the family filed in. Abdul confidently walked in first with Mohammed only a few steps behind him. Both walked with heads held high, unworried. Abdul pushed his hair back behind his ears and thrust out his hand to shake the officer's hand with the greeting he had practiced.

"Good afternoon, sir." Abdul greeted the officer with his accented English. "This is my family with me. My cousin, Mohammed, who lives nearby in Dearborn, and my children are right behind him. My wife, also; her name is Aisha."

He disrespects me. He didn't even look at me when he spoke. He thinks of me always last, and I do not understand why. Allah has made men different, but—

"It is nice to meet you, Abdul." The man had a deep, dry and smoky voice. He pushed away from the desk where he had been leaning while talking on the phone. He stood to shake Abdul's hand. "Quite the family you have here. They told you to bring the whole brood in to see me, did they?"

"Well, sir, they didn't tell us many details," Mohammed spoke up, putting his hand out to shake the man's hand also. "Our family was just sent this way."

"Well, you must be Uncle Fester, who *festered* his way into my office with this family." The officer shook Mohammed's hand as well and laughed at a joke that no one else seemed to get.

"Oh, no; I'm Abdul's cousin, Mohammed. I was only welcoming them into this great country. I'm just doing my best to see they are p-prepared to e-enter…" He stammered and his voice trailed off.

"Look, it's all right you are here. Just take the extra chair here and have a seat along the wall there while I talk to your cousin and his family." Mohammed dragged the chair, scraping the legs on the floor loudly until it reached the wall beneath a clock. The officer sighed deeply and returned to his chair. He leaned forward and placed his elbows on the desk, lacing his fingers together. He looked back at Mohammed and then returned his concentration to Abdul's family. His eyes started with Aisha, then down to Abdul, and finally rested his focus on Abdul.

"So, let me have everyone's papers, even the children," he said with a smile as he reached a hand out to Abdul. "This is really just a matter of protocol. Whole families that are coming into the states require full review and inspection." Leaning forward even more, he placed his right hand on the edge of the table, waiting for the documents. Abdul set them in the officer's waiting palm. They both looked at Aisha, and she shrugged her shoulders. No one had suggested she needed her documents out after the immigration line. She stepped over, kicked Mohammed's right foot lightly, and woke him, as he had started to fall asleep. She passed Aini to Mohammed, dug for her documents, and then handed her passport and visa to the officer.

"Oh, okay. Thanks," he said with a reassuring smile. "Just set yours right there, please. I will get to it in a moment. I was starting to review the men's documents." She was glad the officer smiled because her husband was frowning in her direction. *I wished my mother had prepared me how to love my husband even when he is displeased or frustrated. It's been almost seven years, and yet I still have not found a true balance in our relationship. Maybe I am too sensitive, and husbands are the same, but sometimes Abdul doesn't seem much like a servant of God.*

"Everyone's documents are in order. My question is regarding your passport. It seems it has expired, my friend."

"Oh, no, sir—not a problem!" Mohammed jumped up from his chair, still half asleep. "We have another."

"That's enough, Fester." The officer glanced at him. "Sit back down under the clock and relax. I'm asking your cousin."

"Mohammed is correct, sir. It is not a problem at all. I have only recently renewed my passport. I must have mistakenly brought both of them," Abdul explained quickly. Reaching for his briefcase, he brought it up to the desk. "Great pardons, sir, while I open my bag."

"Oh, it's no problem at all." The officer sighed. "It's only that my stomach has been complaining. But that's all right. It has had to wait before, and I'm sure it will again tomorrow. So, shuffle away through the filing system." Again, the officer seemed to laugh at his own jokes.

I wasn't quite sure what to think of the American sense of humor, or was it only this officer?

"Here it is, filed with 'important items,'" Abdul smiled slightly. That cleared the air for the family. *I sensed as we all breathed deeply. Even Aini gurgled.*

"Well, it looks like you folks are all cleared to enter at this stage of the process. Welcome to the United States!" The officer gathered up all of their papers.

I wasn't sure what all this meant, but I was happy that we didn't have to get back on another long plane ride.

"I should explain further, that, although I am clearing you now to enter America, you still have one more step where you will collect all your items from the plane to the baggage inspection area for Customs and Plant Protection processing." The officer stood up as he said this. "Look, everyone, I have worked that section of immigration before." He looked at all of us and smiled reassuringly. "You should have fewer questions than you did from this department."

Everyone smiled. Mohammed laughed as our family gathered together in the hallway. Abdul gave us all a group hug.

Perhaps now we are ready to enter Dearborn.

Chapter 2

Abdul

Dearborn, Michigan

The family completed processing at the airport. Mohammed directed them to the baggage claim while he left to retrieve the van from short-term parking. The family stood, staring at the carousel with mild amazement. Baby Aini giggled, while Habib intensely watched as families gathered their bags. Aisha slumped; her shoulders sagged. The time spent holding Aini, in addition to the stress with immigration, had worn her out. The baby dropped lower on her arm; Aini was tucked in a wrap, which was loosely hanging on.

As they waited for their luggage, Abdul noticed her fatigue.

"You are tired." Abdul motioned to Aisha. "Give her to me to hold. There is an empty seat over by the window. You should go sit down."

His words were supportive, but his thoughts were not.

Yes, it was a long flight, and then a connecting flight also. But I was the one to maneuver our bags when we changed flights. I did all of the talking in immigration. I don't understand why she looks so tired and stressed. I did all the planning for this trip. She had only to assist in gathering our family and care for the immediate needs of the children. Perhaps when we are at our new home in Dearborn with my family, she will become settled and calm.

"Flight 105, arriving from Dubai, is now unloading in Carousel Four. Please find your bags as they are unloaded and verify each item is yours before retrieving."

Abdul listened to the announcement, taking special note of the words "Dubai" and "Carousel Four." He watched as other passengers from his flight groaned and shuffled away. A man caught his eye. He'd been on the same plane from Sana'a International Airport and again on the connecting flight from Dubai. After exchanging glances, each man shrugged.

Carousel Four was two carousels away, and many had been waiting at the wrong one. Processing through immigration took so long; I would have thought our bags would be sitting on the floor by now, but others are waiting here, also. I would have thought the airlines would be more efficient with their instructions.

"Habib, follow me and find a seat near your mama," Abdul tapped his son on the head. "You will hold your sister. She really likes to sit on your leg like it is a camel ride."

They reached the seating area.

"Aisha, my love, Habib will sit with you. Our luggage will be ready soon, and we can leave for Dearborn." Abdul leaned in to hug her, then handed Aini to Habib.

"Abdul, you haven't got your bags yet. What is the holdup?" Mohammed hurried in, still trying to catch his breath. "I thought you would have been waiting for me outside."

"No, cousin. Waiting more and more here. It is what yesterday and today have been all about. Now we are to move to carousel number four," Abdul sighed.

"Come. I will help you. We should hurry," Mohammed blurted out. "My mother has called me and told me to hurry. She has a feast,

Yemeni style, waiting in our home in Dearborn, and I have left the van in the parking garage. They charge by the minutes."

The men collected all their bags and found a cart to transport them. They stacked the six suitcases carefully and went to gather the family. Abdul and Mohammed tried to entice them with the special dinner to come.

Suddenly, the group stopped. Mohammed frowned. After all this, he had forgotten his family had to go through Customs. All of the adults sighed in relief, because the processing went easily enough after they showed their papers from the Immigration inspector. After all, everyone was so tired that they were ready to sleep. Even baby Aini rested next to her brother, her head dropping onto his leg every few minutes. So, all got up and trooped behind the men to the elevator and across the bridge to reach the van.

∽

Most of Abdul's family fell asleep on the drive to the new home. Abdul had worked in Dearborn with his family on a work visa for a few months, but he remembered little of the city. As Mohammed drove, he watched out the window and wondered about the Goodyear Tire permanently fixed to the ground near the I-94 freeway.

For what purpose was it here? It is taller than the surrounding power poles.

They continued through Allen Park, then Lincoln Park, and finally turned off at Schaefer Highway in Dearborn. Once they'd driven past many buildings of the Ford plants, and even after Michigan Avenue, Abdul noticed the community change to resemble a solid Arab community.

So many people moved here from the Middle East, and many didn't even need to learn English since the community developed their own subculture. But we will be different. Aisha and I will demonstrate our pride and culture through our willingness to be bilingual. Our children will become proficient in English but remain true to our heritage as we balance our new activities while living in this American dream. We will have great opportunities as a family, but our children, especially, Habib, my baba, will have the ability to go wherever his dreams take him with the education and support we will provide him in America.

After a few miles, they turned right into a quiet neighborhood full of second-story bungalow houses. Mohammed made a right turn and slowed down to pull into the driveway of a large, brick two-story home. A well-kept front yard displayed many flowers that Abdul had never seen. Carpets could be seen covering the floor of the large porch. Several chairs surrounded a low table. An older couple sat there, drinking coffee. A basket of bread rested on the table. As they saw the van, both stood up, arms open wide in greeting. They smiled as the van came to a stop.

This welcoming home makes me smile. Here I saw how my uncle Suhaib and Aunt Rahma thrived in America.

Uncle Suhaib had opened a restaurant business years ago, and the family put down roots in the Arab community. People began to respect him, privately and even more so publicly. They would greet him with deference in the marketplace, and many members of the community dined at his restaurant. Even the local Imam enjoyed the restaurant's cuisine and chided Uncle Suhaib *for his inconsistent attendance to the mosque prayer time. I have wondered since my last visit if I too, could create a respected place in the community. What would that look like? Can Aisha and I build a family and create a life that we will be respected? Even more important, will we be blessed by Allah?*

"Mohammed, open up the van doors and help bring the family out," Suhaib yelled in Arabic and waved us to the house, still hollering across the distance. Such was his joy to see them. "Abdul, peace upon you. It's so good to see you again in Dearborn!"

"Uncle Suhaib, peace upon you also." Abdul, stiff-legged, stepped away from the van and stood up straighter to shake arms and kiss. "I have looked forward to this day for so long. I am so glad you opened your home to me and my family."

"Oh no, my nephew. We are more pleased to welcome you to be part of our home."

Locking arms and hands, they shook firmly and kissed each other. Then Suhaib broke the grasp and hugged him. "Come now, let's see your family." His bushy eyebrows raised in anticipation as he rubbed his trimmed beard. The wind blew Maple leaves across the porch from the tree next door.

"Yes, enough of the men and their greetings," Rahma said. "Where are my girls and young man to hug? I have nieces and nephews to love."

"Peace upon you, Aunt Rahma," Aisha said, holding her baby in her arms. "Here is our youngest, Aini. And to my left, Habib, our baba."

"Oh, she is beautiful. Her eyes shine like the Red Sea when the water is calm in the late evening. Let me hold her for a moment." Rahma reached for Aini.

"Here you are, Aunt Rahma," Aisha slowly handed off the baby girl to the waiting outstretched arms of the older woman. "Habib, give your Aunt Rahma a nice hug," Aisha nudged her son.

"Ya Allah! The baby is hugging me with love. Give her to me so I can show her my love."

Rahma reached again for the baby. Aisha yielded Aini to her, albeit sheepishly, and sighed. Rahma smiled, her face brightened with joy. For her, it was a rare moment to hold a happy child. She looked on as Habib tried to hug her, and she half hugged him with her other arm while squeezing Aini closely to her chest.

"Abdul, can you get the bags in the van? I will show you where your room upstairs will be." Mohammed lightly tapped him on the back.

"Yes, you men take the luggage up to the room. I need to hold the children a moment longer," Rahma said. "Aisha, you also should see your upstairs home. You will need to get accustomed to caring for it."

"Excellent idea," Uncle Suhaib said with a chuckle. "Aisha, follow us upstairs with the bags and you can see your new home."

Abdul placed each bag from our journey on the driveway, and some onto the cement walkway near the van.

Uncle Suhaib and Aunt Rahma seem genuinely happy to see us. Their hospitality is sincere. I don't understand what Aisha is thinking. Aunt Rahma only wants to see our baby. Aisha tried to hold back the frown from her face, but I can see she is upset. Our new home, new family, and new community will be perfect. I'm not sure why she is not happy also. She had always dreamed of a new land and a new home for our family. Here it is, and now she is already discontent.

Chapter 3

Aisha

1996 – Yemen

Without warning, dark clouds poured rain. Lightning tore over the side of the mountain, giving Aisha a breathtaking view. Aisha lived in a valley that stretched further than she could see, with rugged mountains on three sides. There was another village not far away, in the one direction where mountains did not loom. Many of her sixteen-year-old friends were already married, but she was content to remain in her father's home. She actually treasured the time alone.

Aisha often walked up an antelope trail for a few kilometers, until the air became thin. Then she would stop and gaze, in awe of the beautiful view. Photographers never could capture the true, natural splendor of the Middle East. The beauty Aisha reflected on so many times was a bit different, where nature spoke to her through its deep wildness and craggy areas. Flowers managed to flourish among the trees and bushes that grew despite the harsh terrain. She struggled to understand how things grew in such a rough land. The stark reality contrasted with the unspeakable beauty pushed her thoughts inward, where she battled her passion to climb beyond the mountains.

It was raining, soaking through her clothing, she urged herself to walk faster.

Aisha's village in the Sarawat Mountains hid neighboring villages in valleys on each side. If she walked high enough, she could see the top of the homes and buildings in some of these neighboring villages. She often walked alone for peace of mind, but sometimes her younger brother Sami, and sister, *Amira*, followed. She often worried they might trip, so she would mama them as only an older sister could. She enjoyed time with them but wondered what life would be like in her own home one day. How would she manage apart from the direction of her mama's eye? Still, walking with her siblings, she heard her mama's voice in her head. Mama reprimanded her for hiking too far with them. All too often, she heard her mama's voice, whispering reminders, telling her to do her prayers, reminding her to wear proper clothes, and finish her cleaning duties in the home.

Aisha turned away from the antelope trail and quickened her pace. She saw Baba in the distance. He plowed the family's field, keeping an even pace with the lanky, strong-legged donkey. Baba had owned that donkey long before she was born. The rain slackened. Her father looked up and saw her. His face lit up like the sun over the side of the back mountain. Entering the field, she stepped over the rows already plowed. Hugging Aisha, sweat dripped from him, still he kissed her forehead and brushed a strand of hair out of her eyes.

Aziz, her father, didn't need to express his love aloud, she felt love in his touch. She saw the love in the way he looked at her. His love for his family showed in his work ethic. He farmed every season of the year, working twelve to fourteen hours a day to see the fruits of his crops sold in their village, and even neighboring villages. The goats the family raised gave milk, and once a year, they would sell a few goats at the market.

Aziz kissed her a second time and then turned to put his shoulder behind the plow. He pushed on to finish the row, and she stepped past him to continue toward home. Smiling, Aisha hummed a favorite tune as she closed the distance to their simple mud-brick home. Mama would be worrying, having expected Aisha to have finished her chores by now. Her mama, Badia, carried her broom like a warrior carried a sword, only she used it to emphasize her sharp tongue.

"Aisha, I am here cleaning the house, and where are you? I don't doubt you are wandering around the side of a mountain or were you bothering your father again in the field?" Badia stood in the center of the room sweeping the floor. "Just because you didn't have class today, doesn't mean you can wander the whole morning to dream."

"Yes, Mama, but I was actually meditating about our faith," Aisha said, reaching to take the broom from her mama.

"No, you were dreaming of life and the big plans you have for yourself. How many times do I need to remind you to cast aside your foolish dreams? You need to keep your heart close to our mountains." Her mama sighed as she watched Aisha make quick work of sweeping the floor. "We will be open to a good man for you to marry soon enough. Perhaps he will have a small business in a neighboring village, but we will be sure he will provide for you."

"Oh Mama, I am not ready to marry. But when I do, my husband and I will travel far from these mountains. We will see new lands, where we will raise our family," Aisha said as she brought the broom to her chest and hugged it like a child.

One day I will have a family that will love me as much as I will love them.

"Shush with talk like that! I'm sorry, child, but you will raise a family not far from our mountain. I will see my grandchildren often, and they will make my heart sing songs that will make the prophet smile from hearing. Maybe even Allah himself will smile when he hears the joy in my heart. Um…Does Allah smile? I wonder about that. I wish that he would, but it's not what's taught. I don't he think cares much for our families' joy," Badia stopped and seemed to look away for a moment. Shaking her head, she looked back at Aisha. "Now stop with silly talk about faraway lands and help me finish cleaning the dining area. Your father said we may have guests today."

"Well, I hope it's not Uncle Saeed or Uncle Kareem from Quelem, the village across the river," Aisha mumbled. *They smell so bad and stink up all the house when they visit. They talk so loudly that I can't even begin to fall asleep.*

"What did you say?" Badia started to cluck her tongue and raised her arms mockingly. "Your adolescence wit will be no match for my strong arm. I will not tolerate complaints about the elders in our family."

"Yes, Mama." Aisha continued hugging the broom. "I'm just so tired of Uncles Saeed and Kareem sitting with Baba, chewing *qat* late at night in the other room. They say they are chewing to *relieve stress…*"

Badia could hear the sarcasm in Aisha's voice but chose not to interrupt at that moment.

Aisha sighed. "But I think they enjoy not thinking about the problems they face next week. Baba has little time for it, and he has to get up early to farm each day." She stepped toward the table, tapping the broom on the floor to catch stray bits of dust.

Aisha looked up as her sister *Amira* walked in. Her face scrunched up, as if she smelled her brother's flatulence.

"Ugh, smelly men," *Amira* agreed.

"Baba only sits and laughs with them because they are family. I know deep in my heart he'd prefer to go to bed early," Aisha said.

"Yours is not the place to judge men." Badia stroked Aisha's back and adjusted her hijab. "Your place is in doing Allah's will for your life."

"Yes, Mama. I want to do the will of Allah and be obedient to you as well," Aisha whispered.

"Good girl. But your voice was much stronger when you spoke of your dreams and where you will live one day. Now you sound less confident." Badia laughed as she looked through the open door of their home. She smiled, touched her hand to her heart, as her husband neared their home. "Aisha… your father and I, well… about our love. It wasn't always easy. Our arranged marriage left us with some turmoil in the beginning, and I was bitter for a time. But your father was, in fact, a great man who wanted to provide. He also took time to show me, even in little ways, how much he cared. I would talk to other women in the market. When they complained, it was that their husbands never thought of their wives' needs or wants. It seemed there was an expectation that a good wife would seek to only please Allah by pleasing her husband and caring for the family and home. But your father, he wanted us to be a better couple. I could see that in how he treated me, and then later his children."

Aisha's eyes blinked a little, and she wiped the beginnings of a tear. She had never heard this story from her mama.

"Aisha, stop thinking now about my story, and pay attention. Go set our table to prepare for dinner. Your father won't be sitting with your uncles tonight. Remember, he's invited a guest," Badia said. She pointed toward the dining area.

"Mama, who is the guest? Is he bringing a neighboring family? Are there children coming? Do I know them?" Aisha asked the questions rapid-fire, like the stones she often threw, in rapid succession, into the nearby river. The river provided clean water for the village and gave local children a clear, sparkling river in which they could swim, fish, and play.

"Oh, Baba, you're home." Aisha smiled and set the broom in its place.

"How much of the field did you complete today, my love? The sweat is dripping from your face, and you smell like dirt." Badia complained, but with a smile. "I hope there is fruit today to justify this foul-smelling effort."

"Yes, there is. I finished the portion of the field I'd hoped to do today. There was no rain except in the mountains, and Mahri, our faithful donkey, actually listened to my orders to keep plodding. But now I am tired and hungry, and I hope dinner is ready," Aziz looked toward the table. It functioned as the dining room, but also the kitchen.

"That burro is named for being full of energy, but he is so stubborn and often has little energy." Aisha laughed out loud. "Maybe we can trade him in for a better one like the Americans do with their cars."

"Go and clean yourself up before you eat." Badia pointed to the back room. "Your meal is ready, and your friend will be here any moment."

"Ah, yes. Tonight, is the night we agreed to his request for dinner together." Aziz sighed. "I was hoping to relax tonight and enjoy a little time with my family."

"We have a guest to entertain. I have prepared a bit nicer meal with fresh goat, vegetables, and some *muluawah*, the homemade bread. I went to the market this morning for all of the ingredients." Badia followed him into the other room, where both the children and parents shared sleep space. Aziz found a shirt and smelled it to be sure it lacked his sweat from another day.

"Lik! You think I wouldn't have a clean shirt for you? I made sure. He has a purpose to come tonight, and you know where his heart is at," Badia said.

"Yes, I know but I'm not prepared to have this conversation. Even if he is well respected in the village across the river."

"Baba, someone is knocking at the door." Aisha came to the doorway. "Shall I let him in?"

"No, my daughter. I will come in a moment. He can wait," Aziz said to her. He tugged his shirt over his head and shoulders, as a grunt came from inside the shirt. He strode to the front of the house and sighed.

"Aisha, you and your sister go to the bedroom to study together. You two will eat a little later," Aziz waved them away and reached to open the door.

"Oh, hello, my friend, thank you for coming tonight." Aziz opened the door wide. "Welcome to my home."

Voices Through the Window

"Greetings and thank you for the invitation to dinner. It smells wonderful in here." The stranger breathed in deeply from a longer than ordinary nose. He was taller with a well-knit *thobe*, and his sandals showed little dirt on them. Here, he stood in a simple village home, looking a bit out of place.

"Well, come into our dining area and sit. We have freshly squeezed juice."

Badia brought juice for them both. She said nothing but quietly placed the cups on the table. Then she brought homemade bread for them.

"Well, I appreciate that my brother-in-law informed me you would like to do business. I am not quite sure of what business you are in. He informed me that you buy and sell goods to a few different villages."

"Ah, yes. Well, my name is Mustafa. I am a businessman from across the river. And I buy goods from various villages as you said. But I don't want to buy your produce, neither sell you anything," the man stated. He looked like he was almost forty years old but carried himself well.

"So, what is this business that you wish to talk about? If not with my produce, what then?" Aziz asked while biting into some of the warm bread. Badia brought a pot of stew from the small stove. She set the hot stone pot on the table on a slab of wood.

"This is my wife, Badia. She has brought you some stew while you explain your purpose," Aziz said.

Swallowing a mouthful of bread, the stranger spoke bluntly. "I am here about your daughter. I have heard about her beauty from villages all around. I am in need of a strong young woman in my home. She will fit my needs exactly," Mustafa explained.

"So, you would like to purchase my daughter to work? Or something else?" Aziz asked the stranger.

Badia heard steel in her husband's voice, a rare occurrence. A burst of noise came from the bedroom, and they walked back toward it.

"Oh no, my friend. I would like her as my second wife. My first wife is not well, and she cannot do the things I require… as well as she used to. Many times, I may have guests come to our home. Also, she cannot give me more children." He paused for a moment. "I am willing to pay an appropriate amount for her as a dowry."

Aziz took his time chewing a spoonful of stew. "I see, but I need to explain that we have not decided yet when we are prepared to release Aisha to another family. My wife and I have talked about when this conversation might happen," Aziz said.

Muffled words were heard from the bedroom. Aziz recognized the sharp tones of his daughter. His eyes closed as if to rest briefly.

"Pardon me for a moment." Aziz stood and walked to the other room. He opened the door and stepped inside.

"Girls, what is the loud whispering here? I am trying to talk business with our guest. What is the problem?"

"Baba, I am not ready to marry! Especially to that man!" Aisha's eyes started to tear up, and she quickly pushed them away. "He is very old and not handsome at all," Aisha said. "I don't like his face, and especially that nose. I cannot bear to look at him even now. And he wants me to make his meals every day?" Aisha shook her head in denial.

"Aisha, you are my daughter! It's not your place to question, but to do as I say. Obey your parents and do what is expected of you."

"Yes, but to be clear, this businessman wants Aisha for *more* than a housemaid," Badia said, frowning. "We knew that suitors would come, and they would be willing to pay more than they would for other girls." Badia stared at Aziz with arms folded and turned and brushed Aisha's hair. "Aisha, you are beautiful, and your intelligence is spoken of throughout the community. Good men understand that Allah wants them to have a beautiful wife." Badia had tried to whisper, but it came out as a shout. She got worked up about the plight of women. "Instead, she is often the hands that see the dirt and put the broom to work."

Aisha lost her spirit, feeling like a broom in the corner, herself. She began to sob softly. Aziz frowned and stepped forward.

"Calm down, my little one. There is no decision to be made tonight. We are only talking." Her father tried to reassure Aisha. "But, one day soon you will have to start a family of your own. You will have responsibilities that your mama and I need to fully prepare you for."

Aisha continued to sob, but quieter now.

"Enough of this. I need to finish the meal and send away our guest. I will maintain our family's reputation and give him the respect due a man of his intentions. I will tell him that we need a bit more time to prepare our daughter for her future responsibilities." Aziz left, shutting the door quietly.

He straightened out the shirt his wife had carefully set out for him, pulling down the sides. Rubbing his beard along his jawline, he contemplated his beloved daughter. He wasn't ready to do business over Aisha. He was a simple farmer who loved his daughters and hadn't given sufficient thought on the tradition of young girls being married off. Certainly, there was a great financial benefit that would help his family overall. But he maintained his farm well, and everyone was provided for. How did Allah expect him to give his daughter to a stranger, and expect him to do so freely without any love spoken of? Strong pangs of guilt overcame him even as he thought about losing his dear Aisha.

Chapter 4

Abdul

Yemen — 1996

Abdul watched with interest at the bartering going on in the village market. He sat, drinking coffee, in a second-story cafe that overlooked the clamor. He had a bird's eye view of the village where his parents had raised him and could imagine — around the corner and across the river — the neighboring village where he'd spent his youth.

He savored each sip of the rich, flavorful brew. It reminded him of the Arabica coffee beans his family obtained in trade as he'd grown up; they might have been the same beans. This coffee, a variety called Yemeni Udaini, was purported to be the best coffee in the world. It was quite expensive and hard to obtain — even to buy a cup in Yemen, where it was grown. The coffee was indulgent, creamy, and full-bodied, unlike the trendy Macchiatos or Americanos that the masses guzzled in London. Abdul craved the rich, bolder, coffee unadulterated by sugar and milk. Good coffee was one of the extravagances he allowed himself.

After he'd obtained his first degree from the University of Aden in Yemen, at the College of Economics, he'd yearned to learn more. His son, understanding the importance of an education, borrowed funds to pay for Abdul's MBA in London. Cambridge University was willing to accept his bachelor's degree from the university in Yemen as long as he passed the placement testing.

After three years spent living in London, he'd completed and obtained his MBA, with a minor in economics. His hunger to learn motivated him to study for hours at a time, and he had few problems with his classes. The only issue he'd encountered was culture shock while transitioning. In retrospect, there were two major benefits in returning to his home country: the coffee and the culture. He's missed it dearly.

Abdul's server brought a second cup of coffee, and he inhaled the aroma, his thoughts turning to employment. His father had suggested he apprentice in London after graduation, which he did. He felt more comfortable in agriculture, and so he had sought out a company that managed the selling of goods to local farmers and ranchers who raised sheep or goats. This at least was more familiar ground to him, having been raised in the mountains of Yemen. The company was pleased with his work ethic and wanted to see him expand their product into the neighboring rural areas. He felt joy in his small success and the fact that they did not see his ethnicity as a factor to hold him back. But he still missed his family, and even Yemen itself. He missed talking with friends in Arabic, while sitting and chewing qat, a stimulant.

"How is the view? I don't think it has changed in decades." An older man named Fahad scraped a chair away from the table and then sat. The man was in his late fifties with gray scattered throughout his distinguished beard. The man's eyes shone like bits of fire.

"*Marhaba*, Baba. The coffee is as good as it always has been. The view, not as much. I think, as I have aged, the view has become defiled, much like when people add flavor to the coffee. It is best in its pure form."

"*Marhabtayn*, my baba. You have been away at the university, where life is different. There you are shown theory and the history of others who have failed and some who were successful. Now we must arrange for you to practice what you have learned in order to become the shrewd businessman that I need you to be." Fahad, gesturing, knocked over his coffee. He looked around for the server as coffee dripped onto his thobe.

"Here you are, baba." Abdul offered him a napkin. *Stains would not be appropriate for a businessman, even in the mountain villages. My father knows how to present himself in public.*

Fahad impatiently dabbed at his clothing. "Where is that server?"

The server appeared, carrying small towels. "Many apologies, good sir." He handed Fahad a moist cloth to better remove the coffee stains. "I will return with a fresh cup."

Minutes later, the mess had been cleaned up, and Fahad sipped from a fresh, steaming cup.

This delay annoys me. There are many things to discuss. Abdul cleared his throat. "Baba, while at university we had great discussions of commerce and trade that involved more than what we see here in Yemen. The technology has increased so much, and the trends are even now increasing." Abdul's voice grew in intensity as he spoke.

Abdul moved his chair and opened his laptop. He turned the screen so his father could view a file of spreadsheets he created for the company where he had apprenticed. *Certainly, he must appreciate the quality of my work.*

"Baba, see?" Abdul pointed to the laptop's screen. "These are a few of the charts I have created. They demonstrate growth in areas of agriculture and the decline in some crops. We were able to make projections that were fairly accurate based on historical data and current trends."

"These charts are well done, Abdul," Fahad took the mouse and clicked on another spreadsheet. "I see you have applied what you have learned."

"Well, yes. Your investment in me, both at the university and in my apprenticeship has shown fruitfulness. I look forward to the future of our family business. I have already put much thought into how we can expand it from regional to national, and one day, even international."

Fahad had been analyzing spreadsheets. With Abdul's comment, his eyes abruptly became unfocused. The fingers of his left hand drummed a slow, methodical beat. He removed his hand from the computer mouse and sipped his coffee, then turned his head to gaze across the village. A faint smile changed his expression as he studied the familiar commotion in the marketplace.

"Baba, what are you thinking?" Abdul asked. A few minutes passed without an answer.

Fahad sighed as he turned back to his son. "I sat alone this morning… thinking. I also prayed fervently about the plans we had together. I truly feel Allah will bless us,"

Abdul broke his gaze from his father and looked at his hand. He stared at the graduation gift. He began twisting the ring given to him by his father. The custom-designed ring showed their national flag on one side, the family business emblem engraved on the other side, and a beautifully, hued shade of red sapphire in the center. *Between prayers to Allah and the ever-present ring to remind me of home, I always felt sure of the plans for my life. Now, Baba won't answer with his usual confidence.*

"Listen, my baba," Fahad said. "You will put away the supposed visions from Allah. Allah has, in fact, given me a broader plan for you when I was last at the masjid. I felt his wisdom during my prayers."

"Yes, Baba?" Abdul waited, his eyes moving to meet his Fahad's face.

"Well, part of my vision that I feel Allah has put in my head and heart, is that will work with me, of course. But first you will work with my two men, who have traded and handled much of the marketing around our valley and much further. They will mentor you…"

"What? I don't understand." Abdul pushed slowly away from the table. "We had discussed for years how I would study business and then become part of the family's trade business. Now you don't think I'm good enough? I would be an underling? An errand boy for one of your traders?"

"My baba." Fahad sighed. "I'm trying to explain my dreams for you. It's a matter of the steps best to walk before you can truly partner with me. But I have wondered if maybe…"

"No. I believe you don't think I'm ready to work with you. You don't trust my ideas for expanding your business. You claimed you would be confident in me, but now that it is time to place some control into my hands, you lack the will to let me manage even a part." Abdul cleared his throat. *I fear my annoyance might reveal my disappointment. The disappointment I cannot face.* Abdul couldn't admit how much his baba's opinion mattered.

After taking a breath, his temper had not subsided. "You sit there, smugly caught up in your traditional way of doing business. Forgive me for wanting to bring new trends to your business model. Forgive me for having the foresight to bring the family business into the twenty-first century. May Allah forgive me the time and effort I've already put into improving your business. You saw the spreadsheets. Did you think that work was a mindless exercise for me?" Abdul noticed his baba tapping the table again. His breathing was as rapid as if he'd been running. *He always does this when he doesn't want to answer my questions. What is his problem with me?*

"What? Am I boring you?" Abdul's anger grew with every passing moment. *Now my hands are shaking.* He set his hands on his lap to hide his reaction.

"Well, no, my baba. I was waiting for your tirade to wear out. And if so, are you ready to hear my voice?" Fahad spoke softly in contrast to the volume Abdul had risen to.

Abdul nodded once.

"Abdul, I am really proud of all you have accomplished. You are the only one in our family and, in fact, the only one in our community, to go off to the university for a master's degree. You have returned a man with a passion for business who understands more than I thought possible in so little time."

Abdul leaned back and stretched his shoulders to control his emotions. "I didn't know you understood and saw so much," Abdul said quietly.

"Oh, I understood much more than you think. I read your emails and explained to your mama what you were learning. How you applied it so well. I need you to understand my vision. My business model is set between communities in this mountain region and valleys. Though I had thought we could partner together one day, and I could prepare you to take over one day. But it will, in reality, hold you back. Allah has much more in store for you. You would be like a stallion, stabled and bridled, who needs to run free with his ambition to create more than what this local region could ever provide." Fahad sighed deeply and moved his chair back to get up.

"No, baba. *This* is my home. I love it and want to develop it more with a passion. I've waited for the years to come and help your dreams grow larger than ever," Abdul said. "Baba, where are you walking to? Are we done talking? This is important."

"Follow me my baba," Fahad chuckled.

"Is this some lesson to learn on a walk? I would think I could see your point without the walking," Abdul said to Fahad's back with only a silent response. They walked about fifty meters, and then Fahad stepped right into a small restaurant. He nodded at the owner, whom he had done many transactions over the years with, and in fact, he owned a share of the business. Onward he walked to the corner, where a woman sat with her back to the door sipping coffee.

"Ah, see we are just in time, my dear flower," Fahad sat next to his wife with grin. He waved his hand to the server for more coffee. "Assure our baba now that my business will thrive as he will travel outside of this region."

Abdul took a deep breath to calm himself and smiled broadly. He bent over and kissed his mama in greeting. "Mama, you brighten our table with your presence. I didn't expect to dine with you this morning." Abdul happily squeezed his mama's hand as he sat. *She lights up the room with her smile, and I miss her most of all. She has a way of calming me so easily.*

"What a glorious morning, and it was my idea we share a meal outside the house. I knew you were probably off gazing across the valley and sipping coffee." She smiled at the two men. "But you need to stop this talk of how you will bring about growth in your father's company. He has grown it enough. You are destined for more than these mountains. We will be saddened to see you leave us again. But this is no longer your only home. Now your home is the world."

∼

Abdul left lunch with his parents; his face drawn with frustration. Although he was reassured to know his baba was proud of how far he had already come in his education, he was disconcerted about how they'd preplanned his departure from their home village. He had, for years, contemplated the combination of his newfound skills and aptitude for business with his father's vast knowledge and experience. He had assumed, with his father's urging for a college business major and prodding for the apprenticeship, that Baba was doing all he could to prepare Abdul for working as a father-and-son business. For his baba to so methodically map out a different plan for him was not unlike him, but he failed to see how his mama bought into this plan to so easily to be rid of him. It saddened him.

He called two of his long-time friends. They agreed to meet and chew *qat* with him. It had been years since he had sat with his good friends. Sameer and Yasser were both intelligent and full of wit, and both had done well in local businesses. They each had apprenticed with their respective families, finding a passion in trade with a sharp tongue. They also were trying to implement slow change with computer usage to facilitate gathering data from sales easier. Both were free for an afternoon visit, and so they lounged in a cafe under a fan reasoning all their problems for a few hours. After a while, from the lethargic effects of the qat, their conversation had circled around with little concluding thoughts.

"Sameer, you are right," Abdul interrupted his friend's speech. "I know I can be successful here and with my education, I could prosper at the international level too."

"Abdul, you have much knowledge that you have gained from university," Yasser said. "Far more than we have. Yet, with quick tongues and even our basic technology skills, we have moved our family businesses with increasing sales. We also have been documenting and sharing ways to decrease costs."

"So, there is no doubt with the experiences you have from the university and what you learned working in the apprenticeship; you are certainly more qualified than us," Sameer said. "You worry about your family business, but your father isn't that old. He is doing well and wants you to go global."

"I know… and I understand that" Abdul said. "I just had hoped and dreamed to be part of his family business. You two are part of that now, and I won't get that chance."

"Ya Allah! The family business isn't so much of a big deal, my brother." Yasser smiled wryly.

"Yes, neither of our fathers leave much room for input. We spend hours showing where we can save on costs, and thinking about how to increase sales on the computers we invested in." Sameer spat out a wad of chewed qat. "Yet, our fathers, they don't trust this new age of technology, and have little faith in their fathers."

"You two make the idea of traveling to do business outside of our home more appealing by the moment. I'm feeling more than conflicted." Abdul looked at the other two and laughed. "The server has disappeared. I need more coffee while we chew."

Abdul stepped to the counter. The server was dressed in a long robe, and he moved quickly to keep up with other orders. He nodded to Abdul.

"Sometimes the best coffee is the cup we must wait for."

Abdul looked to his side. A man Abdul didn't know had spoken.

"The better things in life are waited for." The man raised an eyebrow.

"Sometimes... Yes, you could be right," Abdul said.

"For instance, I am still waiting for the second wife I need. I'm hoping Allah will provide her soon. Though I had hoped Allah had settled it a week ago."

Abdul sipped at the coffee just handed him. The man piqued his interest.

"Tell me more, my friend." Abdul beckoned with his cup and a curious smile. "How did Allah frown on you a week ago?"

"It was a most interesting situation," the older man said. "By the way, my name is Mustafa. I am a local businessman."

Abdul smiled. "I am Abdul, just returned home from Cambridge University."

"That is wonderful. Congratulations." He sipped his coffee. "As I was saying, I spoke in the market to a local farmer from across the river. I asked if we could meet for business. I had seen and admired his eldest daughter. Her beauty is striking, she is full of energy, and obviously, she would pair well with my household."

"And so, he agreed to meet you?" *This story is fascinating. It's so much a part of the Yemenis tradition that marriages are arranged as a business in order to meet the needs of all parties.* While in England, Abdul noticed marriages were agreed upon much differently.

"Yes, I met at their home," Mustafa explained. "But the father apparently thought I wanted to trade wares. He seemed completely surprised by my suggestion, and even worse, I heard the young beauty snickering behind a door." He pulled a smartphone from the pocket of his jacket. He tapped a few times and turned the phone to face Abdul. "Here she is."

Abdul glanced at the photo, then leaned in and took the phone from the man. *Allah be praised, it is Aisha from the village across the river.*

Cousin Mohammed used to tease her. She was pretty as a child, but now as she has grown into an exquisite woman.

"You see why I chose her. Healthy and young, she would have given me many sons."

"Yes. She is a beauty. Too bad it didn't work out," Abdul muttered, still staring at Aisha's photo, a snapshot of her shopping in the market. Her face was alive with the joy of bargaining over the price of fruit. He reluctantly handed the phone back and tried to reconcile himself that this was one more opportunity that had slipped from his hands. "Well, I can't understand why he said no. You obviously have the means to provide for her, and even give quite a generous gift to the family," Abdul said, his voice stronger now.

"Quite right, young man. My gifts could have helped that family farm for years to come. And she would have met many needs for me, especially as my first wife is struggling. She tries to maintain our household but doesn't understand all that I require." Mustafa shook his head as sadness filled his face.

"Well, perhaps another, more grateful family will find their way to your path, my friend. Then, surely Allah will bless you with more boys to raise in your household." Abdul sipped his coffee and began to stand.

"Allah be with you, young man." Mustafa put out his hand in parting.

Abdul shook his hand. He waved at his friends still sitting at the table and decided to walk home. *I hope that my path finds a different route. Love becomes true, and not a transaction or contract to sign.*

Chapter 5

Aisha

September – 2003 South Dearborn, Michigan

The people on television say that it's spring in Michigan. Aisha watched a variety of talk and news shows to improve her vocabulary. She had Abdul set the TV to display the words in captions so it would be easier to follow a conversation.

Today she had watched a little bit of television and then stepped outside. She considered the view from the small balcony connected to their bedroom. The trees waved at her with their long branches. Aisha brushed back the hair from her eyes, adjusting her hijab, and stood on her toes while holding onto the lawn chair. Searching over the wind-blown trees and many houses, she watched a busy street with fast-moving cars. *People on their way to work.* It was quite a difference from the mornings, years ago, when she walked a trail in her village.

Although the springtime in Dearborn seemed a bit bleak and stark like her home country of Yemen at times, there were not many other similarities. All the changes her family made caused her to wonder and reflect.

Our marriage was arranged, and I appreciated that my parents wanted to pair me with a man whom I could come to love. I had seen him a few times in the village before he came to our home to arrange our marriage. He might have seen my smile behind my hijab. He looked familiar to me, but no idea why. Also, he looked athletic, even handsome in a certain way... and strong. Yet I knew nothing of him, except his reputation. But if I had been in another country, or even with another family, I could have chosen better for myself. How would I choose my life to be?

Abdul isn't as bad as some I might have married. He actually listens to me and asks if I have an opinion for him to factor in when he makes the decisions. Habib and Aini brought true happiness to our family. But learning to raise our children under the watchful eyes of his mama became a challenge for me. Somehow, we found our way as a couple, but having parents constantly chide you about raising your children became a bigger burden. Now we are here, and yet we live under a roof with family still.

For months, she had enjoyed her daily time alone to think. To stand outside, overlooking the city, offered small, peaceful moments, even with the loud, busy traffic this early.

It seems I reflect best with the quiet rumblings of the city after my morning prayers. I really try to follow the rituals as Allah commanded, remembering how often my mama modeled them. Our family would often gather to pray when I was younger, the men in front and the women in the back.

Here, in Dearborn, sometimes Abdul prayed and waited to be sure I prayed as well. But more often, Abdul was merely concerned about preparing for the day than he was with prayers. The other men are so busy also, and do not often do their prayers. But I need to pray daily, as my mama and now Abdul's aunt insist I should. Aunt Rahma has wrapped her watchful and caring arms around my baby as a surrogate mama. Not sure how to adjust to it... this love she has to show for me.

"Aisha! Come inside, it's time to go to your school at the mosque," Abdul's voice in the window woke Aisha from her thoughts. "We don't want you to be late for your first day."

"No problem. I'm ready," she said. Aisha had opened the window earlier to bring the fresh air and a light morning breeze. The soft wind reminded them both of Yemen and Abdul laughed as he turned and walked back to the hall. She smiled as he mumbled, "The wind blows from Yemen."

Aisha closed the sliding balcony door behind her. Slipping into her black heels after checking how her new flowered skirt paired with her turquoise blouse, she seemed to float on the breeze. Almost at the bedroom door, Aisha turned abruptly around. She hurriedly searched the bedroom for her notebook to take to class.

"I have your notebook here," Abdul held it up with a smile.

She grinned, amused with her husband. She picked up her hijab as Abdul tugged on a freshly pressed white shirt that she'd ironed last night.

He needs to be fresh for each day's work at the restaurant.

Abdul affectionately placed her notebook in her outstretched hands, his face breaking from his thoughts for the day to take a moment to smile at her. She tightened the cream and blue speckled hijab to hide her frown.

"Ah, Aisha." Rahma, Abdul's aunt, sighed from the top of the stairs.

Already she is up and pestering our lives. She watches Abdul and me like the village gossip but claims the rights of my mama. His aunt lives on the main floor but so often roams the hall and checks the bathroom we share with Mohammed. Again, Rahma continues to scold me under her breath, commenting again about my hijab. She has been acting like this more frequently in the last few months. Somehow, the warmer weather brought fire into her heart and words.

"Aisha, I don't know about those clothes. How did you find American clothes already? Didn't your mother and grandmother teach you properly about our faith?"

"Aunt Rahma, thank you. I know my faith well," Aisha tried to smile. She pulled the hijab tighter and tucked the end in her top.

Aisha stopped halfway down the stairs and ran back up, passing Rahma, who shook her head and muttered something Aisha didn't understand. Rahma even tugged on her hijab when Aisha passed her.

How is it that her name means mercy? Where is the mercy? It seems farther from her each day. I have my notebook, but where is the pen I used last night to practice writing my name?

"Thanks be to Allah," Aisha sighed as she ran back downstairs without one look at Rahma. She slowed her pace and stopped when she heard Abdul talking to their baba at the bottom of the stairs. His voice was deep and low but carried so much love.

"Habib, your mama is going to class today. You remember she told you last night about how you will walk to the corner for the bus to go to your school?" Abdul had squatted and looked into Habib's eyes.

Aisha knew he was waiting for a response.

"You are a big boy and need to represent our family well." Abdul stood then sighed as Aisha's dress brushed against his hand as she passed them.

My husband is a good father. I must remember that. He loves our children and me.

Abdul went ahead of her out the front door. She increased her gait to match his pace.

If I don't hurry, I may lose the courage to go to my first day of class. It makes me happy how he holds the car door. Such a gentleman at times and other times... he's so distant.

"I know you want me to learn English. I do, too." She leaned over and patted his hand on the center console of the car. She smiled at Abdul, showing her confidence.

Abdul pulled his cousin's Honda out of the driveway, but suddenly stopped. Abdul swore under his breath, as he threw his hands in the air, his frustration clear. He glared at Aisha then nodded as he rolled the passenger window down.

"Allah be praised, you almost forget your notebook! I have it and your purse from your room." Rahma hurriedly tottered across the sidewalk. Her voice loudly pointed out Aisha's mistake. Finally, she reached the passenger window. "I feared you almost forgot it. We wouldn't want people to wonder what type of student you are without your notebook."

"Thank you, Rahma. It was very thoughtful of you," Aisha said while she pulled her hijab closer around her head. Abdul waited for Rahma to turn, then he silently shut the window.

"Don't worry about your children. I will take care of them like they were my own." Rahma's voice could be heard, even through the closed window.

"This is a little more difficult than I had imagined," Abdul said. "Sharing living space is one challenge but having my aunt and uncle act as our parents is one I didn't expect."

"It's fine. She only wants the best for us, and she knows some in the community are judging us as newcomers. She really doesn't like me taking English classes, but at the same time she expects me to walk in as the perfectly prepared student," Aisha said. He nodded as they left the side street and pulled onto Michigan Avenue.

"I only wish that it was not necessary to leave our daughter with her," he muttered as he sped up to pass a woman driver. "I don't like to be indebted to her. She is not your mama and *truly* she is not mine. I appreciate that my uncle has made room for us in his home, but this isn't easy for me at all."

"I understand. It's the same for me, but more," she looked over at him and shook her head. "If I were honest, I find it hard to sleep well. We've only been here a short time and she has many ways to find fault with me."

"Well, Aisha, we will pray to Allah that today will go well for you," he said as he slowed the car then pulled into the parking lot next to the mosque." Many Arabic are taking English and Qur'an classes here."

"Will they help with all the English I need to do my shopping and one day work in the community? I need more than just time studying the Qur'an." She waited for his response before opening her door.

"Don't worry, my love. Women from all age groups are taking the class. They will practice English and spend time in the Qur'an with you. I don't think you will pray there, as I will pick you up before the prayer time starts," Abdul said. His voice had taken on a deeper tone.

"Well, then I am prepared for my day," she muttered and opened her door.

"Study well, my love." Abdul opened the passenger window a bit, then waved at her. She heard his voice through the window as she turned to walk to the door.

I said last night I didn't want him walking in. I want my first day to show a balance of love for Abdul and yet show that I'm ready to be independent. I think he is trying to understand, but he's not quite sure how the others would appreciate my attitude.

As she entered the room, a middle-aged man with a greying beard excused himself from a conversation and walked her way.

Is he the instructor or the imam? Maybe both.

"Good morning, and welcome." The imam greeted her with a smile. "If you would come this way, we have a group of women meeting in the backroom, where my wife is leading the class."

He motioned her to follow him, and they walked through the large, empty room, decorated in red with ornate lights hanging. There were many *sajada* against the wall, available for prayer time. The imam opened the door on the other side of the room. It opened to a hallway with two windows overlooking the streets of Dearborn. She heard the sound of trucks grinding their gears nearby. The imam tapped lightly on the classroom door and a thin, middle-aged woman answered with a big smile.

"Welcome to English 101," she said and waved Aisha in. "We are just beginning for today. We are reviewing greetings used here in America."

"Thank you Zara and I pray your time together is fruitful and Allah gives you fuller understanding in your roles of your families." He smiled and nodded at the class.

"Please sit among the other ladies, and we will be ready to begin." She motioned to the table. Aisha found an empty chair at the end of the long table and sat down. She looked around, at a variety of women, some older, wearing the very traditional hijabs and other younger girls with the more contemporary, stylish ones. She sighed deeply and opened the book entitled "English Fundamentals," with a subtitle in Arabic, "English for the Arabs." It all seemed very pleasant, but she was talking in Arabic. *I wonder when they will start using English.*

Chapter 6

Abdul

Yemen – 1996

I can't get that picture out of my head. That man, Mustafa, I think his name was, he'd taken a photo of Aisha shopping with her father in the market. When he turned his head to speak to the barman, I checked his phone. He had several photos. What kind of man does that? One image showed her walking next to her father. She was laughing, and the wind had blown strands of her long hair from beneath her hijab. The other photos showed her speaking on her father's behalf over a product the family was selling. Her smile, ever-present, barely hid her assertiveness when haggling prices over the farmed vegetables. The last few pictures Abdul had seen was showing her loving expression as her father returned from another table, then shook hands on Aisha's transaction.

Now days later, I can't stop thinking of her. I must see her in person. I must find her.

Sameer kicked the ball with his heel across the ground to Yasser. Yasser stopped the ball easily with his left foot and trotted down the makeshift field, dodging the weeds and rocks. He turned his upper torso to the left, where the goal was set up twenty meters away. Yasser dribbled it for five more meters and kicked the ball toward the goal area. The makeshift goal was the area between a bush, a *Euryops arabicus*, and a sandstone-colored bolder they'd moved into place.

"Abdul, where is your mind? The ball just flew over your head. You never let those get by you," Sameer laughed. Yasser had easily maneuvered the ball and taken his shot. "Goal!" Yasser yelled.

"His head is far away, trying to catch up with thoughts, and now he has to buy dinner for us," Sameer yelled as he pumped his fist in victory over the goal. "He didn't even see the amazing goal when the ball flew right by him." Sameer gave a bear-sized hug to Yasser. "He claimed he could stop anything we shot at him all day long. College soccer must be easier to play on a clean field where you don't have to worry about rocks."

"It's in!" Yasser broke out of Sameer's hug and did a victory wave, his hands in the air. "'All day long,' he said. I scored in less than half an hour after warming up. Ha! College boy is back home." Yasser started to laugh and couldn't stop.

Phooph! The ball bounced off Yasser's side and smacked Sameer in the knees.

"Now who is the college boy? There is still power in these legs you so openly mock," Abdul said. He grinned at them as they rubbed their respective blows. "A man can't think for a moment without his friends heaping ridicule on him?"

"I thought we were playing football. If you wanted to go for a cup of English tea, you only had to ask," Sameer said as he exaggerated the knee pain in his limp.

"Abdul, are you continuing to daydream a way to manipulate yourself into a meeting with the father of that girl from your youth? Clearly, we suggested the best plan yesterday. Yet you are still pondering?" Yasser shrugged. "I don't understand how you can be so decisive for your career, and so uncertain with your heart. You have watched Aisha from across the market and talked with her friends. You heard the story from that man in the coffee house. You need to stand taller and be a man who goes for what he wants."

"You two are more than correct." Abdul grabbed them both around the shoulders in a hug. "I will go tomorrow and make this love mine. I think I caught her looking my way, and she recognized me from years ago. If Allah has blessed us with an eye for each other, I will bring about true union as a man should."

Abdul walked with his friends back to the rusted-out Rover they'd arrived in. His stance seemed taller when he walked.

These are good friends I have. I will take the plan they gave me and make it my own. Aisha, she will know me as more than Mohammed's cousin from childhood. She will now see a well-educated man with strong business sense — a man who will be more than capable of providing for her and our future children. How can she not come to respect and then love me?

Abdul put his plan into motion. The first step was to take his young nephew to play football. This common area between the two villages was an open area for children to play.

"Ashraf, watch me as I bring the ball down the field. See how I'm dribbling the ball from one foot to the other? The balls stay close, in range of my feet, so I can control it easier." Abdul demonstrated dribbling.

Ashraf, his ten-year-old nephew, dashed in and kicked the ball away. Ashraf laughed as he ran after the ball.

My plan has begun to come together. I need to engineer a situation where I can awaken her interest in me. If I could but catch her eye behind her hijab, I'd know for sure if I could succeed.

Abdul had spoken to those who know of her family. He discovered that she has two younger siblings, and her parents work hard on their farm. Her younger brother has been seen kicking the ball in the fields between the two villages.

Ashraf has been asking me to teach him more moves. I had seen Aisha's brother playing football with Ashraf. It will all seem coincidental, but if Allah wills it, Aisha's face will shine when she sees me.

"Sammi, stop my ball," Ashraf yelled to his friend. "Kick it back to me. I'm practicing with my uncle."

"Run fast, Ashraf, and hit it with your head," Sami yelled as he kicked the ball five or six meters. It sailed toward Ashraf in an arc.

A new voice rang through the air. "Sammi, leave the ball alone! We don't have time to play. We need to get to the market stand with some of these vegetables." Aisha's scolding carried across the field to her brother. "Today, Baba expects us to hurry for him." She carried an armful — two bags of fresh corn their family had grown.

"Ashraf, come here and let's practice kicking the ball high in the air, like your friend." As Abdul waited for his nephew to return, he watched Aisha and her brother walk away. She headed toward the neighboring village market. "I will show you how to kick as your friend did." They practiced the maneuver for ten minutes, until Ashraf tired of it.

"Uncle Abdul, let's play a game. I want to run far and fast with the ball." Ashraf ran back after fetching the ball. He leaned over, hands on his knees, panting.

"Ashraf, we can practice again another day. Let's walk to the market next to the river," Abdul suggested as he picked up the ball. His pace was quick, and Ashraf had to run to catch up.

"Good idea. You can buy me fruit. Some mangos. And melon," Ashraf said.

Abdul laughed.

"I'm hungry." Ashraf grinned.

Each of the neighboring villages had its own markets even though the villages sat within a few kilometers of each other. A road went through the valley that connected the two villages, among others. The road crossed a bridge over the river that separated much of the valley between the two villages. Both villages had their market day, one day following the other. Many merchants would sell to both villages. On their day, people streamed in from the surrounding mountains to fill the street with noisy haggling over produce grown, animals raised, or various handmade items. Some of these sold well, with their vibrant colors in the machine-sown materials created for the local women.

Time was a commodity that all locals took for granted, and the effort made to agree on prices was evidence of the balance between civility in the culture and making a business transaction. Abdul enjoyed the apparent chaos on market days, since his baba had raised him in business. But now, his mind was singularly focused. He hurried, nearly dragging Ashraf among the throng of people, weaving among them as he sought the food tables.

"Uncle Abdul, I want a piece of fruit. There is a table over on the left side with many melons and even citrus fruit on the table," Ashraf said.

"First, we will get some vegetables for your mama's favorite stew to make. You will buy for her, and I will give you the money — after I show you which table. It's not far now," Abdul said.

Where is her family's stand? They usually set up a table on the farther end of the street among other local farmers every week. I remember my baba helped her baba years ago. Her baba purchased a used machine for tilling the ground. Then a year later, they needed another donkey, and baba negotiated the deal between Aisha's baba and a herdsman. Where is that table now? It can't be much farther. Did they move their business? Why am I worrying so?

He slowed his gait to a casual walk. He slipped out a few rial from his robe, then bent down and held out the money.

"Now Ashraf, go to the table just a few meters to our right. Your friend Sammi is sitting on a bucket. Say hello and ask the lady if you can buy some of her vegetables."

"Uncle Abdul, Sammi will give us a good deal. That isn't some lady. That's his sister," Ashraf said. He pointed to his chest and boasted, "She's only five years older than me."

"Fine, fine. Just go and buy at that table, so your mama will be happy," Abdul folded the money into the small hand and pushed him lightly, setting him on his way. He stood up and listened to a larger woman, hidden behind her burka. Her voice boomed as she bartered over a handful of potatoes.

Abdul gazed over at Aisha. *Young still, but her passion is clear and full of love for life.* She was bent over, talking to Ashraf. She recognized him and smiled as he tried to get her to come down in price for her father's vegetables on the table. *What a boy he is. Trading is in his blood.* Ashraf held the rial in his fist and shook his head sternly.

Smiling, Aisha's eyes glanced up… over the stubborn child's head. Her gaze caught Abdul's. A few heartbeats later… she was still smiling.

A voice interrupted Abdul's joyous moment.

"Abdul, you didn't tell me you were coming to the market today." Yasser's voice broke through the murmuring of the crowds. "Come and stop by father's tables down the street." He reached for Abdul's arm. "Let us go. We have more linen in stock. You must see how we have arranged our product."

"Oh, Praise be to Allah, Yasser. You caught me listening to this loud woman haggle over potatoes when I need to find my nephew." Abdul turned and took his friend's hands in greeting.

"There he is. That is him running our way now with a handful of vegetables. It looks like he just came from a farmer's table on the west side." Yasser paused a moment. "Wait a moment. Isn't that Aisha's table? The one we spoke of yesterday?"

"Uh, not sure. I need to get my nephew. Good to see you, Yasser," Abdul quickly said.

"Hey Abdul, you can't walk away now. I gave you pieces of this plan. What happened, you silly fool?" Yasser watched him leave, then he smoothed his well-trimmed beard. He prided himself in knowing where to get the best blades for the most contemporary look. "I have been abandoned." He shook his head as he watched Abdul scurry away. "Might as well make a few purchases."

Chapter 7

Abdul

Yemen — 1997

Since I've been home, I've gone to the mosque almost every day to say my prayers. As with many people, I go more often on the weekend. Taking time to pray in the mosque is commanded by Allah, and the Prophet established the standard for us. But occasionally after the prayer, solid networking occurs, and I'm not the only man who takes the opportunity to connect with other local people. Obviously, I appreciate the piety of those who take their prayers seriously. Certainly, Allah wouldn't disapprove of a little networking.

I've stopped many times to chat with local merchants, many of whom I've known from helping my baba years ago. Most days, I pray in the mosque in the village I was raised in. In the last few weeks, I've gone twice a week to the village across the river. The sheikh there was very friendly and spoke with me about my plans for my life. Twice, I saw Aisha returning from her prayer time on the other side of the mosque. I watched her walk with her mama toward the farm. The third time I saw her, I was finishing my conversation with the imam. She glanced my way, but it was almost as if she looked right through me. After she looked my way, I felt Allah had confirmed for me my plans.

The next weekend, Abdul was at the other village's mosque, and he waited for Aisha's baba outside under a low-hanging tree.

"Peace upon you, good sir." Abdul pushed away from the tree as Aziz walked his direction. "May I have a few words with you?"

"Peace upon you as well. What is it you might need of me?" Aziz asked. "I have little time to speak of local goings-on. I'm returning home for the meal my wife prepares even now."

"Well, yes sir. A meal is what I wanted to discuss. I thought perhaps you and I might share a meal together… and some matters of interest to you." Abdul said while he straightened his robe.

"I see, and what is your name?" Aziz asked. "And how might the conversation of our meal go? Most meals I take in my home."

"Certainly, I understand. Uh, my name is Abdul, and my father is a regional businessman in the valley."

"Young man, I'm not talking business with your father," Aziz said. "What is it you need of me?"

"Well, I recently returned from working in business as an apprentice, after completing my master's degree in business… in England," Abdul said as he smoothed a wrinkle from the shirt beneath his robe. "I have begun to prepare for the next steps in my life."

"Abdul, I'm growing a bit impatient, and my stomach is growling like my family donkey," Aziz grumbled. "What does your life story have to do with me?"

"Yes. Y-yes sir. As I was trying to explain. The next steps for me are to find a wife that will help me create a beautiful family in a home that will be well respected in the community," Abdul said. "Your daughter is the woman I need to help me meet that plan, to share my life and home."

"Ah… you want to meet over a meal to discuss a union with my daughter, Aisha?" Aziz head shook. "Yet you have just returned from the large university. Have you obtained as much as a job nearby?" Aziz asked him.

"Oh, well *today* I haven't." Abdul raised his head and straightened his back. "But I have numerous contacts, and I'm sure with my qualifications, that I will easily find a job."

"Abdul, you seem like a well-educated man who thinks sensibly." Aziz scratched his beard. "You come back and see me in a year. Perhaps after you have worked for a while and established yourself."

"Good sir, you don't understand," Abdul hastily said. "I have worked over a year abroad. Then, even before my time at the university, I worked for my father. And our family is recognized for our history in trade and marketing."

"That's fine. Then, in our business, what might have you to offer? Do you have much more than a strong character to discuss?" Aziz raised an eyebrow and looked him over, waiting.

"Sir, I would soon have much to offer during our meal. More than the fine robe I wear," Abdul said as he stroked the gift his baba had given him. "I would bring gifts for your family and home. Then I would cherish your daughter, as she deserves."

"I'm sorry Abdul. You come back, and we can talk more when you have real employment. Not just stories of what has been or what will come." Aziz began to walk down the well-worn path.

Abdul bent over, his hands on his knees, staring at the farmer in disappointment, and a bit of disbelief.

This isn't how the plan was to have worked out. Her baba should have easily agreed to a meeting. Instead, he questioned my character, and my ability to provide a dowry, or even how I could provide for his daughter in the future. Doesn't he know of my family? All of the surrounding villages in the valley and mountains know of my baba's business. What man wouldn't want to marry his daughter into our family?

The sun and heat have affected his thinking, and now logic is out of reach for him. I must speak to Yasser and Sammir about this. Somehow my plan will be refined. This, too, could be a test from Allah. I will rise above this trouble and stand strong with his daughter in my new home.

~

The three friends lounged outside, at a table behind their favorite coffee house, *Mocha*. The coffee house had been named after the famous port city of Mocha. A few large shrubs grew high enough to give some shade, and they had just purchased a freshly harvested batch of *qat* from one of the mountain-dwelling locals.

All but Abdul sat serenely, contented smiles on their faces. Abdul seemed to the others that he wanted to relax but failed. He chewed more and more, but the stimulant didn't seem to affect his demeanor.

"Abdul, you have sat under the shade and chewed for more than an hour, and yet I haven't seen one smile." Yasser chuckled. He was always the first to laugh at his own jokes. "This week has been warm. The rainy season has not set in yet. Relax, my friend."

"We waited for you to join us, and once you did, it's been a wall of silence over there," Sameer said. He smoothed his well-trimmed beard. "Is it that young village girl you are intent on marrying? Is that what causes you worry? More likely her father?" Sameer winked. "The father is most likely the problem." Sameer chuckled at his wit.

"You two friends, so full of advice I didn't ask for," Abdul mumbled loud enough for them to hear. "How much more will I need to tolerate it?"

"Hard to say. How many more weeks are you going to remain stubborn?" Yassir leaned forward. "We have your best interest in mind."

"Still, you don't fully listen," Sameer added.

"What are you talking about? We all agreed I should take a job as some type of supervisor in one of the businesses here in the valley." Abdul waved a hand in the air as he spoke.

"Yes, we did talk about you taking a job, but we actually graphed the other possibilities. You took pieces of our discussion, and then decided on the better route," Sameer answered.

"And we understand you have a degree from abroad, while our time at Sana'a University, here in Yemen, wasn't quite the same level of business experience. But we have kept a good sense of local business since we returned," Yassir said.

"Oh, I remember the probability chart. Your suggestion was that I should be willing to take a position as some low-level runner of product." Abdul snorted. "Maybe even work a table in the market? Get used to the local trading again? Well, I've been trained from the best for marketing the product more successfully and managing resources with complete focus. Why, I should be supervising and helping a business move forward, so they can see a higher profit and decrease their expenses?" Abdul's eyes shone; his earnest intentions were plain to see.

"Yes, yes, Abdul. Then where is that management position right now?" Sameer asked.

"I don't understand it!" Abdul shook his head then stood abruptly. "I've met with four or five different businessmen. We had great meals, and they all appreciated my input. But afterward, nothing. *Nothing*. I called them, inquired about a second meeting, but they were too busy. I even spoke to both of your fathers. I thought they might consider me, knowing that I had studied abroad, and we are friends. But they didn't even want to share a meal with me."

"Ahh, I thought so. You did try my father," Yassir said. "He made a remark about the work ethic of today, that those of us who went to college think we know more in business than those who actually work in the business."

"He said that after I came to him?" Abdul sat down and put his head into his hands.

"We tried to tell you Abdul… these businessmen don't want a business expert with new trends coming in to try to change their style. It just won't happen here," Sameer said.

"But I worked and was paid well in Lebanon, gaining solid experience under great leadership." Abdul's words were muffled as he spoke through his hands.

"True enough," Yassir said. "But you apprenticed under a *European company* that invested there. Then they brought you on to supervise as they had trained you with their methods. If you had stayed with them, you might have been promoted by now."

"Instead, you came back to Yemen," Sameer added. "Now you wonder what to do about a job and a new wife."

"You are both right. I now know what I must do," Abdul stood again. "I will go speak to my father. I will humble myself and say that I will work in whatever position he has open." Yassir and Sameer stood also.

"Okay, well, that might be a good idea," Yassir said.

"But I would broach it with your mother first," Sameer said. "You know she loves you deeply and has a way of talking to your father."

※

I spoke to my mama at length, in private. She has always opened her heart and listened to me. This has been one of the ways she expresses her love — in how well she listens. There is no doubt she can be shrewd and sharp-tongued, if so inclined, but her love is evident when she speaks only a few words to prod people to share their burdens. Especially with her children and grandchildren. Then, her grace is strong and there isn't any judgment. Now if baba will listen to my words! I did some cleaning around the home and waited for my baba to return. I sat in the chair in the living room, staring at my hot tea. I noticed that my right hand is shaking slightly. I breathed deeply, striving for a calm demeanor, but my thoughts made me increasingly anxious the longer I waited.

A shuffle broke me from my thoughts.

"My baba, I thought you would be out this evening with your friends. Their fathers and I had lunch." Fahad shut the door and walked into the room.

His wife brought him a hot cup of tea. A warm smile of greeting adorned her face.

Fahad received the tea and nodded to his wife. "They said Yasser and Sameer would be meandering the streets."

"Not tonight, baba," Abdul said. "I cleaned outside behind the house and repaired the door. It was not opening easily. Now it works much better."

"Yes, my husband," Abdul mother spoke up. "He has been helping with a few things that you haven't had the time to do."

"Well, excellent. Productivity is to be greatly respected," Fahad sighed as he smiled.

"I know, baba, my attempt was to demonstrate my value to you. Mama isn't the only reason I'm here drinking tea alone," Abdul said.

"Well, your reason must be distracting, because you've spilled tea on our favorite table, and you never do that," Fahad said. He waved a hand to his wife, an unspoken request to clean the table. "What is it we have to discuss, since I already see you several times a week at dinner?"

"You see, Baba… I wanted to discuss the idea of you hiring me. I know we had a similar conversation, but this time I'm willing to work at any of the lower jobs," Abdul said.

"Hmm, most interesting," Fahad said. "The men I dined with, they and I had a little laugh over tea. They told me that you had interviewed with each of them." He raised his eyebrows with amusement.

"Well, as long as you laughed," Abdul said, clenching his teeth as he considered his next thought. *A month ago, I might have had more comments. But now I hope he can find me a willing, able, and teachable worker.* "Baba, I have been humbled. I had thought many would want to hire me because of my newly acquired degree, as well as having worked abroad. But that is of little value to those I have spoken to."

"This, my baba, was why I wanted you to go again and work abroad again. Here, business is done on a smaller scale. These men all have their own traditions — just as I do. So, why won't you leave, other than the love of your family?" Fahad asked.

"It is more than that now. I have a *stronger* interest," Abdul quietly said.

"Ahh... I see now. You have picked a woman to marry." Fahad chuckled.

"Yes, baba. But she is not an ordinary girl from the village. She is girl I knew of years ago when Mohammed was her age. Now, she is not only beautiful, but she is known for her intelligence and strong work ethic. I have already spoken to her baba, and he has suggested we wait for a year to let me become established. But Baba, with you as my support in working, he may change his mind." Abdul poured out his thoughts like tea pouring freely from a long-necked tea pot.

"Well, your mother mentioned, in passing, that this might be the case. She claims you could have strong feelings for this girl. You have only been home for a few months, so I'm not sure how that is, it is something to discuss."

"Baba, you have seen what my experiences have brought me, in addition to the education you have helped provide for me. But now I understand more... I understand that I can still learn even the smallest details of business from you."

What other words can I say to sway his mind? I felt in my heart that this is a blessing from Allah, and it will happen.

Chapter 8

Aisha

1997 October — Yemen

Home is full of chaos today. My two aunts have come over to help my mama and me clean our home and begin preparation for the meal. Uncle Saeed and Uncle Kareem have been busy with my baba today bringing over a second table and chairs. They also put away some of Baba's tools. Then they made room for the tandoor oven that the entire village shared.

It was almost like a party, but some of the adults seemed nervous. I have heard them talking in low tones, speculating the outcome of the meal today, and even the future. They are speaking in nervous and hushed whispers, but it's even worse for me with the constant fluttering in my stomach. It feels almost like a swarm of mosquitos buzzing and waiting to land on me.

I wonder if I'm ready. Honestly, I don't think I'm ready for the responsibility that comes with marriage. My mama and I talked about it. She said she will help me to learn how to handle myself properly when I am to marry and be placed in a new home. My aunts smile at the thought and cluck their tongues in anticipation.

The area that functioned as our kitchen area began filling the air with aromatics. Aisha's older aunt, Najam, was spreading a dry rub, hawaij, over the lamb meat her father had butchered yesterday. She combined the chopped mutton with vegetables from our garden. Aisha helped chop for the stew. Mama added the chopped potatoes to the pot for our family's version of salad. Then, Mama cleaned the table and started to make the flatbread for the tandoor oven outside. The family was not used to making such large meals, and so everyone has come together to help prepare for this occasion.

As the afternoon moved toward evening, the pots gently simmered to keep the stew warm. Men lounged in chairs outside with their qat while they told stories of their youth. All around there was an air of anticipation of what was to come.

"Aisha, you're pacing the room like a baba waiting for his child to be born. All the food is ready, and now we are only waiting for his family to come. You need to relax now," Badia said with a smile.

"But mama, I'm nervous, and I feel like I should be doing more." Aisha wrung her hands.

"There is nothing more that can be done but trust that Allah will provide for you. You can't be in the dining room when they arrive, so go now into the bedroom, and read one of your favorite books," Badia said. "Your aunts and I have served people before, and all the men will be pleased."

"But how is it that I can't be in the room and meet the family? It is me they will be talking over like I'm vegetables traded in the market. I should have a presence here," Aisha said.

"Your presence will be felt in spirit as you listen from another room. I'm sure the men will not be whispering about their intentions," Badia laughed.

"You will sit and play with me on the bed and tell me stories of faraway lands," Amira added with a little grin.

"Girls, it's time for you to go in the other room now," Aziz walked aside his brother. "There is a train of men walking. I can see them coming along the river."

"But mama, let me help serve the tea. I will be veiled, and they will not know it is me," Aisha suggested.

"No, hurry now. You'll cover yourself completely with your dark hijab and then you will go the bedroom quietly to be with your sister. I need to go and heat the water for the tea," Badia said. "My sister has all our cups ready. I don't know if some will stand or if some will sit outside. We don't have enough seats for all those people." Badia hurried to the kitchen area.

The steps of those men seemed to take much too long. My younger brother got to stay outside, and I don't understand it. But baba only smiled as I frowned when Khalil ran outside with his ball to kick it along the river as the train of men arrived. I could just imagine Abdul stopping the ball easily with his foot, laughing as he dribbles, and it kicks it back to Khalil. I stood and stared at the wall in mild frustration, arms folded. I wondered about Allah's will for my life.

"Aisha! I hear the men talking outside. They must be coming close," Najam tapped her on the shoulder.

"Okay, Aunt Najam," Aisha said. She tightened her hijab.

"Greetings. Allah be praised. Come into my home," Aziz said loudly, as he opened the door to usher in the line of men. "Come, come and relax. My name is Aziz. I have hot tea on the table for all."

"Greetings! We have come with the finest sweets our wives could make for you." Fahad spoke first. "Where shall I put them?"

"Ah, three sets of hands are full. We will taste many moments of joy," Aziz laughed. "Set all of them on the table."

Yasser and Sameer walked with Abdul's cousin, Jabir, to the table with homemade bint al sahn. The sweet honey bread almost overpowered the aroma of the tea.

"My name is Fahad. This is my older brother, Taymullah," Fahad as he extended his right hand to shake with Aziz.

"Peace be upon you," Aziz said.

"Upon you be peace also," answered the two older brothers in unison. The other men were gathering in anticipation of their tea but nodded in their host's direction and sought the basin to wash their hands.

As she shut the door, Aisha stood against the door to hear the men's conversation. *Amira poked at my back incessantly because she wanted me to play but I was in no mood for her princess stories.* She silently opened the door a few centimeters so she could see the men.

"How are you this warm day in our great valley?" Fahad asked.

"Fine, praise Allah," Aziz responded. "My bones are weary some, but they are still strong enough to carry me for the work I do."

"Well, I have the best answer for tired bones. Taymullah has brought you some coffee," Fahad said with a smile. "He owns two coffee farms in the neighboring valley."

"Oh but, you are the Taymullah that my nephew, Kadar, speaks of. He has worked on one of the coffee farms you own. He has said you have high standards for the workers yet are fair and just among them. You pay well for their work and on time," Aziz said.

"Kadar, that is your nephew. He is a good young man. With that limp, he still works like a gazelle. It's amazing how fast he is," Taymullah exclaimed.

"That is my son," Saeed spoke up with a loud tone. "The limping gazelle, we call him. He got that limp when our mule explained to him a better way to plow my field." Saeed bent over, mimicking how the mule had stomped on the shins of his baba. "He learned that day a farm animal that has worked the field for years will not yield easily to take directions from a new hand." All the men laughed as he repeated the stomp. So enthusiastic was his recreation of the mule's stomp that his cup of tea spilled.

"Careful, my brother. My wife has made only so much tea," Aziz said through his laughter.

"Speaking of tea, it is one of the products we trade. Abdul has done a good job increasing our market with tea. He has many ideas how to expand our trading. It is Allah's blessing that he is such a smart man." Fahad bragged of Abdul's work ethic. Fahad had hired Abdul into an entry-level position. Fahad had assigned him to work under one of his better tradesmen, and that mentor spoke well of Abdul. And the man knew enough of Fahad not to speak highly of the owner's son only because Abdul was the son. Abdul trusted his supervisors and their judgement. "He brought us a few new ideas I am considering. They may work well in our business."

Aziz nodded. He'd heard how well Abdul is doing. "He has already mastered the tasks at entry-level and was a go-getter. That is one reason I agreed to this meeting." He smiled graciously. "Let's begin the meal. I know many of you must be hungry."

"Bismillah," all the men said in quiet unison before they walked toward the stack of plates.

The conversation continued to move around the room of men. It seemed as if everyone knew somebody else's cousin or brother. I couldn't believe how easily the men talked. Many times, I saw them so stoic and silent. I heard them compare the sheikhs between different villages in our valley. One sheik's voice could be heard across the road, while another had a stern look. I wasn't aware how much these men noticed. I thought they were only concerned with their work. After a half-hour the mutton that had been simmering was served in the vegetables and potatoes. I could hear my aunt bring the bread from outside where it had cooled from the special tandoor oven. The talking quieted as the men ate. I knew some would eat outside because our home was not large enough for all ten of them.

"This food is delicious," Fahad said. "I can taste all the fresh flavors. They must be treasured hands that prepared it." All of the men in the room had mouths full. They all nodded in agreement. Abdul ate also, but he sat back away from his baba and uncle. Although his uncle had turned back on occasion to silently stare at him.

They all took some of the fresh bread and wiped a portion of the plates. But they purposefully left some food untouched. Smiles filled the room as their stomachs were content, but they didn't want to suggest they were still hungry. It was important that you didn't appear poor and clean your plate empty. But clearly the men had seemed to enjoy the food.

Yet the room remained quiet.

"Bismillah, because we would be honored to have your blessing for our son to marry your daughter." Taymullah finally spoke up. All of the men looked up from their empty plates to see the expression on Aziz's face.

"Quite an honor," Aziz said. His voice shook slightly, and he took his left hand to steady his teacup in his right hand. "We are honored, indeed." But his expression didn't change.

"Your family is known throughout our community," Saeed said. "You are blessed many times over."

"Humbly I thank you. Our family has worked industriously over the years to meet the needs of the various communities among the surrounding valleys, "Fahad quietly said.

"It's obvious you want to invest in the people, and care about them. So, it's only reasonable that you have such a respectful baba in Abdul, "Aziz said.

I heard Uncle Saeed speak up again and he talked for a while again about the impact Fahad's family has made in their valley. There were quiet murmurs of agreement. Finally, the conversation turned over to the politics and weather. They spoke of the earthquake years ago, and how it affected our region. Then I heard them laugh about the honey bread, and the flavors it brought. Aisha opened the door a bit and snuck a peek as the men gathered themselves in preparation to depart. They laughed as they finished the last few sips of tea. These few hours seemed like a whole day. I heard the noise of Khalil kicking the ball against our house. Then Mama called my name to come clean all the plates.

One week later – October

"Aisha, stop asking, the answer will not change," Badia sternly said. "Now sit and relax in the chair. You should be content that I am allowing you to sit in the room and listen."

"Hah! Am I not the topic of the conversation between my aunts, you, and these strange women from another village? And you expect me to go hide in the bedroom? I need to hear what's being said of me," Aisha said with arms folded across her chest in the chair. "So, being in the room isn't too much to ask of my family?"

"Aisha, take the scowl off of your face. You think you are an adult now because you may be getting married soon, but you still are a child," Badia said.

"Yes, little one. You have much more to learn, while you are thinking you are so mature," Najam, her mama's sister interjected. "Wait till you have to run a house, care for children, and make your husband happy. All to please Allah, of course."

"Keep your tongue still now, my daughter. I see them walking up now," Badia said. "I must turn the water on for the tea."

"Oh, I see one of them has a large basket in her hands. I hope it's a tasty dessert for us," Aisha said. "I have been craving some after smelling the food the men had last week."

"You will do as your mama says and sit in the back quietly, or you may pay the price for your impudence," Najam said, her eyebrows raised.

I sat there and listened while my mama hosted these guests. The group of women came in and introduced themselves to my family. They all looked at me but did not say a single word. A few of the five women even stared as if I were an assortment of produce from the market and they were not sure what to make of me. Tea was served and the conversation began to flow.

Somehow, one of the women was a cousin to my Aunt Najam, and then laughter began.

Najam had had two daughters, and she had begged Allah to provide sons for her. So, her son later became known as the token prize within the family. He was like a king. They all laughed, and then looked at me to see if I smiled. But instead, I only sat silently, as I was instructed. Ghada, Abdul's mama, was more subtle. But I could see she was watching me. She caught me looking at the fresh fruit basket with raisins scattered among the other fruit that they had brought to our home. I knew the men would speak of me as something to be traded, but this was somehow worse. I'm being judged and I'm not sure if I will meet the standard or if it will get back to the men. Perhaps one of these women might not find me acceptable. But Mama continued to smile as she carried the flow of the conversation about my faithfulness to Islam, my obvious beauty, and my ability to discern wisdom and share it properly with others. I hope she is not building me up so much to be something I can't reach.

November

"Badia, dinner was again well done," Aziz patted his stomach. "You make food that is always so good out of the simple ingredients we grow, or you find within our budget at the market. A better wife I would not find around the mountains or even in Sana'a, our capital."

"I'm pleased when I know that you're full from a meal that I've prepared," Badia said with a smile. "But I would be fully pleased if you would tell me how the meeting at the coffee shop went today. Did they agree to your terms?"

"Yes, I was planning on telling you the details. But where is Aisha? She doesn't need to know all of my discussion," Aziz looked behind him to the cooking area.

"She is in the bedroom, claiming to be reading. And she probably has her ear to the door," Badia said. "But we don't need to whisper. I think it would be good for her hear of the business about her."

"Okay, my love. Fahad, the young man's father- he and his brother met with me. Fahad explained how he had hired his son, and that his son worked well at his tasks and without complaint. He spoke of the home that is not far from Fahad's home where they would live, and one day raise a family."

"Excellent, my husband. But what of your price?" Badia asked.

"Yes, I wrote down the amount. The rial amounted to 10,000 American dollars, and he didn't even blink about my dowry demand. I'm not sure what to think," Aziz said.

"But did he agree to a third meeting?"

"Yes, what did he say? I need to know," Aisha said through the partially open door.

"Hah, I knew you were listening," Badia laughed. "Where is the wisdom we spoke about last week?"

"Yes, mama. I know, but I was full of rumblings in my stomach, waiting," Aisha said.

"Rest easy, my girl. He said he would meet me early next week," Aziz laughed. "So now you can sleep tonight. Or maybe you can't sleep with this on your mind?"

January-1998

The last two months have become swift memories for me. They were filled with emotions that swirled about my soul, like the pot of stew my mama boils. Baba informed they had agreed to an amount for my dowry. Then there was the great betrothal feast. Fahad brought the engagement ring, and many clothes to give to mama and me. He made quite a gesture in giving them to baba. He also brought fresh dates for my mama and me. They were delicious, and freshly picked from one of Abdul's contacts. They brought a portion of the dowry amount, and it was explained among the men that the remaining amount would be given once we were married. Abdul's family is known throughout the valley, and there was no doubt among my family the remainder would be paid in full. My mama and Aunt Najam explained to me that much of the money given would be mine to be jewelry, and other valuables. These things I could keep as mine, even if divorce would be spoken of. During the betrothal feast, the men decided on a date for the marriage ceremony, with a month to prepare.

The month came quickly, and I still didn't feel completely ready. But every time I stole a glance in the market, or I saw him walking among the villagers, Abdul seemed completely confident and at ease. My emotions moved up and down, filled with uncertainty.

The week of our wedding was a three-day celebration that began on Wednesday. I stood veiled apart from the men. Abdul came to the home with his baba and uncle. This time he spoke. 'Will you give me your daughter in marriage?' Baba answered immediately. 'Yes, I will give you my daughter to be your wife.' It seemed he spoke rather quickly, as if he were ready for me to leave. The qadi then asked baba if I agreed to the marriage, and baba nodded. Then baba and Abdul clasped their right hands. The qadi laid a white cloth over their arms, and spoke loudly the Fatiha, the first sura of the Quran. Then raisins were thrown from those watching, to ensure a happy marriage for us. The next two days were a combining of our families to celebrate. Somehow it seemed right, this man whom I was given.

My family helped me move into our new home. Abdul had already been living there for four months. He and his baba had prepared it so that it would be ready for us as a couple. I could see the work he had done to try to make me happy. My aunt had even told me his mama had talked to her about my favorite colors to place in the home. As we prepared to come together as husband and wife, I felt blessed by Allah. Perhaps this union for us would be a true blessing. What could I have to fear from a man like this? He is a good man.

Chapter 9

Abdul

Dearborn — 2003

The restaurant was very busy today. Customers were lined up out the door because every table was full. I like it when we're busy. It keeps my mind off other problems, but I still notice what goes on around me. It's in my nature to observe people – I can't help it.

Many of the people who work at Ford came here for lunch. They enjoy our unique foods. Uncle Suhaib has chosen the menu carefully for Americans' taste as well as Middle Eastern.

I cleared another table and listened with curiosity at the different groups chatting around me. I finished one table and then brought out waters to a new table — all the while listening to those around me. Two women agreed on a time to meet at the gym, and still make dinner for their respective families. A second mixed group seemed to all have a different story to tell about their children. Everyone seemed to want to outdo the others as to the excellence of their children, either in sports or academia.

Four men at another table argued about where to stop for drinks after work, while one excused himself from the bar meet-up. By the other three's mocking laughter, I could tell it wasn't his first time bowing out. They jeered about his being tied to his wife's leash.

Americans led such busy lives, and I couldn't believe all the different choices people made. Women who insisted on exercising each day and yet finding time to cook for their families. Proud parents who seem to justify how much greater they are through their children. Men who preferred to spend even more time with their coworkers after work, than enjoy the quiet of their own home. I just don't understand their thinking at all.

"Abdul hurry, cousin! More people are waiting at the door to be seated, and there are two tables against the wall need to be cleared," Mohammed loudly whispered to him. He held a stack of menus in his arm, waiting to seat a new group.

"I'm doing the best I can, Mohammed. I have cleaned four tables and gotten water for two others," Abdul whispered back. *Uncle Suhaib goes to buy more supplies for the kitchen at Restaurant Depot, and Mohammed is left in charge. Then his head is puffed up, and I have to counter his overbearing confidence. I would have thought by now he would find his sense of self here. Instead, he likes me to know he is the supervisor, only under his baba. In small ways and most often the words he speaks under his breath, he shows me that he is the manager.*

"Abdul – move quickly and take these menus. Then go seat those people waiting at the door at one of the tables you just cleaned. I'm going to see where the two waiters are," Mohammed muttered. He looked around the room to check all was well.

"Good afternoon," Abdul said to the group of men with Ford badges attached to their button-down shirts. "Please follow me to your table," Abdul smiled and motioned to the large table along the wall.

"This table will work great for us, since it has more room for my laptop." A thinner man with a clean beard jutting from his narrow chin smiled. "Can we get a few glasses of wine, or do you have that here?"

"No, sorry gentlemen," Abdul said. "But I will quickly get your server for some beverages to begin with. In fact, I can get you water now."

"Thank you." The thin man seemed to want to speak for the group. He nodded to Abdul.

Americans must think they need some alcohol at all times of the day to make good conversation. Is there no sense of real awareness without outside stimuli? Then I remembered qat.... Humph! I need to hurry for water, and Uncle Suhaib still has me bussing tables. He could at least help serve as a waiter. My English has gotten good again, and we are in Dearborn where many Arabic restaurants are.

"Careful traying those glasses up, Abdul," Suhaib said while pushing a hand truck of plates, glasses, and carryout supplies from the back door in the hallway. "Each glass cost the restaurant money and they are easy to break."

"I've got it under control," Abdul spoke under his breath as he put the fourth glass on his forearm. "I practiced for two days carrying trays with Mohamed. I'm pretty sure I've got it handled." Abdul wanted to say it loudly to his uncle, but he ended up mumbling to himself.

Uncle Suhaib and I had long conversations about my management degree, and how much value I had brought to the company I had worked for after interning through the university. With a business management focus and a minor in marketing, I had helped raise sales by five percent in the years I worked there. Then they had transitioned management. My previous direct supervisors really appreciated my work efforts and could see the impact I was making. But the new leadership didn't care so much for me, and I was just another young, hungry supervisor. It made me feel disillusioned. On top of that, I really missed Yemen and my family. I Skyped with my mama and emailed my parents. But it had been a few years since I'd actually seen them.

I know Uncle Suhaib doesn't really understand my potential. Instead of sitting down and considering all of my education, work experience, and new ideas for marketing at the restaurant, my uncle has relegated me to learn the basics of the business by starting as a busboy and host. He did not grasp all that I was capable of, and how much influence I could offer the family restaurant. I know I could have sought out other employment in the Dearborn area, perhaps even at the Ford Motor Company. But my baba had insisted I put in time helping his brother at his restaurant, especially since their family had willingly offered to take in my family. Baba even implied Uncle Suhaib could use some of my expertise. But that doesn't seem to be the case.

"You dropped the water off, and then stood as still as a statue looking out the window," Mohammed pushed him, and he almost lost his balance. "There – three more tables that need to be bussed and cleaned, cousin."

"Look Mohammed, thank you for all your training. But you know I was a supervisor for years after I completed my education."

"I know, cousin. But it is much different working in our restaurant than the business you did after university."

"Yes, you need to remember you are in a restaurant, and even the slightest mistake could bring down our sales. You need a change of perspective," Uncle Suhaib said. "Stop living in what you did in Europe and Lebanon. I need to see you working here in Dearborn."

"Well, I'm doing the best I can in the position you placed me," Abdul said. "I need to leave in a few minutes to pick up Aisha from her English class at the Mosque. I will drop her off and return before dinner begins."

Chapter 10

Aisha

Dearborn — October 2003

I walked with Aini in the stroller after I came home to feed her and make myself something small to eat. We walked in the crisp fall day, where the wind blew the leaves around the neighborhood. Another Arabic mama was out for a walk also, and we talked for a few minutes. We talked about the English classes I was taking, and she said she preferred the ones where native English teachers taught. There was a place that taught English, helped new immigrants with their paperwork, located shopping nearby, and even provided resources for working. My new friend was from Saudi Arabia, and she said the place was only two blocks from the mosque where I went to classes.

Although I'm not happy about the name, Heavenly Home, this community center was very well regarded by my new friend, and I looked it up on the internet using the computer in Uncle Shuaib's workroom when no one was looking. The website said its main goal is to help meet the needs of immigrants as they attempt to become acclimated to American culture. They focus on language, soft skills, and a boutique to help immigrants fit better into the American culture. There were even two separate rooms for men and women with cots for those looking for a bed. Abdul dropped me off today at the mosque, and I waited until he pulled away. Then I walk the two blocks away from the mosque and found a single-story plain building. The sign read, 'Heavenly Home.' The sign had a carved angel with a piece of red-hot coal in his hand, and below 'Heavenly Home' it read: 'And I heard the voice of the Lord saying, "Whom shall I send, and who will go for us?"'

A tall, pear-shaped woman with long, beautiful blond hair opened the door for me as I approached. I had rehearsed my first greeting again and again. Would I even get that correct? I prayed that I might pronounce it correctly. I mean, we had practiced greetings with a sheik's wife, but this was an English teacher.

"Thank y-you," I stuttered a little, but still smiled. "How are you today?" Just as I had practiced in the mirror in our new room.

"You're welcome, and very well," she said with a large smile. "Come right in and go to the table where we have people preparing for your day. There is a small fee of ten dollars today only," she said slowly word by word.

I understood almost everything she said because she spoke slowly. Aisha congratulated herself and smiled. *Because of my internet learning, I have become more proficient in English.* She pointed me in the direction down the hall. *Ten dollars? I have no money in my purse. I had not thought of money. Abdul had taken care of any fee at the mosque. Should I turn and go back?*

I walked to the table where a line of people stood. There were ten to twelve other Arabs, a few Latinos, and three or four people from Asia. I stood on my toes to see over the taller Arab man in front of me, who looked like he could be from Saudi Arabia. I tried to see what paperwork was at the table. Was someone helping the people with the forms I sighed deeply while stepping back in line. I do not know if they will even allow me to stay today without the money.

"What is your name, Miss?" a woman asked me. Looking up, I saw she was a pale, thin white woman with dark hair sprinkled with grey. She motioned to me with a pen in her right hand. "I will need your full name on this paper." She pointed to a line with an encouraging smile. I printed my name in English as I had practiced many times in our room. "Now if you could step to your left and pay the ten dollars for the class Aisha, we can complete the process."

"No, I have no money," I said slowly. I opened my purse and shook my head. "Maybe I should come back another day."

"Oh, no. Don't leave. If you don't have the money today, that's fine." She smiled again. "We can do an 'I owe you' for today and you can pay us by the end of the week. I will just make a note here by your name. Go ahead and find a seat at one of the tables." She pointed across the room that opened to a classroom setting, with a large whiteboard in the front.

"Come, come sit with us." Two Arabic women sat at a back table. They gestured at Aisha; their loud whispers carried across the room. *There are two empty seats left at their table. Smiling at them, I picked the one closest to them.* "This is the first day, but we are repeating the class again because it is so good," the older one explained.

"Yes, the class has at least twenty people in it, and we are all trying to learn here in America." The girl next to me said, giggling softly. She touched my arm lightly. "You will enjoy it so much," she added.

"My name is Aisha," *I said with a little laugh.* "I am from Yemen, but I am very happy to see people outside of my new home speaking Arabic. I was not certain that others would be here to welcome me."

"Oh, we have been waiting for two months for the class to begin again. I have been only cooking and cleaning for my family, and it's so nice to be out of the house," the girl next to me explained to me. "My name is Caliana, and I am from Lebanon."

"And my name is Jada, and I am from Lebanon also. We are so happy you can join us." The older woman looked like she was thirty years old. "I called Caliana last week to be sure she was coming today, and here we are," she said while looking around. "I think our other friend from the last class is coming also from her morning job where she serves coffee."

"That's nice. She is able to work just for a few hours?" I asked.

"Oh yes." Caliana smiled. "Many of us have a small job, as long as we can still maintain our homes and meals, our husbands don't mind. A little shopping money, you know. We will have so much fun together, and—"

"Okay, class. Everyone stop the little talking." An older white woman with long, curly, gray hair tapped the whiteboard. "My name is Karin Freemen, and I will be one of your teachers here at Heavenly Home."

"She is such a nice lady," Caliana whispered to me.

"And she is a great teacher also," Jada nodded.

"All right, everyone. Please write on a piece of paper the sentence on the board. Print it just as I have written it," Ms. Freemen instructed us. I opened my notebook where I'd practiced my name and started to print, 'Today is Monday.' I looked to my left and both girls were whispering.

"Where is your paper?" I whispered to Caliana and pointed to my notebook.

"Oh, we were so happy to see each other, we forgot our paper today. But this part we already know," Jada laughed lightly.

"Ladies in the back," Karin pointed at us with the long pointer. "I love that you three are getting acquainted, but we will be doing that with real introductions after everyone is registered." I opened my notebook again and started to carefully outline the letters in English, while the girls just started to talk again. I sighed and shook my head. I hope I did not get reprimanded because of them. But even more I wondered about a job for me. I could earn some money myself, and shop for my own clothes without asking permission to get what I needed.

∼

Rahma asked me to assist in the preparation of the lunch meal. Although many in America eat a lighter lunch, our family here has a larger meal in the middle of the day, as was the custom in our home country. The men dine with us after their busy lunch business, and so we eat at two-thirty. They leave a few other men to watch the restaurant and come home to eat with us. Rahma plans the meals. I love the smells we create together. The simmering spices bring back such memories of our home and my family. I miss them so much. The hot and spicy blends are readily available in local markets, and we use them often.

Today, while I was in class, Rahma had already started one of my favorite main dishes in Yemen. She had started the chicken slow cooking in the pot two hours earlier and then added potatoes and carrots before I came home from my class. Abdul stopped the car in front of the house and smiled when I said I would help with lunch then I would see him back hungry again in a few hours. But here I was, singing softly to myself while cutting up zucchini and tomatoes to add to the ogdat stew. My head lifted a little with my voice as I dropped the zucchini in the pot. My nostrils filled with the aromatic and prominent blend of turmeric, coriander seeds, cumin, and fresh cilantro. I dipped down for another whiff and felt just a small amount of roasted chili pepper momentarily take over my senses. I set down the bowl that I had emptied into the pot and leaned back against the kitchen counter. Hands on the counter, I stared out across the kitchen, remembering my mama's kitchen. I was wondering what she was doing today, and what of my sister? What version of this stew would my mama be making? Most likely, with lamb. I could taste the lamb, and I licked my upper lip and inhaled deeply thinking of her cooking. I shook my head when I heard a sound. Aini, my baby daughter, was crying through the speaker on the counter.

"Do not concern yourself with cooking, and take care of your sweet baby," Rahma spoke up while cutting the khubz, our homemade flatbread, that we would dip into the stew. "I have already cleaned her diaper. You should see if she is thirsty now."

"Yes, Rahma. I will go check on her," I replied. *I hurriedly walked up the stairs to follow the sound of her cries. I know she probably only wants to be held, and so there isn't much of an immediate need. But even for the moment, I need to be away from Rahma. Sometimes I feel her staring at me. Perhaps it's because I'm another woman in her home. And her helpful comments don't feel very helpful. She's not my mama.*

"Aini, my daughter, quiet down, my love," I cooed to her as I picked her. I wrapped her blanket lightly around her face, and she spit while gurgling happiness into it. A little smile takes over her face. "Oh, my beloved one, you make my heart so full when you smile! You are such a gift from Allah. I thank him so often for you."

"Aisha, you and she belong in a picture frame," Abdul startled me, and Aini burped as my upper body moved. "Stay there while I go for my camera," he said with a laugh. All of our memories were on that camera.

"No, please don't go looking through that closet I only yesterday finished organizing," I called after him. "Go downstairs and prepare to eat the stew your aunt has made. She even found a bit of prep work for me to do. I suppose to help me feel useful."

"Ah, useful? Well, you are loved among the men in the house. My cousin and uncle see how you care for our children, and the kindness in your voice for those around you. Even the poise in which you carry yourself. I am proud to have you as my wife! Let my aunt live with a little joy and hope for our tomorrows," Abdul finished with higher tone. Both Aini and I looked at him, our eyes glowing.

"Well, the camera is in a box on the shelf of the closet. Get it quickly and take your photo," I said with a laugh. "In moments like this I thank my baba for approving of our wedding."

"Aisha, bring your family down here for the meal, and help me bring it to the table," Rahma stood at the stairway. She held a spoon and tapped the handrail to get our attention.

"Smile and look this way, girls!" Abdul snapped two photos quickly. *He checked the photo with a satisfied smile, and then we all walked toward the hallway. Aini giggled as her baba took her from me in the hall, and I waved at Rahma, still standing at the foot of the stairs. We all walked down together, laughing lightly at Aini's smile.*

"You look at me and walk around my kitchen, so I have you help me prepare our meal. Then you waste time coddling the baby, while our food is getting cold," she mumbled to me as I walk into the kitchen. "Here is the stew. Take the bowl carefully, it's full and hot. I have the toasted khubz."

"Uh, thank you, R-rahma," I stuttered while picking up the steaming bowl. *What does it mean, waste time with my baby? She was the one who told me to go spend time with Aini. It makes no sense.*

I walked to the large dining room table, where the three men were already seated. I tripped on the rug that was curling up under one of the chairs, and much of the broth from the bowl spilled out like the Wadi Sudd in Yemen.

"Aisha, be careful, you clumsy girl! The stew is all over the table now," Rahma pointed with the platter of bread in her hands. *I quickly grabbed napkins from the center of the table to stop the hot stew from reaching the men and staining their expensive imported rug.*

"Oh, that's quite all right, Aisha," Uncle Suhaib smiled reassuringly in my direction. "We can easily move our chairs back, and I will pull the rug back," he laughed while kicking back the rug and moving his chair at the same time. *I didn't think it was funny at all.*

Why wouldn't anyone else help me clean up the spill? My nerves were already on edge from Rahma chastising me. I am no young girl who is untrained. I am a married woman.

"Here Aisha, take my apron to clean your spill. And Suhaib, stop that laughing and bring your chair back to the table to eat." Rahma sternly looked at her husband.

"All is well," Abdul said, while biting into the flatbread he picked up off the platter Rahma had set down, Aini was giggling in his other arm.

"No, it's not. We worked hard on the stew, and much of it is gone." *I frantically finished drying the table with the apron and walked into the kitchen. Rinsing the apron in the sink, I began to sob. I am made a mockery of by Rahma, and the men think it is only a joke. This home is not much of a home for me. I wish I were back in Yemen with my mama, who loved me.*

~

I said my morning prayers and prayed silently to Allah for guidance. I felt no peace in this home. It was so different when Abdul and I were first married. We had our own small home that I maintained well. I would even go and help his mama host when businessmen came to their home. Both Abdul's mama and my aunt and mama gave me great council for meeting my husband's needs in the home and bedroom. Within a few months, I was pregnant with Habib, and I knew it would be a boy. I was so happy then, and Abdul's face shone in our home. But I knew his eyes were meant for more than business in our valley. I heard his baba speak to him and ask when he would do what Allah had purposed for his life.

Now in this home, I felt little joy. Even the neighbors watched me, almost waiting to see how much I would do as a proper wife and mama in this home. I felt their eyes on me from all side of our home. They stared from their windows. I would look out in time to see them shut their blinds.

I walked back into our room silently with Abdul. Today, again, I was to go to class. The ride was silent, and Abdul knew from the week before I wasn't really pleased at the mosque. But he doesn't know I'm going to Heavenly Home instead. Today, I sat in the back away from the other girls I had befriended. They had told me about the Arabic coffee shop just another block away, where one girl worked. I had worked up the courage, and I was going to that coffee shop. I'd leave an hour early from the computer time in the ESL class. The teacher wouldn't see me silently walk out the side door.

"Good morning! How can I help you?" A forty-something woman with a nice smile and loose-fitting hijab asked me.

"Peace be upon you," Aisha answered with a smile in Arabic. "I'm wondering if you are looking for people to work a few hours a day. A friend said to me that she works two hours and then comes to my class."

"Oh my, yes. We want to work with different schedules, and offer new residents a chance to work," the woman stated. "Can I get you an application?"

"Yes, please. I would like to fill it out," I said. *We had practiced filling out blank applications at the Heavenly Home class, and I knew how to answer all of the questions. This is so exciting. I've dreamed of having a job. What would my mama say to this? I could never tell my family. They wouldn't understand at all.*

Chapter 11

Aisha

January — 2003

"Listen well and try to enjoy yourself in class today," Abdul said with a gentle tap on my hand. He smiled. "I know you wish the class could be different, but you are still learning. You have a passion for learning. I hope that is enough for you."

"Certainly, my love," I said and returned his smile. "The sheikh and his wife are doing a good job of blending the teaching of English and reinforcing the important necessary concepts of Islam for women. Also, the book they use is a nice resource."

"Ah, well then. You are making the effort to continue. That is what I want for you," Abdul said.

"Well, enough talking, I must go before I miss the first segment of class," Aisha said and opened her door. "Thank you for your concern, Abdul." Aisha stepped away from the car and walked slowly toward the mosque. The wind whipped between the buildings. The last of the leaves fell from a few trees nearby. Abdul honked the horn once as he pulled away.

He must report for work at the restaurant.

Aisha's eyes followed an orange leaf as it swirled and danced.

The wind reminds me of my walks on the mountain trails above our valley in Yemen. Life was simpler there, but I remember how I dreamed of being in another country. Then, after our baba was born in our new home, Abdul was so happy. But I still felt a yearning. I tried not to let him notice, so I smiled and acted happy with my duties around the home. Then, after a few more years, our daughter was born. By then, Abdul was beginning to feel even more unhappy with his working world. He didn't share his concerns with me, but I could feel his discontent. So, it wasn't a surprise when he announced he was going to visit his uncle and cousin in the United States to work for a few months. I knew that Allah was planning something more for us. Later, we all moved to the United States.

Once we arrived here, I realized I have not been happy here in America either.

But now I feel strong pangs of guilt. In my yearning for respect from those I love, and a need for independence, I may have crossed a boundary line.

It's almost like the rope we used when the river was too high to cross, and if we weren't careful, one could be swept down the river. Now I'm caught in a current of my village's doing, but it's somehow what I wanted. I can't stop these decisions. But the real guilt comes from not telling my husband, or even giving him the clues to notice. Instead, I deceive everyone. I live in fear of what he and his family will think or do if they discover my secrets. How long can I go this way?

My first big transgression was when I clearly stepped away from the mosque's classes. The new classes I'm in teach more English and have helped me to adapt to American society. Secondly, I got a job that allows me to work two or three hours a day. It's only a few minutes' walk from the Heavenly Home classes, and I still have a full hour of English. But I'm learning more by working than by being in the class. It's called the Java Blue Café.

I work the counter there, selling mostly coffee and some sweets. I try to practice my English, but often the customers are speaking only Arabic. Today, I told the supervisor I could work an extra hour because the English class had been canceled. They had us practice on the computers for a short time, and then dismissed us.

"Aisha, how are you today? You were able to come in early. Thank you so much." Malak, the supervisor smiled warmly.

Malak was the supervisor who managed at the Java Blue Cafe. Malak was Lebanese, who seemed to always wear a pleasant smile with the guests and other employees. That was something I noticed immediately.

Aisha stood behind the counter, serving coffee from the machine as she'd been trained. Almost all of the customers spoke Arabic, and so it was not difficult to keep up.

I enjoy my work, moving about quickly, and interacting with the customers. After three hours of working, it felt like only a few minutes. I had asked Abdul to pick me up by the Mosque at 2:00 clock when I would finish the afternoon class.

She glanced at the clock and grimaced. *Now it's 1:30 and I will have to leave here soon.*

A customer stepped up to her counter. "Hello, what can I get you today?" Aisha replaced her frown with a smile. She was still practicing correct greetings in English, so she spoke slower than the Americans and the Arabs that spoke fluent English.

"Good afternoon. I would like a large coffee with a *knafeh*." A dark-haired man in his fifties ordered.

His hair showed a few streaks of gray, but he was clearly not an Arab, which was a little unusual for the Java Blue Café.

"Yes, sir," she answered, then reached beneath the counter for the pastry, using tongs. Malak had told her staff to be sure to pick up the food with the tongs. Aisha quickly poured and handed him the coffee.

"It's been only a few weeks, but you have gotten quicker at serving here," the man said, smiling. "I come in here every week and see peoples' comings and goings."

"Oh, thank you," Aisha said. She bagged the *knafeh* and handed it to him. He adjusted the books to tuck them under his arm, took the bag and walked to a table. She watched him settle himself. He moved the coffee to the corner of the table. He opened each book and set them side by side. Fascinated, she watched him pull a yellow marker from his pocket. He carefully highlighted portions of each book.

When the next guest came in the man was still sitting there reading his books and casually observing people.

"Malak, I have to go. My husband is coming for me," Aisha said.

"Oh, okay, Aisha. Thank you for coming in an hour early. You're doing a good job at the counter," Malak said with a smile. "You have learned this job very quickly. You're a natural. Even though you're a bit shy, you greet customers with wonderful hospitality."

"Umm, thank you," Aisha said.

"Here, give me your apron and have a nice afternoon," Malak said.

Aisha picked up her jacket. The Michigan weather had changed and gotten colder. Walking toward the door, she curiously looked at the man with two books. She stopped.

"Why are there two books you are reading?" Aisha asked him. She had paused a few feet away from him.

"One is the Qur'an, and one is the Bible, or Injil. I'm comparing what each book says about Jesus," the man said, smiling.

"So, you are Christian?" Aisha asked him. She knew her curiosity would get her into trouble but couldn't resist asking.

"Yes."

"Why read our book?" Aisha asked curiously.

"Well, I have a lot of Muslim friends who always ask if I have read the Qur'an. I want to say yes. Also, they tell me that Jesus is in it and even more than Mohammad. So, I am really curious to see for myself."

"Oh, well, I'm reading both to see who they say Jesus is. The two books don't seem to agree. My name is Sam." Sam stood and waved at the books as an invitation. "Look and read for yourself."

"Yes, the Qur'an speaks about Jesus. He was a great prophet," Aisha said. She took a step closer.

"So, I see. But it's very different from how the Bible does. In the Gospels, or Injil, Jesus Himself stated He is the Son of God. That God sent Him from Heaven for a reason," Sam said.

"Hello Sam," Aisha said. "I know a little about this but I, don't understand it," Aisha said. "I have to go home now. My husband is waiting."

"Let me give you a card." Sam pulled a card from his Bible to hand to Aisha.

She stepped back, shaking her head. "Uhm… No, thank you," Aisha said

"It's not my card. It's my friends who are married. Before you go, take the card and put it in that English textbook you have in your arm as a bookmark. My friends teach a Bible study and also teach English. Think about it," Sam with a reassuring smile.

Aisha took the card and put it in her grammar book. She walked out without another word.

～

I almost ran the three blocks over to the front of the mosque and hoped I wouldn't bring the coffee smell in the SUV. Abdul picked me up as scheduled. I had told him I was staying for a second class at the mosque so it would be later than the usual time. We drove to the home we shared with his family in silence. It was obvious he was upset, and I knew it wasn't because of me. I wanted to ask, but he seemed to ignore me and focus on the streets of South Dearborn. We arrived home, where the others were all waiting to have our daily meal together. An obvious, tangible tension was in the air. I could feel the strain bubble up as we entered the room. It was as if a pot might boil over. Habib didn't eat this meal with us because he would still be at school till three.

My family in Yemen did not act this way. My mama would say her mind quietly to my baba. He would listen and nod. He took her counsel, but still made the family decision.

At the restaurant, Uncle Suhaib rules with authority when managing the business. But here in the house, Rahma rules. She rules with a stern voice, a quick retort, and harsh looks, even to her husband.

As we sat, Mohammed and Uncle Suhaib looked at Abdul. They exchanged a glance between them. No words were spoken. Rahma stared at me as if she had a plate full of bitter words to serve me. But with everyone at the table, she waited. I could see it in her eyes, the urge to speak.

"O Allah! Bless the food you have provided us and save us from the punishment of the hellfire," Uncle Suhaib prayed before we began to eat.

"Baba, baba," Aini gurgled. She waved at Abdul from her wooden highchair.

"My beauty," Abdul let her grip his index finger tightly and swing it back and forth. Aisha smiled but the other faces around the table remained stoic.

"Aini, eat the food your Aunt Rahma has cooked for you," Aisha said.

"Yes, the food I made separately for her, that I cooked and mashed for *your* daughter *alone* in the kitchen we now share. But it is no matter. I know you have… *important* things to do." Rahma lowered her voice until she spoke the last words with barely a whisper. Abdul looked up but said nothing. Aisha looked at Abdul, trying to show him the anger Rahma holds just for Aisha.

"We must return to the restaurant," Uncle Suhaib said. He abruptly pushed his empty plate forward. "It's been a busy day, and we all are needed to get ready for a busy night shift." Mohammed's plate was already pushed away, but Abdul's was only half-eaten. He looked at his unfinished meal and set down his fork. The men got up from the table and walked out to the van.

"Good, they're gone. I know you want to learn English, but you don't need so many hours of learning." Rahma glared at Aisha. "You could practice on the computer here in our home,"

"The classes help me learn much more than watching a video on the computer, and it helps me to talk to other people in person," Aisha replied.

"But you aren't doing what is needed in the home. I see the condition that you leave the baby's room. And don't let me speak of your room," Rahma said. "A disgrace."

Aisha felt pinned in her seat like a butterfly to a board in a lab. She waited, knowing Rahma's scolding was not yet over.

"Also, you could be helping to cook for the family," Rahma said. "More of the people in this home now belong to you, and yet I'm doing most of the work for them."

"No, Aunt Rahma. When I come home from my classes I care for both of my children. I make their later meal when Habib comes home from his school," Aisha said.

"Some pita bread, chicken, and vegetables, on the occasion that you actually cook," Rahma pointed to the kitchen. "And you think it's enough for your children as they grow."

"Pardon beyond pardons, Aunt Rahma. But I think Aini's diaper needs to be changed." Aisha had picked up Aini and felt her bottom.

"Oh yes. That's most convenient. Only when the conversation becomes uncomfortable does the baby suddenly needs to be cleaned," Rahma said. Her face held an ugly sneer.

"It can't be helped, and I won't have my baby sit here in her own mess," Aisha sighed. She took her beloved upstairs quickly, her feet pounding the steps a bit louder than usual.

The stress of our home life is growing. Abdul refuses to discuss the obvious problem at work. He has now come to bed for a few nights in a row, his body nearly rigid with tension. I wait for him but usually cry myself to sleep. Each day, Rahma continues to find fault in everything I do and don't do.

In Yemen, Abdul seemed so self-assured in our home. He knew how to build me up and assure me that I was meeting all the needs of our household. Now he seems so distant. My heart craves for peace, but Allah seems not to hear my prayers.

After two days of staring at the card in my grammar text every morning, I asked Caliana if I could use her cellphone. I dialed the number of the couple, Jenni and Jerry, for the discussion about English and Jesus. A woman answered. I stepped into the hallway and whispered my questions. She sounded pleased that I called and said they would be happy to meet with me at the coffee shop. I told her I might have a half-hour if I could leave my shift early. Tuesday was a slower day. They agreed and said we would meet at Java Blue Café. I worked the counter with an attitude of uncertainty.

What would my mama say about this plan? I know my baba would disapprove, especially as I haven't discussed it with Abdul.

I watched for Jenni and Jerry. They would probably be the only non-Arabic people. They came in ten minutes before the time and ordered two cups of coffee, with some baklava to share.

"Aisha, you are free to go when you wish," Malak said to me. "Our lunch crowd has died down. There won't be much more coffee and sweets sold today."

"Okay, thank you," Aisha said and removed her apron. Gathering her books from under the counter, she almost walked out without speaking to the couple. Stopping at the door, she tightened her hijab. She turned around and sighed imperceptibly.

"Hello," she said. She moved with grace to the middle-aged couple who sat side by side in a booth. "I am Aisha."

"Oh hello, Aisha." The woman had long dark hair with a few streaks of gray. She stood to shake Aisha's hand. "My name is Jenni, and this is my husband, Jerry."

"We're so happy to meet you," Jerry said as he stood. He pulled a chair out for her. Then he dismissed himself from the introduction and went to the car.

"Jerry knows I like a little privacy when doing girl talk, even if it's practicing English or if we talk about Jesus," Jenni smiled reassuringly.

"You two seem like nice couple. The love must be strong. I can see your peace in you," Aisha said.

"Ah well, we've been married a long time. And our love is truly strong. But it's bound together not in emotions, but something much more," Jenni said.

"Well, that's interesting. I thought American couples are truly happy with each other. So, I have to a-ask," Aisha stuttered nervously. "Where do you find the peace and joy? You don't have it in each other?"

"Awe, we have joy in each other Aisha. But we don't rest only in each other for it. My husband can't me truly happy. Again, it's much more," Jenni emphasized.

"Yes, I saw it in the other man's face. You two also have it." She sat, and with that Jenni opened a small New Testament in Arabic. They started looking at the words of Jesus Himself.

They spoke about Jesus' words and Jenni showed her the places Jesus said he would leave His people with peace. A few moments later a chair scraped, and Jerry sat down without a word.

"See here? In the book of John, chapter fourteen, verse twenty-seven. It says, 'Peace I leave with you; my peace I give you.'" Jenni held the small New Testament and pointed.

Aisha wondered aloud about that could Jesus really give peace. Jenni continued to show her other passages in their Bible, like how Jesus healed people. But more often the verses told how Jesus brought joy to people's lives. It was so different from what she had been told about Christianity. She'd been told about so many words of Paul and other ordinary men, but not of the words of Jesus Himself.

After thirty minutes, Aisha left the café deep in thought. She'd never heard or seen anybody with such a sense of identity related to Jesus.

How had they found this treasure? Was it possible that I could have that kind of inner peace? How could I find a personal sense of identity for myself?

Chapter 12

Abdul

February

"Thank you for the ride, my love," Aisha said. "I know it's not easy to drive me to the mosque, go to work, leave for me, then go back to work."

"I'm just happy you are working to learn more English." Abdul smiled as the car came to a stop in front of the mosque. "You can be more prepared in this country. Also, you are willing to take the classes for Muslim women."

"Okay, I'll see you in four hours. It's another two-class day," Aisha said and kissed him good-bye. Abdul pulled away to drive to the restaurant.

Aisha seems to be learning more, but I know something is not quite right with her. She acts as if all is well… yet I can't determine the exact problem. Her English is getting better, and she still does her prayers. But there is real tension between her and Rahma.

Abdul tightened his fingers around the steering wheel as he watched the heavy morning traffic, looking for an empty lane.

Maybe there's a way to help her find peace, if Allah wills it. But first I must overcome my own struggle for it. Truly, the only peace I have lately is when I hold Aini close in my arms, or wrestle with Habib in the evening. I have asked Allah for direction, but I wait. Perhaps Allah is teaching me patience.

"Abdul, you are late again. You had said you would be here by 9:30. Yet it is 9:45, and just now you arrive." Suhaib scowled as he watched Abdul punch his timecard.

"I know Uncle, but I had to drive Aisha to her class, be sure Habib was at the bus stop, and there was heavy traffic on Ford Road," Abdul said.

"Excuses, nephew. You spoke of the responsibilities you carried when you worked in Lebanon, and even under your baba's management. But now you work in a restaurant, where the expectations are different. I know you think you have much to offer my business, but first I need you to fit into this company. One misstep leads to another, and soon I have a few less guests dining here." Suhaib took a breath. "I have talked at length with your baba, and he agrees that although you did great with him, you need to match my management style. You need to abide by our ways."

"Yes, Uncle," Abdul said.

"Excellent, we agree. Now go help my son put away the stock properly. Remember to rotate it, using that FIFO system I explained to you. First in, first out. Fresh product always. Go." Suhaib pointed down the hall to three stacks of goods on the floor next to the walk-in refrigerator.

Mohammed was leaning against one stack, holding it in place. He winked at Abdul and waved him forward. "Good morning, cousin," Mohammed said. "How do you feel today?"

"I'm fine. Let's move and put this product away," Abdul answered. "Your father is in a foul mood, and I don't want to worsen it."

"Sure, sure, Abdul," Mohammed said. He threw a bag of bell peppers at Abdul. The bag broke and spilled peppers into Abdul's arms, while a few fell to the floor.

"LaGrasso Produce may not give us new peppers tomorrow! Be careful, Mo," Abdul grunted as he balanced the torn bag. "Your father will go on a rant about food cost if he sees vegetables rolling around."

"Relax, cousin." Mohammed shot him a glance. "I would just say that it came damaged from the driver."

They focused on the remaining cooler items, then put away the frozen food. Though Mohammed enjoyed talking, they still worked well together in tandem. Their movements flowed well, and stock was put away and properly rotated.

"Mohammed, there is a large party coming tonight, and I'm worried we may run out of the meat. I have called Sysco. You will pick up two cases after lunch from the warehouse in Canton," Suhaib's raised voice was heard easily even from his office in the hall.

"Yes, Baba. I think we can use some more napkins as well," Mohammed said. "And I can take Abdul with me to help me load the van."

"Uh, no. I have to pick up Aisha from her class and take her home before the dinner party," Abdul said.

"You will be back from Canton close to the time," Suhaib said. "If she has to wait in the mosque for a half hour, that's okay. She causes your work schedule to fall behind too often, Abdul."

"But if lunch is busy today, it will not be enough time," Abdul said.

"Abdul don't worry. I have it taken care of. I called in Hussein early to help bus and even serve if I need him to. You two can leave after the main rush of people has come in," Suhaib said.

Abdul didn't like Suhaib's words, but he hid his annoyance from the man.

I went from supervising a marketing and trade group, and then planning with my baba his trade business to a designated errand boy. And most other days I work as a mere busboy waiting to earn the privilege to be a server who represents the restaurant. I saw Mohammed go back to the kitchen and help the lead cook. He started to cut some fresh lettuce and cucumbers for the salad today. I thought I might help also, since I saw some basmati rice simmering. My mama made rice often, and I would finish it for her.

But the tasks required in the dining area to open are many, and Uncle Suhaib no longer watched me as closely. There was no need, as I had timed the opening duties and effectively done them for weeks. Mohammed even said I was much quicker than Hussein, who they moved to the night shift after I arrived.

The restaurant opened without any problem, like any other day. Abdul served water to the guests as the dining room filled. Mohammed came and looked through the doors to see if more cars were driving up. Sometimes they had a short calm period during lunch. Not today it was guest after guest filing in the door.

Mohammed turned around and caught my eye as I was sanitizing a table. We would be able to leave soon, after all. Uncle Suhaib was right. He must have looked at his sales history.

Mohammed strolled over and whispered. "Abdul, stop cleaning the same table again and again. Half the room has emptied, and my father told me we can go now."

"Okay, but I hope a group doesn't walk in after we leave. That's happened before with a late lunch crowd," Abdul mumbled.

"Just go hang your apron and get your jacket. Winter has gone on, and spring has moved in with a few days of warmth, but today it feels like January again. They say Michigan can bring three seasons in one week or even a day, so we need to be ready." Mohammed pulled his coat tighter. "Meet me in the van outside."

Mohammed put the van in gear after Abdul climbed inside, and his hands immediately chilled on the frigid steering wheel.

"You have lived here longer than me, and yet you aren't used to the change in weather?" Abdul asked as he put on the seatbelt. *Better to be safe when Mohammed is driving. I have children and a wife to come home to.*

"I'm a little cold. I need a good hot coffee while driving. I know just the place to stop. They have good Arabic coffees, sweets, and a few pretty servers. We will stop," Mohammed said.

"Fine, but your father is watching the clock. And I still need to pick up my wife. I'd prefer she not wait too long," Abdul answered.

Mohammed drove for another ten minutes, then suddenly pulled in a shopping area. A big sign in bright blue large lettering stood tall above the building.

"Java Blue Café has been here for a few years, and it brings in homemade desserts from a local bakery. I tried to convince father we should buy our desserts from the same bakery," Mohammed said.

"The street seems familiar to me. Isn't the mosque nearby?" Abdul wondered out loud. He looked down the street.

"Abdul, you wait here while I go inside. I'll bring something for you. The coffee will taste better than what my mama's bland taste and even better than at our restaurant. Don't worry," Mohammed said, grinning.

~

Mohammed

Bells hanging on the door jingled as I entered. The last time I came here, the place was full of local Arabs, talking and leaning on tables, each group deep into their conversations. Many seemed like local college students, and I envied them a little. I was never given much of a chance for college. I was pushed right into the family business where I was needed the most, our Yemeni Dearborn restaurant.

I have learned much from my baba, and he has begun to give me more responsibilities. Soon, I will have earned his trust enough to be a supervisor or even manager. Then I will earn more respect when I walk about, and I will be known as more than the owner's son.

Today, the Java Blue Café seemed less crowded than before. Nobody was standing around, and only a few tables were filled. Although, I might have thought more students would be here studying. I noticed an older group in the back corner. And I saw a beautiful woman working the counter. She's dressed a little nicer, probably the manager. She must be really skilled, to be given such an important position. I hope this place is worth the four-mile detour.

"How can I help you, sir?" A long-haired, Middle Eastern woman smiled pleasantly.

"Hello. Yes, I will take a coffee. It reminds me of home when I drink it," Mohammed said.

"How about one of our pastries also?" she asked.

"Oh, yes. I will also have a couple of the *mamoul* cookies and the baklava. I need the sugar for the drive." Mohammed laughed.

"Ah. Yes, I see your restaurant's van out front. I think I've heard of it from one of our servers," the woman said.

He stuck out his chest, proud of his family's fine tradition of authentic meals. "Our food is well known throughout Dearborn and many nearby cities. You should come by," Mohammed suggested.

"Perhaps one day," she answered with a shy smile and a shrug.

"Okay, thank you, and see you at my restaurant." Mohammed handed her one of the business cards. *Well, she did take the card. My baba had no problem with me having the cards made, and he winked when I put my name under his name.*

He turned to walk out but paused when he heard the pleasant sound of joyful laughter. He turned around and looked toward a back corner table. A middle-aged American couple sat across from a woman in a hijab The woman had her back to him. Curiosity aroused, he stood for a moment and listened as they asked the woman another question. He noticed two open books.

"Aisha, do you see how Jesus is identified by God as His son here? God clearly states it, and says He is pleased with Him." The older woman spoke softly but firmly, and she pointed to a page.

Mohammed recognized the name the American woman spoke. *Is that Abdul's wife, Aisha? It cannot be.* He strode quickly past empty tables.

"Yes, I see it there. It's much different from what the Qur'an says," Aisha said.

Suddenly Mohammed presented himself and interrupted.

"Cousin, are you sitting here with Christians and reading their holy book?" Mohammed asked with dismay "Where is your head, my cousin? What is this about?"

"Mohammed…" Aisha changed to speaking Arabic. "W-what are you doing here? Is Abdul here? Why aren't you at the restaurant?" Aisha glanced around, her eyes widened and scared.

Mohammed saw fear in her eyes. "Your husband is outside, waiting for me in the van. He has done nothing but speak of his love for you and his family. And this is how you repay him? You betray him and our faith!" Mohammed answered in Arabic, his voice becoming louder and angrier the more he talked. "And what is that uniform shirt you wear?" He gestured with his coffee, noticing her shirt. "Do you work here, also?"

"Oh, Mohammed." Aisha lowered her head, her hands at her face.

"What other secrets are you hiding?"

Aisha stood. Her eyes teared and reddened, she faced him. "I… I… was just—"

"Woman!" Mohammed interrupted her. "Do *not* make excuses for yourself."

Aisha began crying but remembered courtesy to her new friends. "Thank you for your time. I must go." She scraped her chair back, stood, and hurriedly ran behind the counter to the restaurant's kitchen.

Mohammed turned his wrath on the Christians. "What have you been doing to my cousin? Are you trying to convert her? She doesn't need your religion. Islam is her religion, and it provides all she needs." Mohammed pointed to the Qur'an.

"We understand you're upset, sir," Jerry said. "But we were only offering an explanation of the contrast in our scriptures. We were looking at who Jesus was and still is."

"Jesus was a great prophet, but not more than a prophet. He was not God. I have heard of your preaching and will have none of it. So, stay away from my family." Mohammed pointed at them with the box of sweets in his hand and his coffee in the other. He stormed out and got in the van.

"You didn't get a coffee for me? Only for yourself?" Abdul asked. Mohammed shook his head and edged the box of cookies and baklava at him. "I mean you bragged for so long about it here, my heart is aching for it now." Abdul sat back, laughing.

"We need to go to Sysco Foods Warehouse. Then you can go for Aisha. I must talk with my father and mother," Mohammed said. He gripped the steering wheel so hard, his knuckles paled.

"What happened in there? What is the problem? Why is your face red, and your hand shaking?" Abdul asked as Mohammed's coffee spilt on the car seat.

"I don't know how to answer you," Mohammed said. "You will see tonight. I can't speak of this anymore." He started the van and shoved the gearshift into drive. As he quickly pulled out, gravel shot from the tires. His mind raced, trying to grasp the magnitude of Aisha's actions.

I can't believe Aisha would do this. She got a job on her own. She hid it from all of us. Then, at the job she is working, she is sitting there with those Christians. Those people want to convert her and pull her from Islam, her family, and her community. What evil has gone inside on of her? Was she hearing voices in the upper window of our home? I remember her voice late in the night. Has Iblees spoken to her? How could this happen, when I heard her doing her prayers to Allah? And Abdul is taking her to the Mosque for English and religious classes. What has filled her head? How does Abdul not even have a clue? Look at him now. He is listening to the radio. He's completely unaware about the dangerous line Aisha has crossed.

∽

"Well, thanks for the silent ride," Abdul sighed. "Can you carry the two cases of meat into the restaurant? I'm late to pick up Aisha."

"Yeah, fine. There were a few in the cafe that gave me looks and it made me angry. They weren't Arabs. These people come to our local Dearborn shops, and then they look around showing attitudes to us. Some people want to enjoy our best coffee and food, but don't respect us," Mohammed said.

"But most of the people who come into the restaurant show respect to me and the other servers. I'm not sure I see what you're talking about," Abdul said.

"Well, you probably have had better experiences. I'm just trying to explain that some of these people resent us, and it's quite easy to see," Mohammed said as he shut the back door of the van. "Anyway, the Americans in that coffee shop were full of pride, it was obvious… But you go pick up your wife. I'll take in the stock and talk to my father."

Abdul was starting to sound like his wife. Soon he will probably want to become a citizen. Our community here takes care of each other, and we maintain our culture and heritage. Some people who come to America focus on fitting in too much. They can lose their identity and the culture of their homeland. I need to show him what it means to be an Arab living here in Michigan. Learning some of the American language and social necessities is important, but even more relevant is building and maintaining your image in the local Arab community. What kind of success and community recognition can anyone gain if they don't practice Islam fully, have their wives and daughters dress properly, and respect other Arabs in Dearborn? The wives and daughters need the standard of the Qur'an, but they stray from it. I know this well, although I know of the latitude men are given before they marry. What will baba say now? I'm sure he will want to call mama.

"Mohammed, you are here. Excellent! Take one package of the meat over to the cook, so he can put it on the broiler rotisserie, and put the rest in the walk-in cooler. Why are you late? I expected you fifteen minutes ago," Suhaib asked. "And why have you put the meat down on the prep counter? What's the problem now?"

"Baba, we must talk. Come with me into the office quickly," Mohammed said.

"Okay, fine." He turned. "Hamid! Stop slicing onions and take one of the meats from this case. Start prepping it for cooking." He turned back to Mohammed. "Let's hear your problem," Suhaib said.

"Baba, it's not my problem. It's our family, specifically. The family that lives with us." Mohammed shut the door firmly. It rattled the doorframe.

"So, tell me about our family problem. What's so urgent? I have a few things to prepare for before the dinner staff comes in." Suhaib leaned back against his desk and sighed.

"Well, it's crazy and… I wouldn't have believed it if I hadn't seen it myself in person," Mohammed said. "Aisha has been hiding things from us… her family, and even her husband."

"What things are you talking about? She's only been here for what? A year?" Suhaib asked. "Tell me what you saw."

"We were on our way to Sysco to get the meat Hamid needed today. But I needed a coffee for the long drive to Canton, and we stopped at the cafe I like—"

Suhaib cut him off. "Ah-ha, so, this is the real reason you were late,"

"Let me finish, Baba. Abdul stayed in the van while I went in. When I started to walk out, I heard a familiar voice. It was Aisha's. She was talking at a corner table with some Americans." Mohammed waved his hands in the air as he talked. "They were reading a Bible and discussing religion with her. I wasn't positive it was her, because she had a uniform on for the coffee shop. Baba, she's working there as an employee!"

"This isn't good, my baba. She has a job. She was talking to Christians. This is troubling." Suhaib paused. "Are you sure it was Aisha?"

"Yes, Baba. I went over. I saw her face." Mohammed blew out his breath and closed his eyes. "I spoke to her."

"When does she have time for this job? She has been attending classes at the mosque. How could she be there?" Suhaib rubbed his chin.

"She was. She even asked a few questions. They were comparing Jesus in the Bible to the Qur'an."

"How can her mind and emotions be so easily changed and open to *Iblees* – the Devil – attacking her? We must call your mama," Suhaib said. He slowly shook his head. "We must intervene."

"Yes, Mama needs to hear this. I will call and put her on the speaker so we can tell her what's happened," Mohammed said.

∼

Baba told Hamid we had a family emergency and that he was in charge of the night shift. Hamid was informed that we may not return today.

The ride home was silent, except for the mumbled words from Suhaib, "Abdul, oh Abdul. What will we do with your wife? This is very suspicious behavior."

"Hello, my love. Greetings, my baba. Dinner is ready in the dining room. I'm sure you are hungry," Rahma said.

"Abdul isn't home yet? I thought he would have arrived home before us." Mohammed asked. "Maybe he went for a drive with his wife."

"Ah!" Suhaib said. "I see the SUV now coming up the driveway. Abdul has stopped the car." He continued to watch through the window. "He is talking to her. Now they're walking up. Everyone moves about and seem busy, like we're not waiting for them." Suhaib waved them to sit down as the key went in the door.

"Aisha, talk to me through those tears. What is the problem? First Mohammed is much quieter than usual, and now you've not stopped crying," Abdul asked. He'd opened the door for Aisha, and he stood, waiting for a reply that didn't come. They walked into the house, Aisha's only response was more tears.

Rahma stood in the hallway wearing her apron, and an angry scowl on her face. Her expression said more than a thousand words. Suhaib looked at her and nodded his head to the chair not far behind her in the doorway to the dining room.

"Hello, Abdul. Your dinner is waiting," Rahma said. She spewed bitterness, like words from a viper. "But I have nothing for your wife. She isn't welcome to eat in my dining room."

"Aunt Rahma... I don't understand. I know you have had differences with my wife. But refusing to let her eat at your table?" Abdul asked.

Mohammed's shoulders slumped with despair. *Still, she has not told her husband the truth. I see the deception in her face, the confusion on his face.*

"Send her to your room! She will stay there. I don't want her in this living area. She isn't welcome on the main floor," Rahma barked.

Aisha tightened her hijab as she walked past them, pulling it to hide her face. She had to walk by Rahma and tried to turn her face toward Abdul.

"Don't look around! Just go upstairs and pray to Allah," Rahma barked at her back.

Abdul turned to Rahma, horrified. "What has caused you to behave like this?"

Aisha hurried to the stairs.

So many secrets she has hidden from us, her family. Who does she think she is to bring obvious shame on our family? She will learn what is acceptable in our family and community. Mama is not one to easily forgive, even if Aisha quickly repents.

"Yes, leave this floor. You deceitful one who has betrayed us," Rahma yelled after her.

Aisha arrived on the landing.

"My love, wait. Come back and explain to me," Abdul yelled to her.

She did not stop. Her answer was clear as she rushed up the last few steps.

"My son, let her be. It is best for the family," Suhaib said. He stood by Abdul's side, his arm firmly around Abdul's shoulders. "If she doesn't change her ways, you may have to take a more drastic action. She has shamed us, Abdul."

"That's enough! Uncle Suhaib you try to sound reasonable, but now I need to speak to my wife. And Aunt Rahma, you have no right to speak to her that way. It's not your place!"

"Not right? This is my home, and I will be sure the rules of Islam are followed. You fail as a husband and you want to blame me," Rahma's said as her hands shook.

"Rahma, calm down now! Abdul, go on up and speak to your wife if you must. We should all try to relax here now," said Suhaib as he gripped the edge of the dining room table.

"Look at him go, running after the wife! He should have had a better reign on her. Like a horseman who uses a bite to control his horse, a man should have control over his wife. I'm going to be sure to hear this"

"Mohammed, stay here in the kitchen with us. You don't need to listen in," Suhaib added.

"Baba, I'm just walking to the bottom of the stairs," he replied.

"Aisha, open this door now!" Abdul demanded. "You must talk to me, I'm your husband!"

"No Abdul, I'm sorry. I can't open it. I can't even get up off the floor!" Aisha yelled back between tears

"Get up and open this door now Aisha!"

"No, no, no…." Aisha sobbed.

Mohammed hurried back to the kitchen when he heard Abdul muttering to himself and coming back downstairs.

"See, I told you to just let her run upstairs by herself," Rahma said with a smirk and wink at Mohammed while Abdul slumped down into the empty chair.

"Rahma, that's enough," asserted Suhaib. "Now Abdul, do you mean Aisha didn't give you any idea of what has happened on the drive home?" Suhaib's voice softened and looked directly at Abdul.

"No, not all. She simply cried all of the way home."

"Mohammed, you must tell him," Rahma said firmly.

"Fine then! I will be the one that brings hidden truths into my cousin's life," Mohammed said as he took his head out of his hands and looked directly at Abdul.

"There are hidden truths?" Abdul whispered. "You mean lies Aisha has told or something?"

"Yes, or not told," Rahma hissed softly.

"Let Mohammed quickly tell it," Suhaib patted his wife's hand.

"Yes, ok. Well, when I went into the café Aisha was there. She was sitting with some Christians and talking about religion."

"What's wrong with talking to Christians?" Abdul objected.

"Well, nothing if she was defending Islam properly," Mohammed retorted. "But it didn't seem like that to me. It seemed like they were doing the talking and she was doing the listening, as though she was actually interested. What's more, she had on the uniform for the café. She's been working there in secret who knows how long. That's what I know," Mohammed said with gravity.

"And what are we to think?" Rahma interjected. "What else might she be hiding from us? She's not to be trusted now!"

"I'm afraid she is right," Suhaib wondered aloud. "We can't be sure what is true and what's false. How many Christians has she talked to, and how often? And what of her classes at the Mosque?"

"I can't answer any of these questions," Abdul said with dismay. "But she and I will talk."

Chapter 13

Abdul

After Aisha went upstairs, and all of my family went to their room, I didn't feel like sleeping. I walked to the living room and sat in my uncle's chair, staring out the bay window. The darkness seemed to surround me. How could Aisha do these things? She got a job without telling me. Why would she hide that from me? And now she has locked me out of my room. What does she think...? That I will leave her alone so much that I would sleep on the couch in the living room? There is no way that I will let my family see I've allowed my wife to lock me out of our room. They definitely won't see me here in the morning... I thought houses made small noises late at night, like appliances and utilities humming and beams settling, or small animals outside. But it's so silent. All is quiet in the house, but so many voices continued to speak in my head that I have begun to shake a little. Aunt Rahma's bitter words, her scowl, then firmer but stronger words from Uncle Suhaib, then Mohammed's explanation with a little sneer, and Aisha's inability to answer continued to barge into my head. First, one person's words would enter, and I would start to question myself, and then another would come in behind them; until a tangled narrative ensued full of questions and doubts. After a while, the stress got to me, and I stood up putting my hands on the damp windowsill, shouting silently into the darkness, 'Why?' But no one heard my despair. I sat back down for another hour, and still no answers came.

That's it! I'm going to my room! Standing up, I suddenly ran up the stairs two at a time. She'll open that door for me! Reaching the door I stopped, unsure for a moment the best action to take. I didn't really want to wake the whole household.

"Aisha, it's Abdul," he whispered. "Wake up now and open the door." Abdul tapped on the door lightly.

"Abdul, leave me. Sleep downstairs or even with Habib. But just go away," Aisha mumbled.

"That's not acceptable. Get up and unlock this door." Abdul began to tap louder. He stopped and waited for another minute when he heard a few steps.

"Baba, are you okay? Is Mama alright? I heard voices," Habib said from his open doorway down the hall.

"Baba, go back to your room and shut the door," Abdul turned around and pointed back to his son's bed. "Get back in bed and don't worry, and please shut the door. You know I'm your father. Everything will be fine." Abdul waited until Habib's door was shut. He turned back around and put his shoulder to the door. It didn't budge much. Bracing his feet and gritting his teeth with a little grunt, he lunged forward into the locked door. The door gave way, and he stumbled in.

"Abdul, what are you thinking? "Aisha sputtered. Throwing the blankets aside, she ran to the door and shut it quietly. "You couldn't wait until tomorrow to see me, you had to break Rahma's door down? One more thing for her to complain about." Abdul angrily moved forward and glared at her. She shrank away and got back into bed, pulling the blanket over herself in a fetal position.

"Sit up Aisha, and please look at me. I'm your husband! I deserve respect," Abdul said as his voice raised a decibel. She refused to move in his direction, and her body was shaking in convulsions.

"What is going on and what are these secrets you're keeping from me? I drop you off daily at the mosque, and somehow you end getting a job. I hear about it from my family, and I have no idea what they're talking about. Who do you think you are? Answer me!" Abdul grabbed her feet, and she finally sat up, but refused to look at him.

"Still, you have no words for me! This from my wife, who said she loved me. Ha!" Abdul stepped closer to the bed and raised his open hands, his right arm swinging back.

"Abdul, don't do it. I'm your wife. Don't hurt me." She stuttered through the blanket she held partly over her chin.

Abdul's arm stopped in mid-motion, and his whole upper body began to shake. "Yoo! I refuse to strike you, though any other good husband would have done so by now. But I'm a better man than that."

"Yes, you are a better man than others," she replied as she flung the blanket off the bed. Swinging her legs over the edge of the bed, she wiped a few tears away and pushed her body from the mattress, her pillow still gripped in her left hand. She finally stepped toward him with bloodshot eyes full of pain, love, and a little fire.

"Abdul, I remember in our first home, I had such peace. I found joy walking the trails in the nearby mountains and fields and often going to the market. I was content caring for our home and children, and even serving you when you returned from work. Now where I am?" Aisha flung the pillow at the wall. "Trapped in this house with a very kind husband but with a domineering aunt!" Aisha stopped and looked at him. "Now I'm a slave to her and I hate my life! I hate it! I would be happy anywhere but here!" She flung her body back on the bed with her head in the already saturated pillow. She began to cry again, softly. Abdul took the other pillow from the bed and laid down on the bed opposite her.

∼

Two days came and went. While alone with her I tried again to get her to explain all those choices she had made, but each time she would turn away when I tried to broach the subject. Aisha was confined by Aunt Rahma to the house, although Rahma made it clear Aisha had more time in the home to assist in cleaning. I confronted Rahma about completely banishing my wife from the outdoors, and that she had no right to do so. But she had said it was her home and had gotten Suhaib's approval to leave us all on the streets if I didn't agree. For the moment I let it be.

I came up to the room, and Aisha sat on our bed with hand cream, trying to soften the callouses. Rahma had told me how she had Aisha scrub the kitchen, including the inside of the oven and refrigerator.

"My love, how was your day at work?" Aisha looked up and tried to smile.

"Ah, today you're talking to me." Abdul sighed. He looked at her with a sad smile from the edge of a trimmed beard. "Yesterday, you said but only a few words."

"Abdul, you're my husband and I will always talk to you. But yesterday you asked so many questions I'm not sure how to answer. I don't think I know the answers myself, and so how can I expect you to fully understand?"

"Aisha, from the time I have known you, seeing you help in the market, and later begin raising a family with me; I've always loved you. But these lies you have created have brought distrust between us, and even more within our family and community." Abdul sighed again.

"I've never lied to you." Aisha started to sob.

"Truth, my love? You have never lied directly to me, but you have let me and all of us believe another set of truths. There is a difference, and you have changed to think there isn't. Now let's be honest and tell me everything."

"I cannot..."

"Where is your heart? Have you changed so much?" Abdul pulled the chair from the desk and abruptly sat across from her. "Do you even love me still?"

"Oh Abdul, you're a good husband and an excellent father. I could never stop loving you." Aisha started to cry more.

"Allah be praised! But we must talk, at least you and me about all these things." Abdul's open hands reached for her, shaking.

"No, I cannot. I'm not ready!" Aisha sobbed and turned away, pulling the blanket over her head, her sobs getting louder. Abdul pushed his chair back and walked down to the bathroom, muttering to himself.

∼

Uncle Suhaib and Mohammed insisted that I come home for lunch with them still. I tried to keep busy, and I didn't want to go home. What was there to do? Aisha would eat at another time, and I wouldn't see her till I came to bed. The dinner table was usually a time to share our hearts as a family, but it's obvious to me that my aunt and uncle and cousin will use the time to lecture me on my family.

"Ah, you are home," Rahma said to the men when they walked in. "Excellent. I have your dinner prepared. Come, come into the dining room and sit," Rahma beckoned as she smiled warmly to them as they strode in. "Dinner is coming out. Aisha even helped peel the potatoes this morning."

"And how is Aisha doing today? While she was working with you, and did you have any problems with her?" Suhaib asked.

"Oh, not at all. Once I reminded her of her role in this house and some of the better ways to raise her family, she easily did as I asked of her." Rahma smiled as she replied.

"See Abdul, Aisha only needs gentle reminders of what it means to be a proper Muslim wife and housekeeper. You two might have your own home one day, and she should be trusted to care for it and you properly," Suhaib said firmly while spooning cuts of beef with his favorite sauce on his plate.

"I'm sure she appreciates the efforts from Aunt Rahma, but she handled our home and family quite well while in Yemen," Abdul answered quietly.

"Oh, I'm sure she did well enough there. But her mother was close by to help her as she began the new life with you. Mamas know how to best demonstrate to their daughters what it truly means to start a family," Rahma nodded her head.

"Ah…Well, I understand, but—"

"You think you understand but you don't, Abdul. Now that she's away from her family, it's apparent that Aisha has forgotten her sense of identity. She must remember what it means to be a woman of Islam, and not forsake Islam or herself. And I have asked a few ladies in our community to come and meet with her and me in our home. We must maintain our culture," Rahma explained.

"And of course, we as a family will continue to support her and you, Abdul. You too must consider changing. You're the man in the family, and it should be evident to those around you. You must lead with a tone and demeanor of strength," Suhaib said. Mohammed sat tacitly eating, nodding on occasion in agreement.

"Abdul, finish your plate. The stew cooked all morning, and I wouldn't want to tell your wife you couldn't eat what she assisted in preparing today." Rahma pointed at his plate.

"The food was good as usual. I'm just not as hungry today," Abdul turned to get up from the table and stood at the bottom of the stairway.

"Abdul, we don't have time for you to go talk to her now, we need to return to the restaurant in a few minutes," Suhaib said. He ate a few more bites and looked at Mohammed. They both got up from the table.

"Yeah, let's head back now. We need to finish dinner preparation for tonight at the restaurant," Mohammed jingled the keys toward Abdul.

Abdul followed to the van and sat with his fingers dancing on the passenger seat.

"Everything all right Abdul?" Suhaib asked, moving his shoulders in the seat. Mohammed started the van, smiling as Abdul's hands sounded a familiar rhythm.

"No, it's not all right," Abdul's hands picked up speed. "I'm not sure what you meant earlier. I don't see how I can change. I'm working hard in the restaurant, and I'm raising my children well."

"Oh, so now you speak up, and you have a problem with how we see you handling your wife," Suhaib laughed. "You couldn't say so at the table. Afraid my wife's words might bite you?"

"No, not at all. But when we talk about my responsibilities as a man, I prefer to talk with men. I know what it is to be a man, for my baba has instilled in me the way to walk like a man."

"Listen to me, Abdul. There are times you must be more assertive. It may require your voice to be more authoritative and say what you expect. Even in some extreme times, you may have to show your authority," Suhaib's pitch raised.

"You suggest I might have to strike my wife. Never will I strike my wife, nor my children once they are not toddlers any longer. Although emotions often rise, logic and reasoning prevail; and it doesn't make any sense to do so. I studied psychology at the university, and we discussed behaviors in people. That goes against the better part of my nature," Abdul said.

"This is where you must change your thinking nephew. Sometimes we must do what is distasteful so that a man can maintain order in his home."

"I don't agree with that at all. My marriage is better than that, and I'm a better man by choice," Abdul muttered.

"You think so. Your aunt has pushed me at times, and I've had to only raise my hand. She understood quickly."

"Many husbands have struggled with this, but it's our culture and what we should do as men," Mohammed shrugged.

"I don't need your input, Mohammed. You've never been married, and you struggle even trying to talk to women at the restaurant," Abdul responded with a smirk.

"What are you talking about? When I serve women, they ask for my section. And I see some stare at me from across the dining room," Mohammed's voice raised in defense.

"Yes, until you try to talk to one. Then the conversation falters flat like our bread we serve," Abdul laughed aloud.

"Enough from both of you," Suhaib angrily said as they pulled up to the restaurant. "You two go work on the prep list for tonight. I need to do a produce order for tomorrow."

Aisha

I don't care about working in the home. Aunt Rahma has a list that is getting longer by the day with tasks that need to be done to keep this house clean. But each day she is getting harsher in her tone, and at times I feel like matching her in response. But I can't do that. She has the authority here, and who am I? What is worse is that I heard her talking to Uncle Suhaib on the phone while I was cleaning the baseboards in the living room. She was in the kitchen chopping vegetables for dinner.

"He complained about our conversation my husband," Rahma said while slicing onions. She had set the phone on speaker.

"Yes, he was rather offended that we suggested he change," Suhaib sighed.

"But did you explain it's part of his duty as a husband," Rahma said. "Ugh... Oh my!"

"What did you do my love, slice your finger?"

"Almost cut off my finger with this knife you sharpened for me," Rahma cried out.

"Be more careful, and I'm distracting you now. Stop and listen. Abdul thinks that he can reason with Aisha to change her. So, you will need to be even stronger with her because I will have to continue to convince him in his failed college thinking."

"Yes, I will make her be the woman she is called to be," Rahma's voice raised through the sighs of pain.

"Good, our families' name is at risk in the community, and I will not allow that," Suhaib exclaimed.

"Yes, my husband." The line disconnected and Rahma began to hum.

Chapter 14

Aisha

March — two weeks later

"Thank you so much for meeting today with me." Aisha greeted her new friend. "I'm so worried… I don't know what to do."

"Oh Aisha, it will be all right. Jesus has his hand on you. Jerry is at a Bible study tonight. I was just surprised you wanted to meet so soon after what happened. Honestly, I wasn't even sure we would see you again," Jen said.

"Yes, well. It's a story to tell. And I hope you have time." Aisha sighed.

"Oh yes, certainly I have time. You're important, and who could say no to your sweet voice? Let me order some coffee for us," Jennifer said.

"Please no. I don't have a lot of money and I can't pay," Aisha said.

"It's okay. It's my treat." She hugged Aisha. "Oh, you're trembling. And your cheeks are tear stained. I think you need a cup of strong coffee. Also… would you mind if I prayed for you?"

"Here? Now? In the coffee shop? Someone could walk in, or the cashier could come back out." Aisha resembled a frightened deer, ready to bolt.

"I will be quick and soft. This is only for God's ears," Jennifer said.

After they sat down, Jennifer bowed her head and, in a low voice, prayed. "Father, come in and be present now in this moment with us. Jesus, comfort Aisha in her time of stress. Your Word says if we ask for wisdom, you will provide it liberally. I'm asking now, Lord. Give us wisdom for whatever problems Aisha has, amen."

Aisha took a deep breath. "Thank you, Jen. I don't understand how you can pray to God and Jesus in the same moment. I know we spoke of this, but I don't get it," Aisha said. "But I do feel better." She smiled a little

"I'm glad you feel better. Jesus is comforting you. Later, we can discuss how God and Jesus listen at the same time." She patted Aisha's hand. "First, I want to ask why you called. And why are you dressed in pajamas? Does this have anything to do with that man who came into Java Blue and upset you?" Jennifer asked quietly.

"Yes. He is my husband's cousin. Since that day, I have been banned from leaving our house. My husband's aunt and uncle have locked me in the bedroom. Abdul has been made to agree to it. He often tried to talk to me. But I just wasn't ready to explain to him how I was feeling. Frustrated, he finally sent me to sleep with the baby in her room. After a few days they had installed locks to imprison me. I escaped through an unlocked window today. Aini is sleeping for an hour in her baby bed. I needed to talk to someone. I didn't… k-know anyone else to talk to." Her voice broke as she talked.

"Take a deep breath and continue when you can."

Aisha inhaled and blew out her breath. "I had seen this coffee shop a little way from our home. So, I called you — no one else. Then I walked here." Aisha began to sob. "I'm hoping they don't look at my phone and see your number. "

"Well, Aisha, I don't know how exactly I can help you. In this matter, I'm not sure what I can do. First, let's depend on wisdom from God. He has said, if we only ask in His, Jesus', name, He would give it," Jen explained.

"I don't know what to do Jen," Aisha started to cry softly. "My thoughts are in many places. I want to know more of the Jesus you love. But I love my husband so much. Also, I'm fearful."

"I'm sure Abdul loves you, Aisha. Why should you be so full of fear? He surely wouldn't do you any harm," Jen said.

"Oh no. Abdul wouldn't want to hurt me. But after some time, his family and maybe… people from the mosque would have many conversations with him. Soon, I may start to get beaten. But they would do it, so others wouldn't notice. I have spoken to friends who have known women who spoke about doubts of Islam, or even their status in the home. These women were shown the proper conduct in their home," Aisha said, then sobbed even harder.

"Well, I have heard there is often conflict in the home when Islam and Christianity are spoken of, but I hadn't heard of such extremes in Dearborn."

"I feel no peace," Aisha said. "Sam and I spoke about the peace Jesus gives, and I thought about that last night. The thought kept returning, even when I tried to p-put it away." Aisha stuttered, but her tears had stopped.

"Thank you, Jen, for your time. But I must return to the house quickly, before Aini wakes. Or before Rahma returns from shopping and sees I'm gone," Aisha said.

"I know God will provide a way," Jen said. "How can I contact you?"

"I think I'm safe for a week. We will meet again in three days. Rahma goes every Wednesday to the restaurant for a few hours after lunch. She helps with the bookkeeping in the office," Aisha said.

∼

"Baba, why does mama eat in the other room alone? She has always eaten in here. She always talked to me during dinner, and even afterward. Now, she doesn't say many words to me. Only when I'm ready to sleep, she tells me how much she loves me, right before my dreams begin," Habib said. "Have I done something wrong?"

"Habib, listen to me. Your mama will never stop loving you," Abdul said as he slid his chair closer to his baba. "Her love for you is strong. Since you were born and in the days and years as you have grown, she has never stopped loving you," Abdul said.

"Okay, then why can't she come in here with us during dinner? Why does Aunt Rahma only stare at Mama? Uncle Suhaib won't even look at her. She is part of our family, and they act as if she isn't anymore," Habib said. "And another question, why do I have to come to you to unlock the door to go play outside? I thought in America we were free to go outside."

I could hear the conversation from the dining room. I started to cry softly, but not too loud that Abdul or Habib might hear me. Rahma had left to go to her room. I sat in the other room until all had finished with their meal. Then I would clean up after everyone and clean the kitchen. This was now my life. Day after day was the same. I feel so completely alone. I had a job that I enjoyed, and I was learning English so quickly. All day I have only my thoughts to dwell on, until Abdul comes up to our room. But he doesn't know what to say, and I can't find words to explain to him. So, we silently find our sides in the bed. When I awake, I clean and care for the home, but I am unable to talk to or show love to my own family. Except my daughter, she alone was my solace and comfort. She stopped her cries once I picked her up and held her. I must get a message to Jen and try to meet with her. Maybe she has answers for this miserable life. And though I'm no prophet, I know it will get worse. Rahma will infect the others' attitudes so much, that eventually any punishment done to me will be justified and rationalized easily.

∼

"Jen, you are here. I was a little worried you might not get my email. They have taken my phone, so they can be sure I'm not calling friends from school or the job I once had," Aisha said. She smiled broadly as Jen pulled a chair out. She hugged Jen tightly for a moment. "I've no friends but you, now. At first, I was locked in my room all day, and Abdul spoke up said it was unacceptable. So, then Rahma's answer was to give me duties around the home. No one speaks to me still, except to tell me what to clean in the house. I had to use Uncle Suhaib's computer to email you in secret."

"Aisha, I'm so happy to see you. I'm glad you are okay. I've been praying earnestly for you since last week," Jen said. "In fact, my husband and I have been both praying for you and your family. I know God is working in your life."

"Well… Maybe. Something *is* going on. But I don't see any easy answers. All I know is that I need to leave their house and community soon." Aisha looked around the small coffee shop, her eyes moved from table to table. "Things are getting worse in the house. Soon, my baba will not be able to talk to me at all. Rahma, Abdul's aunt, has started to raise her hand, like she might hit me when I don't move quickly enough while cleaning. I also overheard her ask Abdul when he would be prepared to beat me. I heard him mumble that that time may never come. But I know there will be pressure on him."

Jen sighed. "I have talked to my husband about this. We know that you feel you have no other way but to leave and go far from Dearborn. We have friends you could meet. There is a church about an hour's drive from here. They minister to many immigrants. Most of them are Latino, but some are from Africa and even the Philippines. They work with the church and have done many kinds of outreach in the community. I could call them for you, if you want." Jen explained.

"That would be excellent! It feels like a good plan that could keep me safe," Aisha said. "But we wouldn't be able to continue our study, will we?"

"Oh, Aisha, I'm so happy you are thinking about Jesus still. Even amid the stress you are facing, you want to know more," Jen marveled.

"Yes, of course. He is somehow at the center of this, and I think of what you and Sam have said about Him often," Aisha said. "But I still worry. I remember hearing my mama and aunt tell of a story. It was how the prophet said a woman spent the night deserting her husband's bed, she did not sleep with him. Then the angels would send their curses on her till she comes back to her husband."

"Well, we will find a way to continue to talk about Jesus. And rest assured, you will not be cursed by angels now. God has you in His arms to care for you. I know that He will certainly put others on the road you are walking that will want to talk with you more. If we can meet in two days, we can discuss the details for a safe plan for you," Jen said.

∽

It's been a month since I've moved out from our home in Dearborn. Of course, I miss Habib, and he's on my mind constantly. I wonder how he's doing in his classes. I wonder about his friends at the school, and if he feels like he is fitting in. And of course, I miss Abdul. I miss his smile and easy way about himself when he's at peace with the children and me.

Jen told me how hard it would be to move out. And I felt it. But I didn't know so many little, small things would come to mind. His booming laughter always lit my days, and he would see humor in the oddest things. His intelligence was striking, and he would come from his room to talk and ask me questions he must have thought about all day. I miss our moments together as mama and baba.

And I thought I would be okay without Abdul. His moods would swing from end to end but I daily sought ways to support him. But there is the space in the bed I sleep in, where he should be. His nearness had always assured me that things would be good in the morning, even when we argued. His light touch when he held my hand while driving. I never thought that I would ache so deeply for more than only images of these faces. I didn't know it would affect me so much, even physically. I don't feel like eating much anymore, and my stomach is knotted up like when my mama was making a thobe for baba. My only solace is found with Aini. She is starting to say a few words, like Mama. Her smile brings the only time I feel a bit of joy. Even bathing and cleaning her brings me moments of joy.

I don't how it worked out so easily. Allah, or maybe even Jesus had worked a small miracle. I had begun steadily to fear for myself, and I hated being locked in the house like a prisoner after I had begun to feel a sense of purpose at work and the ESL classes. People respected my work at the Java Blue Café and recognized my efforts in learning English at the Heavenly House.

The miracle was that I was able to escape my home without any detection from my family while still taking Aini. I carried her and one suitcase of things that I couldn't do without. The suitcase had been hidden under our bed for over a year, and Abdul had forgotten it. I'd quickly walked to the same local coffee shop to meet Jen and Jerry. I pushed Aini in the stroller and pulled the suitcase with a blanket over it. I saw one Yemeni woman peek out her window, watching me intently. But I acted like I didn't see her and walked on. She was an intrusive woman who several times had tried to tell me how to wear my hijab properly and even asked about my daily prayers to Allah. I had wondered how devout she really was. Jerry and Jen had hugged me lightly and were crying a little when we met. I had felt they truly understood the stress I felt, but I shed no tears that day.

Jerry drove us away from Dearborn on north 75 through Detroit, past Wayne State University, and Crain's Business. I saw the stadiums further off. My thoughts had drifted as I stared at the cars passing us. Was I doing the right thing, listening to the voices in the window in my mind, and my heart? Deep down inside, a stronger voice was pulling this way. But a few other voices suggest doubts. Would Allah approve? What would my mama say about this? What about my aunt from our village? I can hear their tongues with that clucking noise they would make when they disapproved. Then again, the stronger voices. What of Jesus, Aisha? What Word of Jesus have you heard? Remember how those words echo in your heart? What will it be like when I truly meet more of this Jesus?

"Aisha, wake up, we are in Waterford Township now. This is the home of a young couple who attend the church that my friends minister in. My friends, Matthew and Theresa are just amazing people," Jerry said. He pulled into a mobile home park. He slowed down as he drove over two different speed bumps, then stopped to look at Jen.

"Oh, I'm sorry. I had forgotten I was the navigator at this part. Turn left at the next stop sign, and then it's on the left," Jen looked at her notes to be sure. "Ah, look how nice these homes are, Aisha. There are much bigger than I remember. Jerry and I lived in one many years ago."

"Here we are. I believe this is Roberto and Carmen's home," Jen said with a satisfied tone. "And you didn't trust my mapping skills. Technology is moving so fast; I wonder if cell phones will one day be able to direct the car?"

"Oh, I read many people already have it on their cellphones, and we could have used MapQuest. Instead, you insisted on taking the directions from Theresa."

"Pssh with MapQuest. I just love talking to her, and it gave me a reason to talk with her," Jen said.

"*Buenos tarde*, my brothers and sisters," Roberto greeted them as they opened the door. "This is my wife, Carmen."

"*Hola*, everyone. Aisha, we are so happy to meet you especially. We are so blessed to open our home to you and your daughter."

"*Hola. Mucho gusto*. We're so happy that you have made your home open to me and my daughter." Aisha tried using their language.

"Mucho gusto to you as well," Roberto chuckled. "Everyone come inside. We have some juice and coffee made, along with Carmen's homemade guacamole with chips and a little rojo salsa."

∼

"Hey, 'Berto, what are you doing here on your day off? You told me you were relaxing from both jobs today." A tall waitress with long blond hair greeted Roberto. "Oh, hello, who might you be?" she asked, giving Aisha a warm smile.

"This is Aisha, my new friend. She has experience working in a busy coffee shop in Dearborn. I thought maybe she could talk to Charlene and see about an interview," Roberto said. "Aisha, this is my friend Sandy. She has worked her at Porter's Houseboat Restaurant for a few years more than me."

"Well, we won't count the years." She laughed. "Anyway, it is so nice to meet you, Aisha. I hope that we can—"

She was cut off by a loud voice. "Coming through, I got a six top waiting for their late lunch. And Roberto, you know better than to stand in the aisle talking when we're open." It was an older lady with short, stocky legs who chided him for being in the way.

"Oh, she seems very busy," Aisha muttered. "I don't know that I can carry a tray of food so big and walk so fast."

"Good, she speaks her mind," Karen said. "You'll need to be able to speak up on occasion. Don't worry about Frieda. She can be a bit sharp with her tongue, but she has a big heart and loves all her front house staff."

"Oh, she is the boss?" Aisha asked.

"Well, not the *big* boss. She is the head server for the dining room, and I help her supervise. We don't usually work the same shift. But I couldn't work tonight since my daughter has a dance recital. Our big boss is Charlene or Samuel, and even bigger is the owner, Mr. Porter," Sandy said.

"Hey look, Charlene is headed back," Roberto said. "Charlene, can I talk to you for a moment?" Roberto called. Charlene came around the aisle and met them.

"Why, hello, Roberto. You clean up well outside of your chef clothes. It's not often I see our cooks out of uniform," the woman said.

Charlene looked to be over thirty years old and carried herself like a true American professional woman. She was dressed in a slim grey pants suit with a matching jacket, and a pressed white blouse. Her hair was long and curly, but it was tucked in and tied in the back, with a few strands hanging around her face. Her voice was crisp and clean, just like on the television news. When I first came here, she was the type of professional woman I had thought I could have been one day. But then again, I had two children to care for and a husband to please.

"Hi, Charlene. This is Aisha, my new friend. I was hoping you could spare a few minutes this afternoon to speak with her. She is new to this area and has had some experience. Frieda had mentioned to me last week, you might need a few new host staff," Roberto said.

"Certainly, we are always accepting applications. I see you have given her an application already. I happen to have ten minutes before I review a plan for shift change. Aisha, is it?"

"Yes, thank you," Aisha said.

"Well, let's go sit in the corner away from the bar and talk. Thank you, Sandy and Roberto for helping her," Charlene said.

"Charlene, talk a little slower for her. She understands English well, but it's better when it's not so fast. I don't mean any disrespect, but remember how Michiganders tend to talk faster?" Roberto smiled.

"Don't you fret, Roberto. We'll have a nice conversation and see what we can do. She does have all her documents, right?"

"Oh, yes. She has her two-year green card, and she has no problem working," Roberto replied.

∽

New International Version: The Parable of the Good Samaritan

25 On one occasion an expert in the law stood up to test Jesus. "Teacher," he asked, "what must I do to inherit eternal life?"

26 "What is written in the Law?" he replied. "How do you read it?"

27 He answered, "'Love the Lord your God with all your heart and with all your soul and with all your strength and with all your mind'; and 'Love your neighbor as yourself.'"

28 "You have answered correctly," Jesus replied. "Do this and you will live."

29 But he wanted to justify himself, so he asked Jesus, "And who is my neighbor?"

30 In reply Jesus said: "A man was going down from Jerusalem to Jericho, when he was attacked by robbers. They stripped him of his clothes, beat him and went away, leaving him half dead. **31** A priest happened to be going down the same road, and when he saw the man, he passed by on the other side. **32** So too, a Levite, when he came to the place and saw him, passed by on the other side. **33** But a Samaritan, as he traveled, came where the man was; and when he saw him, he took pity on him. **34** He went to him and bandaged his wounds, pouring on oil and wine. Then he put the man on his own donkey, brought him to an inn and took care of him. **35** The next day he took out two denarii and gave them to the innkeeper. 'Look after him,' he said, 'and when I return, I will reimburse you for any extra expense you may have.'

36 "Which of these three do you think was a neighbor to the man who fell into the hands of robbers?"

37 The expert in the law replied, "The one who had mercy on him."

Jesus told him, "Go and do likewise."

"People will forget what you said. They will forget what you did. But they will never forget how you made them feel."

— MAYA ANGELOU

"Having been in the restaurant business, our job in the restaurant business is to be responsible for our customers' happiness. It is the nature of the hospitality business. You need to take care of people. You take care of customers above all others. Customers are your lifeblood."

— Andrew Zimmern

Chapter 15

Abdul

March — 2004

"Abdul, here we are in the storeroom again." Mohammed shook his head. "This time, though, it's different. Doing inventory with you is better than with Hamid. Hamid wants to examine each box, its expiration date, and sell date. Those things should be checked, but not when we have to do inventory."

"Well, I'm randomly checking the dates on these while we count and checking to be sure they've been rotated. But inventory goes faster as a two-man job, one to count and the other to log items on the clipboard," Abdul said.

"Okay, at least the storeroom is done. Let's do the walk-in next. I'm getting a coat from the office because it gets cold after a while," said Mohammed.

"Here is your jacket, baba. But you need both scales on the cart to weigh all the cheese, meats, and chicken. Those are my higher-cost items, and every ounce makes a difference," Suhaib handed Mohammed and Abdul each their jackets as they walked toward the office.

"There's a cart over there next to the prep sink. Tell Hamid to move his vegetables off of it and put them in a hotel pan."

"Did he think we *wouldn't* get the scales? This isn't the first time I've done inventory," Mohammed muttered under his breath as he shouldered into his jacket.

"Relax. This is your father's business. At least he's having us do inventory for him. Months ago, he didn't want anyone but him to touch it," Abdul said.

"Well, last year was better when he would sit and drag me into the office. He would point to pages of ledger paper that compared our sales from month to month and then compared to food and labor cost. Then he'd show me the percentage of profit we'd made," Mohammed said.

"Yes, I know. Paper and pencil are still the trusted method for some businesses," Abdul said.

"Then he went to that Michigan Restaurant Association Food Show, and that hospitality computer salesman convinced him to buy this whole package. He has everyone clock in through the computer, even me. Harrumph! Then he would come to show me how we are doing on hourly checks for labor costs. But that PC they got him to buy stock takes up half the desk, and the tech guy spent all day explaining the system to him and me." Mohammed stopped his ranting to open the walk-in door.

"I know how those salesmen work. They convince you that the package deal with all its accessories and special capabilities is something your business has to have. It's all in the marketing," Abdul said.

"Well, now everything is precisely tracked weekly. Abdul, didn't you help him with a few questions on the PC when he was inputting on Excel? See, that degree you got in business over the years comes in handy." Mohammed shrugged. "Well, now at least you can see the value in it."

"Yeah, I see the value in it," Abdul said. He rotated a case of chicken to the bottom shelf.

"Little recognition and even less pay to show in my check," he muttered under his breath.

"Watch that chicken, like I told you guys. Excellent!" Suhaib's voice boomed from the open doorway. "Maybe one of you two will be ready to take the food safety test, and we can have a second SERV Safe manager certificate on the wall," Suhaib said.

"Baba, there's no need to stand in the doorway inspecting us. We know what needs to be done and how you want it done," Mohammed said.

"Yes, yes, I know. Just leave what you have done on my desk, so I can start inputting them in the computer," Suhaib said.

"Uncle, I would like to borrow the car after we're done with the inventory. I have a short errand to run," Abdul said.

"Yes, that's fine. But you know you have the freezer after the walk-in, and don't rush through it," Suhaib said.

"Okay, Baba. We know you will be checking the numbers for any possible discrepancies," Mohammed said with a smile.

This inventory seems like it's taking longer to count than last month. It doesn't help that Mohammed wants to talk like my aunts did in our village. And Suhaib should know by now that he can trust his baba and me, I'm the one who studied business and marketing and then actually worked in a professional field. His restaurant is looking more professional, but I worked with a large company that was respected in more than a few countries. Now I'm chided like I can't remember the basics of business. And his constant follow-ups on the few responsibilities he has begun to delegate is tedious. He watches over everything we do like the hawk flying over his prey coming down from the mountainside.

I've thought about little else in the two weeks since Aisha has been gone. I overheard Rahma say how neighborhood people are complaining about how I handled Aisha. I feel like the other employees at the restaurant are talking about me when I walk in the room, and I see them look away when I walk in. Suhaib muttered something about people from the mosque. So, now I know I must do something. If only for my own sanity. I'm going to that café where she worked. What was the name? I see it in my mind every day. Java Blue Café... yes, that's it! I have to speak to the manager. And maybe I can see those Christians. What would Jesus say about tearing apart families? They've pulled a mama from her baba who needs her to guide him and raise him. How can people like that call themselves godly? I'm glad it's only another a few blocks. I can see the pillars of the mosque, so I know it's close by.

The bells on the door jingled as Abdul walked in.

"Hello, welcome to the Java Blue Café," a dark-haired woman said.

Abdul looked around the fully seated area, hope showing clear in his face.

"What can I offer you today? Our Gulf region blend or the darker Levantine Arabic blend? Both are good, but I think you might prefer the first. You look like someone from that region of Saudi or Yemen," the woman said. She smiled. "I'm Malak."

"Whatever you sell most, I'll take," he said. "My name is Abdul." *I don't see anyone studying at a table.*

"Are you searching for someone? Maybe I can help. I work here most of the time," Malak said.

"Yes, well, I'm looking for a bearded fifty-something-year-old Christian man. I think he comes here and waits to bother people," Abdul said

"Oh, you must mean Sam. He's no bother at all. Actually, he's a very nice gentleman," Malak said.

"Okay, well, have you seen him today? I really have to ask him a few questions," Abdul said.

"Sure. Actually, he's coming out of the restroom now," Malak said.

Abdul strode back across the room to a half booth on the far side. Sam had walked from the bathroom to the table with his books and laptop.

"Pardon me, sir. Are you Sam?"

"Why, yes, I am Sam. And what is your name, sir?"

Abdul tried to control his anger.

"My name is Abdul. And I've heard that you and your friends try to belittle our holy book while suggesting your Bible is more sacred. But even worse, you then try to confuse the minds and emotions of less-educated people. Months ago, you even did that to my wife who was secretly working here. Do you think you should do that? Do you think you should try to pull them away from Allah who is supreme?" Abdul asked

"Nice to meet you, Abdul. You seem upset. Would you sit down with me so we can talk? You must mean Aisha. Yes, she was my server a few times. She saw me reading my Bible and apparently got curious. She had some questions. But wait, has something happened?"

"Yes, something has happened, and mostly it's none of your business! But it never would have happened if you had just kept your religion to yourself," Abdul waved, pointing his forefinger.

"Abdul, I'm very sorry if I have caused some kind of problem that has made you so angry. Are you and your wife all right? Please help me understand what happened?" Sam implored; his voice faltered slightly.

"Well," Abdul replied with much hesitation. "First of all, she was keeping secrets from me. She was not supposed to get a job. We have enough money, so there was no reason for it. Why would she do it in the first place?"

"Oh," Sam slowly replied, his eyes widening and lightly touching his hands to his forehead. "This is starting to make more sense now. No wonder you feel the way you do. But that's not all of the story, is it? What else can you tell me?"

"No, it's not." Something about Sam's demeanor and sympathetic tone was disarming. "I know she enjoys working and I'm sure the idea appealed to her. She's quite intelligent and finds it easy to read people and their situations around them. So, I don't doubt she would be good at a server job. *And now she has left us!* She took the baby and went out the window, and I have no idea where she went, and who took her. This is a disaster and a shame on me and our family, and I think it's your fault."

"What?" exclaimed Sam. "Oh Abdul, I'm so sorry. The last time I saw her was right here when she was working. I admit that we were talking about the Bible. Then a man came in who saw her talking with me and spoke to her very sternly. He clearly did not approve of what he saw and acted like he was surprised to even see her there. Then she suddenly rushed out with a terrified look on her face."

"That was the fateful day," Abdul groaned. "But why? I provide for her, and she doesn't need anything. How did she feel it was okay to get a job but not tell me? And why would she even talk to you? She should feel content in Islam, and I believe she was. Her parents brought her up to be faithful to Allah, and to her husband. Now that we're in America we live with my uncle and Aunt Rahma. Rahma is a very strong woman in the home and wants to push Aisha to be compliant to her rules, but I fear she is overbearing. Aisha resents it and pushes back. But until now she has never pushed back against me. *I treat her well!* I have taken her to English classes, and also classes for the Qur'an at the masjid with other women there. So, I don't know where this idea to get a job and keep secrets came from. How did she start questioning her faith that she has been trained in since just a girl?" Abdul dropped his hands, no longer pointing. He sat down and sighed. His right hand stroked his neatly trimmed beard, and he bent his head into the palm of his left hand. "I pride myself in how I stay calm and reasonable. So, you must excuse my raised voice earlier."

"Well, Abdul, I understand you're in pain. Again, I'm so sorry that Aisha has taken such extreme measures. I know I would feel exactly the same way if I were in your situation. In fact, once or twice my wife was so upset with me that I thought she might leave me too. Tell me how I can help?"

"You don't seem like a bad man. Explain to me why you even come to this place, *it's for Arabs!* Don't you feel out of place? But if you must come here, why don't you find men to talk to?" Abdul's upper lip quivered, and he put his palm to his face, his voice cracking. "We Muslims believe in Jesus and *all* the prophets. We must, the Qur'an commands it! And we believe the Bible, the Torah and the Injil *in their original form.* But your scripture has been changed numerous times and by too many authors. Now you have four Bibles at least, and you can't even know what's actually true. Jesus was a great prophet, but he was not God or the son of God. Yet, you presumed to challenge the faith of my wife and lead her off the straight path. *Allah forbid it!* And Jesus will not bless you for it!"

"Abdul, I hardly know what to say," Sam replied. "My heart is broken for you, and I regret that this is how we had to meet for the first time. You're speaking very boldly right now, and I think it's out of anger. I don't think this is the right time to argue. I want to just say that God loves you and he cares about you. He cares about this crisis you're going through, and he knows how to meet you there. This is a time to pray to the Lord and ask Him to intervene in some way that only he can. He can solve any problem. I have already started to pray in my heart. There are many examples in the Bible of how people cried out to God asking him to solve their problems. *God is good!* "

"Yes, I know, all Muslims believe that," Abdul retorted. "The only things that happen are what Allah wills!"

"Yes, I believe that too, Abdul," said Sam. "In his infinite wisdom, God is doing something in your life through this hard situation. The Bible often reminds people of that. There was even a prophet named Hosea whose wife left him and committed adultery, then Hosea had to buy her back! Can you imagine? God told him that it was part of His plan to teach him his great love for his people even when they act like that. In the Injil, Jesus also reminded people of God's wisdom. Once He told people that they should build their house on rock, not on sand. But even when people disregard that rule, He is there to help them when the storm hits. Thankfully, he also intervened for people a lot. He saved thousands from their disease and despair, and He even cast out demons from people. That's how I know He can help you."

"Yes, of course Jesus was like that," exclaimed Abdul. "Our prophet Muhammad, peace be upon him, and all the prophets were. But I can tell that you want to point to Jesus as God, when he was not more than any other prophet."

"Abdul, truly I'm not attempting to argue with you. I want to listen to your perspective on truth, and want to share mine with you," Sam explained.

"Truth? Well, here is my truth. You have somehow caused real confusion in my wife's head. You and your partners. So, now you have helped Satan get in the middle of my family, my marriage, and my home. I don't know how you can claim Jesus in all of this when God *or* Jesus wouldn't want to allow a broken home?"

"Abdul, will you please sit down with me so we can drink our coffee together," Sam invited.

"No, thank you. I like my coffee hot. And this distasteful discussion has made it cool down." Then Abdul turned to leave.

"Wait, how can I reach you again?" Sam asked. "I think we need to talk about this again. I care about you, and I don't want to lose touch. Maybe I can help find Aisha!"

"No. I don't need your help," Abdul replied, and strode out the door.

∾

I left the Java Blue Cafe and drove back to work. The rest of the day was uneventful, and I talked as little as possible through the afternoon shift. I chose not to go home for the late lunch at the house, and just worked at the restaurant until it closed. While I worked, my mind drifted like the wind that pulled the football we kicked around the fields when I used to practice with Sameer and Yasser back home. Often, we kicked it in a north or south direction, but it would be taken by the wind quickly to the west or east.

My mind went from wondering about Aisha, and what she was doing to remembering Ani's smile and imagining how she has grown over the months. I have missed her. Then with a scowl, I pondered Sam's words. I thought again how he referenced Jesus' words. I hadn't known that Jesus had talked about building foundations. Look at my foundation. It has crumbled down around me.

Mohammed, Suhaib, and I drove home together in silence. I didn't want to talk with either of them. But Mohammed turned around and looked at me a few times as if he might start a conversation. Both times I nodded and turned my face to the window.

"Finally, home," Suhaib mumbled. "Some days seem longer than others."

"Yes, those last few customers, the ones who came right at 8:30, they didn't make it easy for closing down. They just seemed to want to talk forever," Mohammed said while he opened the passenger side door.

"Yes, well, sometimes you have to balance the will of the customer with our lives. After I asked Abdul to refill their beverages two times, I went to the table and took them carry-out boxes. I offered them a smile and a handshake good-bye," Suhaib laughed. "Abdul, you didn't even break a smile when you went to the table. I'm proud of you, nephew," he said. He slapped Abdul heartily on the back as they walked up to the house.

"I know what you like and expect, Uncle," Abdul said. "Sleep well until the morning."

"May Allah give you rest, nephew. And you as well, my baba," Suhaib said then walked to the living room. Abdul followed Mohammed as he climbed the stairs.

"I wish you could have cleaned a few more of those dishes from that last table," Mohammed mumbled. "I waited to take care of them since Baba had already sent the dishwasher home."

"I know, Mo. You told me that in the restaurant, and I got it," Abdul said.

Five more steps until I can be free of his incessant complaining... for today. I can almost guarantee he will find something to complain about each night. Even as a boy, he was never happy in the moment. I would have thought, with his American bravado, that he had outgrown it. But the attitude still comes about, like the spoiled rich boys that came into trade with my baba. I'm so grateful for my own room and peace in it.

After firmly shutting the door, Abdul walked to the balcony and stared into the night.

In my mind, the voices in the window come alive again. I hear Aisha ask about my fears. I hear the gurgling cries of Aini, and finally, the nagging questions about faith. Opening the window, I look about... but the voices have become silent in the wind. Staring at the bright moon, I feel no answers to my own discontent. I need to talk to someone. Someone other than Mohammed, who feels like a friend many days but other days, is more like a brother I wish I had left behind. Baba... Would he understand? What would he say about my situation? I know my family has told him. But I haven't talked to him yet. I made time for mama, but not him, yet.

"Good morning, baba," Abdul said. "I know it's early."

"Abdul, it's so good to hear your voice. We haven't spoken in a few months. Your mother told me she had a few minutes with you, but I've missed you, my baba," Fahad said into his new cell phone.

"Baba, I'm sorry I haven't called you. It's been a rather disturbing time, and I've not thought how to talk to you about it," Abdul said.

"I know much of your situation, my baba. You know your aunt and even your uncle, who I should remind you, are on your mother's side, they insist on talking to your mother often. Even your uncle has gotten on the phone with me once, demanding that I should talk to you. He stated that I need to clear your head, and have you prepared to do what is right in the eyes of Allah, the sheikh, and your community," Fahad explained.

"Baba, I don't how you live so calmly. I've always respected how you carry yourself. Other men look at you and see a man that has no worries. Mama has loved you, and you have never raised your voice or a hand to her. Yet, I know of many men in our village who have done so. How do you maintain your composure so well?" Abdul asked.

"Abdul, my life hasn't ever been easy. You know and have seen how hard I've worked to get to where I am. I've worked hard to put the same ambition in you. But I've also logically thought through how to represent myself as a businessman in the community, as well as a husband and baba. I've learned the importance of balance. Even with Islam… For years I prayed five times a day and went to the mosque often. Now I don't do so as much. So, I've also learned to share with your mama things that are important, and we spend time together." A sigh came clearly through the distance. "Thus, I've never had to be harsh with your mama. She knows how I love her, and she shows me the love in return."

"Yes, Baba, I know. I've seen it between you two. I thought I had that between Aisha and me. At least, I was working towards that. Now she is gone, along with my precious daughter. I just can't believe she would hurt me like this. I don't understand where it comes from."

Abdul stood up; the phone pressed to his ear. He began to pace about the room, stopping by the window. He stared out through the window that he'd often seen Aisha gazing out. *What had she seen? What voices had she heard? I wonder…*

"Abdul! Can you hear me?" Fahad's raised voice came through the speaker on Abdul's end.

"Yes, Baba. I'm sorry. I can hear you. I just thought I heard a voice through the window. I need to go," and Abdul pressed the button to hang up the phone. He walked past the window to the door, opened the door to the balcony, and stepped out. "Aisha! Come back to me!" Abdul softly whispered to the wind.

∞

"Good afternoon. I think I remember you. And I believe you enjoyed enough of our good coffee to come for a second cup," Malak said.

"Oh, yes. That was very good. I need a cup right now, since it reminded me of home so much. I just spoke with my father, and he and I drank a brand quite similar to yours," Abdul said.

"Happy to bring memories to you today. It'll be just a minute. I need to brew a fresh batch," Malak said. "I see you're dressing in uniform. You work in a restaurant nearby?"

"Yes. My family owns a Yemini restaurant not far from here," Abdul said.

"We are known around the community for our flavors from the homeland."

"Ah, yes. I think I met someone who owns that place. He invited me to lunch. But I think it was to see him," Malak smiled. "A bit younger than me, but still…"

"Yes, my cousin, Mohammed. He's very talkative and persuasive. But he has a heart with only good intentions," Abdul said.

"Oh, I can see that. Though he was rather insistent that I come to taste the family food," Malak laughed. "Speaking of insistence." She cleared her throat. "Sam insisted that if I saw you again to give you a gift. He left a book for you," Malak poked under the counter to come with a book. It was inside a Kroger plastic bag.

"He even left his card in here. He suggested if you want to talk some more, that you can email or call him," Malak pointed with the bag.

"Thank you. Perhaps I'll call him this week. I think I do have a few more questions for him."

～

I might listen to Sam this time. I know he must be a man of real faith, and he feels the needs to share it with others. But where did he get the idea that Aisha was seeking more than what Islam provides? Was it something she said, or questions she asked? I mean, if it was, then I don't know my wife. She is not the woman that I married. It's always been clear she loves our children, and it seems she still cared for me. But how can she so easily leave her culture, and her faith? The mosque where she was taking English classes is only a few streets from here. A walk in the Michigan spring air is good for me. So many questions yet in my head, maybe the sheikh will have answers.

"Peace be unto you. I was hoping you could speak with me for a few minutes," Abdul said to the sheikh who was holding the door open for him to enter. "I know you may be busy."

"Not at all, Abdul. We were just finishing one of our classes here at the mosque. You're not at work today at Suhaib's restaurant?" the sheikh asked. "My wife and I really enjoy dining there. I think you served us… maybe a month ago?"

"I may have, I've been serving quite a bit in the last month or so. I've split numerous duties at the restaurant, and work more than I used to."

"Well, how nice. What can I help you with today?"

"Ah, yes. Well, it was really your wife more so than you I needed to talk to," Abdul said.

"Certainly, my friend. Zara, my flower, please come here," he called down the hall in the mosque.

"Yes, my husband?" She came from around a corner into the hall. "What is it I can help with so soon after my class?"

"Abdul, our restaurant friend, has a question or two for you. If you could take a moment before your next class."

"Greetings. I'll answer what I can," Zara said with a smile. "Sometimes, my husband is better with some things."

"Oh, yes, I understand. But you teach a few classes for English?" Abdul asked.

"English, yes. Then, we add in studies for women of our faith in Islam. I find it helpful for women to balance their view in where they see themselves in our homes, culture, and new society here in Dearborn," Zara explained.

"I understand. But my question is about my wife, Aisha. I had been dropping her off for almost a year here in front of the mosque for classes. It was obvious she was learning at a fast pace. Did she demonstrate that in class?"

"Well, it's hard for me to say. Although, she did pay attention in our classes and take notes," Zara said.

"Why is it hard for you to explain? I don't understand it," Abdul said.

"Well, to be honest with you, Abdul, she stopped coming to our classes after only two or three weeks." Zara smiled politely. Obviously, she was uncomfortable. "I can't explain since she didn't see me about it. She just stopped coming."

"Okay, so where would she go for a few hours? I know she worked, but she didn't start right away after I left here. Is there somewhere else to learn English nearby?" Abdul murmured. It was spoken more to himself than to the couple standing in the doorway.

"Abdul, only a few streets away is a community center called Heavenly House. I know part of its mission statement is based on their Jesus's sayings," the sheikh said.

"Oh, I'm sure about that. Anyway, no doubt they push their beliefs on people," Abdul said.

"Yes, well, they do have strong support in the community. They have worked with us, our leadership in the mosque, in paving the way for immigrants to obtain their papers. They also help immigrants find jobs in the area, once they have obtained their work authorization card. So, in addition to helping learn English, they have partnered with us in the community numerous times. Although, we don't agree with their religious views, we appreciate their help," Zara explained.

"I see. Where exactly is this community center?" Abdul asked.

"If you walk two blocks in that direction," the sheikh pointed to the right. "Then you turn at the corner and walk another block, you will see it on the side you are walking. There is a sign with an angel around it. Once you come close, you won't miss it."

"Thank you very much for your help this morning. Goodbye," Abdul said.

"Oh, you're welcome. See you for prayer time next time," the sheikh said with a smile.

Abdul turned back and waved at both of them in the doorway as he moved down the sidewalk.

My pace increased as I thought about what I might ask the administrator or even the teachers. This is more involved than I'd thought. Not only had Aisha gotten a job without telling me, which was a lie of omission... but she had also deceived me in having me believe she still was attending classes at the mosque. Instead, she must have waited until I'd driven away and then hurried to this community center. Who knows what ideas those people filled her mind and heart with? Obviously, her decision to leave wasn't only based on her time with those Christians from her job. There's the angel he spoke of. It's hanging from the sign with a rock in its hand.

"Can I help you, sir?" A pale, white-skinned woman asked with a smile. She sat at the desk just inside the doorway. The desk had assorted documents for immigrants, from government contacts to local attorneys, to various local job openings, and a map of the building for the classrooms.

"Hello. I'm looking for a supervisor. I need to ask some questions about your center," Abdul said.

"Oh, I'm quite sorry, but they're all finishing up their morning classes. You could wait for one of them, but often students stay after class with questions for the teacher. So, it could be fifteen minutes or longer. Perhaps I could answer your questions." The woman stood, smiling.

"Do you know this woman?" Abdul asked as he pulled out his cell phone. He showed her a picture of Aisha.

"Oh, yes. That's Aisha. She's one of our best students. The two teachers who worked with her, they just sang her praises. She was always studying and hungered to learn more. Though I haven't seen her in a while, and I've been wondering…"

"Goodbye, Ms. Sherry. See you tomorrow." A person walked past them.

"Yes, goodbye, Ms. Sherry. We will see you tomorrow." A second young woman repeated the farewell.

"Oh, have a good day. Jada and Caliana, I hope your class went well," Sherry said.

"Excuse me." Abdul turned to the two women. "Jada and Caliana? I think you might know my wife, Aisha. I heard her talk about practicing English with you two. I just thought it was somewhere else." Abdul chuckled, but it sounded forced.

"Yes, we know Aisha. She is the sweetest girl. You must be Abdul, her husband. She spoke of you often, and with nice things to say," Jada grinned, trying to make light of the situation.

This is about as awkward as it can get. I would rather be anywhere else than here, having this conversation. But if I leave, I won't get answers.

"Well, anyway, we're all friends. We help each other out with English and things," Caliana added since Abdul hadn't smiled at Jada's joke.

"It's a pleasure to meet you two. Did you forget your hijabs today? I'm just wondering because I saw a few other women leave here with their hijabs worn properly," Abdul asked.

"Umm, Abdul, you know we're in America now, and it's the twenty-first century. Many women don't wear their hijabs out all the time. I wear my hijab when I know my family will be around or when I go to the mosque," Jada explained.

"Yes, we are fitting in with the community. We have some nice hijabs in our purses," Caliana opened her purse and pulled out a piece of fabric. "See how beautifully designed this one is? I bought this one at a nice shop on Livernois Street."

"It's quite lovely. Do you women know the coffee house where Aisha worked? I think it's close by," Abdul asked.

"Yes, I work there, too," Jada laughed lightly.

"Oh, I see. So, you maybe you helped her get the job?" Abdul said softly, a scowl forming.

"Well, I might have mentioned how the manager is very flexible with the hours, and we could use another part time worker. And Aisha is so nice, I just knew she would work well there," Jada answered quickly.

"So, she would often leave the ESL class so she could work more?"

"Oh no, not all," Jada exclaimed. "She loved our class and tried hard to do both every week."

"Oh, yes, she was one of our best students," Sherry said.

"I see. Thank you, girls. And Ms. Sherry, I believe. Have a nice afternoon." Abdul waved at them as he hurried out the door.

So, Jada works at the Java Blue Cafe also. I must have missed her when I went there. What kind of influence did these girls have on my wife? Where has their faith in Islam gone? It should have been more visible than that. They didn't even want to keep their hijabs on. Where is the influence of their mamas? Rahma would surely chide these girls for failing to keep with tradition.

I debate with myself about Aisha's character and choices for independence. There's no way I can bring her home, even if I find her. Rahma won't stand for having her in the house again after what she's done. She won't ever back down or even understand Aisha's reasons.

Chapter 16

Aisha

"Hello? Can I help you?" Aisha said as she held the phone to her ear while bobbling Aini with her left arm. Aini had been crawling around the apartment floor, and now Aisha held her back as she reached for objects on the kitchen counter.

"Hello, Aisha. It's Jen calling," Jen's voice was strong but tender at once.

"Oh, hi, Jen. How are you today? I was just watching Aini. She's crawling around the room, and I need to be careful where she goes," Aisha said.

"Do you have time to talk now? I can call back later tonight."

"No, I mean yes, now is good. I just need to put her down in a safe place. The church donated a nice crib to us."

"Okay, that's great. How are things going for you and the baby now that you've had a few days to get settled? I know it can't be easy. You've left everything familiar behind. Do you feel more comfortable? Are you less worried about safety now?"

"Uhm…that's a lot of questions." Aisha giggled. "I'm doing okay here. Roberto and Carmen are so nice. They've made room in their second bedroom for Aini and me. All of the books that were there, they moved to the living room. But Carmen is especially nice. She and I have had some good talks already. She also took me to her church, and we went to her friend's house for a Bible study."

"That's good. How do you feel about missing Dearborn?"

"Oh, Jen. I miss almost everything about Dearborn. Everywhere I walk or go, most people there spoke in Arabic, the smells of food cooking in the neighborhood, and the sweet, flavored desserts in the bakeries. These things all helped to bring me just a taste of our home country, which I still miss most days. And, of course, I miss my baba, and even Abdul. I think of them daily."

"You are still praying to Allah? Every day? All five times?"

"Well, not all five times, and not every day. I have tried to be a devout Muslim, but I wonder. My lifelong habits are still there, but I've thought about Jesus also."

"Aisha, Jesus is able to hear all things that are said and thought. I know that it is not easy to understand. Have you had a chance to read the book of John from the Bible? You know, the one I stuffed into your bag when we were driving? That was the book we read a few verses from that first time we met in person."

"Oh, I opened it and read a few pages. And I appreciate that you gave me a Bible in Arabic. It's still not as easy to translate words in my head, especially ones that are this important to the questions I'm asking. Carmen saw me holding and staring at it last night. Then, she offered to read it and study together."

"That's wonderful! I was praying that the Holy Spirit would lead more people into your path and that you would feel comfortable talking with them. And now look, after only a few days, a Bible study with Carmen."

"Well, I'm not sure about all that but she did say we could start studying together two or three times a week."

"Aisha, I'm just so happy that God is working in your life."

"If you think so. Also, Roberto took me to the restaurant where he works. I met a manager, and it looks like they might hire me. We still have to meet again. I need to decide who would watch Aini, so, I'm not sure, But I would like to work again."

"That sounds so nice. I'm sure things will start working out for you. You know we can talk anytime. Call me on my cellphone or you can leave a voicemail and let me know. I want to be there for you."

"Thank you, Jen. I understand. But I need to go and take Aini for a walk now. The sun is out, and she has been looking out the window."

"Well, have a nice afternoon. I will be praying for you. Talk to you soon."

"Goodbye, Jen."

She's so nice to call me. I truly do appreciate her love and caring for me as a person and helping me find myself... I've missed walking outside with Aini. Michigan's weather is never what it should be.

Almost like my life, it's not what it should be either. I was supposed to be living a new life of joy, the American dream. Last week it got colder, and I was happy for it. It made me want to hide inside the blankets Carmen gave me. The deeper I went under them, the more I seemed to hide from life's problems for a while. But today, the sun is shining, and I don't feel the cold. Instead, I feel hope. Hope for the days to come. I think my talk with Jen brought some of that new hope.

After Aisha brought the stroller out, found a jacket, and grabbed the door key, she pushed the stroller onto the sidewalk out of the complex. Aini started gurgling as she waved at the lines of shade from the trees. A bluebird chirped as it hopped in the grass, which was beginning to turn green.

A couple holding hands passed by and turned their eyes away to avoid a greeting. Aisha realized she was new to the neighborhood and tried not to take offense. They turned onto another street, and the sun brightened as the clouds moved away. Aisha folded her hijab and arranged it over the stroller to block Ani's eyes from direct sunlight.

The bright sunshine on my face lifts my spirit. I feel like I should be thankful for this day. I'm simply content to be walking with my daughter.

A voice broke her thoughts. "Excuse me, but you have the most beautiful baby. May I say *hi* to her?" Aisha looked up to see a blond-haired woman standing next to a man. She spoke with a different kind of American accent than she'd heard before. The woman bent over in front of Aini.

"Lila, let the child be and let them both enjoy this bright spring day." The broad-shouldered man spoke.

"I know, Johnny, but she's so adorable. I only wanted to peek inside and say hello," Lila answered.

Aisha recovered from her surprise. "It is okay. You can say hello. Her name is Aini, and she likes to smile for new people," Aisha said.

"Oh, how nice, you speak English," Lila said.

"Yes, I started learning it as a child, but I've been practicing it for over a year now," Aisha smiled. "Didn't you think I would speak English?"

"Well, many of you don't even need to learn English at all. That's all I meant," Lila said.

"'Many of you'? There is only one of me, and I'm here now."

"She's trying to say, your group of people in places like Dearborn. Many of you folks live over there that you don't even need English most days. But it's great you have learned," Johnny said and nodded slightly at her hijab worn loosely.

"I'm not the only one learning English. There are many people who are trying to learn, and many who have mastered it. And I want to be part of the American community," Aisha said.

"From what I've heard, most of your people only want to be part of their own neighborhood. They're not trying to mingle with the rest of us Americans," Johnny's voice was louder.

"That's not true." Aisha spoke defensively.

Just then Roberto appeared and got out of his Mustang.

"Hey, is there a problem? It sounds like you guys have a problem with my friend,"

"Naw, *this scary lady* here was trying to explain how she's fitting into America now," Johnny yelled.

"Well, there's no need to be so loud about it. You should wait until you know what you're talking about," Roberto stepped between the stroller and the couple.

"Maybe both of you should go back to your own countries. You're probably here as illegals. Especially *her*. Maybe she has family in the Taliban, or Al Qaeda. We *real* Americans worry about them bombing something," Johnny said.

"What! Taliban? I don't understand at all," Aisha said.

"Yeah, Taliban. My brother fought in Afghanistan and came back messed up. He was wounded over there and lost a part of his leg. He told me all about the reasons Muslims want to come here," Johnny exclaimed.

"Look sir, you need to calm down. She's not even from that part of the world, and she has no family that's part of a terrorist organization," Roberto said.

"How do you even know? Maybe her cousin or brothers are in a secret cell. You don't know everything," Johnny complained.

Another voice broke into the discussion. "What's going on over here? I need voices lowered, and I need to see ID from everyone." Two police officers walked up.

"Oh great, the Township Police are here. Any other day I can't get you here fast enough, when we really need you," Johnny complained.

"Well, we had a call come in, and we were close by. So, I guess we're on the job right for once," the younger officer replied with a tone.

"Sir, you have your papers, right?" The older officer pointed at Roberto.

"Yes, sir. I have more than papers. I have a green card, and I'm married to a citizen. See? Here it is," Roberto handed him both the green card and license.

"Most people don't carry both on them. But thank you… Roberto," the officer said as he read the documents.

"I carry them both in case someone wants to suggest otherwise," Roberto commented.

"Here is **my** work authorization card and my permanent residence card," Aisha gave both to him.

"Okay, you both have legal status. And you two? John and Lila, you live down the street, right?" The female officer took their identification while the other officer handed the cards back to Roberto and Aisha.

"So, Lila, you're pretty calm. Can you tell us what's going on here?" The officer asked. "The quick summary."

"Well, I only wanted to see the baby. She's so adorable. Then we were just surprised by how the mama knew English. And Johnny was just wondering why she'd want to live so far north. Dearborn is where most of her people are." Lila explained, and Johnny nodded in agreement.

"Oh, I see," said the female officer. "So, you're telling us that she has to live in Dearborn with the rest of 'her kind'? Is that what we Americans want?"

"Yeah, pretty much," Johnny mumbled.

"Well, she has proper documents. She can live anywhere in the United States she wants to," the older officer said. "You don't see anything wrong with what you said? America is filled with immigrants — you understand that?"

"And I bet if we looked at your family tree, we'd find a branch of folks that sometime came on a boat or plane some years ago," the female officer added.

"Yeah, that was almost a hundred years ago. But now immigration is getting out of hand, and—"

"Look, John, we don't need to debate the politics of it. The point is this. Both of these people are here legally, with at least two legitimate documents each. We should show hospitality until they demonstrate that they shouldn't be here."

"So, everyone, move on. Let's enjoy the sunshine," the younger female officer pointed to the sun.

"Come on Aisha, let's go back to the apartment," Roberto invited. "Later on, I'll come back for my car. We can walk back together."

"Thank you, officers," he enjoined. "I just saw Carmen drive past, so we can sit all down together."

Roberto pushed the stroller and hummed a tune as we walked the three streets back to the apartment. After a moment, he started talking about the day. I looked at him and felt in my heart that he wanted me to not think about the incident with the loud man and his wife. But I'm not sure what to think or how to take it. I thought Americans would be more welcoming, that they wanted people to be part of this better life they so enjoy, this American dream that I always hear about. I mean, Roberto has told me how he sends money back to his mama's family, and they have a better home now. How does he deal with some of these attitudes he has faced here? I think this is one way for him he pushes negative thoughts away.

"It's good that I wasn't scheduled to work at McDonald's tonight, and only the dayshift at Porter's Houseboat. You know sometimes they call it just *Porter's*. Today it got really busy. There were problems with servers and cooks yelling at each other, and four tickets were five minutes late. One ticket for a table was even lost on the floor. It got the table time *really* behind. Some people complain when it's busy there, and all you can hear are voices in the window. It seems crazy, even chaotic, for some, but *I* live for more moments like that. Although, a kitchen blow up can happen so easily. Like, when expo runs out of paper in the printer, or if one guy misses two calls that hold up two tables, or even a couple of servers who forget to ring in their food. I laugh to myself as the problems occur and focus on when the chef comes on the line to get everyone straightened out. He barks orders like General Patton, and everyone suddenly works faster."

Aisha laughed.

"It takes a few minutes, but after a bit, the wheels of our kitchen machine begin to turn around again. Food is pulled, and other food is plated. Tickets are pulled and not left on the printer and sold by the handful. Normalcy begins as we all get in step with the flow. It's like magic when it happens like it should."

Aisha sobered and shook her head. "I don't know, Roberto. Maybe I should not work there. It seems too stressful for me. We never had problems like that at the coffee shop. Busy days meant a line of people waiting for coffee. But Malak and I handled it without any big deal."

"Oh, don't you worry. You'll be trained well, and you won't have to deal with problems like that right away." Roberto smiled.

"Don't scare her with stories of the restaurant before she's even started working there Roberto," Carmen yelled through the screen door. "Come on in. I've made a cool drink, *Limonada con soda*, one of your family favorites. Aisha, I'm sure you'll like it."

"Okay, we're *strolling* in now," Roberto laughed at his pun. "Aisha, you're not laughing?"

Voices Through the Window

"No, I just want to take Aini out before you run over the step in the doorway."

Aisha picked up the child and walked through the door. She set Aini in the crib, now fast asleep. She looked at the dining room table with ice water and limes, and a few open books. One of them was her Arabic Bible.

Just then Carmen chimed in, "*Mi amor*, after you bring the stroller and fold it up, take your Limonada and go watch some football in our bedroom. I think I recorded a Guatemalan football game from the Centroamerica TV station for you. *Te amo*, Roberto." Carmen winked and took Aisha's arm. "Come with me and sit down. I really want to talk about Jesus with you. The Holy Spirit has put something on my heart."

"Okay, well don't mind me at all then. I'm going to shower first, and then watch Carlos *The Fish* Gutiérrez. I heard that he just made one of his best goals. Ladies, you relax while the little one naps," Roberto said.

"Carmen, you are so kind to prepare cold drinks for us. We had a little problem while I was walking Aini with some other walkers; then Roberto came, and the police showed up too It was like a sandstorm that started suddenly, and I'm a little worried. People didn't speak to me like that in Dearborn," Aisha said.

"Oh my! Think about this. Most of the people you talked to were Arabs, and those who weren't often **chose** to come to Dearborn, aware that it was more populated with Arab people. This part of Michigan doesn't see many Arabs, but they do see Hispanics. That couple is what we call *a bad apple in the bunch*. Many Americans worry about immigrants with bad intentions, and that's what fills their minds sometimes," Carmen explained.

"I know, and I can understand how people might feel that way. Even now, I judge many of my husband's family and their friends and see how their perspective could impact my Abdul. I mean... that was one of my fears when I left Dearborn and now, I have hope for a new job in this restaurant. And I *am* curious to learn more of Jesus from the Bible," Aisha sighed.

"Oh, good. I had hoped so. I've been praying for this moment. And now, after your day, I can see you're anxious. I want to talk about how Jesus meets our needs completely and is ready to take away our anxiety. Let's find the Gospel of John in your Arabic bible, chapter four," Carmen said.

"Oh, this is nice. Jen only this morning suggested I read that," Aisha commented.

"Excellent! We're going to read about Jesus, who is not just a prophet, He is the Son of God. He stopped to talk to a woman at a well, and most people from his culture would have condemned him for it, because she was a woman, a Samaritan, and not a true Jew," Carmen began. "The Book of John is closer to the end of the Bible."

"Okay we can talk about Jesus, and I want to learn what the Bible says. I know He was a great prophet. The Quran speaks of His greatness. But the Quran also says that there is only one God," Aisha said. "But Jesus has been on my mind a lot lately, so I am happy we're reading it today."

"So, before we start, let me just say this. Christians believe there is only one God also. He is a relational God, in three persons, the Father, Jesus His Son, and the Spirit of God. I know it's not easy to digest. But God, as one of all three of their Persons were there at the beginning of time. Before the world was spoken into creation, and we began existence, all three existed in community. Genesis tells us of the Spirit hovering over creation as it had spoken it into existence and Jesus stated that Moses spoke about Him. The Gospel of John, in chapter one, speaks directly to the fact Jesus was there at the beginning of time."

"Can we look at those passages? I would like to hear more of this."

"Sure, at first, I thought we could discuss the Samaritan woman, but now I think that can wait…"

"Yes, that would be so nice. It sounds interesting to me, and I would like to see the pages in my new Arabic Bible."

"Well, there are numerous times that Jesus is referred to earlier in the Bible, and oftentimes events in His life are predicted hundreds of years before they happened. But there are some times where Jesus specifically points out where He was spoken about. We can start with those passages." Carmen opened her study Bible to the back, where there were references. She also moved another book closer, Strong's Concordance. "So, I remember Jesus said something like 'you believed,' so let's start there. And here we look under the word *believed*, and the verse is John 5:46. Actually, let's start at 45 and go to 47." Carmen cleared her throat. "Verse forty-five. 'But do not think I will accuse you before the Son. Your accuser is Moses, on whom your hopes are set. If you believed Moses, you would believe me, for he wrote about me. But since you do not believe what he wrote, how are you going to believe what I say?'" She looked up at Aisha, to see if she was following. "Jesus was talking about Moses, who the Jews looked up to as a great prophet and man of God. He wrote under God's direction the first portion of the Bible. So, we can look in Strong's tool book again, under *prophet*. Here it is, in Deuteronomy 18:18. We can read from 17-19."

'The Lord said to me: "What they say is good. I will raise up for them a prophet like you from among their fellow Israelites, and I will put my words in his mouth. He will tell them everything I command him to. I, myself, will call to account anyone who does not listen to my words that the prophet speaks in my name.'

"Aisha see, the comparison between what Jesus and Moses said, and here Moses speaks of the Messiah that God the Son will put His words in the mouth of Jesus. We have the record of Jesus' words in the first four books of the New Testament."

"That's interesting, but it doesn't say Jesus there or even Messiah," Aisha pointed out.

"Yes, that's correct. My study Bible has another verse for us to see in the book of Acts. Here it is in chapter 3:17-23, one of my favorites, where the Apostle Peter is preaching to the Jewish people.

'Now, fellow Israelites, I know that you acted in ignorance, as did your leaders. But this is how God fulfilled what he had foretold through all the prophets, saying that his Messiah would suffer. Repent, then, and turn to God, so that your sins may be wiped out, that times of refreshing may come from the Lord, and that he may send the Messiah, who has been appointed for you — even Jesus. Heaven must receive him until the time comes for God to restore everything, as he promised long ago through his holy prophets. For Moses said, 'The Lord your God will raise up for you a prophet like me from among your own people; you must listen to everything he tells you. Anyone who does not listen to him will be completely cut off from their people."

Aisha nodded as the reading continued.

"Verse twenty-four, 'Indeed, beginning with Samuel, all the prophets who have spoken have foretold these days. 25 And you are heirs of the prophets and of the covenant God made with your sons. He said to Abraham, 'Through your offspring all peoples on earth will be blessed.' 26 When God raised up his servant, he sent him first to you to bless you by turning each of you from your wicked ways."

"Wow! So, Jesus refers to Himself in the first part of the Bible! But who is Peter?" Aisha asks.

"Ah, well, Jesus called twelve men to be his followers. And after Jesus went into Heaven after He was raised from the dead, His followers spread the news of the truth of Jesus coming as the Messiah. It's called the *Gospel*, or the *Good News*. Peter was an Apostle who became a great preacher, filled with the Holy Spirit. That part in the Book of Acts is a part of his plea to the Jews to turn, repent, and come to Jesus. He explains about Moses, and his prophecy, where God would raise up a prophet that would tell them all things. Peter reminds his listeners of the Abrahamic covenant, where 'And in your seed all the families of the earth shall be bless.'" So, you see, there is a direct line we can see drawn on the prophecies from Jesus. There are many more we could look at."

"And these people seem to all agree with what they are saying. How did that happen?" Aisha asks.

"Only because God's hand is in it. Under the inspiration of the Holy Spirit, He directed each person, and God knew ahead of time. He has knowledge to see before and ahead of time," Carmen pointed out. "Jesus states later in a vision to John that He is the beginning and the end of everything!"

"This is really different from what the Quran says about Jesus. Even how God feels about us. I was taught that Allah was just, but I didn't feel his love so much," Aisha said.

"Aisha, when people say God is love, it is so true. The trueness is in the intimacy He wants with us. He models that in the intimacy between the persons of who God is. God the Son spoke of His love for His father to people when Jesus was baptized. Jesus spoke of His love for the Father and spent hours in prayer with Him. Jesus also speaks of the Spirit, who would be sent. We can see a clear love relationship between the persons of God, and God gives that to us," Carmen explained.

"This is not easy for me to see all three persons of God, the Trinity you're talking about. I need to understand more," Aisha said.

"I know. At our next Bible study with the ladies, we can talk about how God works among them through the persons of the Trinity."

"Carmen, thank you so much for your time. I need to check on Aini in the bedroom," Aisha said, and Carmen squeezed her hand.

The next day…

"All right Aisha, I think I'm comfortable having you start today. I spoke to Roberto at length, and I trust his judgement. He told me about your experience at the café in Dearborn, and that you handled lines of customers with a smile. So, I'm confident you'll be ready for our level of business. Our host staff don't have an official uniform for you to wear. We ask them to wear what is called business casual attire.

Usually, a pair of pants or slacks, and a nice blouse or even a dress is fine. I see you're wearing a hijab; would you like to wear it at work? And the clothes you have on today are fine also." *Charlene stacked the application I had completed with a 1-9 form. Carmen was off today and is watching Aini.*

"That's good. I think I'm ready to begin," Aisha said. "And for now, I would like to wear my hijab please."

"Great, well, Karen is not too busy right now. I think you met her last week. She will get you started in a few minutes after she checks on the opening side work the other servers need to complete. Take a look at the menu items in the packet, and our orientation material in the front. It talks about Mr. Porter and the reason for our concept close to the lake. You may not know this, but Michigan is known for its lakes and rivers, and we are part of the Great Lakes Region with its five large lakes. But this restaurant adjoins a much smaller community lake, and we cater to the local community with our fresh seafood, chicken, and broiled steak dishes. I hope you will feel part of our family here," Charlene extended her hand as stood up.

Karen spent a half-hour showing me the seating chart, and then took me table to table throughout the dining room. She explained how the seating chart helped the host understand who would generally get seated next so servers wouldn't get double- or triple-sat. She even showed me the problems for some servers who feel overwhelmed when they are seated more than one table at a time. She demonstrated the way management wants guests to be seated, and how to highlight items on the menu that sounded appealing to me. She told me that each day for my shift I would need to eat something off the menu so I could more easily discuss it. After we spent time in the empty dining room, we returned to the host stand to review. Then she introduced me to Jan, who had just graduated from Mott High School in Waterford. Jan had been hosting for a few months in high school. So, she and I worked together. In the beginning, I followed her. But soon, I understood the steps when we did it a few times, rotating seats from server to server by their section. As it got busier, we got into a type of flow, and I would seat someone in line right after she left with the first group. Lunch time went quickly, and I was surprised how the second-hand fish clock had turned so quickly. Two o'clock came fast, and by two-thirty Roberto yelled my name. I went to the cook's window. A few voices were talking on one side, but Roberto waved me over to the far side. He pushed through a plate of chicken and vegetable stir-fry over a bed of rice, with toasted sesame seeds on top. The smells of fresh herbs and sweet and sour sauce filled my nose, and I realized I hadn't eaten. I placed the plate with rolled silverware at a corner booth. Karen said I could eat my lunch there. I bowed my head. I said Du'a, where I spoke with Allah. Then wondered about it, and if Allah even listens to me.

Chapter 17

Aisha

The weeks went by quickly. I didn't realize how much could happen when you start to live life in a small community. Over the weeks, I've found new sets of families. I have a group of people who already respect my work ethic and praise me for my efforts. They listen to me, and they could see that I understand what is expected of me. Only after two weeks, Charlene told me that they would be training for the server position soon. They needed someone on the dayshift, and they said I was learning quickly. And Carmen's father had offered to watch Aini on the days that Carmen was working. Then, we are going to church every Sunday. Everyone there is nice and pleasant to talk to. They love Aini, and they ask how my English is coming. Some of the same ladies from the Sunday service, also come to the weekly Tuesday night study we have at Margarita's home. Margarita is only a little older than Carmen and has her first baby also. He's a two-year-old boy with a beautiful smile. They have me bring Aini, and she plays in the other room with Gabriel, the two-year-old boy, while we discuss the Bible. But they always just talk for a half-hour about the last week. Each of us shares while the whole group listens. Everyone seems to really care for each other. I find myself waiting with anticipation each week for these meetings. After attending Sunday services at church, and the Bible studies; somehow, I don't feel so inclined to wear my hijab. Lastly,

Carmen and I have made time to sit each week and read more of the Bible. We had put off talking in-depth about the Samaritan woman, and so tonight Carmen said we would.

"I'm going to read in English slowly for most of chapter four in the book of John, and I will stop at verse forty-two. This will give you a whole picture of the story, as Jesus interacts in a real way in a conversation with this Samaritan woman. I'll start," Carmen began. She read word by word, and Aisha followed line-by-line in her Arabic Bible.

"Aisha, notice how after asking her to get Him a drink of water that He brings the conversation to how He can provide her living water. He has to help her understand that His water is greatly different; while the well water satisfies, people need to drink again. His water is a 'spring of water welling up to eternal life.' Have you ever been thirsty, Aisha?"

"Yes, of course. I've been on walks in Yemen and the sun was so bright, I felt sweat all over my body. I'd begin to count the minutes until I could get home for fresh water," Aisha said.

"Jesus, as the son of God, is able to truly provide your needs. He can provide physical needs and spiritual needs. Spiritually, He provides peace now and assurance of eternal life as you follow Him," Carmen said.

"I know Jen, and even Sam talked about the joy found in Jesus. But I've never really had real peace and joy. So, I'm not so sure," Aisha said

"Well, let's look a little more. See how Jesus asks about her husbands and then tells her about her previous five husbands. She then says, surprised, *Wow, you have got to be a prophet.* Why do you think she said that?"

"I'm not sure…" Aisha's eyebrows were furrowed in thought. "Well, how could He know those details? But you see Muslims believe Jesus is a prophet, just like this woman did."

"Well, not exactly, Aisha! See, next He explains the relationship between the Son and the Spirit, and what that worship will look like.

She then says the *'Messiah is coming, and He will explain everything to us.' Jesus answers her, 'I am that one.'* This is important. Now He is declaring that He is the one they had waited for. This shows He is the only one that gives the true water that He promised. The hard part for many to understand is that He was both God and man at the same time. He has another name we celebrate at Christmas. He is called *Emmanuel*, God with us. "

"Yes. I heard that music at Christmas time on the radio. I wasn't sure what they were singing about," Aisha said.

"Oh, I know, many sing about it. But not everyone actually understands. Let's look back in chapter three, where Jesus explains God's truest love that sent Jesus, God's only son, and He would save those who believed in Him from their sins. They would then have eternal life. We call this the *Gospel*. Our whole Christian faith is wrapped in the person of Jesus. We believe completely in God the Father who sent Him, and His Holy Spirit who was sent by Jesus. But our Bible prophesied Jesus, and tells of His life, death, resurrection, and ascension, His work in His followers, and the time when He will return."

"I didn't realize that your Bible gave words of faith about things that have been and things to come. That's interesting," Aisha muttered.

"Well, another time I can show you many promises that God made and how they came true. In fact, there are over forty promises specifically about Jesus in the first part of the Bible that then are demonstrated true in the second part."

"That's hard to believe," Aisha shook her head.

"Okay, let's look at one I can show you now. In Isaiah 7:14 of the old part, compared to Matthew 1:23 in the new part. *'Therefore, the Lord himself will give you a sign: The virgin will conceive and give birth to a son and will call him Immanuel.'* This is from the Isaiah passage. While this passage is from Matthew: *'The virgin will conceive and give birth to a son, and they will call him Immanuel,'* which means 'God with us.'"

"Oh," said Aisha. She leaned forward to absorb the words Carmen was saying.

"These and other prophesies told of Jesus coming, with over seven hundred years apart from Matthew's writing. Isaiah said they would call Him that name, Immanuel because it meant that God would be with us. It is so amazing, and I thank God for the precious gift every day when I pray," Carmen sighed.

"You are good, since you pray every day, Carmen. I struggle to pray five times a day, as Mohammed has told us to. And lately, I've been so confused, and I haven't prayed much at all," Aisha looked over at the mat rolled up in the corner.

"Aisha, it's okay. But I want to talk more about Jesus and this Samaritan woman for a moment, so you understand the big picture. At the time, the religious groups and the cultural norm wouldn't have allowed Jesus and His followers to speak to her. She was a foreign, non-Jewish single woman at the well. Most Jews would have purposefully walked the long way so that they wouldn't even have a chance to meet a Samaritan. Jesus purposefully went that way, because He knew God had a plan for Him that day. When Jesus walked toward that well, there would be gender lines, cultural lines, religious lines, and ethnic lines all surrounding it. And Jesus broke the walls down and walked across those lines that people create." Carmen placed her hand over Aisha's. "He is waiting now to walk this line and come to *you*."

"I don't know Carmen. I have had so many problems. And I've been a Muslim since a child. Why would He want to come to me?"

"Aisha, He cares more for you than what any person can think. He loves you so much He died on the cross, a horrible Roman crucifixion, and He took your sin and my sin to bear before God the Father. And God had to turn away. Then He died. But then, He came back alive three days later. No one else in history has ever done that. This is why He is my Savior. He could be yours too, Aisha. You then could have that peace that passes any and all understanding. He wants you to come and walk with Him today, and one day in Heaven."

"First, Aisha you need to confess or say with your mouth that you know and admit you are sinner. No matter what the sin is, it is unacceptable before God. That's why God the Father turned away from His son on the cross."

"Carmen, I understand sin. Sin is just a mistake we make," Aisha nodded.

"A better view is anything against God's will is sin. And although God is full of mercy and grace, He is still just. God is so holy, any and all sin is horrible in His view." Carmen calmly said.

"Yes, I understand that from what we read just now. But what next?"

"Well, Jesus said to one man that you must be born again. To be born again means you must put all your faith in Jesus and trust Him alone as your Savior that died and rose again for you. Once you declare He is Lord of your life, then you have been born again from your sins. You will have peace today, and eternal life when you die. That is the promise He gave," Carmen said. "Do you want to pray with me now to trust Jesus as your Savior?"

"Wait a minute, you said 'born again?' How can someone even be born *again*? That doesn't make sense to me."

"Yes, I see how it can be confusing. But it really just means that a person can be a brand-new person, like a butterfly that comes out of the cocoon. Have you seen a butterfly here in Michigan yet? They're beautiful. But they start as a wiggly, small caterpillar, and are transformed into something new. I thought of that because the magazine we have on the table had contrasting photos. Anyway, the butterfly becomes completely different, with a new look to his body and shape. God changes us in a similar way into new creatures."

"Well, these photos are just beautiful," Aisha held Nature magazine, staring at it. "You mean God expects people to change their lives so other people can see a difference?"

"Exactly, Aisha!" She smiled with true joy. "Can we talk more about you making that first step to a change for God today?"

"No, I do not think I can yet," Aisha shakily said. "This is a very strong point, but I can't make the commitment you ask me to."

"Oh, that's okay, Aisha. God is waiting, and I'm not pushing you," Carmen smiled weakly and pushed a few hairs out of her eyes.

"Uh, Carmen, you need to know, our time together is so good for me. I look forward to our Bible study, the drive to the church, and I really like the weekly study at your friend's house."

"I know, we call this fellowship. God calls us to build a community where we can love each other as Jesus called us to."

"Well, we Muslims have a close community also. The difference is in love. It's different somehow."

"I know, Aisha. The real difference is in Jesus. Faith in Him, and what He has done for us on the cross for us. Jesus told us the greatest commands were to love God with all we have in us, our heart, soul, and mind. And then to love our neighbor as ourselves. Then Jesus told much more how to show that true love to God and those around us."

"I remember Margarita talked a little about that in our group study. But I want to study more about what you said Jesus was told about years before," Aisha turned the pages back in her Bible. "And I still want to know more about who God really is."

"Yes, Aisha. Next time we will study those verses and try to let them speak to you," Carmen smiled. "One of the great ways God, through the Holy Spirit speaks to us is by His word, verses in His Bible."

∼

"Okay Aisha, you have your uniform on and look like one of us. Black slacks and our polo shirt with the emblem of the houseboat and a large fish. The logo is a little silly to me, but we've had it for years. Maybe Mr. Porter will listen to his younger management about changing it. Anyway, you look ready to go. Just follow me. I may be short, but I can move quickly when I need to. Today you will be following me, and at times you will run for food or beverages," Frieda pointed through the doorway of the wait hall.

"Thank you, Frieda. Yesterday Karen worked with me for an hour, practicing tray carrying for beverages on the smaller round tray, and the larger oval tray for food with the tray jack thing. I'm pretty sure I can do that," Aisha tried to sound confident.

"Yep, she told me you caught on fine. But its rather different once you have to carry food on the tray, and people are waiting behind you to get their food from the window. Then there's the guest who is still waiting on their refills and the new table who hasn't gotten their drinks yet."

"Oh no, I can't do that all today. That's too much for me," Aisha looked around the empty dining room.

She chuckled. "Nobody expects you to be able to do it all on your first day. In fact, you shouldn't have hardly any stress today, since you will be following me in step. We practice the technique so that you can learn to do it on your own next week." Frieda squeezed her hand. "Don't worry, honey."

"Well, that's good. I was a little worried," Aisha said quietly.

"Oh look, they've been seated in our section. Let's go introduce ourselves," Frieda walked with purpose as she strode toward a row of booths along the window looking out onto the water. Lead servers often got the pick of the sections when they opened, and she had picked the favored tables that face the lake. Those booths tend to fill up quickly as the restaurant gets busy. "Good day, folks. Welcome to Porter's Houseboat Restaurant. My name is Frieda, and this is Aisha, my trainee today. Have you dined with us before? Might we tell you about the menu?"

"Oh, yes. That would be helpful," a middle-aged dark-haired woman said. "My friend who lives only a few miles away suggested we dine here. So, I brought my mama to a girl's luncheon." The older woman smiled and tucked a few strands of her gray hair bound up.

"Well, our name gives it away a bit. But because we are situated on water, often seeing fishing of smaller boats and the dock, we specialize in fish. We have a great beer-battered fish and chips, with either cod or perch. We have broiled tuna, whitefish, and shrimp kabobs. Then we have several pastas with a variety of choices, from seafood to chicken or beef tips. Then, we have an assortment of chicken and steak dishes, and some salads that ladies especially enjoy. Shall we begin with a hot or iced tea? Maybe a lemonade or soda?"

"Well, that sounds nice. I will take iced tea with extra lemon, and some hot tea for mom. Thank you," the middle-aged woman said. Aisha wrote both down both drink orders on a small pad in the abbreviations she had practiced with Karen, while Frieda placed two small napkins down. Aisha started to walk toward the wait hall until Frieda gently pulled on her sleeve. She nodded back along the wall and walked the few more steps that way.

"Hello gentlemen. Welcome back for lunch. Two coffees and one Coke for the table?"

"Yes, Frieda. You know us too well. It's like we come here every week. We might need a new spot for our mid-week lunch meetings, before Frieda counts on us every Wednesday," the taller man in the center of the table laughed.

"Oh no, guys. I will never take you for granted. Our regulars are special, and to me you could be my other sons, like family." Frieda shook her head, smiling. "This is my trainee, Aisha. Give her some love and welcome her here to our community. She's still getting used to it."

"Hello gentlemen," Aisha waved behind Frieda and shrugged her shoulders.

"Welcome to Waterford," all three said in unison and laughed heartily. "We're going on the road soon," the tall one spoke up again.

"Off for the drinks, but any appetizers today, guys?" Frieda put three small napkins on the table while they shook their heads and opened their portfolio packets on the table. "See, most people are friendly. They will understand you have a job here, but they want to enjoy themselves while they're here. Whatever the reason they've decided to eat out."

"I see that's not much different from people who come into a coffee shop. They each have a reason, and a focus, while here," Aisha said.

"Yes, now you get the tea for the ladies, while I get the drinks for my regulars. Then, I will meet you at the booth to take their order. The guys usually take their time."

I walked quickly to the wait hall and filled a glass from the tea urn with sweet tea. Then picked up the small wicker basket of assorted teas, filled a small hot water urn, and a teacup. Then, glancing at my notes, I got lemon sliced for the tea and figured her mom might like some for her hot tea also. I carried the teas out to the ladies without any problem, setting each on their right. Out of the corner of my eye, I see Charlene walk by, tapping the beverage napkin from where the guys sat. Frieda had said the napkin was where we set cold beverages, but it also notified others we have been to the table and talked to them. I also noticed the dining room had partially filled up. Booths behind me had couples, and a few tables in the center were filled. I could hear the bartender making a few drinks, and the TV got turned up above the bar. I took a deep breath.

"Ladies, Frieda will be here in just a second to take your lunch order. Did you see the rest of the menu? I've tried the Chicken Stir-Fry with Sweet and Sour Sauce and the Pesto Chicken Pasta with Spinach and Sun-Dried Tomatoes. Both were very good," Aisha easily flipped one of the menu pages and showed the photo of the Pesto Chicken.

I stood back and watched as Frieda took their order, and then quickly went back to the table of three men. She said that they often got the same items and were ready to order. We stopped at a new table to greet them on our way to the kitchen, dropping a napkin. We pre-checked both tables into the computer in the wait hall, and I could see a line of girls for the other computer to place their order. Frieda quickly punched in the two tables' orders, and we went to take the beverage order for the new table. She sent me to get their water and soda, and she went onto the fourth table that had just been sat. They were regulars also, with little time, and I heard her take their complete order immediately. She smiled as she strode into the wait hall and waved onward with the drinks for the third table.

She whispered, "Check refills on the first two, okay," and hurried over to the computer. I heard Roberto yelling for help from the chef, and I hurried with my drinks. After setting the drinks down with a smile, I stepped back for a moment, unsure of myself.

"Aisha, we can't be like a potted flower in the aisle, my dear. We just got seated a fifth table. Go ahead and practice greeting them and try to take their beverage order. I'll catch up to the table that you just dropped the soda," *Frieda whispered in my ear.*

How did she keep smiling and run around so much? I can't remember who was first, and she's saying a fifth table now. I think she said table twelve. Where is that again?

"Over there, dear. The third table with the man and woman in business attire. I know you can do it. Go ahead."

"Alright, Frieda. Yes. I can do it. It's just like taking a coffee order, except in English," Aisha laughed softly and made the ten steps over toward the booth closer to the restaurant door in their section.

"Good afternoon, and welcome to Porter's Restaurant. My name is Aisha. I will be helping with your beverage order."

"Oh, you're not our server, Aisha? We're ready to order," the businesswoman with curly blond hair spoke up. She was quick with a smile.

"Yes, you see, we have a quick lunch, and we have to return to work." An African American man with a trimmed beard spoke.

"Okay, sure. You have been here before and know what you want. I will write it down. Frieda and I are working together, and we will get the order in quickly."

"Yes, I would like the Michigan Grilled Chicken Salad with dressing on the side, and a Diet Coke, please." The curly-haired woman nodded to the man.

"And I'll take the Pub Sandwich with cod, coleslaw, and fries. No, take the fries off and get me a side salad instead. Watching my starch intake some," he smiled across the table.

"That's nice Aisha, now repeat everything they said, right back to them. You have to be sure you have it correct on your pad before you ring it on. Hi folks, we're working on some training, and Aisha is doing great."

Frieda smiled and put her arm around my shoulder and squeezed. Not sure how I feel about getting hugged, but I guess she likes me. We turned around together after she was sure I got the order correct. Then she told me I could practice putting orders in another day, but we needed to hurry now. Our food was up.

"Roberto, where are tables thirteen and fourteen? They should be up by now. I see my pasta in the other window and my Cobb Salad in the cold window. Can you sell table thirteen, so I can get that out there? And how about fourteen, my regulars? They should be up. A couple of sandwiches and a salad also? Come on now, Berto!" Frieda tapped the window with her fingers and waved for the ticket with her other hand.

"Frieda, what's going on? We just opened a half-hour ago, and you're already yelling in our window," Chef John asked.

"Oh, hello, John. My first tables, and you guys are already behind. These people are on lunch and can't wait," Frieda said with a forced smile.

"Here, you're right. Table thirteen is up, and Roberto just brought over the Pesto Chicken. So run that out, and I'll check on the other one," Sous Chef John said through the window.

"Okay, okay. Thank you. I will be back soon," Frieda trayed up the plates and ran off.

"Chef John, Broiled Lunch Whitey is up. You can sell it," Henry yelled on the line.

"Good! Now come down and put fries on these sandwiches 'Berto just plated up. 'Berto, is that Caesar Salad ready? Can I sell it or what?"

"Yes, Chef! Aisha, get a big tray ready. Your second table is coming up," Roberto whispered loudly through the cold window.

"Excuse me, Miss? Aisha, isn't it? Are you training today? Get ready to run," Chef John said through the expo window.

"Aisha, where's your tray? Table fourteen is looking around for their food. Frieda waved at me to check on you, Aisha." Charlene gently asked her.

"Aisha, Aisha?" Roberto's voice got louder in the window.

"Oh, I'm sorry. Yes, yes. We have the two sandwiches and the salad. I got them. Oh, that's hot to my hand," Aisha said. *Did my voice just jump? All of these voices in the window. Cooks yelling, my manager, and even Roberto. Okay Aisha... Deep breath. You can do this.*

"Yes, ma'am. Our plates get hot. We keep them hot for hot food," John said with a little grin.

"Aisha, you remember how to carry these? Center it on your hand and the back end on your shoulder. Steady it now with your right hand. You got it now. And the tray jack, just like I saw Karen practicing with you the other day," Charlene had her fingers under the tray as she lifted up carefully. "Off you go now, and please don't drop it."

∼

Carmen drove us over in her Focus, and we talked about our days. She was off today and watched Aini for me. She and Aini practiced reading some children's books Carmen had gotten from the library. She knew I was frustrated when I came home with Roberto, and he just shook his head when we came in. But now, while she drove, I expressed my frustrations to her. I had never been in such a stressful situation, and wasn't sure if I could handle it, much less to handle it with a pleasant smile on my face. But I did make it through my first real day of training as a server. I certainly did more than just follow, like I had thought. Maybe they thought I could handle it, or maybe it just got a little busier than they thought it would. For whatever reason, it was more stressful than I was ready for.

But once we reached Margarita's house, my day disappeared. All the ladies came up and hugged each of us. In the car, I think I had started to cry a bit. Somehow someone noticed my emotional pain and hugged me a little longer. Once we were seated, Margarita opened in prayer.

"Before we start talking about the Bible verses from Beth Moore's book, *Jesus, the One and only*, I wonder if we can reflect on our lives. How has God, as Father as Jesus, and as the Holy Spirit worked in your life?"

"I would like to start with God, who we see as our Father," Ms. Thersea said. "He is a God of love, joy, peace, mercy, forgiveness, and grace. Just like the Israelites, who rebelled often, God forgave them with mercy and grace. Just like the prodigal son, He has welcomed us into His arms each time I have stepped in the wrong direction."

"And God chose to send His Son, Jesus, as the substitute for our sin. He knew no other sacrifice for our sin would do and that Jesus was the only answer. I thank Him every day for His choosing to send His only Son Jesus," Carmen said. "But Theresa, how did you feel about God the Father?"

"Well, He is the best father ever. He is my rock and fortress that I go to for each of my needs. It doesn't matter how big or small they are. He is the father that will rebuke in love but show mercy to me. I'm not afraid that He will hold any sin against me. I've gone to Him many times in my life, bearing my heart open wide. And I've felt such peace afterward, when we had a sweet time of prayer, and I felt a voice in my heart come over me." Theresa sighed.

"Gloria, how about you? How do you feel that Jesus has been in your life?" Margarita pointed with a homemade chocolate chip cookie. Her son ran by with one in his mouth, coming from the kitchen.

"Well, I pray to Jesus as my Savior. I thank Him for sacrificing Himself on the cross. But then He said also I can call Him *friend*, so I go to Him and talk to Him throughout the day. Then I pray to Him about my needs, because He said He is my advocate to the Father. And when I pray, I pray in His name, because there is power in the name of Jesus."

"Okay excellent. Praise Jesus for that. Who could go out on a limb and tell us how they pray in the Spirit, and even to the Holy Spirit?" Margarita smiled around the circle of chairs.

"Well, I know others may have some thoughts, but I feel led to speak up," Theresa smiled and patted her legs.

"Thank you and go ahead."

"This is just an element but feeling led is one way the Holy Spirit speaks to me. Just like now, I feel He is telling me to speak up. He brings to mind thoughts and verses I have memorized. There have been a few times when I couldn't think of the verse, and I prayed *in the moment* to find He had put more than a few verses into my mind to share with a new friend." Theresa looked up and smiled.

"We are all walking forward in step with Jesus. We should be growing more in Him, imitating Him each day. ~And we should understand how the Father cares for us, so much that He sent Jesus, the truest sacrifice of love. And we need to remember how much the Holy Spirit is working in us also, and that He is the promise Jesus said would come soon before He went to the cross," Margarita summed up. "I know a couple of you didn't get to speak, but next week we will give time again for this. We want to continue to share and think about how God has been working in your lives. Now let's watch the Beth Moore video clip, and then get into the workbook for this week."

~

"Mama, I'm so happy to hear your voice. I was w-worried you would be at the market when I t-tried to call," Aisha said. Her voice faltered.

"Aisha, it's so good to hear your voice too. We were worried about you. We haven't heard from you in a few months," Badia said. "I wish your baba were here on his midday break. He will miss hearing your sweet voice."

"Mama, who is on the phone? Is that Aisha? Let me talk to her, please. Please, please, please!" Amira tugged on Badia's robe.

"Quiet, child. In a moment!"

"Mama, I don't have a long time to talk. I'm using someone's phone, and I don't want their long-distance bill to be too much."

"Okay, just say hello to Amira."

"Aisha! I miss you so much! I wish we could walk up the mountain trail together. How are you? How are my cousins?"

"Amira, we are all fine. I miss you too. I love you. I miss your beautiful smile, my sweet princess," Aisha rushed her words and sighed.

"I'm sorry, little one. But Aisha doesn't have much time. And I need to talk to her—big girl things. Go on outside," Badia said.

"Yes, I'm going to tell Baba that Aisha is on the phone, and he will come," Amira started to run to the door.

"You can run out to the fields, but we will be finished before he can come," Badia scolded.

"Okay, but I'm going to tell Baba, and Mahri." Amira giggled at the door.

"You always want to talk to that burro, and the only reason he listens is because you bring him some grain to eat. Now run on," Badia turned the mouthpiece of the phone back up to her mouth. "I'm sorry, I know you are waiting, my dear. How are you doing? Ghada, Abdul's mother, told me you have suddenly left Rahma's home. Your father's brother opened his home for you and Abdul, and you choose to leave? I don't understand it, Aisha. This is not how I raised my daughter to care for her children and husband… by leaving for another city." Badia's voice raised slightly.

"I know, Mama. It's hard to explain. But Aunt Rahma thought she could be a mother to me and even control me. Every day she was scolding me. One day I was not a good mother, another day a poor wife, and always I failed as a true Muslim woman. Then I took some classes at the mosque, but there was a place a little way down the street that was so much better. They did not teach religion, only helped me to learn English quicker, and even talked about learning to fit in here in America. And then my new friend, Jada, helped get a job at the coffee house not far from where we took classes, a few hours a day. I just loved working in a professional place. I mean I love being a mother, but I feel so much more alive when I'm working. I'm not sure if you'll understand Mama," Aisha's words poured out like the sudden rains that broke loose up in the mountains.

"Aisha, take a breath. So much you are thinking. You know how we have taught you what Allah says, and where our place should be in the home. I know you have a fire in your spirit, and you feel it burning inside. But you should pray more in order to find your true peace," Badia said.

"Oh, yes. Peace? I haven't had a sense of real peace except when I've been talking to people about Jesus, and the Injil. Have you ever even looked in their Bible about Jesus, Mama? He has promised true peace. And I've thought about it," Aisha sighed.

"Aisha, you have heard from the imams, and they tell us all we need to know in the Qur'an. They have studied and know what we should believe. Not some foreigner," Badia sighed into the phone deeply.

"But what if they are wrong? What if they have been misled? I have looked at verses in the Qur'an, and I have looked at many verses in the Injil. I must tell you about Jesus. I think He may be more than the prophet we have been told."

"Aisha, I'm not ready to argue Islam with you, especially when you were trained in it and know it as well as me. But what will you do about Abdul, your husband? You must return to him." Badia's voice sputtered at the end.

"Mama, I don't know. I thought you could help me. I really hoped this call could give me something… some answers… some peace." A few seconds passed in silence. "Anyway, please ask Abdul's mama to tell him Aini is fine. She is growing up fast. She is crawling now. Will you give Ghada the message?"

"Yes, I will. But my dear, you must return home where you belong. Will you do that?"

"Wait... Mama... I hear a voice from the window that is open. *'Hello, hello? Is anyone there?'*" Aisha stilled herself for a moment. "Mama, I thought I heard my name being called... I have to go."

"Aisha, don't hang up. Come back to the phone, please!" Badia pleaded.

"Hello, is anyone out here? Abdul, Abdul! You're not here, are you?" Aisha leaned against the open doorway, staring out into the starlit parking lot. She started to cry. "Is that you, Jesus? Are you calling me? I'm not ready yet. I don't know where my heart is, and do you want it? No, not now. Not now..."

Chapter 18

Abdul

May — 2004

I left the house early this morning. I had requested to use the SUV from Uncle Suhaib. I made sure Habib was up and preparing to go to school. Then I went off for my coffee appointment with Sam. He and I had emailed to sort out where Aisha had gone. Sam suggested in the last email that we meet for coffee. I recommended The Java Blue Cafe. At first, it brought a little bitterness, thinking where many of the problems may have really brewed first. Oh, I made my own pun! It's odd how I can joke with myself, but I can't seem to laugh with anyone else anymore.

However, I hoped that the same coffee house where Aisha had worked might just bring me closer to her. Unanswered questions about our situation are hanging, but I don't think they will be answered without knowing her heart and hearing her voice. And now there are other voices in my head, presenting even more questions. Why would Aisha be willing to talk about Jesus? What does Jesus offer? He was a great prophet, but that's all. What about these Christians who claim him as their God? They think he is the answer. There is no other god but Allah, so how do these people want to say differently? I think today I will just ask Sam who Jesus is to him.

. . .

"Abdul, what a nice surprise to see you early," Malak said when Abdul walked through the doorway. "I thought you were the afternoon kind of guy, and here you are." Malak smiled at Abdul while pouring coffees for two college students in line.

"Uh, today I will break a weekly habit and get a coffee early. Isn't that what the Americans call it, a 'pick-me-up'? Well, I need one at least twice a day," Abdul laughed. *Second laugh today — that might be a new habit, but I doubt it. Without my dear wife, I don't want to laugh.*

"Sam said you could be coming in. He's over there by the window. I'll bring your coffee over to you. Would you like something to eat also?" Malak motioned to the counter with baked goods.

"No, thank you. Coffee will be enough; you know the one you served me before that tastes like Yemen." Abdul nodded and walked over to where Sam was sitting.

"Abdul, thank you for coming. I didn't see you walk in. Did you order something? I wanted to order for you, but I wasn't sure the flavor you preferred." Sam stood to shake his hand.

"Good morning, Sam. Yes, Malak knows the brew I like, and she has it just right. She must have trained Aisha well." Abdul sat down.

"Yes, sir. Aisha was fast and efficient here. She could quickly tell what customers liked with their coffee, and she remembered repeat customers' preferences."

"Yes, I know she works well. Back in Yemen she maintained our home well and yet prepared carefully when we had guests of business come to visit. She is able to carry many tasks at one time, and that's one reason why I supported her quick tutoring of English."

"I notice your English is good, Abdul."

"Well, I came to America two years ago before I brought my family, and since then, I've tried to practice English. Also, it helps that it's necessary for me to speak English in my uncle's restaurant, even though it's an Arabic restaurant," Abdul moved his shoulder as his coffee was served. "Thank you, Malak."

"So, Abdul. How are you? Are you working at the restaurant today? Do you find it stressful?" Sam picked up his coffee to sip as he waited for Abdul to speak.

"Umm, I'm alright. I try to put aside my worry over Aisha when I work so I can keep a pleasant face. But I admit, usually that face is a mask. I had hoped when I returned to America with my family that I would find real happiness. My father had pushed me to leave and find my way here in America. But here I've become dependent on my uncle and his family and wish I had my own business." He paused to pick up his coffee. "I really hadn't planned on telling you this."

"That's no problem, Abdul. I was only asking about your welfare. I know life can't be easy for you. But what do you want to talk about?"

"Okay, Sam. Aisha mentioned her interest in Jesus. Can you tell me, who is He… to you?"

"This isn't the first time that people have asked that. About 2000 years ago, Jesus Himself asked his followers almost the same question. He asked, 'Who do you say that I am?' I bring that up because, at some point, we should all ask that question."

"Okay, but what about you?" Abdul furrowed his eyebrows.

"Yes, sir," Sam smiled. "So, for my answer: First, Jesus is my Savior, my Master, my Lord, and my King. But He is not far away. Instead, He is closer than a brother, and He said that I can be called His friend."

"How can He be both a master or king to you and a friend closer than a brother? I don't understand that. I've never heard of being close like a brother to God. God should be so awesome that he has little space to be your friend."

"Abdul, I know it's not easy to understand, but you've asked me. Simply put, I have faith in Jesus. I know that He is God and is able to save me for eternity. Also, I have faith in His Word, where He said He would be my friend and take notice of me when I come to Him daily with any worry or need."

"Sam, that's not reasonable. You put faith in Jesus to save you and get you to Heaven. And then He promises you that you can come to Him daily? I don't see the logic in that. Your Christian website claims to stand on logic, but I just can't see it."

"I can show you how the Bible is supported in logic. But, also, so much of it is based on faith. It becomes a faith that is logical and makes sense in so many ways. But it is faith. My faith is based on the work of Jesus, His miracles then and even now. But even more, my faith is based on His work on the cross that has saved me. There is a reasonable logic to this faith."

"Now you're preaching, Sam. Like the guys on cable TV on Sunday morning. Are you and they the same? Are you trying to sell me something now?"

"No, Abdul. I'm not selling anything. And those preachers, if they are asking outright for money, they should explain the purposes for it — what they do with the donations. Anyway, you've asked me what I believe about Jesus. This is it."

"Well, I appreciate you telling me who Jesus is to you though I can't get past the contradictions and understand," Abdul shook his head.

"Abdul, Jesus's purpose and plan have never been easy for people to completely understand. He has been called The Son of Man, Immanuel, the second Adam, the Alpha and the Omega, and many other names. And his logic requires a special faith that sees Him as these things."

"I'm not ready to ask about those other names now. I have to get ready for work soon, and I need to help open the dining room today," Abdul sighed.

"Abdul, I'm not trying to pressure you. But I would like to be able to answer more questions. Even if you can't meet in person, we can continue our discussion through email."

"That would be good, Sam. Let me think about what you've said. It is a lot to consider already. Have a good day." Abdul got up from the table and nodded a good-bye.

I went to work, focused on setting up the dining room. While I did that, I planned for tomorrow. I would talk to Uncle Suhaib. He needed to hear me out.

∽

"Alright, Abdul, what is so important that you want to meet in the office? I have some paperwork to do, and I can't be taking time for long unscheduled meetings. This could wait for when we have the restaurant meeting once a month, can't it?" Suhaib loosened his tie just a bit. "And the lunch business is coming in soon. You need to be prepared on the floor."

"Yes, Uncle Suhaib, I've looked at the dining room. It's all ready for lunch. And I didn't want to wait until our monthly meeting to air out my thoughts. This is for you and me." Abdul pulled out a small pad of paper from his pocket.

"Well, go on then. I see you have some bullet points, so, it must be important to you," Suhaib grinned.

"You know I've been in America working for you over a year now. I started bussing tables, and now I'm serving. But you know my management experience, and my university degree. Yet you don't want to allow me to help with any management functions."

"Ya Allah...you're singing this song again. We've talked about this, Abdul. First, you must learn all parts of the business. Second, you should master problem solving in this type of business and be able to apply it. Do that well in the areas you are working, and then we see what you do with your management suggestions." Suhaib checked his watch.

"Well, Uncle. I have done well in all parts of the business, except cooking. You have your main cooks, and you. I have done some food preparation. But I have shown some of this problem-solving in the dining room," Abdul replied.

"I know that. I've seen you handle some interesting issues and not have to bring them to me. Also, you have handled inventory with Mohammed well."

"Yes. But I have extensive background with computers and their business applications too. And--"

"Listen Abdul, all in good time for you," Suhaib interrupted. "But we need to get ready to open the doors."

"But—"

"But what? We need to open soon!"

"My *but* is that you should at least let me spend time on the computers. Let me update the spreadsheets for you. Let me review what you have in place. Also, let me show you about websites that are out there. We should consider creating one."

"You will not touch the office computer! At home, you can look and research things on your own time. But I will not have you trying to get mixed up in the system I have in place. Now go to check your section."

I walked away from the office in frustration and returned to the dining room. I'm going to serve as a waiter in his restaurant, but I should be his manager, and all he's done is promote me from busboy to server and Mohammed's helper with a few minimal functions. Mohammed had opened the dining room and seated a few parties. It began to get busy, and my thoughts had little time for my conversation with my uncle. Even after lunch died down the other servers were sent home while I stayed, working on the floor. It left me little time to stew about this morning. Soon, before I'd even realized it, dinner service was over, and I'd missed going home for the daily meal Rahma makes. It was fine, since I really wasn't feeling much like our family time together. I had eaten a cup of lentil soup between tables, with some Malawah bread. We closed the restaurant, and still, I didn't want to talk with my family.

Uncle Suhaib absently nodded when I said I wanted to spend a few minutes on his computer in the home office. I opened my email and noticed that Sam had sent me one. After I had met him in person, I thought about how he had seemed to truly care for Aisha and me. So, I had found his card and thanked him in an email. Since then, we have had a small string of emails. After we observed pleasantries in them, we went back and forth for a while regarding the divinity of Jesus. But only a few weeks ago, Christians had celebrated their holiday of Easter where they replay the death and claimed resurrection of the Messiah, Jesus. So, I insisted, this was one more reason Jesus could not be God in our email exchange.

I wrote to him explaining my views.

Sam,

Jesus was only a prophet. There is nothing to prove that He actually died on the cross, rose from the dead, and was resurrected. Even your Bible says that the body was taken from the tomb.

Abdul

His return email was quite detailed and dissected my argument.

Alright, Abdul,

Let's talk about evidence. First, we will look at Jesus death, which some people cast doubt on: 1) The Bible as its own source has all four Gospels that explain in explicit detail the death of Jesus. 2) There are outside historical sources that verify in their writings that Jesus died, such as Roman historian Tacitus and Jewish historian Josephus. Neither of whom claimed faith in Jesus. Now Let's review the resurrection facts: 1) The tomb of Jesus was found empty. 2) Jesus appeared alive after His death. 3) The disciples claimed to have seen Jesus after His death. So much so, they were all willing to be persecuted, and many of them put to death for their faith.

I will begin with your point about the empty tomb. The Bible speaks about someone taking the body, but that shows the religious leaders in fear that He was truly the Messiah that had been prophesied of. So, the scripture tells of what men said. There were eyewitnesses who came to the empty tomb — two women first, and then two men saw the tomb empty. And as the script played out, the religious leaders were trying to shush the amazement of the Roman soldiers who had no clue what happened to the body. They explained how the large stone was rolled away, and they were stunned and dumbfounded.

Yours in Christ,

Sam

Hello Sam,

That whole story is based on your Bible one singular document that you and others claim is inspired from God, and to the belief that he appeared to people after he had died. Well, that's still your people spouting their beliefs.

Abdul

Well Abdul,

We could spend days talking about the validity of the Bible. But let me just suggest this: There are numerous outside resources other than the Bible that verify what is said about Jesus's death is true. There are non-Christian, secular, and Jewish historians that have documented it. So, it wasn't only the twelve main followers of Jesus spouting these things. One in the New Testament states He appeared to over five hundred different people at once after His resurrection. But one of the main points of support is that the scriptures speak with the authority of

God. You can see and feel it when you read it, especially the words of Jesus Himself, as well as His deeds. Jesus Himself told His followers that He would be crucified and rise again. The apostles wrote as eyewitnesses to this. And His resurrection has incredible explanatory power too. What else could explain the unprecedented growth of Christianity in those years.

Yours in Christ,

Sam

Well Sam,

The Qur'an verifies that Jesus was only a prophet. I have no problem with that. His verification by over five hundred is again from your Bible, and thus is it really that reliable?

Abdul

Yes, Jesus was a great prophet, so shouldn't we listen to all that He said? He said that He came to die and rise again, only to become even greater! He demonstrated power death and sacrificed love.

Yours in Christ,

Sam

Okay Sam. Until next time. We can pick this up this line of thought again in a few days.

My last email was a few days ago, so I wanted to see what he had to say this time. I left the restaurant and thought about our conversations a few days ago. If Sam is still on the internet tonight, then I may ask another question or two. It's very intriguing to me. The browser opened and I entered my email... earlier today.

Hello, Abdul,

This is the stuff I enjoy, great conversation. I can give you numerous examples about the authenticity of the Bible as God's true revelation. First, it verifies itself and never contradicts itself. Although many look for gaps, they are simply the inspired perspectives of the various apostles informed by the Holy Spirit, and their personal eyewitness encounters with Jesus. Also there have even been archaeological digs that verify what has been revealed in the gospels. Our New Testament has the greatest stream of authentic manuscripts of all ancient sources of antiquity compared to other historical documents. Even the Qur'an has some verses that verify the validity of the Bible. (The Torah and the Injil) So there are very strong reasons why you should at least read the gospels. I would love to read some of them with you.

Sincerely,

Sam

Sam,

Maybe you can show me these pieces of evidence you're talking about, sometime. But let's address the third point you made a few days ago about his followers being willing to be persecuted and even die for their belief system. Surely you can't think this is much different from some Muslims who died at the hand of Christians during the crusades, or willing Muslims who are extremists of Islam, and suicide bombers. I certainly don't hold to their extremism, but how is that any different? Or even during World War II, where Japanese pilots flew kamikaze for their emperor, whom they thought had some spiritual effect on them.

Abdul

In reflecting on our conversation through email I felt I had some good responses. I had been thinking in the back of my head about this email, and I kind of planned for it. I gazed out the window, thinking of Aisha. A ping brought me back to reality. Oh, it looks like Sam is still near his computer.

Voices Through the Window

. . .

Abdul, you're available to talk. Excellent. First, even the Qur'an seems to assume that somebody was crucified who looked exactly like Jesus, and then rose from the dead. Who? Would God deceive even Mary, Jesus's mother? Would God raise an imposter? Then, about these apostles of Jesus, His followers. Traditionally, the only resurrection that Jews believed in was the resurrection prophesied in their scriptures at the end of times. On top of that, when Jesus was on the cross, He visibly appeared to be cursed by God. What righteous and true Jewish man would want to put their faith in a shamed man on the cross when no one was supposed to be rising from the dead until end times? But then these assorted followers — from a despised tax collector to fishermen, and then the Apostle Paul, who was a well-educated Pharisee; all of these men became changed for Jesus, and without violence or gain whatsoever. Nobody would do that for what they knew was a hoax. Would God have deceived them? These Apostles then spread His Word to thousands of people, and they actually suffered for their efforts. The whole known world was impacted. Then, after His resurrection, these men were willing to be persecuted and die for Jesus. Paul was in fact a man who previously had felt compelled to persecute the Christians, and Jesus called him to a new life in Him. Paul was transformed to a new way of thinking, and then he became a great missionary for the Gospel, the Good News of Jesus. And he spread that news to non-Jews too, whom God loves just as much as Jews.

Sincerely,

Sam

I quickly wrote back and signed off.

Wow. That's a lot to digest and take in. Let me think on these things. Good night, Sam.

Abdul

I dropped by the Java Blue Cafe for coffee and talked to Malak again. I asked her about the Christian couple that had met with my Aisha once or twice, Jerry and Jen. Did she know anything about them? Did they come in here often? She said they had left her a card to post on the board in the doorway for ESL classes at a church in Dearborn. I took a picture of it with phone.

Later that day, while I was eating, I called Jerry and asked if I could meet up with him. He said I could come by the church in the morning before or after their English class if I wanted to talk. So, I said I would meet him at 9:30am right before it began tomorrow. The next day I pulled up to the church and wondered if this was a good idea or not. I really didn't want to cause a scene in a church. I had questions, and maybe they weren't all about Aisha. Could I stay calm, and not let my temper rise? I think so. And somehow, I felt that a few of my doubts about my wife's love for me and our family were resolving. It's almost like the snow I saw for the first time, when it fell on my cheeks. The snowflakes were there and then gone...

After talking to the teacher at the community center, the ladies who claimed her friendship there, and then her supervisor at Java Blue, some of my doubts dissipated. More than that, there are times when I weigh Rahma's comments to me when I come in the door from work, and I realize how Aisha felt. How she couldn't endure them anymore. Nobody would want to; they were that toxic and demeaning.

I opened the door to the church, and I shook my head in disbelief. If the imam from my family's village, knew where I was walking into... What would he say?

Inside I saw a woman sitting at a desk. "Excuse me, do you know where I can find the English class?" She pulled her glasses up over her nose and smiled at me.

"Good morning, sir, Jerry is expecting you. Our ESL classes are in the basement. You walk down this hallway, turn left and go down the stairs. Jerry is down there preparing for this morning's session." She pointed the way with an outstretched arm.

"Thank you."

I walked down the hallway and glanced into their large worship room. I looked deeper, seeing a cross. But it said above it, "He is risen!" I wondered and remembered my conversation with Sam. On the way to the stairs, I passed another office where a man in a polo shirt was working behind a desk with many shelves of books to his left. He heard me walking and smiled a greeting to me. These people have little concern about strangers walking their halls. They must be used to it with their classes. Downstairs I found Jerry just where the woman had said he would be.

"Good morning," he said. "Are you Abdul?"

"Yes," Abdul replied.

"It's a pleasure to meet you." A tall American man approached speaking wonderful Arabic. "As-salaam-alaykum" Jerry put out his hand to shake hands.

"And peace be upon you," Abdul answered in English with a grin and held out his hand.

"I'm Jerry and this is my wife, Jen. She also teaches here."

"Hello Abdul." Jen walked up next to Jerry.

"So, you saw our ESL posting somewhere around Dearborn and you are interested?"

"Well, maybe Jerry. I actually saw the flyer at the coffee house that my wife, Aisha, used to work at. Now she doesn't any longer," Abdul sighed. "She left me and seems to be in another city but I'm not sure where exactly."

"I'm so sorry to hear that. We have about fifteen minutes before the class begins… Can I get you coffee and donuts while we talk?" Jerry asked.

"No, thank you." Abdul stood there; his tension was betrayed by his clenched jaw.

"How can we help?" Jerry asked.

"Well, I don't know… maybe you helped her to leave. I saw a few emails on the computer between Aisha and Jen. But I'm not here to demand that you bring her back. Sam and I have already talked about it… I think you know him. I know it was her idea – Aisha, I mean. I know she had a job, and she wanted more independence. But I'm still not fully sure why she had to leave."

"I know you don't want to hear this, Abdul," Jerry said. "Yes, we helped her leave. She was miserable with your aunt. She couldn't stand it anymore."

"You see, Abdul," Jerry continued. "After Jen met with Aisha the first time, we could really sense her pain and distress. She asked us to help her escape from her situation, and it broke our hearts. We have never done this type of thing before, and we didn't plan it. We normally would never want to do something like this. We believe in marriage and good families. Plus, she said you are a very good man and good husband. She said she loves you and your children. But we felt that God wanted us to act. And when God speaks to both of us, then we must do His will."

"All right." Abdul's jaw loosened the tightness. "I'm not sure how to answer that. Except I have my doubts about God actually telling you to do that. I won't argue the point with you. And I… I thought I might ask you more questions about how you understand God. But I don't think now is the time."

"Well, Abdul anytime you want," Jerry said. "I'd be happy to meet you again anytime."

"Okay, I'll think about it. But I do have a parting question. How do you know Arabic so well? From your greeting, I can tell you have practice outside of a classroom."

"Ahh... yes. Well, five years ago God called us to go to the Middle East. We lived there for over many years to work in a hospital and speak of the Good News to people." Jerry shrugged his shoulders. Jen smiled. "And now we serve the community here."

"Well, then. Thank you again. Ila-liqaa."

"Yes, until we meet again, Abdul." Jerry and Jen spoke in unison and smiled at each other.

Abdul turned to go.

"Abdul, again she told me how much she loved you, but she was starting to worry about her safety. And she worried that you might be influenced to mistreat her too." Jen's eyes were filled with compassion. "She is so sorry to have hurt you like this."

Abdul stopped and turned back to see her face. To see if she was honestly telling the truth. *Does Aisha still love me? I think I see true compassion in her eyes and hear it in her voice.*

"I believe she was overthinking this," he said. "Even though many Yemeni husbands don't want their wives working, we could have talked it through. And my family would have had to accept it. I know somehow, she trusted you, Jen. She trusted you enough to leave me," Abdul's voice wavered as he spoke, and he left the room silently.

∽

"Abdul, may I speak with you for a moment?" Rahma asked Abdul as he walked in the door behind Suhaib and Mohammed.

"Yes, Aunt Rahma. What is it? I am very tired, and it is late."

"Here, Abdul, have a fresh cup of tea. It may relax you some. You know that I care for you like you are a second baba for us." Rahma motioned to him to sit with tea in her hand.

"Thank you, Aunt. It is good to sit after working all day." Abdul took a sip of the tea and stirred.

"Abdul, why is it you don't come home for the afternoon meal after the restaurant's lunch time? You used to come home with your Uncle Suhaib and Mohammed for a meal with all of us. How can you prefer the restaurant food over my food? Even though I've shown that cook there all of my recipes." Rahma sighed softly over her teacup. Then, after brooding for a moment, she looked again at Abdul. "Just because Aisha left us, you are still welcome here. You are part of our family, and we love you."

Ahh... Both you and Uncle Suhaib remind me of how much I should appreciate what you two have done for me. Constantly I hear of the problems other immigrants face, and I have it much easier, being here in an established home and business.

"I know you set a place for me each afternoon. I appreciate that. But often I would rather work serving for the late tables after lunch, and let the other servers go on break. I need to make my way and show my worth to you and Uncle." Abdul took another sip and looked out the window across the room.

"Well, as I said, you're loved. We only want what is best for you. Dearborn is different from Yemen, but not so different. Our community here wants to care for each other. Many of our friends have asked about you, and the sheik also." Rahma shakily put her cup down on the end table.

"I know, Aunt. I see your efforts. But I'm tired and not ready to discuss more tonight," Abdul said. He set his cup down, empty. He looked into it, seeming to be lost in thought, then excused himself and walked upstairs. There he noticed a light on in Habib's room.

"My baba, why is your light on still?" Abdul turned in the hall. "You should be asleep now."

"Yes, Baba. I was waiting for you." Habib sat up in his bed. "I wanted to talk with you."

"Where are your thoughts my baba, to keep you from sleeping?" Abdul sat on the bed and pushed back Habib's hair out of his eyes.

"I miss Mama so much. She would talk to me each day, and I would tell her the many things I was learning at school. She cared about what I was thinking."

"You know you can talk to me. I care what is going on in your life too, my baba," Abdul pulled Habib's chin up toward his face. "You know I love you very much and none of what is happening is your fault."

"Yes, Baba. But you often work late, and Aunt Rahma sends me to bed most days before you even get home. And she... She doesn't want to listen to me or ask me questions. She only tells me things. She tells me how bad my mama is. One day her friend from down the street, Mina, came over and sat in the kitchen with her, drinking coffee. They both kept on saying what a terrible shame it is that Mama left us without any good reasons. Then, she gives me my dinner left from their dinner, and watches me eat. I don't like her standing over me and waiting for me to miss a vegetable on my fork. Then she checks on me watching the tv all the time. I know the shows you said I can watch. I remember, Baba."

"Habib, my baba. Things will not be like this always. Soon, we'll have a home of our own. But she is part of our family, and you must listen to her and respect her." Abdul patted his son's head.

"I know Baba, but I'm not happy. She isn't even my grandma, but she thinks she is. And when will we have a home of our own? Will it have a backyard like my friend's house, where I can play? Will Mama come back and stay with us then?"

"Habib, you must mind your place and rest in the fact that I love you. I cannot answer all those other questions right now. Even though your mama left, she still loves you deeply. And you will see her soon, my baba." Abdul pulled the covers up and ruffled his son's hair.

"Good night, Baba."

I walked across the hall to my room after turning off Habib's light and shutting his door. Sitting on the bed, I thought about my emails with Sam. We had a few more exchanges about Jesus, and I thought of Jerry's words that God had spoken to them. I thought God only spoke to prophets. I will need to ask Sam about that. Why would God speak to common people? I just don't see that. Jen and Jerry said God was speaking to them about Aisha. How is that even possible? And Aisha... What is Aisha doing now? Does she know how much Habib misses her? He wants to please her. Does she realize how much he needs her? How much I need her?

I wonder what my mama would say about all this. I know she would love to see her grandson. I should call her. She will be getting up and making coffee now. And she will watch the community slowly wake up. And then maybe make Baba some breakfast if he doesn't leave too early. Where is my phone? Ah yes, in my coat pocket over the chair.

Abdul dialed the number, and he waited for her to answer, tapping his foot silently.

"Good morning, Mama," Abdul greeted her, "I hope I haven't woken you up."

"Abdul, it's so good to hear your voice. I was going to call you, but I'm sure you got my email," Ghada said as her coffee cup clinked on the saucer. "Aisha sent me a message through her mama, Badia, and she says she is well. And Aini is growing so fast. She is starting to crawl now. Aisha does miss you, my baba."

"I believe that. Habib misses her terribly, though I do too, I suppose," Abdul said.

"What, my baba? You suppose? I knew when you two were married that Allah would bless you two. And he did bless you with the most beautiful children. Your family will be whole again soon, don't you worry."

"I think so too, Mama. I just don't know how to make it happen. I've found out so many new things about Aisha. She seemed to be searching for something more than I was giving her. First it was her job, where I know she showed great skill and progress, but she still didn't need to work outside of the house. Then it was her new Arab friends that talked of all the things they did differently here in America. But the most disturbing thing has been her seeking new ideas about the Prophet, Jesus, and her obvious discontent with Islam. I just don't understand it and I'm not sure if we can come back from it. She may not even want to go back, and I don't know where that leaves me. I've spoken to these people she met with," Abdul explained.

"What... you did, baba? She may question, but don't worry. She will realize her lack of faith in Islam, and her community, and her family, and her true friends; once she sees what is most important. And *you* need to be doing your prayers and reading more of the Quran! Be devout, my baba. You shouldn't be led astray yourself."

"Yes, Mama. I hear you. Thank you for listening. I love you. Greet Baba with a kiss for me."

"Goodbye for now, my baba, and don't worry." Ghada said in a reassuring tone.

Chapter 19

Mohammed

The lunch rush has died down. The dining room is clear of customers except for the regular sales group from Ford. Down the hall I see Baba walking with today's POS receipts into the office. He's in a good mood today. Sales are up slightly, and we have kept hourly labor down. I helped prep in the kitchen today, and then hung my apron so I could seat and handle the dining room for lunch. Baba helps cook during lunch, but he's been trying to cross-train Abdul and me in order to cut back on some of the kitchen staff when the daily sales projections are mediocre.

I'm in the mood for my favorite coffee, and I think I can get out of here today. Maybe I will skip our family meal at home. I'll call Mama and tell her I need a little time to myself today. I think the manager from the Java Blue Cafe smiled at me the other day. She might be interested in a little conversation, even though I might be younger, we have some things in common. Though that day was bad for our family, it still flashes in my head like a movie. That manager, Malak, she's like the movie trailer for the theatre that brings anticipation of greater moments to come. I think we could share some moments bicycling along the Detroit River downtown and stop at one of the newer restaurants. Or I could take her to West Dearborn to walk through Fairlane Mall and walk around Henry Ford's Estate. Maybe we could do Greenfield Village and Henry Ford Museum, where all the tourists go but some locals haven't been. I heard it is really interesting to see America's history, and some of the inventors who have changed the future for today. Those things might make a good first impression, and she could see me as a bit of a romantic. I know I won't ask Abdul to go along. He's kept to himself lately and hasn't joked with me much like he used to. We work together, and he's helping with some of the management functions Baba delegates to us. Yet, he acts more distant' It's almost as if he somehow blames me for what happened with Aisha after that day at the Blue J Cafe. I mean I had to tell our family, and him. The family needed to know she was working. She had been living a lie. What else could I have done? I heard she only worked a few hours a day, but what did she think? People in this community had seen her walking her baby, and knew she was a recent immigrant. Sooner or later, someone will have had her wait on them for coffee, and they would wonder. She should have learned to fit in like all the other women in our Yemeni community. And when she chose not to, there would have to be consequences. Mama had to be clear about it, and eventually Baba, and even Abdul, would have had to clarify it for her.

"Good afternoon. You look like you could use one of our Yemeni favorites, a blend that's grown near the Sarawat Mountains and the Red Sea. And maybe you could take some back to the restaurant, I'm sure the family would enjoy it," Malak said.

"Hello! And I thought you wouldn't remember me. It's been a month or two since I've come by. Still, you got the flavor I've been waiting to drink," Mohammed smiled.

"Well, I have to confess I've been given a few clues to remind me. Your cousin has stopped in here a few times, and we've talked a little. So, he's kept your family fresh in my mind," Malak laughed and pushed a few strands of her hair back. *She doesn't wear her hijab here at work. She has a smile that widens more when she pulls her hair back — like the Red Sea when ships push back the waves. Momentum is created, and for a second, the waves stand still. That's her smile, when it's released, the sea around her is still.*

"Oh, Abdul has come back here? I wonder why? We have coffee houses closer to our restaurant." Mohammed looked around and back at her. *I can't be jealous that Abdul has been talking to her. I mean there has to be a reason. He's married, and he's not the kind of man to want to talk to women other than his wife.*

"I see now. And for what reason do you come here, then, if there are other places closer to your restaurant?" Malak smirked.

"Umm... Your coffee has a reputation that brings me back. And I like the customer service here." Mohammed smiled with a nod.

"Well, I appreciate that. But I think it is less about the coffee or the customer service for Abdul. He was here with questions about Aisha. And then he happened to meet Sam and they had a few conversations."

"Who is Sam? Is he the man with the woman that was with Aisha the day I came by?"

"Oh, no, I don't see those people much. Sam is a friend of theirs, I think. He comes in often to work on his laptop. Occasionally he talks to other people. I think he even talked with Aisha."

"Well, that's fine. Abdul is struggling a bit right now. Marriage isn't an easy thing for people, let alone a couple with two children."

"Oh my, I didn't know they were having marital issues. I hate to hear that, especially with Aisha. She was my best worker, and I loved working with her," Malak handed Mohammed the coffee.

"Well, I'm not sure if it was so much about the marriage as it was that she needed to find herself here in America. I think many people who come here to America have a hard time figuring out how to adjust to life here, but it's even harder for women. Many women want to be so much more than what they were in their home country now that they see the independent American woman."

"I'm sorry, Mohammed. I'll have to disagree with you. Men actually struggle more. The American culture and society ask them to change and acclimate to a new language, new habits in the workplace, and even different social mores. Most immigrant men would rather not change, and instead embed themselves in a cocoon of their own particular culture here in the states. Many cities like Dearborn have pockets of demographics where an immigrant wouldn't even need to learn English. In those areas, all of their needs, from business to shopping, and certainly religion all could maintain their own language, and sometimes even dialects."

"Wow, I didn't think we would get so socio-political. I was commenting on what I see here in Dearborn, and even when I visited Mexican Town in Detroit. I see you don't only think about coffees, and their origins, but you are a philosopher as well."

"I know. Maybe I said too much. But I've taken a few classes at U of M, Dearborn. Often it becomes a topic of conversation on the campus and even in some of the classes."

"I had hoped to invite you to our family restaurant for dinner. Now I feel I might not be ready for the dinner conversation," Mohammed laughed lightly.

"Umm… We can think about it. We could really try to keep the tone of the conversation lighter in the restaurant. We wouldn't want any guests at nearby tables listening in and try to make their way into our private conversation. That just wouldn't be nice." Malak laughed.

"So, could you picture yourself sitting across from me, and thinking about what we'd talk about over dinner? That's a good sign. Allah be praised." Mohammed smiled and brushed his long hair back over his head. "Now I will have to put some thought into the perfect dishes from our menu specials to have you try. Maybe a couple dishes that we might share. You'll just love it."

"You know I've grown up where my mama made Saudi dishes for us all the time. But I'm sure Yemeni food will be just as flavorful, even if it'll be made by your men in the restaurant." Malak pointed at Mohammed, still smiling.

"Well, then if I could have your number, I can check my schedule next week and see what day I'm off. Then I will call you after you get off of work. Is it okay to call after nine? Sometimes we get home then, and we could have more time to talk on the phone."

"Sure, that works for me. But you could text me during the day at work when you see your schedule, so I can plan the day. Sometimes I get together with friends after work. You know I don't just sit at a table brooding after work, waiting on restaurant managers to take me to dinner at their place." *Malak laughed softly to herself, and it lit up her face for me. I love to watch her laugh.*

"Oh, I'm sure you keep busy. You seem quite content with life and confident of yourself. I can't wait to relax with you over dinner. But now I've got to get ready to go into work for the day. Thanks for the coffee. What I've sipped has been worth the trip. It's almost as satisfying as sharing your laughter."

"Really? That's your line? How long have you waited to use that one? But it's still cute, I'll grant you that. I'll wait for your text and then your call. Just don't wait till midnight to call, because I get up early to open up here."

"No problem at all. See you soon," Mohammed smiled as he turned to leave.

∽

Aisha

Charlene calls it my availability. I just call it peace of mind. We have planned out the shifts I can work for the schedule ahead of time, opposite of either Roberto or, preferably, Carmen. I insist they take some of my tips each week for rent, food, and for helping watch Aini. They are so kind to me, and I don't really understand why. I just know I'm indebted to them. But they smile, and say they are serving as God has asked them to. I don't quite get that either, as if God is talking personally to them and telling them to help so much. Jen and Jerry implied something similar, and this Hispanic couple felt led to be so kind and loving to Aini and me. The God I've known expects so much, but I never felt a relationship with him. I listen to the women at the Bible study and hear how God is changing their lives. He is working inside them, and they seem to feel joy and contentment while He is changing them. One said something about molding her to be more like the potter. I wondered how she had thought up that metaphor, but she smiled and tapped her Bible emphatically. Today, Roberto finished cooking at three, and he got home around three-twenty. Carmen is home already, and she is able to babysit. Roberto had to go back work and cook and said we could drive together. I like to be a few minutes early, so I can check my section and any side work I might have been assigned during the shift. There's nothing worse than running out of glasses or rolled silverware during the dinner rush. The lead servers are always so organized and have a plan when each server punches in.

"Aisha! So glad you're here a few minutes early. We're down two servers tonight, and I need you to take the bigger section in the back," Karen looked up at her from the clipboard she held with a color-coded seating chart.

"Oh, I don't know Karen. That's one of the bigger sections when we're in a six-server chart. I'm not sure I'm ready for that," Aisha said while she tied her bistro style apron and glanced toward the larger booths in the back. "Usually, I have a couple of booths and a couple two-tops."

"Aisha, Frieda and I have been watching you. We've seen you get stronger as you have handled getting double and even triple sat. That section has the four booths, and the one large family booth. You'll be fine. And I'll be on the same side of the dining room if you need help. Plus, if you need beverages run for a table, I can ask the host to drop them for you. No worries."

"Okay, if you think I'm ready. Then I'll take care of the guests, just like you've trained me to. And a bigger section might mean more tips?"

"Oh, yes, sure. As long as you give that consistent service, I've seen in you. You'll see the effort pay off when you count your cash tips and Charlene runs your charge tips at the end of our shift. But focus on service, and don't let the money be your motivator."

"Oh, I know, Karen. I work as hard as I can, because it's what is right, and not for the money."

"I know you do, Aisha. Sometimes even the best of us sees the dollars ring up in our head, like the grocer who quickly adds a cart of food for a hundred-dollar total. Some of my servers see that hundred-dollar total from the registrar in their mind and try to pick more tables than they can handle. They end up sacrificing quality for quantity in their service. That's not what we're about in our mission here at Porter's Houseboat Restaurant. Even Mr. Porter himself will remind a server of that when he sees them overwhelmed, to 'Take a deep breath and remember why we're here. We're here to have a guest feel like they're part of our family, and we're so pleased they've joined us. So, breathe and smile for my guest.' That's what he has said to a few servers over the years. Or at least something like that."

Karen smiled and looked across the room toward the kitchen. "The manager's office is in the back of the kitchen. But Mr. Porter spends more of his time walking about the dining room than in the office. He leaves the office duties for cashing out bartenders and servers, shift planning, and ordering to his Samuel and Charlene. Of course, Chef Curtis does the ordering for the kitchen, but the front of the house managers deal with the bar orders and carry out supplies."

"I hope he doesn't have to tell me to take a breath. I wouldn't want him or anyone else thinking I'm out of breath. I think I might be afraid to have him pull me aside and talk to me," Aisha said softly.

"Oh, don't you worry. He's very kind and down to earth. He just wants us to always give excellent service, even if we're a bit behind. And he usually doesn't work the night shift much, unless it's a busier night. Samuel or Charlene, his managers, work the dining room with the same standards Mr. Porter expects, so he usually goes home when he sees they have it handled."

"Uh… Well, that's good. I'm not ready for too many more surprises."

"Just go check your section, Aisha. Make sure the day shift filled the sugar caddies, salt and pepper shakers, and see that the general area around the table is clean. Then check the list I posted in the back for the two side work assignments for tonight." Karen nodded to the wait hall around the corner.

Mohammed

Today is my day off. It was slow this week and Baba said I could take Tuesday off. Abdul is content to work on the computer at home and work almost every day at the restaurant. It's like he's trying to bury his family problems, and instead he should be dealing with them like a man. I've heard a few people in our neighborhood suggest he's not the man he should be, knowing he couldn't keep a rein on his wife. And, of course, Mama mumbles comments without much regard for him at most of our afternoon meals, and he looks at her without any answer. His face solemn, and hard to read.

But today I was happy to be away from that corner of my life. I'd watched the news and had trusted the weatherman that Southeast Michigan would have a sunny 70-degree spring day. I was a little worried because over the weekend it had rained, and then Sunday it dropped below 40 degrees. They say Michigan is one of the states where you could have all four seasons in one week. Even the first week of May it had snowed. But Fox News was right, and I was happy. I gassed up the SUV and picked up Malak with Tim Horton's bagel and coffee in hand. I wasn't quite sure she would agree, since it wasn't common for Arabic couples to do so. So, with a quiet smile on my face, we snacked on them while driving back down Michigan Avenue toward Greenfield Village. I knew this would be the place to get some interesting conversation going and enjoy a nice spring walk. Days like today came and went, and people liked to do something memorable when they could get outside.

We strolled along, looking at colonial buildings. I wondered if I could get her talking with the passion I heard before. Would she debate about the gender roles from yesterday to today? Inside the Village, parts didn't seem too far off from some of the poor villages in Yemen. And women often carried much of the workload. Villages near the mountains often don't have the luxuries we have in the city, although my village I grew up in wasn't too far from the city. I had running water, and electricity. And I had known some children who didn't have water in their home in Yemen. But here in Dearborn it's all taken for granted. So, we walked in and out of the famous people's homes. We saw how colonial Americans cooked food over fire, and we rode the Model-T cars with Malak driving. Afterward, we tired of the village and took the train back to the gate.

From there we drove over to my family's restaurant, knowing that the lunch rush had died down. I gave her a tour of the restaurant, and showed her the kitchen, the walk-in, and waved at my father sitting in the office. He nodded with a smile and told her to enjoy her meal. I knew he had already returned from the family meal at home, so I didn't ask him to dine with us. We shared Maraq, our lamb stew, and then some Mandi, our chicken and rice dish, with some Malawah bread. Once we were done, she agreed to take a drive to downtown Detroit. We strode along the Riverwalk on the Detroit River as the sun came down. We held hands and walked around Hart Plaza, watching the sun come down over the Ambassador Bridge.

It was a day that I couldn't have imagined being better.

Then I came home to my mama and Fatima, the neighbor next door, having tea in our living room. When I walked in, both of them looked up from their tea. I looked at my watch, and confirmed it wasn't too late. But it seemed late for tea with visiting friends. I felt something brewing, and knew it wasn't a second pot of tea.

"Mohammed! I'm so glad you're home. Fatima and I were just talking about you," Rahma clapped her hands.

"Mama, I hope you haven't found a new girl for me to meet. Pardon me, Fatima. My mama wants to marry me off soon, and not let me say a word about it."

"Oh Mohammed, please stop," Rahma dipped her head slightly.

"It's true what you do, Mama. By the way, I had the best day with a young lady today. So, you don't need to worry," Mohammed shook his head.

"Pardon me, but I think I will go now," Fatima said. "Rahma, you know my thoughts, and my heart for the community." Fatima looked at Rahma as she got up to leave.

"Fatima don't leave because I'm home. You two visit. I'm going up to my room," Mohammed said.

"No, that's all right, Mohammed. I need to go home to my family, and I think your mama has something to discuss with you." Fatima gave Rahma a kiss on the cheek goodbye and tightened her hijab.

"Oh, I see, you two have decided something, and now I need to hear all about it. Won't this be good?" Mohammed's head dropped in frustration and sighed.

"Oh, my baba. Sit down at the table and relax. This isn't about you. You are my special one, and I hope to see the girl you met soon over family dinner. I know she was the reason you missed the last few dinners in our home. But now we must talk about your cousin, Abdul, and his wife, Aisha."

"Well, somehow, I knew it. You've been planning and deciding what's best for Abdul and Aisha. I know Aisha shouldn't have left us the way she did. But Mama, you could find a better way to tell them how to live more for Allah. The muttering comments, the darting looks, and the outright demands you placed on Aisha might have pushed her away. You should have let Abdul try to handle it. It is his responsibility, and he would have found his own way to do what is right."

"Well, Abdul wasn't thinking enough of what he should do." Rahma lightly clattered her teacup on the table. "Even the rest of their family in Yemen, they agreed that we should speak up to Abdul. He needs to step up and be the man here. He can't allow Aisha to disgrace our family. What will our community think once they know she is gone working and without our permission? And she is taking English with those Americans, and certainly talking to Christians at her job. Before she left, she was even asking questions about Jesus and the Christian Injil writings."

"What? How do you know these things? She told you?" Mohammed looked quietly in his mother's eyes. "I know Abdul didn't tell you. He hasn't talked to any of us lately. And especially you, after you continue to berate him to be a better Muslim husband."

"No, of course not. She wouldn't tell me. We hadn't had a friendly conversation, especially since I saw her shirking her duties at home. I would nod to her, and even explain what she should do for her family, and as part of this home. But she walked about as if it were a Tihamah storm in the Yemeni desert along the Red Sea. The only real concern she showed was for the baby and talking to Habib about his schoolwork. A mama needs to do more than listen to a child's day at school."

"Okay. But how did you learn these things about Aisha?" Mohammed tried to not roll his eyes.

"I walked by the office one night on my way to the kitchen, and Abdul was mumbling to himself while he was typing. He was probably doing some kind of journal he is saving on that computer. But I heard him repeat again and again, questioning himself or Allah in his mumbling tone. I don't know which. That was a week ago. That's one of the reasons why I started to tell him more how he should find Aisha and bring her home where she belongs. Then he could demonstrate his authority, as a husband should."

"Ah... now I understand," Mohammed said. "And I agree, he should stand up in his marriage and be the authority as the prophet, Muhammed said in the Quran."

"She should know that he is the man, in voice and hand, if necessary." Rahma tapped her teacup again. "It's our responsibility to help guide as family."

"So, I suppose you have more of a plan," Mohammed wondered aloud. "You and Fatima probably have the details all thought out."

"Oh well, she only listened and suggested how the community would notice our efforts to maintain unity within our family. It's important to be sure our culture isn't lost while we are here in America. That includes our faith in Islam, and the family values we share."

"Fine, Mama. What else do you know that has you planning things? I'm starting to get tired, and I want to go relax in my own room," Mohammed complained.

"I know, my baba. But you must listen to this. Aisha's mama, Badia, called my phone to talk to Habib for a while. And I couldn't help but listen a few meters away in the kitchen."

"Big surprise there! A grandmama who wants to talk to her grandson who she hasn't seen in over a year or so," Mohammed laughed. "And even more of a surprise that you happened to be listening."

"Stop and listen for a few more moments, my baba. They talked about life and school for Habib. But then he said how he missed his mama and wanted to see and talk to her. He was also worried about her."

"Mama, that's only natural for him to say that. Would you expect otherwise in this situation?"

"I know, but then she tried to reassure him. She said she had talked to Aisha and explained how Aisha missed him terribly. But she told her mama to tell Habib that she was okay. In fact, she was working at a new restaurant and serving people."

"What? She is working now. How can that be?" Mohammed asked.

"Yes, apparently, she is a waitress in a nice restaurant. I even heard Habib say the funny name, Porter's House Restaurant. And I can't help but wonder about the baby, Aini. Who is caring for her needs if Aisha is off working?"

"Wow, that's surprising. Does Abdul know? When will we tell him?" Mohammed questioned Rahma again. "We must do something about this."

"Oh, yes, we will do something. We will help Abdul where he has failed. We are family."

Mama smiled knowingly at me and tapped my hand like she does when we share something. But this is more. She is the matriarch in this family, and Baba allows her to be strong in this house. She knows the importance of family. But what will her plan be?

Voices Through the Window

~

A week later….

*I can't believe we're actually doing this. My mama had pushed me into a corner. She had manipulated and found a way to insist I be part of her plan. First, she kept after me at every meal when I brought in my dirty plate. She told me again and again how it was so important to find out where Aisha's new job is. So, I finally relented, and looked it up on the internet. I found it be a fancy restaurant, with consistent reviews. And it was miles away in a city I wasn't familiar with. But I was able to find the specific location, and how to get there. I even called and asked a few questions about seating arrangements for her. But then said if I didn't take her and Fatima to the restaurant, she **would tell** our community, including the imam, how I had been dating without the family's consent. Smiling smugly, she had muttered something about the newer generation. And now today, while driving she quietly explained in detail the plan. How she and Fatima would quietly explain how imperative it would be for Aisha to return home. In order to save face, she should return home immediately so that the family and community will no longer be shamed. And if her stubborn nature still resided within her, then Mama had a more specific plan. I was to keep the van parked close to the back door and wait in the hall by the door. At a set time, I would come out and stand by the long bar the host had told me about on the phone. And if Aisha dismissed their request, Mama would wave at me from across the room. Once she signaled, I would walk towards their table, rope hidden behind my back. All of this was too much, and I wasn't sure I could do what my mama insisted need be done. The thing that pushed most was when she questioned my manhood **if I** wasn't willing to take Ais**ha if it was** so required.*

Aisha

The beginning of the shift started off well. I had seen Charlene check with Karen about where she placed the servers, and if all the servers could handle their sections. I heard Karen say that her four strong servers were placed in each corner section of the restaurant, and the two weaker ones were between them. One was a nineteen-year-old girl who waited tables at Coney Island but was still getting used to larger tables and serving alcohol from the bar. The other was a twenty-year-old guy who had never worked in a restaurant before but was studying nursing and needed extra money for tuition and books. It struck me that I had somehow made it to the experienced server status after only four months working here. It was nice to overhear it said out loud between two supervisors, and really unexpected. I was sat a few families in the first half-hour, and then got double sat. And then a fifth table was seated right after I had just finished getting drink orders for the two tables double sat. Instead of feeling stress, I was feeling almost exhilarated. I spoke to the newest table and took the order from the two after bringing their beverages from the wait hall. I got in a rhythm as I moved about from my section to the wait hall, and to the window to pick up food. There were voices talking in and through the cook's window, but I felt part of it. This time fear didn't catch me, and the voices in the window seemed to be natural. Everyone was happy with their food, and I was able to help them find just the right menu item for each of them.

"Hey, Aisha, thanks for pre-bussing. I just finished clearing your two window booths." Bev, the cute college hostess, whispered to me as she tossed a towel in the red bucket at the server stand. "The tips are on the edge of the table. I've got a few waiting at the door, so you're getting sat really quick,"

"Thanks, Bev, I'll be right over to greet them after I check on my food in the window," Aisha whispered back as she strode past her.

"Roberto, how about tables 88 and 89? I've been waiting a while for them," Aisha tapped her hands in the window and poked her head in a little. "Most of them got entree salads, and a couple of burgers. They should be up soon, *si*, or no?"

"So now you're practicing a little Spanish here in the window with me?" Roberto laughed. "You ring in two four-tops in back-to-back, and then want them up ASAP. You're fitting right in with the rest of our serving staff."

"Relax a little bit in the window, Roberto. As the expo, you're supposed to remain calm for the whole kitchen. Just like Sous Chef John does. And where is he, by the way? The restaurant is starting to fill up, and he should be up here," Samuel asked Roberto as he moved plates around the hot and cold windows to tray up on a tray jack. "Karen, you're food's up. Let's go run it out while it's hot."

"Samuel, I'm running soups and side salads out. Can you get a runner for me?" Karen asked over her shoulder. Her arms were filled with a banquet food tray and tray jack.

"Samuel, Chef John is filleting the fish for tonight's special. We've almost 86ed the Encrusted Salmon, and he's almost done trimming more," Roberto yelled over the plated burger he tossed in the window.

"Hey, new guy, that's enough of stocking on the salad condiments. Come run this food out that I trayed up. Take it out to Karen's section; it's table 80 on the opposite end of the restaurant," Samuel turned his head back around to the salad bar to look at him.

"Samuel, what about my food? You know tables 88 and 89?" Aisha asked.

"Aisha, we just sat you again. They asked for you, so hustle on over to windows," Charlene yelled into the wait hall with menus in her hand.

"Go, Alisha… Roberto just gave me the five-minute sign for your two tables," Samuel said.

"Oh, no, five minutes. Really? Okay. And who is asking for me as their server, I don't have any regulars yet."

"Who knows Aisha? Maybe one of those great comment cards someone turned in about you specifically came back and wanted you as their server," Samuel said. "Anyway, head on over to at least greet them."

"I will Samuel, and I'll let tables 88 and 89 know their food is coming soon," Aisha picked up three glasses of water and added a lemon slice to one of them. She strode back out to the dining room.

"Here are a couple of waters for you, and I'll be back in a moment to see what we can start after you have looked at the menu then." Aisha said to her one table she had already greeted, "and I wanted to let you know that your food is coming out shortly."

"Oh, that's fine. We're still finishing the chips and salsa. No worries, Aisha." The son from table 88 said, and the man from table 89 nodded and waved slightly, acknowledging he heard the same for them. She turned to greet her newest table.

"Hello Aisha, it's nice to see you're doing well and alive. We would have never known otherwise," Rahma said as Aisha came walking up to the table.

"What? What are you doing here Rahma? With Fatima? Hello Fatima. You came here to eat?"

"Oh no, we came with Habib's report card. We both thought a mama should know how her son is doing in school," Rahma pushed a yellow envelope across the table. Fatima smiled and gave it another push to the edge of the table.

"I see it took you and Fatima to bring it. And you had to come here… to my work?"

"Well, obviously we couldn't bring it to your house, or even mail it. We don't know where you even live," Rahma smirked, and she continued in Arabic.

"Look Aunt Rahma… I can't just stop and visit with you two right now. I have other tables to care for," Aisha said.

"That's alright, Aisha dear, go get us some hot tea and we will wait here for you to come sit and talk with us." Fatima smiled endearingly in English.

"Yoo! No, you don't understand. I'm busy and I can't sit with you. But fine, I'll get some hot tea for you," Aisha walked quickly away. She brushed against Karen, waiting for drinks as she strode past the bar aisle.

"Hey girl, are you okay? You need help for a minute? Your face looks stressed," Karen pulled on her apron to stop her.

"I'm okay. I think. It's just family problems I wasn't expecting. I need to go check on my food, it should be in the window," Aisha pulled away from her and almost ran to the wait hall.

"Take a breath," Karen yelled after her.

"Roberto, please tell me tables 88 and 89 are up. I see my entree salads, the wrap sandwich, and the kid's meal. What about my burgers?" Aisha pushed her head into the hot window. Then thinking, she turned to the beverage dispensing machine and sighed. "Hi Bev, can you please get two hot teas for me, with a 2oz cup of cream on the side? I would really appreciate it."

"I got the hot tea coming up, Aisha. Don't you worry," Bev smiled at her as she stepped over to the pot of hot water.

"Excellent, can you drop them at table 78 just around the corner?" Aisha asked.

"Done! And I remember those table numbers, girl," Bev laughed lightly.

"Aisha, here are your burgers, one with bacon and cheese, the second one is picked MW with mushrooms and Swiss on it. Don't mix it up from the Patty Melt with Swiss and onions already up in the window, though, the melt is on light rye." Roberto pushed two platters to her side.

"Aisha, are you okay? Your face is a little flushed," Samuel turned to look at her from the other hot window as he cleaned the rim on two rib-eyes that had just come up.

"Aisha, you never look this way. What's going on out there?" Roberto stopped pulling tickets from the printer. "Come over and talk to me for a second on the cook's line."

"Look guys, I think I'm okay. I have family at my table, and I'm not sure why they came." She stopped and took a deep breath. "Just let me take my food out."

223

After she left, Roberto turned to Samuel. "This isn't good. You need to check on them," Roberto tapped lightly on the window with a spatula.

"Aisha, both tables are up. I will follow behind you with the second table." Samuel picked up a food tray and glanced through the window at Roberto. He nodded toward the back kitchen.

"Aisha, table 78 is ready to order. The menus are on the edge of the table, and they're looking around. You want me to have Karen pick them up." Charlene stepped into wait hall.

"No, I'll get them right after I take out this food. Thank you," Aisha picked up her tray and jack and walked swiftly out to her section. Samuel followed in step behind her.

"Here we are everyone, your Michigan Cherry Salad with grilled chicken and extra goat cheese, the Bacon-Cheese Burger well done, chicken tender kid's meal, and a Caesar Salad. I believe we have it all right," Aisha passed the plates around after setting the tray on the tray jack.

"Everything looks great, Aisha. Well done." The son at table 88 smiled.

"Oh, Jim, that's enough. She's just doing her job."

"I know that, Jan. But remember I used to wait tables years ago. That's how we met, and I never want to take for granted how difficult serving many tables at once can be." Jim answered her with a grin.

"Okay, thank you and enjoy your meal," Aisha tried to smile and turned around to table 78. "Aunt Rahma and Fatima, you got your tea. Good."

"Yes, we got the tea. But it's not as good as we can get in Dearborn," Fatima said.

"Yes… Dearborn, where our flavors are full and always mindful of our homeland. What are you doing here? This is not your home or where you belong." Rahma looked around the restaurant. She had switched to English, and her voice had raised slightly. Ben, the bartender, heard her and caught Samuel's eyes. Samuel had stopped to pre-buss another table across the aisle. Samuel moved behind the bar and picked up the house phone.

"Rahma, what is it you really want? Why are you here?" Aisha took one step back.

"Aisha, if you will not sit down and talk, then you must know this: You are coming home *today* to Dearborn." Rahma's voice was deep and commanding. Fatima vigorously nodded in agreement.

"I will not talk to you now. This isn't the place for this discussion," Aisha stepped away and over to the next table. "Ladies, you have the waters, you ready to order?"

"Excuse me, Aisha. You won't be rude to your aunt. We aren't done talking," Rahma stood up next to her and grabbed her hair. "And where is your hijab? Have you forgotten who you are?" Rahma nodded beyond Aisha to Mohammed who was just a few tables away nervously gazing around the room. Once he saw Rahma nod at him, he quickly stepped toward Aisha.

"Rahma, let go of my hair," Aisha's voice got louder. "Hey, my hands. Let go! Untie my hands!" Aisha yelled.

"Relax cousin, it isn't that tight. You're okay," Mohammed muttered loud enough for her to hear, as he made it snug behind her.

"What are you doing, Mohammed! You know you can't do this," Aisha yelled. "Roberto, come help me! Roberto!"

"Quiet down, Aisha. Everything will be fine once we get you to Dearborn." Now that Aisha was restrained, Rahma talked calmly, in an attempt to keep her quiet.

"Hey, what's going on here? Let Aisha go." Roberto came running out from the kitchen with his apron tucked. "She works here, and she isn't leaving."

"Keep talking to him, Berto." Samuel held the phone up.

"Says you, Mexican! She's coming with us!" Mohammed shook his head and started dragging her through the dining room. "Everything will be fine once we get you home to Abdul," he whispered.

"Stop, I said!" Roberto tried to block Mohammed. But Mohammed sidestepped and pushed right by him.

"Aisha, who's that… a new friend? Wait until you have to explain your friendship to Abdul," Mohammed snidely said to her.

"Mohammed, I thought you had matured from that boy who tried to steal the ball from me when we were younger. But here you are pulling me like I'm a goat from the village."

"Here, this will quiet the betrayer," Rahma said as she put duct tape over Aisha's mouth. "Mohammed, now hurry and pull her outside to the van. Then she can tell us where she has the baby hidden."

"'Berto, are you okay out here? Where are they taking Aisha?" Sous Chef John shouldered up next to Roberto.

"They're trying to take her back to Dearborn." Roberto glanced at the back door.

"Roberto, can you help me?" Aisha yelled through the tape. She was deeply frightened.

I still have twenty meters to find a way out of this, to get help or out of Mohammed's strong grip. He and Rahma were dragging me to the back door to the waiting van. All the guests in the dining room stared but didn't offer help. Everything had come to a standstill. How could this be happening to me? Where are the voices now? All is still and silent. The only sound was that of my shoes scraping the wooden floor as I was dragged through the restaurant.

Chapter 20

Aisha

"Mohammed, you don't really want to do this. You're embarrassing yourself. I know your mama put you up to this. Untie me and let me go, now!" Aisha's voice raised an octave.

"Yeah, but what does it matter if it was her idea? I realized it's for the best. Abdul isn't the same without you, and people are asking in the neighborhood where you are," Mohammed said between breaths. He dragged her while she kicked wildly, trying to stop him or at least slow him. Her feet only skidded on the wooden floor.

"Roberto, where are you? Can't you do something?" She screamed for help. "Karen? Samuel? Chef Jon? Anybody?" Aisha, now frantic, tried to see around Mohammed.

"Yes, we're here!" Roberto, Karen, and Chef John replied in unison. They had all hurried from the back room. Roberto and John stood, arms akimbo. The two men effectively formed a solid barricade to the exit. But Karen was clearly intimidated. She stood back, holding onto the edge of an empty booth.

"Look out! We aren't playing a game." Mohammed grunted, turned his left shoulder, and pushed right between them. "Much like the American football, I believe I just broke your defensive line." Mohammed laughed at his own joke.

"Mohammed! Be careful, but hurry," Rahma said. She and Fatima were pacing him on the next row over. Both wore grim expressions.

"Ugh... *What?*" Mohammed barked. He and Aisha tumbled to the floor. "Who did that?"

Karen pulled her foot back and smiled sheepishly. Aisha realized Karen had tripped Mohammed. She took advantage of the distraction and jerked away from his grip. Roberto helped her up. John turned and stepped with his full weight on Mohammed's chest.

"Relax there for a second, sir. We'll get a refill on that ice water for you. Karen, can you get this gentleman a water, please?" John turned his head to Karen and grinned.

"Take your foot off my son! He will not be treated like that," Rahma yelled across the aisle.

"What's going on in this dining room? Chef, why do you have your foot on a guest?" A larger, heavy set Waterford Township Police officer had arrived and strode toward them.

"And what's that server doing tied up? The one who would be on the floor if not for the cook, holding her steady," his female partner sidled up next to him and barked out, surprising the silent dining room with her sharp tone.

Samuel came from the kitchen. "I'm the one who called 911!" He walked over to the officers. "Thank God, you made it before things got out of control!"

"And this *isn't* out of control? Your chef has his foot on a customer's chest, holding him down. Everyone here looks agitated. I don't even want to guess why that server is hog-tied and barely standing straight. Sam, frankly, it looks like a three-ring circus has pulled into town and set up camp in your dining room. Would you be the ringmaster of this circus?" The burly officer, his thumbs hooked in his belt, cocked an eyebrow at Samuel.

"Well, yes, I suppose. I'm the manager and the server who's been tied up is Aisha. Chef John is our sous chef, while Roberto is a lead line cook. The guy on the floor… him, we don't know, although I assume he is somehow related to Aisha." He pointed at Aisha, still bound. "But obviously, she wants no part of him or his mother." Samuel pointed at Rahma. "The other one?" He indicated Fatima, "I have no idea who she is."

Aisha glanced at Rahma and Fatima. Both looked annoyed, but Rahma was so angry she was barely holding her temper in check. Aisha understood that, since Rahma's plan hadn't worked, everyone around her would feel her wrath — later. For now, she was smart enough to breathe through her rage. Aisha believed that only the threat of jail prevented her from leaping on her and clawing her face.

"Excuse me, sir! Yes, you are there." The sharp-tongued female officer pointed to Jim, the father of two that Aisha had been waiting on. "Can you untie that waitress?"

"You mean me? Okay, sure, sure," Jim stood and stepped over to Aisha and began to untie her. His hands shook with residual adrenaline.

"Jim, just sit down and stay out of it," his wife muttered.

"I'm almost done. Relax, honey. You see how stressed she is?"

"Her? What about your young children? That crazy man could hop up and do God knows what to the rest of us. Hurry and sit back down." His wife whispered angrily. "I always tell you to mind your own business. Interfering will only bring us trouble."

"Thank you, Jim," Aisha whispered as he untied her. Then she squeezed Roberto's arm and sighed.

"Aisha, tell them what's going on here. The police need to know. This is a public disturbance, and they will need to decide what to do." Karen looked into Aisha's eyes and nodded.

"Well, officers, my husband's aunt and her son were trying to forcibly take me back to Dearborn. My husband and I are currently trying to decide how to best reconcile. But *they* thought they knew best." She pointed at Mohammed and Rahma. "As you can see, I want nothing to do with them." Once Aisha found her voice, she was ready to spit out the whole story.

"First of all, let's find a spot to all talk. Samuel, is there someplace more private we can talk? And sir, you on the floor, can we trust you to remain calm or do I need to restrain you?" the male officer asked. Mohammed grunted his assent.

"I'm sure all of the guests dining here would like to complete their dinners without further distractions," the second office pointed out.

"Certainly, let me show you our small banquet room. It's empty right now, and you can interview everyone there." Samuel pointed to the back corner.

"Okay all. Chef, cook, and the server who was just untied, I want you all in the banquet room first," the female officer said. "Everyone else, back to working or eating."

"You sir, off the floor. Come with me." The larger officer watched Mohammed as he got up and sat in an empty booth. "Ma'am, you and your friend sit down in this booth as well. Let's relax for a minute."

"I think I recognize you two," the female officer said. "Didn't we meet you a month or so ago on a street altercation? Yes, I think so." She furrowed her eyebrows. "Won't this be fun to hear all about?"

"I'm not sure we're the same people. I'm sure you deal with a lot of issues on the streets." Roberto said, turning his back to the officer as they walked.

"Samuel, you and your chef go on ahead to that room, I need to tell Aisha something quickly." The officer gently pulled her over to an empty booth far from Rahma and her group. "I'm Officer Dabrowski." She smiled. "It seems there have been dark clouds following you around. The township has professionals that can help you deal with things." She looked her straight in the eye. "You know, help you sort out things and find sunshine beyond these dark clouds."

"Well, I don't know if I need that." Aisha said as she sat down with a weak smile.

"Well, I think you might be surprised what they can do." The officer took her hand and assured her, while deftly pulling a card from her shirt pocket. "And you know, I can give you my card even if you don't need a professional to share with you. But you just need someone that can listen. I'm a good listener, though I need to be tough on the job." She smiled kindly.

"I don't think you understand, officer. I see rays of sunshine already. And I feel hope—"

"No, I don't think I do understand. How can you feel hope? Both times I've seen you, you've just been attacked. Yet here you are trying to smile and say that it's okay. Most women would be hysterical, crying puddles by now."

"Well, I've found a job that satisfies me, and I have people that care for me. Then, I have more support with the people I live with, and even more from the church I go to." Aisha's smile grew until she radiated with confidence.

"Oh, so you're one of those that think church gives you all the answers for life. Now I see," the officer said as she drew back her hands slightly.

"Yes, the church is wonderful! I used to be a Muslim, but now I feel Jesus has been maybe calling me to be His child." Aisha warmly said. "I've seen so much contentment in people, even during the stress in their lives. This God they have is relational and I see that in the church as well in their homes."

"Wow, you're like an onion, with layers that are peeling back more than I thought. I pulled you aside to help you, and now you've got me thinking."

"I think I see the stress of life in your eyes, and I know that helping people deal with their bad stuff is not easy." Aisha pulled the officer's hand back. "You know what, you should join us for our ladies' Bible study. All the women are strong like you, but God is clearly working in them."

"You're not even one of these Christians yet, but here you are inviting me to a Bible study. I can't get past that." The office's voice faltered.

"Maybe you're like me and you need to get God out of a box you've put Him in. God seems to be working outside of a box we seem to often put Him in, where He's distant and directing with a somber face. Instead, the face of God I've seen lately is one of concern, enduring love, patience, and a sense of wanting to know me. Allah had never wanted to come to meet with me. All of these Christians who truly speak of a living faith in their lives, they talk about a God speaking to them and walking with them. That's what I think I want, and you could have it, too."

"Well, maybe I will join your ladies' group one night. It might be better than the night I go out with the other women. I usually wake up discouraged and down afterward," the officer sat back and reflected.

"Excuse me, officer, are you going to detain my cooking staff much longer? Our kitchen needs them soon, and we need to get back to business," Samuel asked.

"Certainly. We were just doing the first interview here in the booth for a bit of privacy. I'll get to your kitchen staff immediately. Thank you, sir."

∼

After an hour or so, all parties were interviewed, and Mohammed was released with a stern warning from the police. Both officers were empathetic towards me, and the female officer smiled with confidence as they left. Soon the restaurant got busy again and business moved on. Although, in my head I started to hear voices of uncertainty and worry. I tried to show an attitude of joy, but it was incomplete. Karen could tell something was wrong, and I felt a little off while working. But I was surprised how well she went right back to work as if this were a normal day. We got a late dinner rush, and I had little time to think about my family. A few images of my husband and son popped in my mind, and I wondered about them.

Rahma and Fatima pushed Mohammed to try and take me away. That was really incredible, and I couldn't believe they'd do such a thing. But it was easier to not think about them then it was to put aside thoughts of the two men I loved, Abdul and Habib.

The dinner rush died down, and as we pre-closed, my mind wandered again and again to my two men. But amid those thoughts, peace on the faces of my friends came to me also. Then the Words of Jesus that we had discussed in Bible study started to come to me as I was cleaning tables. This was so different, a God that wanted to interact with you. Allah always seemed so far off to me, and especially if I didn't maintain the ways of Islam. I wonder how Roberto's life started to change when he came to Jesus.

"Roberto, thank you for being the friend that you are," Aisha said as he put the Mustang into drive. "You and Carmen mean so much to me. And of course, Karen, Samuel, and Chef John, too."

"Aisha don't even think about it. We truly care for you, and you're our friend now." Roberto answered her with a smile on his face.

"And I appreciate it. Can I ask you something though? How did you know Jesus was calling you?"

"Oh, that's easy," Roberto said. "It all comes back to Jesus. I could see the joy of the people I met, like Carmen, Santo, Ms. Theresa and her husband, Matthew. I wanted that too. But I wasn't quite sure, until I heard Pastor Pedro retelling a story how Jesus explained about seeds getting dropped. I felt like he was talking directly to me. He asked what seed are you? He also explained how Jesus is the Good Shepherd and is willing to hunt for even one sheep apart from 99 more. I felt like the pastor was asking me if I was that one sheep who needed saving. Something moved down inside me, telling me to get up and walk while that song, 'Just as I am' was playing. I had felt a tap on my arm, and it was Ms. Thersea asking if I wanted to walk with her to the altar at the front of the church. There we talked about verses called the

'Roman Road,' and John 3:16, reminding me that God the Son sent Jesus for the whole world, even me. Then I made a commitment that day to have Jesus as my Lord, Master, Friend, and Savior. I haven't looked back in the rearview mirror since then." Roberto adjusted his mirror slightly and laughed.

"And you've been happy since that day? You haven't had any problems in life?" Aisha looked over at him as he shifted gears.

"Hold up, now. I didn't say that." Roberto grinned. "I've had many problems after that day, and still face problems now. The difference is in the one to whom I turn now. Jesus wants me to turn all my days to Him; the good, the bad, and so-so days. In all things I thank Him and praise Him, and then depend on Him. Just as Paul said to do, that is my daily plan. But it's not easy, and I often fall down but with a reaching hand, Jesus helps me back up. Falling is one thing but staying down is something I won't do. And I can't face the idea of hurting the Holy Spirit as He speaks to me."

"Wow, your daily struggles and finding Jesus and the Holy Spirit daily remind me of what the ladies in the weekly Bible study said. They talked about how God the Father, Jesus the Son, and the Holy Spirit all speak to them in their minds, hearts, and through the Bible."

"Well, that's not crazy at all. God doesn't prefer one person or group over another. So, just as He is working to grow me in Him, He is working with others to do the same." Roberto said and smiled. "I learned that quickly. I found out Chef John was a believer in Jesus, and he has helped mentor me to grow stronger in my faith. Even though my friend actually assaulted him, John forgave him and me. Now we are friends, and brothers in Christ."

"Chef John is a Christian, too? Wow, I didn't know that," Aisha said.

"Well, he doesn't get a chance to talk a lot about Jesus with the servers when we are open. Though he did share his testimony after his shift with some front-of-the-house staff while they drank a few beers, and he sipped an Arnold Palmer. He used to drink and smoke. But he's decided to cut off the habits that dragged him down, away from his faithfulness. Many chefs drink and smoke. They'll smoke to get through the long days, and then drink to relax more afterward. He doesn't preach to anyone about it. But the other chefs ask about why he's changed, and he explains with a smile that his focus is on the one he lives for. He laughs some with them and says it's no good to live for yourself. I remember when he really changed his heart. It was after he left the hospital when he was assaulted. He told me later that God spoke to him about forgiveness. He thought about his so-called Christian life before. Then he dedicated his life to Jesus, and he lives for Jesus 'all in' now and not his own life."

Aisha leaned forward, not wanting to miss a word of how this change came about.

"In our Bible study we went on to have, we talked about carrying the cross that Jesus said we must be ready to walk with. He asked me how anyone would want to listen about the difference Jesus has made in their life if he's telling him that while they down drinks after work to decompress. He and I decompress for a few minutes after work in prayer in the parking lot, while others have the tables lined with beer bottles. You know Jesus never said not to drink, but the Bible says not to get drunk." Roberto stopped at a red light and turned to glance at Aisha. "The problem is… well, Chef John used to get drunk. Frequently. He told me how he felt sick in his heart afterward. The Holy Spirit spoke to him, and yet he didn't listen for a while. It took time in the hospital for Chef John to really listen to God again."

"Wow, I hope it's alright with him that you shared his story with me. That's a little private," Aisha said.

The light turned green, and they began to move again.

"Oh well, I'll let him know we talked about him. He'll be fine with it. He told me that he wants people to remember that Christians struggle, and God is drawing each of us to Himself. Oh look, there's our street. Carmen has the light on."

"Great, I hope she didn't have problems putting Aini down to bed."

"Well, let's go see. Hopefully she is sleeping well, and we can read the Bible for a few minutes."

"I think that would be nice."

∼

"Roberto and Aisha, you two are home. Excellent! How was the shift at the restaurant? Just another day, working?" Carmen opened the apartment door with a smile.

"Oh, no, don't even ask." Roberto laughed. "But God is good, and the night is over." Roberto sighed.

"Oh, yes, God is good all the time," Carmen quipped. "Aisha, the night was just as bad in the dining room for you?"

"Ah, yes, I think you could say that. But the weight of the world was starting to feel lifted as we drove home."

"So, do we want to vent and reflect about it from a Godly point of view? Or do we want to simply let dead dogs lie," Carmen asked. "Or something like that. It's some silly American saying I learned from someone at work."

"Uh well, I don't know about dead dogs. But let me check on Aini, and then I'd like to talk about something important." Aisha ran off to the bedroom she and Aini used.

"Are you sure everything is okay with her, Berto? She seems a little rattled," Carmen observed soberly.

"Actually, she is so much better than earlier tonight at work. I can't believe how well she is actually doing right now," Roberto sighed.

"I imagine it's a long story you won't have time to explain, since it sounds like she wants to talk about something else," Carman said.

"Let's just say some of her family tracked her down, and there was quite a conflict at the restaurant. Right in the dining room." Roberto shook his head and softly laughed.

"Oh, I see. And is she still safe here in our home with us, and the baby?"

"Yeah, it's no problem at all. The tracking got as far as the name of her workplace only. Our names weren't on their list," Roberto explained.

"Aini is sleeping well. Carmen, you'll make a great mother one day. I can see it in the way you guide her by the hand and talk to her. I wonder when that will be," Aisha smiled.

"Oh, I wonder too," Carmen returned her smile and looked up for a moment and back down with clasped hands.

"Please, don't pray too much yet. I don't know if I'm ready." Roberto moaned playfully. "Though I can't deny I'm a little excited at the thought of one day having a child to raise. What would God bring for us, a boy or a girl? And what would their personality be like? I wonder about that sometimes."

"I knew you were ready now," Carmen smiled. "We had talked about it one day. Maybe that one day will be soon?"

"Enough, mi amor. Our guest has more on her heart than preparing us for parenting," Roberto's voice got a little deeper, but he paired it with his easy smile.

"Sit, Aisha, and tell us what weighs on you. We'll gather around the dining room table. I just made some cold tea, although I know you're used to hot tea to relax." Carmen stepped into the small kitchen for the tea and plastic cups from the cupboard.

"Cold tea is fine," Aisha said loud enough for Carmen to hear. "It was hot in the restaurant, and it's warm out now. Roberto said summer is coming soon. It feels close to it now."

"August, well that's when it really feels like summer. So, the end of May and some of June will be a mixed bag. I like the unexpected and thank God for it as it comes our way," Carmen said.

"Mi amor, you are always the philosopher. I thank God for each day. I prefer a sunny day, but not when it's not too hot," Roberto said. "And the rains in May remind me of the rainy season in Guatemala. All I miss about that country is my family. I hope to bring my mother and sister to be close to us soon."

"Now who's **philosophizing**? Let's focus now that we have tea, and pleasant company," Carmen said. "Aisha, what are we going to talk about?"

"Roberto explained how he came to know Jesus. Can you two summarize the story Jesus told about the seeds?"

"Excellent, we both love that parable," Carmen said. "Jesus loved to tell stories so the people could better understand His teachings. In this case He began talking about one who planted seeds. These seeds fell and dropped into different types of ground."

"Yes, four types in fact. The first ground near the road, the second is the rocky soil, the third is thorny soil, and lastly is the good, fertile soil. The seed, the sower, and all the grounds symbolize a point Jesus was making," Roberto explained.

"All right, so what do they mean? My father is a farmer, and I can see how this can easily happen." Aisha shook her head. "Really dry years can ruin the crop."

"Yes, well, the weather is referred to somewhat in that type of ground. But let's get to Jesus' point. Jesus is the farmer, scattering His seeds which are the Word of God. These words are spoken by His people to other people. And if I could point out, the Holy Spirit has led a variety of people in your path, Aisha to put seeds of God's Word in your heart and mind." Carmen looked her in the eyes. "I know Sam dropped a few words from the Bible, Jen wanted to share God's Word with you, and the ladies we have studied with from church. They all have tried to drop seeds to be planted in your mind by the Holy Spirit."

"I guess I can see that, if God is making suggestions to you and others. But how do you know it is His voice?"

"Well, first, anything in HIs Word, we know is from Him. Sometimes also I hear the Holy Spirit speak softly to me, and then I confirm it in

His word. And I have a peaceful certainty that this is what I'm supposed to do," Carmen said. "God had clearly put it on my heart to talk with you and study His Word whenever you wanted. It brought me such joy."

"I don't listen as well as Carmen," Roberto added. "But God's Word is clear about many things; and when I stand on it, I feel I'm in no better place than in God's will. But I'm still growing to seek God in prayer more often, and Chef John has helped me to see that too."

"Anyway, Jesus explained that the first seed near the road is a person who hears the word, but it doesn't impact them at all. The rocky soil hears the word with joy and receives it, but when life's problems come, they lack true faith or commitment. They fall away from their faith. The third soil is one that's thorny, where it hears the word but is preoccupied with the other things. It could be negative, like poor weather or anxiety and depression or it could be positive, such as being caught up in material things. The last seed is the fertile soil that hears God's word, and it affects them so that they can do nothing but love and obey the Master, Jesus." Carmen took a breath.

"So, Roberto…the pastor, he asked you what seed you were?" Aisha smiled.

"Well, he didn't ask me… *personally*. There were over a hundred people there. But it felt like he and I were the only ones there," Roberto said.

"But he wasn't the only one there," Carmen said. "Many of us were praying in the moment for me. I was praying earnestly for me, and God answered my prayer,"

"I can hear the joy when you two talks about that decision. But what really affects me is the constant time you all seek God. And even on nights like this, Chef John and Roberto, took a moment to thank God that I was okay in the kitchen with me. This abiding peace that the ladies from the Bible study seem to have, this peace where you two seem to rest and depend on Jesus," Aisha looked between them and smiled. "I think I want that type of relationship," Aisha said. "I'm ready to ask Jesus into my heart and to be the Lord of my life as my Savior."

∼

"Good morning, Aisha. How do you feel this morning?" Carmen asked. "Some people feel a big difference that overcomes them, and for others it becomes a more still and quiet experience when they begin a personal relationship with Jesus."

"Oh, I don't really know, Carmen. What I think that I feel some of the peace you have spoken of. And I now feel real hope in the future because I'm trusting in God that He has a plan outside of my control. I rest on that." Aisha sat down on the sofa with Aini and leaned back easily with her head on the cushion. "Before I had hoped that days would get better based on my husband, my family, and then my education and job. But those things never really made me happy. I see that now."

"God is moving in you and lighting your way already. There is a verse in the Psalms where God points through the author that His word is a lamp for the feet and a light to the path he walks. In John, Jesus spoke about being the Light of the world, and those people who follow Him will not end up in darkness but instead receive the light of life. You'll be surprised how God reveals Himself to you and makes you happy to encounter Him in His word."

"Yes, well maybe. All I know is that I feel more content with life than ever before. Now I feel prepared for the next steps I have to take," Aisha looked over to the phone on the dining room table and then back down the hall. "Where is Roberto? Usually, he has coffee in the morning."

"Oh, he had to work a double today. If you have to work today, I can take you in. I'm off from work all day today." Carmen smiled.

"I wasn't even thinking about work yet. I'm not scheduled till five. But I'm wondering if I can use your phone to call my home country. I will keep it short. I feel excited and don't know if I should share my new faith with my parents. And then I'm curious how Rahma found out the name of the restaurant I work at. My fear is that my mother might have said something. I just don't know why she would betray me."

"Aisha, I don't have an easy answer for you. My first answer is to always pray about it, and then if we can, we could read a few passages from the Bible." Carmen pointed to her Bible underneath the cell phone. "God speaks to me when I seek Him out in His word."

"That's okay. But I want to talk to her soon, and not wait. There is a time difference. I also need to talk to Abdul. I really wanted to talk with him last night but knew deep down that I should wait a day. I didn't want to say something to him in anger, especially after not talking for months. And I know he goes into work by ten. Maybe I should call him first. I'm so confused."

"Well, after I pray, I usually write down my thoughts. Then I think about what I want to say to someone, especially if it could be a confrontation. After I put it on paper, I organize the ideas for what's important, and think about how the person could respond. Then I decide if I need to change the way I say it. I check with the Holy Spirit and see if He has something to put on my mind."

"Carmen, do you have some paper? That is a good idea, and I think I will write my thoughts for Abdul down. Maybe that will help my confusion. But with my mother, I've decided to tell her about my new faith. That won't make her happy, but she is my mother, and my heart wants to share my peace with her. And maybe I'll ask her not to share with Rahma my choices. That had to be how she found the name of the restaurant."

"Okay, here is the phone and you can call her your mother when you're ready. I'll go get some paper for you," Carmen strode to the kitchen.

"Thank you," Aisha said and stared at the cell phone. She was still staring at it when Carmen brought a pen and paper. Carmen silently went back in the kitchen as Aisha started to write down some notes. After ten minutes of writing and thinking, she looked down at them.

Then her gaze returned to the cell phone. Suddenly she picked it up and started to dial the international number to Yemen.

This won't be easy, but I must tell her. She's my mama and although she loves me, we've had our differences. But I need to tell her about Jesus. He's the most important one now. Abdul and Habib, I dearly love. But Jesus is so near now.

"Hello Mama. How are you today? Is everything well with you? I wish I could kiss and hug you," Aisha began in Arabic.

"Aisha, what a nice surprise to hear from you. It's been a few weeks since we spoke. We are all well here," Badia said.

"I wanted to say I miss you and Baba. We used to have such great times as a family, and you both know me so well," Aisha said.

"You've always been special, and we're very proud of you Aisha. Your father was just saying how he misses your smile."

"Mama, I have something important to tell you. And I need to watch the time, since I'm borrowing a friend's phone."

"What… is Aini sick? Are you okay? Have you been to one of those American doctors? They are very helpful." Badia asked quickly.

"No Mama, everything is wonderful! That is what I must tell you."

"Wonderful? Are you back in Dearborn? And now you feel wonderful again, in your proper place?"

"No, Mama. That's not it," Aisha said with a hint of sadness.

"Then what is it," Badia said with a bit of exasperation rising in her voice.

"Mama, I have decided to follow Jesus. He wants all that want to come to Him, and now I'm a child of His."

"Follow Him where? The prophet Jesus? Don't be silly. You will give up Islam, and be one of those Christians? This is what the Americans have done to you?" Badia asked quickly.

"Mama, I have more joy now than ever before, and I wanted to share some of that joy with you. I know it's hard to understand." Aisha's voice lost some of its confidence.

"Aisha, listen to me. You have been deceived and led astray by the ideas of these Christians. Our family has always worshipped Allah. You can't turn your back on him, and Islam. We have some common things, like many believe Allah and the Christian God are the same. Talk about that, but don't turn away from Islam, my daughter."

"I'm sorry, Mama. I thought this conversation might go better. But I'm only trusting in the God of the Injil now. And Jesus wasn't just a prophet, but He was the son of God, whom I now trust with my life. I'm sorry again, Mama. But I must get off the phone soon."

"Aisha, this is really important. We can't just sweep this conversation out the door, like you used to do with the dirt in our home. We need to talk through this," Badia implored.

"Mama, we can talk next week. Before I hang up, I need to ask you please not share any of our conversations with Aunt Rahma," Aisha pleaded.

"What? I haven't talked to your father's family in Dearborn in some time. Your father talks more with his brother. So, I don't know what you are talking about," Badia said.

"Somehow Aunt Rahma found out the name of the restaurant I am working at now. I thought you may have told her," Aisha said.

"No, but I did share it with Habib. It has such a funny name, and he was asking so many questions about you."

"Ahh… Habib was probably using Rahma's phone. And she heard him repeat it. They might have talked again once he was done talking to you."

"What does it matter about the name, Aisha? I don't understand the big problem," Badia asked.

"Look Mama, I'm not telling you the whole story on the phone. Maybe another time. You might find it strange, but I have to go. This call might cost me half a night of tips," Aisha groaned. "I love you, Mama."

"I will always love you, Aisha. But I don't approve of this decision about Jesus, and we will continue this conversation," Badia sighed.

Chapter 21

Abdul

"Hello? Who is this? I don't recognize the number," Abdul asked as he answered his cell phone. He walked back down the hall of the restaurant to the back dry storage room so he could hear better and have a little privacy. "I'm sorry. Hello again — who is this?" He pressed a finger over his ear to block out the clanging from the dishwasher.

"Abdul, it's Aisha. Can you hear me? I know you're probably working at your uncle's restaurant," Aisha said in a hushed voice.

"Aisha, my love. It's you! I can't believe we're talking. I've missed your voice so much," Abdul turned around in the dry room and looked down the hall. He shut the door and moved a *Cambro* bucket of flour off of a dunnage rack and sat on it.

"I needed to talk with you and… I wasn't sure about the best time. I should have called last night," Aisha said. "Can you hear me okay?"

He stared at the cell phone in disbelief before answering her. "Yes, Aisha. I can hear you. I'm still here. I went to the back storage room so I wouldn't be disturbed. Why are you calling suddenly… and today? Why not two to three months ago to explain what you did to your son and me?" Abdul's chest heaved from the sudden onslaught of stress.

Aisha calling like this, out of the blue. His mind raced with questions. Leaning against the wall, he rested a foot on the dunnage rack. "You… left me… without any explanation. And what about your son? All he does is talk about you. Every day he questions me, wondering where you are and when you are coming home. He's tired of getting no answers."

"Oh, Abdul, I feel so bad to cause you both so much pain. You know I love you and Habib so much. "

"So why? Why did you? How could you do such a thing?" His voice raised, showing the first signs of pent-up anger releasing. "These things aren't done in our culture, and still you chose to… leave," Abdul voice cracked on the last word. He took a moment to compose himself. "I'm sure even your own family has told you it was wrong to—"

Aisha's words rushed over Abdul, cutting him off. "I don't know if I can explain it well enough for you. And I know you have to return to work very soon. But I can only tell you that I felt imprisoned in your uncle's home, and your aunt cut me off from the family. I knew she would soon pressure you into taking other, stricter measures to demonstrate my place in the home. I began to fear for my safety. I was already imprisoned in the house, so I felt I had no other choice but to leave with Aini. I knew if I'd left with Habib, too, your family would really be angry."

"But, Aisha, you should know me. You know I love you. Family is important to me. But you are more important, and I could never hurt you. I've not raised my voice or my hand to you, ever. You think I would change so much?"

"I don't know, Abdul. I saw how much your aunt wanted me to change and expected you to make me behave a certain way. Then what would others think? The community and the rest of the family?"

"What are you talking about? Those people are talking now about you and me. But I still love you and miss you. We are still a family, Aisha."

"Yes, I know. But I must tell you some things and… I need you to listen. I've thought it out, and I'm afraid you will interrupt with questions. Please let me say what I have to say."

"Alright. Say what is heavy on your mind," Abdul mumbled loud enough for her to hear.

"I've found true peace in my life, like never before. It's not because I've run from your family. It's not because I'm working and found some independence. No, my true peace I have is because I've chosen Jesus as my Lord, my Savior, and my friend. I don't trust in Allah anymore, and I don't think he is the same as the God of the Bible. Instead, I believe in God, the Father, Jesus the Son, and the Holy Spirit. I trust them for my daily peace and my space one day in heaven."

"Aisha, is this some game you're playing? Maybe you're reading from the Injil just to frustrate me right now."

"No, not all, Abdul. I'm not playing with you. And I'm not reading lines from the Bible. I'm telling you how I feel, and that my hope for tomorrow is more than what you or your family can provide. I stand on the hope Jesus has promised. I'm sure of what my God will do in my life."

Abdul sighed. "I'm not sure how you want me to answer you right now. You know this is heresy against Islam, and it will cause a rift in the family." Abdul shook his head. "But I knew I might hear this from you. In fact, I first thought that was the main reason you left."

"Oh, you had some ideas?" Aisha asked.

"Yes, but please tell me about your other problem. I fear that Uncle Suhaib will be looking for me soon. And then we can schedule another time to talk."

"Well, my other problem is what happened at work yesterday. Mohammed and Aunt Rahma found me at my job. They literally tried to drag me out of the restaurant and take me away. They *tied me up*, Abdul." Her tone conveyed the seriousness of her violation.

"What!" Abdul barked out the word. "Mohammed put his hands on you. I can't believe it."

"Yes, he did. Rahma, Fatima the neighbor lady, and Mohammed all came and sat at one of my tables. I got them water, and Rahma said she had school paperwork for me to see… it was about Habib so I couldn't refuse. Then, as we were talking, Mohammed grabbed me and began pulling me away… to the door. It was unbelievable," Aisha said.

"Yes, this is unbelievable. Although now I know why the house was very quiet when I got home last night. And this morning, the car ride into work was completely silent. But I can't believe Mohammed thought he could touch you. Wait until I talk to him," Abdul said sternly.

"I'm sure Aunt Rahma found a way to convince him that I deserved to be treated like an animal — tied up and dragged away. But God surrounded me with friends who care for me, and they stood up to him and Rahma. My friends helped stop them until the police got there. Finally, I was untied. Then, though I could have had them arrested, they were let go with a ticket for disturbing the peace. I think it's over a hundred-dollar penalty."

"Wow, that's just crazy. I don't know what to think," Abdul said.

"Abdul, what will you say to them? What will you do?"

"I'm not sure. I may speak to Uncle Suhaib and Mohammed after lunch while here at the restaurant."

"I think it would be better to speak to all three of them. Aunt Rahma really was the one who spoke up during the situation. Uncle Suhaib wasn't even there," Aisha said.

"Maybe you're right. I don't know if I can work the whole shift, knowing Mohammed put his hands on you." Abdul gritted his teeth a little.

"My husband, we will find a way through this. Remember, God is working in our lives."

"Oh yes, you and Sam have probably been talking," Abdul muttered.

"What? Sam? No, I haven't talked with him in months. I don't know what you mean," Aisha said.

"Never mind. It's just that I met Sam a bit, and he's tried to share some things about Jesus with me. I only spoke to him so I could find answers about you," Abdul admitted.

"Okay, Abdul. I understand. I will be thinking about and praying for you. Think about what you will do, please. Can we talk later this week?"

"Yes, you can call me back and we can plan a time to talk. In fact, you could try texting on this phone and tell me when you're ready to talk again. Goodbye, Aisha. I'll tell Habib you have asked about him. Give a lot of kisses to Aini for me."

~

The rest of the day was especially hard as I worked with Mohammed in the dining room. Every time I saw him, I pictured him dragging my wife across a dining room. Her feet would have been flailing like one of Aini's dolls. I can picture Aisha's tender legs and small, delicate feet kicking out in frustration. But the more I thought about it, the more I realized my wife's words were very wise.

It would do no good to confront Mohammed or Uncle Suhaib here at work. But bitter thoughts kept piling up in my mind, and it took real effort for my somber, professional look to avoid turning into a grim, angry face. Uncle Suhaib had even pushed me lightly and asked me to smile while serving his customers. I doubt he even knew what his wife and son had blatantly done, shaming me and stepping outside of their family boundaries.

I turned around to look back at him with a weak smile, then continued clearing the tables after lunch. I told them I wanted to work through the afternoon and preferred to not go home for our daily late lunch. Now it struck me as funny that Mohammed had asked for the evening off yester-

day, claiming he had a date with Malak. It was evidently quite a ruse for Suhaib and me. But today, he acted like nothing was any different. He should have thought about professional acting — he had me fooled.

He hasn't talked much to me today, and I kept our conversations tied to mostly work events. And I can tell he misses the camaraderie we used to share, but I didn't care to joke with him. The times I'd thought about Aisha, and even learned more about Jesus through conversations with Sam over the last few weeks made me pull away from Mohammed.

The shift finally ended as dinner service slowed down, and Mohammed locked the doors at last. I helped clean up the dining room with another server, while Mohammed helped the closing cook finish in the kitchen. Uncle Suhaib was busy as he totaled out today's sales, documented it on his computer system, and bagged the deposit to take to the bank tomorrow. It was a silent ride home again for me, with my family.

"Long day. I can't wait to get to my room and relax. A bottle of water and I will be free upstairs," Mohammed complained as he shut the passenger door of the restaurant van.

"Wait until you reach my age, and the arthritis is talking back to you from two different limbs," Suhaib said.

"Before we go relax, I would like to meet in the dining room. Uncle, if you could kindly ask Aunt Rahma to come with us, I would really appreciate it," Abdul spoke up as he forcefully shut the sliding van door.

"Abdul, this isn't the time for complaints about more of your management dreams. The day is about over, and I'm too tired to listen to you ramble on," Suhaib said.

"You've been really quiet all day, and now suddenly you want to talk? What's so important, Abdul?" Mohammed's voice almost began to whine.

"It's not about work, but something else. And Aunt Rahma needs to hear what I have to say," Abdul said as he held the door for Suhaib. Mohammed had already walked in.

"Mama, are you up? We've been summoned for a *family meeting* in the dining room." Mohammed laughed like it was a joke.

"What is the problem? My men are home, my tea is made, and I'm comfortable," Rahma said as she came from the kitchen. "*Oh, I see.* Abdul has a voice tonight and wants to speak up. Let's see what he has to say."

"Do you have more tea for us, Rahma? Or at least some for your husband?" Suhaib pulled out a chair and sat with some effort. His knee cracked, and he winced as he sat down.

"This is why you need to let Mohammed run about the restaurant more and you should monitor from the registrar," Rahma said. "Your knees don't like you walking and standing on that hard floor." She walked back for the tea in the kitchen and poured a second cup.

"Hah, you don't think I run about enough, Mama? You should come and watch me race around," Mohammed added while he opened a cold bottle of water from the refrigerator. He sat down quickly and leaned the chair back, swallowing the water deeply.

Rahma glared at him sternly, and then turned to Abdul. "The family is all here, except, of course, your wife, who has chosen to leave her city, culture, and most importantly, her family. But what is my opinion? I'm only the aunt of the wronged husband," Rahma handed Suhaib his tea with a smile. She then sat down and pulled her chair forward. It scraped on the tiled floor.

"Quiet, my wife. Let's hear out Abdul now. He's asked for our time, and we'll give him that now," Suhaib nodded to his nephew.

"Thank you, Uncle Suhaib. I know we're all tired. But I need to ask something," Abdul said.

"Okay, what is it? Time won't stop for the night," Suhaib replied.

"Well, really, my questions are specifically for Aunt Rahma and Mohammed." Abdul turned his chair slightly and looked directly into Rahma's eyes. "Did you and Mohammed go and find my wife, Aisha? At her new job? And then did you tie her up and try to carry her out of the restaurant?"

"Yes, we did. We did this yesterday," Rahma defiantly said. She crossed her arms over her bosom. "I suggested you do something to find her, but you chose to bury yourself in work and hope she would come home. Your cousin and I, *we* did something. And she would be here tonight with us if the police hadn't come so quickly."

"Abdul, we had to do *something!*" Mohammed's voice raised. When he jumped to his feet, the chair fell backward to the floor. "A man should have authority over his family, and you have lost yours."

"It's unbelievable that you two would go this far. I don't know how you found out where she was working, but it's just crazy. You thought you would speak for me?" Abdul looked from his aunt to his cousin.

"No, we didn't just speak for you. We spoke up for this family, and this community. We spoke in action. Your wife needed to know the embarrassment she's caused our good name," Rahma firmly said.

"This is not a good thing to have done, Rahma" Suhaib said with conviction. "I don't agree with how Aisha left, but Abdul is correct. You were in the *wrong*. You didn't even consult with me on this matter. I *am* your *husband!*" Suhaib looked at her squarely, his jaw set in a firm line.

"And this is *exactly* why I didn't tell you, husband. You always approach issues with such rational planning. Well, life isn't always like some business model you have created. Sometimes, you just know what's right in your head and heart and must do it. We had the name of the restaurant, and Mohammed was able to find it on some MapQuest program. It called for action, and not much more thought." Rahma tightened her hijab and smiled smugly.

"So, if it was the best plan, why don't I see her sitting with us? Where is the sweet little girl, Aini, who is like a granddaughter to me? You've turned Aisha against our family and blamed it on her independence. Sometimes you've no reign on that tongue as it gallops away in the wind, and you then scheme to recover for it."

"Where is your faith, husband? Allah wouldn't approve of us, our family letting one woman walk away from her responsibility so easily. Mohammed and I were doing what needed to be done," Rahma grimly said. Mohammed nodded in agreement.

"Our culture of old may have dictated such actions," Abdul said. "But we're in America now. And many Muslims are trying to acclimate to a perspective on what's expected in the home. Women have wanted a voice and have desperately needed to be heard. Not with the hollowness that men have traditionally shown. Like a sweet-sounding bird that's craved to sing, women now have a voice that cries to be heard outside the window." Abdul looked beyond them toward the window Aisha had escaped from.

"What do you know of the cries of the heart of the woman?" Rahma said with a smirk. "What do you know of the voices a woman might hear in the window? You're a man who has no clue of women, and how to even handle his own wife," Rahma said, then smirked.

"I'm sorry, Aunt Rahma, but unlike many husbands, I chose to listen to my wife," replied Abdul. "No offense to you, Uncle. But it's obvious Aunt Rahma has no problem at home speaking her mind," Abdul looked over to his uncle. "I wanted to see the desires of her heart met, and I have tried to listen to any concerns she had. In our own home in Yemen, we were a happy couple. It wasn't until we came here, and we were told how to be better Muslims, better Yemenis, and live better roles as parents and spouses. Somehow, you've found ways to dismantle our sense of security, and Aisha finally broke away from it all."

"This is stupid, Abdul," Mohammed protested. "You can't seriously think you can blame all your family problems on Mama and me. How dare you?" He rubbed his head in frustration.

"Enough right now! It's getting late," Suhaib spoke, cutting through raised voices. "Abdul, what is it you want now? You want an apology from your aunt and cousin? Or did you just want to vent? Or are you hoping for some guarantee it won't happen again?"

Rahma and Mohammed sat silently, waiting and staring at Abdul.

"I don't expect an apology, because I know they are knee-deep believing they are right. But I do want a promise today that they won't scheme anymore about my relationship."

"Oh, and now you have better pants to wear, and will be the man?" Rahma asked. Her voice had lowered but still held the sting of a tarantula.

"No, Aunt Rahma. My pants are the same, and my legs still go in one at a time. But what is different now is that Aisha and I are talking things through. We will do this with love, and not an iron fist which is clenched, determined for control!" Abdul squeezed his hand into a fist and released it.

"Fine. But recover your love quickly. And soon! But bring our family no shame while doing so," Rahma said. "The community should see you following what Allah would want."

"If the air is cleared, perhaps we can all be off to bed?" Suhaib asked and sipped the last of his tea.

"Fine, whatever!" Mohammed pushed off the edge of the table and walked away with a smirk.

"Yes, it is fine. Good night, Abdul. Husband, don't forget to turn the lights off when you come to bed," Rahma said quietly.

"Abdul, I can understand your frustration," Suhaib consoled. "You and I are quite similar. Our minds think much alike. The truth is, I have thought about giving you more responsibility in my business. But the keyword is that it is *my* business, and I don't want to give much of it up. My point is that I see and understand how you think logically. I also see your love for your family, and the heart full of passion you carry. I've seen that passion at work, too. It's evident with your family, and how you feel for your wife."

"Thank you for those words, Uncle Suhaib. It means a lot to me," Abdul answered.

"Yes, well, it's true. But it's also true that you can't turn your back completely on our culture and our religion. Islam is deeply part of our lives and it's who we are. Think about that as you start to think about being in this new American culture. We are still Muslims. Your Aunt Rahma may have let emotions rule her thinking, but down deep she is correct. We must stick to our faith in Islam."

"Okay, Uncle. I hear you," Abdul got up. "But I'm not sure I fully agree. Good night." Abdul walked away and turned to head up the stairs.

"Good night then, Abdul," Suhaib got up and walked into the kitchen to rinse his teacup. He walked through the kitchen, dimming the lights, and down the hall, turning off the bright dining room lamp as his wife had told him. He stopped for a moment, the moonlight streaming in through the living room window.

~

After all that's happened today, I really wanted to talk with my parents, But I was torn. They both loved me. I know that Rahma talks to Mama often, trying to tell her of my failure, and Suhaib has occasionally spoken with Baba. I know my parents take and balance what they hear from them because they know who I am. Their family loyalty doesn't blind them. I think they know how conservative Suhaib and Rahma are, while my parents like to see themselves locally as more moderate in Yemen. Yet they still hold to their faith with Islam firmly.

Given all that, I'm not sure I really want to talk to either of my parents much. But I must talk to someone. I think I will email Sam and see if we can talk tomorrow evening after work. I don't want to come home tomorrow to be with the family. I'll see if he's available and where he might want to have some coffee. I don't feel like going back downstairs to use the PC in Uncle Suhaib's office. But Sam did give me his phone number so, I will text him on my phone. I hope it's not too late and maybe he'll be up. I think as long as he agrees, he can text me the name of the place he could meet me.

"Hello Abdul, how are you? I hope this restaurant is fine. Maybe you're tired of the business, but this place has a great reputation," Sam said as he met Abdul at the door.

"Oh yes, I've heard of La Shish. It's well known, and I've wanted to try it and compare it to our restaurant. I'm a type of mystery shopper, and I can go back to my family with the details," Abdul smiled and walked through the door Sam held open.

"Tonight will be my treat, Abdul. I'm so pleased you called. I hope you don't mind that I've invited a friend of mine to join us. He's coming a little later, if that's okay." Sam stepped past Abdul and guided him to the table. "His name is Ibrahim."

"Um... Well, you and I shared some thoughts about Jesus. But you also know some of the details about Aisha, and I needed to talk to someone. But I guess it's okay," Abdul shrugged.

"He won't be coming for a half hour or so. We can catch up for a while and order appetizers," Sam said. "It'll be fine, Ibrahim is an easy-going guy who enjoys thoughtful conversation."

"Alright, Sam, let's sit down and eat." Abdul nonchalantly looked around the restaurant as an older Arabic man took them to their table.

"Here you are, gentlemen." The restaurant manager set down the menus at opposite ends. "Enjoy your meal. We have our daily specials listed here in the middle." The manager turned to walk away.

Abdul noticed a curious look on the man's face.

"Thank you, sir," Sam said. "We'll have someone joining us in a little while," He added. "So, the sampler platter is good. I'm not sure how it will fare compared to your uncle's restaurant. But really, it's not so much about the food as it is the good company."

"Sampler platter will be fine. I would like to taste their hummus, grape leaves, and one of their fried *kibbee*. I wonder how the coffee is here?"

"Well, I'm sure it's not as good as what Malak or Aisha used to make," Sam smiled. "But life is sometimes about risks and living on faith."

"We'll see then. I can compare this food to our home family recipes," Abdul said.

"So, what's going on in your life, Abdul? We haven't actually talked in a week or two. But the emails prove to be most interesting for me. I enjoy the back-and-forth discussion, even if we can't meet in person. But I've been concerned about you. I know you're worried about Aisha and your children," Sam said.

"The emails got rather intriguing for me too," Abdul replied. "They gave me room to think and question what I've been taught. As a college student in England, we were taught to be skeptical, and push ourselves to question all things. So, it's been a good thing for me to exchange ideas over days in email. But now I need to ask your opinion about some issues. I've come to respect you, and I think you see with an objective insight."

"Well, I look to God for wisdom and grace, and part of me tends to try to balance logic and faith. Anyway, I'm all ears."

"All ears? You Americans have these funny sayings. You only have two ears?" Abdul smiled. "With just one mouth, let me tell a quick story before your friend shows up."

"Please do. We have the time," Sam reassured him.

"So, I got a call from an unknown number on my cell phone when I started my shift a few days ago. It was Aisha. We hadn't actually talked in months. I was amazed and silenced for a few seconds. I wasn't sure what to say. But after a minute the questions spilled out, like my friend's practice time with a handgun, shooting across the field. I asked her why she didn't call me sooner and told her how our son is always missing her. And I asked how she could put aside her culture in which she was raised and the family expectations."

"Wow, that's great. Isn't that what you wanted? I mean, you wanted to hear from her, and be sure she is fine. And then to ask where her head and heart are? Did you do that?"

"Well, I guess so. She told me how she has missed both Habib and me, and she loves us very much. She explained how she had feared for her safety, that my family might push me to reprimand her more and more. And she mentioned you and your friends. Actually, she mentioned her new faith in Jesus."

"What? Her faith in Jesus? Has she made a decision for Jesus?" Sam asked, leaning forward slightly.

"Yeah, well, I told her that I had first thought that's why she left. Leaving Islam and worrying about our families' reaction. But we talked about how it was more than that, and that it wasn't until recently she had become a Christian."

"I understand, but why then did she call you? Was it only to tell you about her new faith?"

"I thought that also, but no. She went on to say my aunt and cousin showed up unexpectedly at her job. They actually tried to physically pull her from the job and take her away. But the police came and intervened. I'm thankful she wasn't hurt," Abdul said.

"Wow. That's startling... I'm sure she was frightened by it all." Sam tilted his head. "How did they even find her place of employment?"

"Well, apparently, my aunt had overheard the name of the restaurant when my son was talking to Aisha's mother, Badia. She remembered it and had Mohammed do a MapQuest search for it. And off they went to capture her and find my baby girl."

"Sorry to interrupt gentlemen, but here are your meals. I will be back to refill your coffee. Enjoy." The waiter set a larger platter in the center of the table.

"Well, this looks more like a meal in itself to share and not just appetizers. I suppose we can leave some for Ibrahim when he comes," Sam chuckled. "Would you mind if I thanked God for this food before we begin eating?"

"I'm sure that there will be some left for your friend. Go ahead and pray, if you wish," Abdul mumbled.

"Father in heaven, thank You for this food before us. Give us a pleasant meal together. In Jesus' name, amen." Sam looked up and around the platter indecisively. "So did they arrest your aunt and cousin for assaulting Aisha in the restaurant?"

"No, Aisha wasn't injured and didn't want to press charges. The scene did cause problems in the restaurant, though they were ticketed for disturbing the peace and told to leave after they were interviewed."

"Really, and Aisha told you all these details? See, you two are starting to really communicate," Sam said between bites of the fried *kibbee*. "These are my favorite snack."

"No, not completely. Mohammed begrudgingly gave up some more details when we were putting stock away today. Last night, though, I confronted my family. I wanted to know what right they thought they had tracking my wife down without my consent. Just as I thought, my uncle had no knowledge of it, and was surprised to hear of it. He even gave a slight reprimand to my aunt. But in the end, he ultimately agreed that she should have been brought back home." Abdul took a breath and then a bite of the grape leaves. "I like to taste the flavor of the filling. Everyone's just a little different."

"But down deep, is that what you wanted, Abdul? Did you want her forcibly brought home?" Sam broke off a piece of the warm bread, dipping it in the hummus, and motioned during his questions.

"No, but I've been conflicted about that. I've missed her and thought about her coming home, but I know she was unhappy. And I haven't been planning how I might make her return home or even by force. I mean, our son misses her terribly, so I could have done that, but I chose to let her be, and hoped she would come home to reconcile soon."

"Well, what's the plan now? Did she say she wants to come home? Or are you going to meet her? What are you thinking, Abdul?" Sam tried the baba ghanoush next with another piece of bread. "I'm never sure which I prefer, hummus or this one."

"I don't have a plan. Not like my aunt, who schemed to take her away against her will. If she rejoins our family, it will be on her terms. Although I know Habib longs to see her. We are supposed to talk again later this week on the phone." Abdul smiled and sipped the coffee.

"Hello, gentlemen. Apologies that I'm late. I had to finish up a few things at work," Ibrahim approached the booth. He was an Arabic man of medium height and clean-shaven face, except for the finely trimmed mustache and thin goatee on his chin. Smiling, he loosened his tie. "It'll be nice to sit down after standing most of the day."

"Ibrahim, hello! Have a seat here. This is my friend, Abdul. His family owns a Yemini restaurant, so tonight we are mystery diners," Sam winked and motioned for him to sit, as he moved over a bit.

"Well, we're comparing the flavors. But I'm not getting paid to report back to my family about this place," Abdul chuckled. "Nice to meet you, Ibrahim." Abdul leaned halfway over the booth and put his hand out to shake.

"The Pleasure is mine, Abdul. As-salaam alaykum," Ibrahim said and shook his hand. "Glad to meet you. Sam mentioned you in passing to me and said you were coming."

"Wa-Alaikum-as-salaam wa-Rahmatullah," Abdul answered.

"Ahh... Thank you, Abdul. I wish peace upon you, but I prefer not to have peace, mercy, and blessings from Allah." Ibrahim grinned.

"No, and why is that? You're Arabic and Muslim, no? We would all like Allah's blessings on our life," Abdul said.

"Ah well, my God, whom I seek for peace, mercy, and blessings is much different from Allah." Ibrahim smiled. "I've chosen to believe Jesus is more than the prophet spoken of in the Quran."

"Oh, what is this? A setup, Sam? You agree to meet me when I'm feeling down, and you bring a convert to Christianity to preach to me? And I thought we were beginning to be friends. I don't think I appreciate this." Abdul looked between Sam and Ibrahim.

"Hold on, Abdul. You've got the wrong idea," Sam said. "I didn't invite Ibrahim to dinner with us to preach to you. I only thought he could share some of his story with you. I didn't mean to step outside of the bounds of our friendship."

"Let's order chicken shawarma with almond rice and relax. Nothing like some good shawarma for the soul." Ibrahim smiled. "Abdul, I'd appreciate you'd let me tell you, sometimes I had questioned Allah and Jesus. I don't want to debate or argue, but only tell you some of the encounters I've had."

"All right, I will listen. But don't expect me to choose your Jesus tonight, just because you've done so." Abdul shook his head. "That's not happening. I'm a family man who is looking to rebuild that family, not to turn my back on my culture. And I never pass on some chicken shawarma," Abdul grinned himself.

"Okay, Abdul, if I could start with a famous question that many Muslims ask. Do Muslims and Christians worship the same God? I actually asked a Christian friend of ours who knows Sam also. He explained that Yahweh is worshipped by Christians, while Muslims worship Allah. My friend Jim, he showed me in the Quran how Islam denies how relational God is. We looked at how the trinity is condemned, and that God can't be a son or a baba. Jim went on to show me that because Christians worship a triune God, it really affects how they see themselves and the people around them. It truly changes their whole perspective." Ibrahim stopped and picked up some bread from the basket and dipped it into the hummus plate. "It was quite a lot for me to digest. But Jim and I started comparing the Injil to the Quran in specific passages."

"Yes, I can see how that is a question to deal with. We worship Allah. He seems distant, but he is still God. I had always known that the Quran gave respect to Jesus as a prophet. This is a little new to me," Abdul said. "And what do you mean by 'triune God'?"

"It means that God is one being with three persons," Sam interjected.

"Yes, that is quite important, and I'm not trying to skim over that concept. But if we could return to who Jesus is, because it is quite interesting. The Quran does say Jesus was a great prophet, and I've heard many Muslims complain that Christians don't respect Allah like they respect Jesus. But then some have suggested that Jesus is weak because He died on a cross. What kind of God would deny his own glory and be tortured like that? But then Jim and I talked about His holiness, as seen in examples of His presence in the Old Testament, as what's called theophanies. God appeared to Abraham and talked to him. God talked to Moses at the burning bush and demonstrated His holiness. And then God was with the three men in a fiery furnace, where a person who seemed that might have been Jesus came and stood with them. But ultimately, it was the sacrifice that's foretold in the Old Testament of Jesus coming as a child from heaven. Then in the New Testament in John, Jesus became flesh and walked with us. This is the mystery, and yet as Christians we believe that Jesus obeyed the Father and came to give Himself as our substitute on the cross."

"I'm sorry, but this is beginning to sound like some TV preaching now. It's a bit familiar to me at the end," Abdul said.

"Well, that's the problem. So many people have told the story about Jesus, but not about the love in the sacrifice. The true unselfishness that the Father had in sending His Son, Jesus to come. Then the willingness in Jesus to agree to be a sacrifice for all people is amazing! So, when people talk about how God could die on the cross, it is a great question. But that was the only answer for our sin. Another man's sacrifice would not have worked because he would be just as sinful. It had to be God coming *as a man* to make the sacrifice. A lot of people ask, isn't it unjust to send Jesus, He who is without sin, to the cross? But that was a gift from the Son to all mankind."

"And here are the shawarmas, gentlemen." The waiter brought out three plates and a hot steaming, bowl of almond rice pilaf.

"Excellent! Ibrahim, we've already asked God to bless the food." Sam said.

"Okay, so it had to be God to come down to earth from heaven for man. When Jesus died, where then was God? Christians say He died for three days, and then rose again. Since God always exists, then where was He when Jesus died?" Abdul asked.

"Great question, and one that I also talked with Jim about. But really what so many are asking is who was in charge if Jesus died. The answer is the Father who sent Jesus. We end back at this idea of the relationship between the Father, the Son, and the Holy Spirit. They all work together. In fact, in the gospel of John it explains how each person abides in each other. Jesus said He abides in the Father and the Father in Him. As Christians, we have the right to be called children of God, and then Jesus calls us friends. That is truly a great thing. I'm in a relationship with God, and not just worshipping a god far away and unknown to me."

"So, you see Abdul, as Christians we are part of a community that stands differently. Our faith is founded on the person of Jesus, who He is and what He has done, and what He continues to do in us and for us. Then He called us to love other people more than ourselves." Sam said and smiled. "It's a great thing to know others who truly love Jesus."

"In Islam, we have a great community of people, but to be honest we don't really share in the type of relationship you're talking about."

"Yes, it's quite different, Abdul. God calls us to love Him, and then love each other unconditionally. It's not easy, and really, we only do it through the help of the Holy Spirit." Ibrahim looked up and thanked God.

"Alright, gentlemen, it's getting late, and I need to open at the restaurant in the morning," Abdul said as he pushed his empty plate away. He looked around the table at the other empty plates. The other two had mostly completed their meals as well. "This conversation was more than I'd anticipated, but it's been really interesting. It seems it often is that way when I talk with you, Sam." Abdul smiled.

"Well, I'm sorry if we surprised you, Abdul. But I really wanted you to meet Ibrahim. Thank you for joining us," Sam said.

"Yes, thank you for listening to me, and for your thoughtful questions," Ibrahim said.

Chapter 22

Habib

I'm happy school is over tomorrow. This year was not easy for me at all. I knew little English, and I was put in an English-speaking school. Really, last year was the tougher year, because we came to America and the school still had four or five months to go. So, when I came to Dearborn, they had me finish the last year in the elementary school. I didn't know anyone. It wasn't easy to make friends right away. The only nice thing was that many other students were bilingual, and a few were willing to help me learn English. And I had a special time for ESL class once a week with a special teacher. She was very nice, and I'm glad she works at the new school. This year I went to the middle school, even though I didn't feel ready. But Mama talked to me every day before and after school. She made sure I was ready for the day, and all my supplies were packed. She checked my book bag to be sure I had put the homework we had done together and the books inside. Last year, Baba would take me to school. Now I ride the bus.

Once I came home, Mama would catch me when I walked in every day. She'd make me sit to tell her all about my day. Aini could be crying, or Mama could be cleaning; but she would always stop for me. Sometimes I didn't want to talk about school or the teacher, and I just wanted to go play. But every day she spent time with me. She kissed my head and combed my hair before school. Now she's gone. Now I come home, and

Aunt Rahma gives me a snack and then pushes me outside to play or up to my room. I think she forgot how to talk to young men like me. But she knows how to talk. I hear her on the phone a lot and talking to the people outside like Fatima. I remember how I thought last year was the worst school time ever. But now... Now I feel like this is the worst year ever. I didn't know I could miss someone so much. I miss laughing with Mama. She always laughed at my silly jokes. Jokes about people from television or even ones I made up. Other times I would play army man, and she would rub her arm where I accidentally shot her. She asked me to kiss her arm, and I laughed. No one else in our home plays make-believe with me. One time, I asked Cousin Mohammed to play, but he shrugged his shoulder and said fighting is no game. It's a serious thing. He said he would show me how to play cards, but I just shook my head. I saw a ball in Cousin Mohammed's room, but he told me to not touch it. It's his favorite football. He explained that in America, they call it soccer, and he promised one day he would practice with me. Instead, I play at school. Baba has tried to talk to me more. But he comes home almost every day when it's time for me to get ready for bed. I know he sees me looking around for Mama. I don't want to admit to him how sad I really am. Last week, Baba saw me staring at Mohammed's ball in his room. It sets on a table next to a trophy from his school days. Two days later, a new soccer ball was on my bed when I came home from school. That was a great day. I wish I had someone to play soccer with.

"Habib, come inside now. It's getting late. You've been playing with that ball for over an hour," Rahma yelled out the front screen door. "I said you could practice for a while, but not all night long. You can see it's getting dark, and you still have one more day of school."

"Yes, Aunt Rahma. I'm coming. Just five more minutes, please," Habib yelled while dribbling the soccer ball.

"Okay, five minutes. Then you need to clean the dishes you forgot from your dinner. I made you a nice plate and you leave it sitting on the table to run and play. Manners, you need to learn *manners*." Rahma shut the door, mumbling the last part. She put his dishes in the sink and wiped the dining room table.

Voices Through the Window

"Where are my dinner dishes? I will clean them now," Habib said between heavy breaths. He bounced the ball on the tiled floor.

"Habib, no balls in the house! Especially one you've been kicking around in the dirt outside." Rahma swatted her towel in the direction of Habib's bouncing ball. "If your mama were here, maybe you'd listen to her. A good boy would clean his dishes and tidy his bedroom, not play ball in the house. I don't know how, but maybe things would be different with your mama here."

"Oh yes, things would be different," Habib said. *There would be love in this house. Kind words would be said. Someone would want to take time to play with me. Somebody would ask me about school, and my teacher. Somebody would care again.*

"Oh, so you agree, Nephew? Good. Maybe you can try to do as I tell you to. Go on upstairs to your room after you finish your dishes. You can organize your room before your father comes home to say goodnight."

"Yes, Aunt Rahma. After I put the dishes on the tray to dry, I'll go clean my room," Habib said as he squirted soap on his plate and silverware, emptying the last of the bottle. It sudsed up and he laughed to himself.

"Don't use up all my dish soap on two dishes, Habib," Rahma said as she walked out of the kitchen. "I'm going to relax in the living room until the men come home. Be a good boy and do what I told you."

"No problem, Aunt Rahma. Goodnight," Habib smirked as he replied. *That was a little late to tell me about the dish soap. I wonder if she has more somewhere. I think the plate will be really clean with the extra soap. Just a lot of water to rinse, now. How come the water isn't going down the drain? Oh, I see. There's a piece at the bottom. But can I reach it from here? I don't know if I can clear the hole.*

Habib rinsed his dishes and the sink after finally reaching the food particle in the drain stopper. He turned and picked up his soccer ball, humming as he jumped one step at a time. He started quickly, and the last few steps were slower as his energetic play caught up with him. Now tired, he was ready for bed. When he walked into his bedroom, he tapped the airplane he and his mama had put together and hung from the ceiling. He flopped onto his bed. He stared at the picture on his wall of the Yemeni national football player; he was waving a flag from atop of the team's shoulders. Back in Yemen he remembered his family was all together. They all lived in one house — their own house. His grandparents lived just a short way away but not in the same house. He laid in the bed and thought back to when his mama convinced his father to play in the yard with them. What a great memory from when they were a better family. A few tears fell as he drifted off to sleep.

"Habib, you're sleeping early, and you still have your clothes on. Where are your pajamas?" Abdul whispered from the door. "And you're not even under the blankets." Abdul walked over and lightly rubbed his son's hair.

"Baba, you're home. How are you?"

"I'm well, my baba. Aunt Rahma said you were going to organize your bedroom. You must have gotten distracted because I see yesterday's clothes left on the floor, and your schoolbooks are piled all over your desk."

"Well, baba, I'm sorry. Please don't be angry. I laid down for a moment and was remembering our family in Yemen, and then I fell asleep. Was it a busy day at the restaurant?"

"I'm not angry, but you should try to do something before you leave for school because Aunt Rahma will no doubt check the room tomorrow. And my day, well… It was most interesting."

"What happened? Did you get a big tip from some nice people, or did someone talk about how great the food was again?"

"Actually, I spoke to your mother today. She sends her deep love for you, Habib."

"What?" Habib quickly sat up. "You talked to Mama. How is she? How is Aini?"

"They are both doing well. Aini is moving about the floor."

"Baba, I want to see mama. I listened and heard you talking to Aunt Rahma. She talked to Mama. And Mohammed too. We can go to the restaurant and see her. I need to hug her and hold her tight."

"Uhm… I'm not so sure." Abdul tapped the airplane.

"Why not, Baba? I know the name of her restaurant. If Mohammed can find it, I know you can. You're the smartest man I know."

"I don't know if it's a good idea, Habib. She would be working and can't sit down to visit with us."

"But Baba, she misses us. You said so. She could be our waitress, and we can have dinner. It could be a great surprise for her. I just know it."

"Okay, Habib, I'll think about it. It would be nice to see her. Now get your pajamas on. Then decide if you'll pick up around this room tonight or in the morning. I think it'd be better tonight, because you don't like to get up. But the decision is yours, as is the responsibility." Abdul kissed him on the forehead and started to walk to the doorway.

"I love you, Baba. Thank you for listening to me," Habib said softly.

"I will always love you, my son. Good night," Abdul whispered in return.

∼

Abdul

"Hello?"

"Baba, how are you?" Abdul said when Fahad answered the phone.

"Abdul, it's pleasant to hear from you. Business is good, and your mama is quiet and seems content. What more could I ask? But we haven't talked in a few weeks. How are you?" Fahad's voice boomed through the phone.

"I'm well, Baba. Life is okay. I'm working and the guests seem to like me," Abdul said.

"Are you sure? Because Suhaib spoke to me. He said you had confronted him a few weeks ago about trying to do more management functions. Remember what I told you: A man who starts his own business, that man is careful about what responsibility he delegates to others, even to trusted family."

"I know, Baba. I had thought at the moment I would try to reason with him, but I've learned to keep my peace," Abdul said.

"Excellent, because peace is what is needed in that house where you're living. Suhaib also mentioned that Rahma and Mohammed found your wife. He said the situation could have been better handled, but he explained his wife had the best intentions," Fahad said.

"Oh yeah, well I don't imagine she actually had the best intentions. She told Mohammed to do whatever it took to bring her to their van. He physically dragged her, embarrassing her in her workplace. And he could have hurt her," Abdul complained.

"He did what needed to be done. I'm surprised it wasn't worse. This was your fault, my son," Fahad noted.

"What? How is it my fault? I understand our culture and faith in Islam, but we're living in a new day and time," Abdul said.

"Baba, you should have dealt with your wife long before Rahma did. Your indecisiveness motivated her to do this, and they obviously felt obligated to do the right thing."

"You call that the right thing! Maybe in Yemen, someone might have dragged their estranged wife back home, but now we're in the twenty-first century. Society dictates we behave differently in America."

"Umph! I need to tell you stories from the people I've traded with here. The twenty-first century hasn't changed our culture or society, and you should know that Dearborn has carried our traditions with it. The only thing different is the location, but the following of Islam and our culture doesn't change. I don't understand what makes you think differently. I sent you away years ago to study abroad in Europe to learn management, so you'd become marketable. I didn't send you away to pick up ideas from others about how you should think and see our traditions."

"But Baba, I've watched you as I grew up. You seemed to adapt and change with society. It seemed you and Mother kept up with the newer trends. Also, I have never seen you raise your voice or hand to Mama. So, I don't see how you feel our culture is still mired in the old traditions."

"Baba, my established income as a man of the market gave me the opportunities to see new things from a wider world viewpoint. And your mama appreciated some of these things as well. And personally, we found our relationship an equitable one of both love and self-interest. So, I never needed to take action to an extreme in our relationship. But you should know, underneath our cultured contemporary faces, we still held our religion close. In its truth, we find security and a close bond among our family and friends."

"Well, Baba, you should know that I'm starting to question some of the sayings of Muhammad in the Qur'an. Some of the things just don't make sense from a reasonable perspective,"

"What! What are you talking about? You can't be serious? I've made sure you were firmly grounded in your religion. Is Aisha trying to convert you to Christianity? Don't even think about wavering in your religion."

"Baba, relax. I'm still a Muslim. I'm only asking questions and wondering about things. I've been in some pretty interesting discussions lately. One man was a Muslim, and then explained how he came to Christianity after months of talking with a few Christians."

"Abdul, first you shamed us with your continuous pandering to run Suhaib's restaurant. Then you can't put a leash on your wife and bring her back home to care for your family. And now this, you question Islam. The faith of our fathers for generations. The faith of this land where we raised you. I don't know how you expected me to react with this thinking. But don't call me again until you can talk more sensibly." Fahad hung up the phone and slammed it on the dining room table.

Wow! I didn't know he would react this way. I guess I should have thought out more how the conversation might go, or maybe I should have talked to Mama. Things might have gone differently. She has always seemed to understand my heart more. Even when I married, she and I talked about loving Aisha with tenderness and kindness; that although Islam often put the responsibility of ruling the house on the man with a strong arm, she explained how my love for her could be shown to her in my words and small actions around her. This is why, when we moved into our first home not far from my parent's home, I felt our marriage was perfect. I know the first few years many couples around the world think so, but it remained with us.

It wasn't until we moved to Dearborn with my family where stress really grew on us, individually and as a family. I considered emailing Sam after calling my father. But now I'm not feeling up to the mental challenge of putting thoughtful words into an email exchange.

Feeling a little sad, I flip open my cell phone and turn to photos. The first picture I opened was Aisha holding Aini in the kitchen, only a month after we came to Dearborn. Then, a photo of Habib finding Aisha hiding behind the tree in the back yard. Finally, my favorite photo, where Mohammed took one of us all together on the front porch. We are smiling, full of love and hope for the future. I snapped the phone shut and fell on the bed. I wouldn't be much better than Habib, sleeping in my clothes. But right now, I wasn't worried about pajamas.

∽

Habib

Voices Through the Window

It's Monday. I got to sleep late because school is out for the summer. I got to stay up last night, and even got Cousin Mohammed and Baba to play soccer with me when they got home from work. It was fun and exciting to see them run across the yard. Uncle Suhaib even came out and stood in one goal. Mohammed set up two Home Depot buckets. Uncle Suhaib roamed between them like a lion. I watched his eyes. His legs moved a little slower, but his eyes were dancing. Baba dribbled the ball downfield through the back yard. Cousin Mohammed chased him, kicking at his feet.

And then it happened, Mohammed stole the ball and ran it back to me. I was guarding the other side. He was fast and I wasn't ready. But I watched his feet and then his eyes. I wondered which direction he would kick. Just as he was about to kick the ball at me, Baba ran in front and took the ball from him. I couldn't believe it. I looked to the back door and heard Aunt Rahma laughing. WE both laughed.

I stopped for a moment. Baba was kicking the ball easily downfield, but all I could think about was this moment. This is our family, and we are happy. I don't know about tomorrow or next year, but this moment is pure. But then the sun went down, and it was dark, and it was time for bed. Now a new day has started. I'm not sure what I will do this morning. But Baba said he didn't have to close at the restaurant, and we're going to surprise Mama. This will be the best day ever. If only I can get through the first part and make Aunt Rahma happy. When Baba comes home, we will have a great dinner. And won't Mama be so happy to see me?

"Habib, you're staring across the yard. Aunt Rahma told me you've been out here for an hour. I still see sticks and branches you missed. And did you clean your room this morning? Completely this time?" Abdul stood just outside the back door. He had looked around the yard, and his eyes fell back to Habib. His eyes were shining, though his voice sounded stern.

"Baba, you're home. Excellent! But I see you walking with a limp. Are you alright? Maybe soccer isn't good for you anymore?" Habib smiled and waved a stick at his father. "You know you're an old man, and you run like you're still a teenager."

"I'm fine, my son. Just a bit sore. I can't let Cousin Mohammed think I've lost my stamina, skill, and speed." Abdul stretched his arms up, then bent over to try and touch his toes. "I could go another match. But he's not home, and I've got to help someone finish picking up the sticks in the yard. You know it's important to have the yard cleared of debris, so it doesn't dull the blade when one of us men cut the lawn. And it's getting long, so it'll be cut soon."

"Yes, Baba, we'll hurry and then we can go for the drive to the restaurant? For dinner and visit with Mama?"

"Yes, my son. Now focus more on branches sticking up in the ground, and don't worry what time we'll leave."

*We finished up fast with Baba helping. We broke the sticks and branches in smaller pieces and stacked them in a large paper bag. Baba helped me pull the bag next to the garage. Then we went inside up to our shared bathroom and cleaned up. Baba made sure I put deodorant on. He even sprayed one of his colognes on my neck. I wanted to smell nice for Mama especially since it had been hot today, and I felt sweat around my neck. I picked Mama's favorite shirt, one that she had bought for me. She said I always looked handsome in it. Ba**ba, jingling his keys, yelled** my name from across the hall. We left the house quickly. But Aunt Rahma tried to stop and question us. Baba just waved her off and told her he was taking me for a drive. I hadn't traveled this far in a car for a while. As we drove, I worried that Mama wouldn't be working today. But Baba just smiled, like he knew something different.*

"Wow, look at the restaurant. It looks like it's sitting on the water. I can see boats behind the restaurant." Habib hopped down from the SUV and gazed out at the water and then back to the restaurant.

"Yeah, this is interesting. I wonder how your mama got a job here. It looks a lot different than a coffee shop," Abdul wondered out loud.

"I don't know. It looks really big," Habib said.

"Well, let's go inside and see how big it is. The parking lot isn't full. So hopefully they have a table where your mama can wait on us." Abdul ruffled Habib's hair, gently pulling him away from the water, and they strode into the side door.

"Good afternoon, gentlemen. Will there just be the two of you today?" The teenage hostess asked.

"Yes, only us two. But we would like to be sat in Aisha's section. She is working today I believe?"

"Oh yes. She has a few nice booths open. Would you like to sit in a booth or at a table?" a teenage hostess said.

"A booth would be nice, and maybe in the back, if it's available." Abdul nodded to the back of the restaurant.

"Oh, yes, certainly. Step this way, please." She put the two large menus under her arm and picked up two rolled silverware from a plastic tub underneath the host stand.

"Thank you so much," Abdul said with a smile.

"Yes, thank you very much," Habib added with his own smile as he took long strides to keep up with them.

"Here is your booth." The hostess opened menus on each side of the table. "Our specials are in the insert here in the middle. Our grilled shark has been selling like hotcakes today. Chef John serves it with sautéed spinach over a bed of rice pilaf accompanied by spring vegetables. It's topped with our homemade BBQ sauce."

"Wow, look at this menu. The outside is decorated like the outside of a house but on water, and a big fish in the middle." Habib pointed, his mouth hanging open.

"Yes, it's interesting. But hold the menu tall, before your mama comes to greet us," Abdul whispered across the table, raising his own menu to cover his face.

"Hello there, folks, I'll be back in a few minutes," Aisha stopped by with a tray full of pop and lemonade in one hand. She dropped two beverage napkins casually on the table and tapped the table with a smile. "I just need to drop these beverages off."

"No problem," Abdul said with a much deeper tone to his voice.

Habib peeked from under his menu and giggled.

"She didn't see us. What will we say to her?"

"Why we'll say 'hello' and smile our best smiles. And she probably didn't recognize us because we were hidden."

"Okay, our menu is interesting, but not that interesting. Let's see who I'm waiting on today," Aisha said with a grin.

"Oh Mama," Habib jumped out of the booth and hugged her. "It's so good to see you," his voice broke as he started to cry.

"Hello Aisha, we thought we would surprise you. I hope it's okay." Abdul put the menu down with a wide smile on his face.

"No, it's more than okay. It's the best gift ever," Aisha said. A few tears of joy slipped from her eyes. "My darling, please don't make me cry because I have to continue working here," Aisha laughed shakily.

"Well, how about two Cokes for us?" Abdul said.

"Yes, of course. Let's get you two something to drink. And I need to take an order for another table." Aisha laughed again, wringing her hands.

"Go ahead, Aisha. We're not in a hurry. Habib has been waiting all week for this visit, and he'll be happy just watching you."

"That's okay, Mama. You go onto work; I'll sit back down." Habib's voice broke a little.

"Okay men, thank you." Aisha hurried to her other table.

"Baba, she seemed happy to see us. What do you think?"

"Oh, I think so. Her tears seemed true enough," Abdul smiled.

"Well, I'm so happy right now I could just burst like a balloon," Habib laughed.

"Don't burst yet, we've haven't really looked at the menu. I'm sure they have a kid's menu. And I'm sure they have a nice dessert with ice cream to really finish the meal." Abdul opened the menu again. Habib opened his menu also, and they both turned over the pages, glancing at the color photos of various items highlighted.

"Ahh.... You've opened the menus. Obviously, you can see there's no Middle Eastern food here. It's all-American fare with seafood, steak, chicken, and some vegetarian options. Plus, they have Mexican entrees for some reason. But here are your Cokes. I made them special for you two." Aisha laughed. Then she sat down and scooted in next to Habib with a laugh. "Is it okay if I sit next to my favorite son?"

"Yes, Mama. Of course. How is work going today?"

"Oh, my son with curious questions. My day was average, and now it's just outstanding with you and your father here."

"Oh, I count too?" Abdul laughed. "That's nice to hear."

"Habib, my son. How is life at school? How about with Aunt Rahma? Are you being a good boy? And your teacher, is she still nice?"

"Now who is shooting questions like the battle games we used to play." Habib laughed. "Yes, I'm being a good boy, Mama."

"Yes, he is, most of the time. He and Aunt Rahma have had a few problems. But some of that, I think, is because our son isn't sure how to feel with you gone. And I think he blames Aunt Rahma."

"Oh, well, that's a problem. But let's not answer all the problems right now. Let's find some good food for you." Aisha smiled and flipped a menu page.

Mama had to go to another table. But she always returned between other tables, with more food for us. I couldn't believe how much food we ate. We had some nachos as an appetizer, then fried fresh chicken fingers with french fries, and then homemade apple pie with ice cream. Mama put her arm around me each time she brought the food, and then she'd sit with us for a few minutes. She would smile so big. Then she saw another lady look at her and wink. She would run over to another table to work. Finally, it was time to leave. Mama gave me a few mints and a big hug. Then she and Baba went and stepped down the hall. They touched hands, and he kissed her cheek. She brushed his shoulder and ran back to the kitchen.

Abdul

We came home and practiced dribbling in the yard. I showed Habib how to follow his opponent and try to steal the ball. Habib then went off to shower and play on his Game Boy Advance I bought him last year. I showered as well, and the water seemed to rinse away any remaining doubts. Aisha still loved me, and we will find our way back together soon. After drying off, I fell on the bed and pulled out my phone. I flipped through pictures of us, our family together, and then us. Suddenly I had an idea, and I texted her. I asked her if she would let me take her out on Sunday afternoon. She had mentioned she was off on Sundays, and Uncle's restaurant closed early on Sundays. She agreed and I suggested she dress casually. Two days of anticipation and I waited each day wondering if she was hoping for a nice time also. I didn't tell my family about my plans, only that I wanted to borrow the SUV for a few hours to get away and think. I was thankful Aunt Rahma didn't prod me with more questions.

~

"I hope you don't mind picking me up here at the church. I brought a bag and changed at the church. Carmen, my friend, has agreed to watch Aini for me. So, I'm all set for your surprise." Aisha smiled.

"No, this is fine. I'm not sure why you're here till 12:30 though? All morning, have you been studying for four hours?" Abdul shook his head.

"It's not four hours, but it has been much of the morning. We have a Bible study that's for newer Christians, and we are talking about what it means to be a true Christian. It's called a discipleship class." Aisha showed him the workbook. "We're on chapter three, and it's so interesting."

"Well, I guess that's the next step. I just didn't think they would move this fast," Abdul said. "You know, these Christians. They want you to change and flip to the other side quickly. How soon will you insist on wanting to go and disrupt people's lives, so they give up themselves?"

"Stop, don't drive out of the parking lot, please. If this is how our date will go, you can take me back to the church door." Aisha looked over at Abdul with a scowl.

"What? I'm just telling you how I still feel. This whole situation still stings, and I'm not completely sure where we stand."

"Look Abdul, I still love you, and I'm still Aisha. They're not out to change me, God is out to change me, from the inside to the outside. It's what I want, and I'm not spoon-fed like our daughter with baby food. Well, actually, I am getting spoon-fed early on from the Bible, and learning more to hunger like a new child. Again, I'm not forced to do what I want to do." Aisha patted her Bible. "I've chosen to love Jesus, and I want to do God's will. Not from obligation, but because He loved me first."

"So, will you still go out for our surprise date?" Abdul looked up from the steering wheel and into her eyes. He saw that she was starting to cry. "{I want us to have a nice time."

"Well, if we can just have a nice afternoon." Aisha sniffled lightly. "Can we have pleasant conversations? If so, then whatever you have planned, I'm sure I will enjoy."

"Okay then, I thought we would dine at this interesting-themed restaurant, Rainforest Café and perhaps shop. There is a large shopping mall with many small shops. And if we have time we might see an American romantic movie, I know you sometimes like them."

"That sounds wonderful, Abdul. I would love to walk with you around a mall. I love to window shop. And I have a little tip money hid in my purse, so I might splurge on something for me." Aisha clapped her hands.

"Well, we needed some alone time, and I wanted to have a little fun with you. It will be good for us," Abdul's face was beaming. "I talked to some customers about our date, and they recommended the Rainforest Café and told me about all the many shops. There is a large shopping mall that stretches long and has a variety of choices. And I've got some tip money set aside too, and I would be pleased to buy a new top or shoes for you"

"This will be like the time we went away to the city back in Yemen. It was only the two of us for that week, and we had such a nice time." Aisha smiled and looked over at Abdul.

Chapter 23

Aisha

"Theresa, thank you for coming by the apartment today. I really wanted to talk with people I trust. Carmen is off today, and I'm so happy you could come by." Aisha opened the apartment door and hugged her.

"Oh, you're here, Theresa. Excellent," Carmen said. She walked into the room, carrying a tray of cheese and crackers with three filled glasses.

"Is that an Arnold Palmer? Oh, you made my favorite for a warm afternoon," Theresa said with a sigh. She pushed strands of graying hair back from her curly long blond hair. "It's a hot Michigan summer day out there. The cool AC feels good here. Our home is a bit warm as we're waiting for someone to repair ours. Matthew put up three oscillating fans, but they just seem to blow hot air around. So, a little time with you girls is like a breath of 'fresh air' for me."

"Well, I cut up a few kinds of cheese for the crackers. But then we made some guacamole topped with Oaxaca cheese to serve with tortilla chips. I wasn't sure about the mood, so I mixed our snacks with American favorites of cheese and my favorites." Carmen smiled and set the tray in the center of the dining room table, placing a glass of mixed tea and lemonade in front of each person.

"I'm feeling so blessed that I have friends like you two that will come and spend time with me. I'm still learning how to walk in my faith in Jesus, and you two seem to love me and cover me with your prayers." Aisha looked to each of her friends. "How did I become so lucky? I will never understand it."

"Aisha, this has all been part of God's plan. He got you here, in this place and in these moments to meet us. And then the Holy Spirit prepared our hearts, speaking to us through His Word and insights," Theresa said.

"Yes, just as we want to pour into you the love of God, Ms. Theresa spent many months investing in me years ago." Carmen smiled sheepishly. "At one point in my life, I was really struggling with things, and Ms. Theresa helped meet my needs. First, she met me with such warmth at a block party in our neighborhood. Then, she somehow convinced me to come to church occasionally and got me to commit to a weekly Bible study. There we dove into God's Word, and I found Jesus and I heard His call. But Ms. Theresa didn't stop there, she continued to pray with me weekly. She helped me build my relationship with Jesus on strong foundations until my house has become weather-ready for the storms of life. And in my house, I pull down my armor each day to battle with the evil one and find the strength to carry truth with me, walking in peace and faithfulness, with the sword, God's Word in my heart and mouth."

"Oh, I remember we talked about the armor of God in Bible study a few weeks ago from Ephesians six. But I'm not really sure about it still," Aisha said.

"Part of our responsibility in serving God is to be ready for any opportunities to listen and obey the leadings of the Holy Spirit. So, we have to be on guard all the time, like a real soldier," Theresa said. "But you are preparing yourself weekly and daily. You're in God's Word, praying to Him throughout the day, and meeting with other believers as part of a community. These things help build up and maintain that armor."

"I know and I appreciate that help with these things. But I'm still having some problems. I need answers for decisions in my life, and I'm not sure what to do," Aisha looked from her small plate of chips and guac.

"My friend, that's why we're here. We can dig into finding answers from God's Word and pray your worries into the lap of Jesus at Heaven's throne." Carmen reached for Aisha's hand and squeezed it. "So, go ahead and say what's on your mind."

"Yes, Aisha. One friend once told me this, 'If not for the grace of God, I too could be facing what you feel.' All of us deal with our own struggles, and that's why Jesus commanded us to love one another." Theresa smiled and patted her Bible. "Paul restates it by stating that we bear one another up and care for each other. We love you, Aisha, and want to support you in whatever way we can."

"It's just that Abdul is making a sincere effort with me. We went out on a few dates in the last two weeks. Then he called to see how Aini, and I were doing during the week."

"Shouldn't that be a good thing?" Theresa asked with a twinkle in her eyes. Carmen smiled silently and nodded.

"Yes, but he doesn't quite approve of my new commitment to Jesus."

"Did he actually say that?" Carmen asked.

"No, not really. Actually, he told me he's been talking and emailing with Sam."

"Oh, wasn't he the first person you talked with about Jesus, at your coffee house?"

"Yes, Carmen. He dropped the first seed." Aisha laughed.

"I think I know of Sam. We met at a few Bible conferences. He was always very nice, but also rather articulate in explaining his perspective on sharing his faith, especially his love for sharing Jesus to people who are Muslims" Theresa explained.

"Well, isn't that good, Aisha, that Abdul is talking about Jesus? Jesus actually talked about this in John 6:44, 'No one can come to me unless the Father who sent me draws him.' That means the Father is drawing him. Some might say He is tugging at his heart, drawing closer him to Himself," Carmen softly said. "God is always working in ways we don't often understand."

"I know, but my heart is split. And I'm not sure how to continue with Abdul. I mean, I still love him, and he's such a good father."

"So, let me ask you, Aisha. Was it really him, or was it his family who made demands on you that pushed you to leave?" Theresa asked. "I know that God was reaching out to you, and that also impacted your decision. But you also mentioned you feared things would get worse."

"Well, I feared Abdul's family and maybe even others in the community might try to influence him to treat me more harshly. His Aunt Rahma has already made it a habit to spit out hateful words with a raised hand in my direction. She kept me locked in the bedroom or working under her supervision. I wasn't sure how much I could take. Or how much worse it could get." She took a sip of her drink, and then, a few deep breaths. The other ladies just waited until she was ready to continue. "And, in the back of my mind, I wondered about Jesus who said I could come to Him with any problem. Jen talked about the peace that is so much found in Him."

"But the question remains, what about Abdul? Does he expect you to return with his family to that environment? What has he asked of you?" Carmen scratched her chin. "I mean, you two have met together recently, and spent quality time with each other."

"Yes, and that's a starting point," added Theresa. "But you should find out what he really has on his mind. What are his hopes and expectations? Have they changed? God is planting seeds in his heart too, and who knows? Perhaps God has put you in this place for such a time as this, as he did it before with Esther. Remember we talked about her in one of our Bible studies in the Book of Esther?" Theresa asked.

"Yes, I remember. But it's not like God has some big plan where I need to save my people from death," Aisha muttered.

"Ahh... Don't sell it short, my friend. Remember Jesus's last commandment was to go and spread His Gospel unto first your community, the nation, and their neighboring nations. God has a bigger picture in mind for which we can't see the wider view just yet." Carmen spread her arms wide and held out each one in emphasis. "That's where your faith comes in. Remember, Pastor Pedro preached about the bread that came down for the Israelites to eat when they wandered around the desert. But then some tried to save some, and it went bad. Moses had to reprimand them as children and tell them that God would provide daily for them. They had to live each day in faith, and God expects us to walk in faith that way."

"Amen, Sister Carmen." Theresa sighed.

"Okay, great. We discussed God working in my life and Abdul. But you haven't told me what to do yet. That's why you're here." Aisha looked between them. "You two are my advisors that I trust. I need some answers."

"Look, we understand your need for clarity and direction. And we're here to support you as we can. But we can't tell you what to do," Theresa smiled.

"Why not? You two have become my gifts from God, and I thought with my sharing you could tell me what to do."

"We're sorry, Aisha. But you need to seek God for answers to these questions. Listen for His still voice and wait on Him." Carmen patted Aisha's hands. "We can pray now together, but you should also pray alone. We could suggest verses, maybe in Psalms, about seeking God. Then lay it before Him, and make your request known to Him. That's what Jesus wants of us."

"Okay, but will one of you start praying with me now? I'm not sure where to start."

"Yes, of course." Carmen and Theresa said in unison.

∾

"Wow, this place is amazing, Abdul. I can't believe you made reservations here. I've heard some of my guests talk about it, and even coworkers have eaten here." Aisha's eyes were wide as she smoothed her dress when they walked in.

"Well, I asked one of my regular customers the best place to take my wife for a special event. He mentioned a few places, but he said he liked The Lark over the others. And here we are. Another customer said it seemed pretentious, but I like it," Abdul said.

"I like it too," Aisha said. "But what is the special event? This isn't my birthday."

"I know." Abdul smiled as he held the door for her. "But it feels special to me, and I want to share it with you."

"Well, it already feels special. Look at how elegant it looks, like an English country inn that I've seen in pictures with these beautiful murals painted onto the tile wall." Aisha floated her fingers along the wall. "My, look at the garden in the center with a fountain." She gasped. The owner smiled proudly and pointed gently to their table. "Oh… and our table looks down over all the fresh vegetables and fruit. It's so beautiful."

A waiter silently appeared. "Good evening, my name is Charles, and I will be your head waiter this evening. Welcome to The Lark." He wore a crisply pressed, immaculate uniform. The attendant poured water into goblets. "We have a few wines the chef recommends with our meal offerings. May I serve you a few tastings for you to decide?"

"No, I don't think so," Abdul said as he helped Aisha slide her chair to the table. "Ice water to begin is fine, and we may like to see your hot tea and the coffee selections later in the meal."

"Certainly, we have a variety of hot teas, and we have a Colombian blend or Cappuccino you could consider to complete your meal. My colleague, Anthony, is highlighting our hors d'oeuvre trolley where he can offer you our popular Curried Duck Salad, Oysters on the Half-

Shell, or Gulf Shrimp Cocktail. Each is delicious." Charles's hand directed their attention to Anthony, who stood behind the trolly with tongs in hand.

"This is all so lovely!" Aisha exclaimed. "I'm not sure I will have the oysters, but I know I would like to try the salad."

"The oysters are an acquired taste to eat raw, and I don't know that any Muslims would eat them," Abdul said.

"Well, I may have to try one then. I'm not under that shadow of Islam anymore," Aisha said firmly.

"Please, try some of each. Our hope is that you would enjoy the variety of flavors we recommend." Charles' voice took on a bit of deeper tone. "Our remaining entree menu for this evening is pre-fixed and will be served in five courses."

"Thank you, Charles, it sounds marvelous," Abdul said.

"Oh, yes, marvelous. That's a great word to describe it, I think." Aisha giggled softly and took the plate of salad and oyster with a soufflé cup of Mignonette sauce handed to her.

"I'm so glad you like this restaurant," Abdul said as he cut up some shrimp cocktail and dipped it into a ramekin of sauce.

"I just love it but I'm not sure why you brought me here. We could have eaten at Big Boy's Restaurant, and I would have been content," Aisha said.

"Well, I have something important to discuss with you, and I wanted the atmosphere to be just right," Abdul said.

"I thought so, and I'm a little worried about this conversation."

"Oh... why? I don't know why you would be worried. I thought our time together has been really enjoyable."

"Oh, it has, but I'm overwhelmed by this place and how expensive it probably is. Perhaps you're hoping this may put me in such a good mood. Maybe you're actually worried about my response." Aisha looked around again at the interesting decor and downward at the herb garden. *This fine dining experience wasn't part of my discussion with the ladies. I didn't think to mention what could happen with Abdul. I've prayed for peace, and now I really feel nervous. But I don't want to show it. God, give me wisdom in choosing my words now.*

"We have some homemade house bread in a basket," Charles interrupted the conversation with a smile.

"Thank you, Charles We haven't quite decided even on our entrees, and we need a few minutes to finish a few thoughts in our conversation." Abdul nodded at him.

"Certainly, sir. One of us will be nearby if you need anything at all." Charles waved Anthony away as he began to step over to clear away any dishes.

"You were beginning to explain the reason we're here." Aisha said and smiled weakly.

"Uh, I put a lot of thought into this. So, here you are," Abdul pulled out a slender box from inside his suit coat pocket. He placed the box in front of Aisha. "This is a gift for you."

"Oh my. Why did you buy a gift?"

"Please, open it and I will explain."

"Okay," Aisha said. She slid the top box down to see a beautiful gold chain with a charm in the shape of a heart. She popped it open and saw a picture of the two of them on their wedding day. "This is thoughtful, Abdul. But I'm not sure why you want to give me this memory."

"Aisha, you have a ring that symbolizes our marriage together. I want you to understand I don't want us to end, but instead continue as a full family. This memory is one more token that we need to be together." Abdul held the open heart in his hand and looked at her intently.

"Abdul, this token I understand, and I hear your words. But I'm not so sure what you mean behind them."

"Why, it's not complicated. I want you and me and the children to be a family again. I want us to live all under one roof, working and living as we should."

"Yes, I understand that. But I cannot live with your family. Not after all that's happened. So, I don't know what you expect has changed." Aisha held the necklace and looked into his eyes.

"I understand that. And I'm not asking you to return to Dearborn. In fact, I don't know how much more Habib and I can take living there either. We would like to find a way to move to this city… to be with you and Aini."

"Really? You want to leave Dearborn b-behind?" Aisha stammered.

"Well, it won't be easy for me. But I don't feel like Uncle Suhaib's home is our home. We need to find our own home. I'll miss Dearborn, but this is what we need to do."

"So, you want to find a home that's here? In this area? Where my new job is? And where my new church and friends are?"

"Yes, my love. That's what I want. I'm not sure how it will all work out. But I have a little hope that this is best for us. What do you think?"

"I say, yes! Yes, to the necklace with our picture. Yes, to us as a family again. But most of all, I say yes to a little faith for us." Aisha laughed loud enough for the table across to glance at them. Her eyes danced with delight in the soft, candle-lit restaurant.

∽

It was completely unexpected. A week ago today. I had no idea that Abdul would offer to come to Waterford Township, the city I live and work in. He said he and Habib have been having some kind of problems with Rahma and Suhaib, although even during dinner, he didn't explain why they are frustrated. Frustration became a tipping point for him, but does it compare to how I feared for myself. I set my hot tea down on the dining room table and gazed out the window. The apartment window gave a view of other apartments where I wondered about the lives of people out there. I thought maybe I could hear their voices from across the way, each one searching for peace. In my heart, I thought each one needed Jesus and the peace that only He gave.

I wonder if God could put one person outside my window when I walk with Aini. Just one person for me to speak a voice of truth into their life. Jesus means so much to me and now I feel I want to share with others the peace I have. One only needed a little faith, as Jesus spoke about the faith as small as a mustard seed. Here in Michigan, they're a deeper color, but in the Middle East, we had a wide variety. We used mustard sometimes in cooking, and I really liked the parable Jesus spoke about there. Sometimes my faith has seemed so small, and then Abdul said he's trying to have a little faith. I didn't want to quote the Bible to him then, but I was so happy to hear him say so. I felt a bit of confirmation from the Holy Spirit, that God was working in my husband's mind and heart. I've been praying for him daily. I know things may not happen suddenly, and so I've waited on God in HIs time. I will continue to pray that one day soon Abdul gives his life completely to Jesus. In a few minutes, Abdul will come here to pick us up.

We've been invited to dinner at Pastor Pedro's house. Although I don't know the pastor very well, he's also invited Ms. Thersea, Carmen, and Roberto. I was surprised to find out he knew Sam through the ministry, and he asked if we wanted to invite him as well. So, it will be quite a dinner, and I was happy that Abdul decided to bring Habib as well. Aini would be passed around the room. She's become such a joy for everyone from the church community.

"Just a moment, please," Aisha yelled across the room at the door. She jumped up as the knocking continued, and her tea spilled. "Oh my, not the tea on their table!" Aisha sighed.

"Please, don't worry about it." Roberto smiled and set his coffee down. "I'll get some paper towels, and get it cleaned up before it spreads." He stepped back toward the kitchen and ran in for the towel, laughing as the knocking didn't stop.

"My, my. Is there a bird or other crazy animal outside my door?" Aisha laughed and opened the door.

"No, Mama! It's me, Habib. Remember me, your son? I've been waiting for the day I could see you again." Habib's hands dropped from the door and his arms wrapped around her waist, his hands not quite reaching to the back.

"Well, here I am. Come hug me in the apartment. It's a little cooler here. And you, Abdul, come inside as well." Her eyes shone, not hiding her excitement.

"He's been a bit jealous, since you and I have had a few dates since we surprised you at work. I tried to explain we needed some time to date, but he wanted to come each time."

"I think it was more than a few, after we added in the walks and dinners. But yes, my son, we needed our dates. The time was special." Aisha pushed Habib a little and looked in his eyes. "But you're just as special to me. You haven't forgotten how much I love you, have you?"

"No, Mama. But I like to hear it again." Habib stepped up on his toes and kissed her cheek. "See, I'm a little taller. I don't have as far to reach to kiss you, Mama."

"Well, look at these good-looking men, and now we need to add the princess into the mix." Roberto spoke loudly as he walked in, bringing Aini from her jumper in the kitchen. "She was bouncing up and down when she heard the voices."

"Ah, my precious princess." Abdul stepped around Habib tangled in Aisha. "I'm sorry, we haven't formally met. But I just have to hold my lovely baby girl." Abdul gently took her from Roberto's arms and squeezed her to his chest. She giggled with a shrill, as he rubbed his beard to her cheek.

"Oh, I'm sorry. Abdul, this is Roberto, He has been so generous to offer us a room in the apartment that he and his wife share. They've opened their home, and lives to us. Carmen, his wife, has become a friend closer than a sister to me." Aisha stepped back from Habib's hug and pointed widely to Roberto and his home.

"It's a real pleasure to meet you, Roberto." Abdul maneuvered Aini to his left side and put out his hand to shake.

"Yes, sir. My pleasure as well." Roberto smiled and shook his hand firmly.

"Well, Roberto, what's the plan? I'm not really sure about the details," Aisha asked.

"How about this, if it works for your family. Carmen drove over to the pastor's house to help with preparing dinner. But Aini's car seat is still in my Mustang. I think we can get Mom and Habib in the back, and maybe Abdul can ride in front with me. It would be easier than having you follow me, Abdul. Does that sound good Abdul?" Roberto smiled at Aini as she gurgled at her father.

"That sounds fine, Roberto." Abdul picked up Aini and twirled her in small circles. "We will be flexible. That's part of the new plan."

"Okay, then. It's settled. Before we go, let me shake this young man's hand." Roberto put out his hand to Habib. Habib reached out and shook it.

"What do you say, son?" Abdul ruffled his hair.

"It's a pleasure to meet you, sir," Habib said quietly.

"I'm no sir. Just call me 'Berto and we'll be friends." Roberto let his hand drop and hugged the boy lightly.

"Okay, so where did you park? I don't want to be late for this meal. Pastor Pedro said he has an announcement and I'm curious about it. You don't know any details, Roberto?" Aisha asked, her eyebrows furrowed.

"Not at all. If I had any clue at all, I might have been sworn to secrecy." Roberto grinned.

"Fine, can you please bring your car around for us? Aini and I would appreciate it."

"Habib and I can walk with you," Abdul added and handed Aini to Aisha.

"Yes, sir. I want to ask 'Berto about the life of a chef," Habib said when he followed them out the door.

Roberto laughed. "Contrary to what your mama may have told you, I'm not the chef yet. Although I was promoted to a supervisor for some shifts," he explained.

∼

"Welcome, Aisha and Abdul. Abdul, it's a real pleasure to meet you." Pastor Pedro opened the door wide. "And these are your children? Bring them all in. Please, please make yourselves at home. *Mi casa, su casa.*" Pastor Pedro laughed as they filed in. "And I think you know Sam. He just arrived five minutes ago."

"Oh, I haven't seen you in months." Aisha said as she nodded towards him.

"Aisha, it's so good to see you again." Sam stepped up to hug them. "And Abdul, it seems like only yesterday that we talked." Sam winked at him.

"Oh, and who is this good-looking young man?" Pastor Pedro bent down to shake Habib's hand. "You must be Habib. I've heard you're a very intelligent boy."

"Yes, sir. Well, I-I try to study and listen," Habib stuttered nervously.

"Oh, now you're making the boy nervous," Martha said. "Leave him be and let's all gather in the dining room. Dinner is almost ready, dear."

"Yes, yes, of course. But where is Theresa? We can't start without her and John. The best meals always include them."

"*Calmate, mi esposa.* They're both in the kitchen helping finish the meal. You know they insist on helping whenever they can." Martha smiled and squeezed Pedro's hand.

"Wow, we're all here. What a nice surprise." Theresa walked in the dining room with a bowl of tortilla chips in one hand and a dish of guacamole in the other. She smiled broadly while placing the food in the center of the long table. "John, careful with those salsas and stepping around all of these guests."

"Yes, dear," John said with a gentle laugh. He waited just a moment, and then walked by as Roberto pulled a chair adjacent to Carmen. John hip-checked Roberto just as he was about to sit.

"Watch it, *Chelios*, you might spill salsa. Then the cooks will wave their knives at you." Roberto laughed as he fell into the seat.

"Oh, pardon me. I didn't think you were so close," John said. "So, you remember the players after all. I thought you only came for the popcorn to watch the Wings game with me," John muttered in Roberto's ear as he set the salsas down.

"Don't play around with our food, John. You'll be eating canned tuna for a week if you drop what we worked so hard to prepare," Theresa scolded him. She smirked while most everyone chuckled.

"So, if we could have our guests of honor closer to the center, we'd appreciate it. We want to hear and see them clearly." Martha clapped to gain everyone's attention. Sam moved over a seat, and Carmen moved down before getting settled in. He moved over with a grin, watching out for John. Martha, set a platter of empanadas down to pass around. "Pedro, can you say grace, please."

"Certainly, *mi amor*. Father, thank You for this time to gather and celebrate a family united. Thank You for the food we are about to feast upon. And Father, thank You for the gift of salvation in sending Your one and only Son. Amen!"

"Amen!" The whole table cried out in unison.

"So, let's enjoy our appetizers. We have enchiladas in the oven that will be done shortly." Martha started to pass the empanadas. She pointed to the two bowls of chips on each end. "Help yourselves to chips, please."

"Pardon me, Martha. But what is the beautifully wrapped box in the center of the table? Is it gourmet candy for dessert?" Aisha asked.

"Well, I'm not quite sure about dessert," Martha said with a twinkle in her eye. "But it's for you and Abdul to open."

"You want us to open it now? In front of all these people?" Abdul asked, his eyebrows raised.

"Oh, it's okay. We're all like family here, Abdul. I know it feels odd, but have a little faith," Theresa said sweetly, her voice lifted like a song.

"Oh, again with a little faith. I suppose you'll tell me about a mustard seed now." Abdul winked at Aisha.

"Please, I waited a few days after you said that until I told you about the parable. I know you think it a coincidence." Aisha smiled.

"I've had a lot of those types of coincidences in my life." Sam laughed and pointed down the table. "But please, open the package. We're all wondering now."

"Go ahead and open it, Aisha. You do enjoy sweets," Abdul said.

"Please hurry. I'd like to eat some," Habib said.

"Okay, okay. Let's see," Aisha shook it lightly and the silent group heard it rattle.

"Does candy usually make that noise?" Habib asked.

"Shh, son." Aisha smiled and started to unwrap the bow from the box. She pulled the box apart. "A set of keys... What? I don't understand?" She held up the keys with a ring and small, pewter house-shaped key fob attached.

"These keys are for a home. We were told in confidence that you would be in need of a home to stay as a family. We have an elder here in our church who sees it as part of his ministry to renovate homes and rent them out in the community at a reasonable price." Pastor Pedro nodded from the end of the table.

"Wow, that's amazing! I don't know what to say." Aisha looked down the table. "This is so thoughtful and kind. Don't you think so, Abdul?"

"I'm not so sure about this. I mean, it is thoughtful. But we are hard workers, and we don't need charity. I'm sure I can find us a home soon." Abdul looked uncomfortable. His gaze swept from Aisha to the pastor and then down to Sam. Sam simply shrugged with a smile and his hands out.

"Oh, no. This isn't charity," Martha spoke up. "We know that your family works hard, and you surely could find a place on your own. But Aisha has become part of our community, and we would love to support her and you both, Abdul. It's our privilege, in fact, to serve you in this way."

"Aisha has served in our church community in many ways that people haven't noticed. She helped set up for a block party and helped with the boutique for families coming to the church. She has even weeded the flower garden around the church building. Aisha has a heart to serve God and others, and we love her. This is just one way we can serve her *and* you," Theresa said.

"Well, I didn't realize how much she has meant to you all. I'm still not quite sure how to take it all in. But Sam and I have talked a little about the community that true Christians claim to have. I didn't really understand it, but now I think I do." Abdul shrugged his shoulders.

"And what's this envelope underneath?" Aisha looked down at the table again.

"Open it up, Mama. Maybe that one is a new car," Habib added.

"Oh, my, I hope not." Aisha laughed and tore the envelope to see a photo. "What's this picture? A large sofa and chair? What does this mean?"

"Uhm... I think this is my cue." Roberto laughed. "Carmen and I help as leaders with the youth group. Last month, we had newer furniture donated to the youth room, and these have been sitting in storage. The youth pastor told us to find a home for them. So, if you want them, they are yours."

"Excellent!" Habib said. "I love it! It looks so comfortable."

"I guess that settles that question." Abdul laughed out loud and smiled at Aisha.

"Well, I would like to see if this guacamole is as good as Carmen's was a week or so ago," Aisha said as she reached for the dip with one hand and jingled the keys with the other hand.

"It had better be, since I made this batch, too." Carmen smiled with a chip full of guac in her hand while Aisha took the dish.

"So, Abdul, you worked at your uncle's restaurant? Will you continue working there, if you don't mind me asking?" Roberto asked.

"Oh, no. It's not a problem. Aisha has already talked to her manager. She told them about my serving and food preparation experience, and they said they always need good help, especially if Aisha speaks for me."

"Well, I'll confirm that with the chef. He loves it when people are cross trained in the front and back of the house. We always need solid preppers," Roberto answered.

"Did you do restaurant work in Yemen, Abdul? Not everyone is cut out for that type of work," John queried.

"No. Well, I actually worked in more formal business. I studied management in England, and they set me up with a company when I graduated in Lebanon. But I missed home and thought I could work with my father. He does regional marketing in Yemen. But he pushed me to find my own way, and so I thought business here in the US"

"Then family business called once you came to the states?" John asked.

"Yes, well… More of an obligation. My Uncle Suhaib took us into his home, and he needed reliable help. Plus, I had come a year before to visit and worked on a work visa for him then."

"But Wayne State and Oakland University are both reviewing his transcripts. It may not take much to see his degree validated here," Aisha interrupted.

"Yes. We'll see. My MBA should take me further and help us with the cost of raising our family here. Especially now since we may not have family support." Abdul's voice sobered. He looked at Aisha and folded his hands.

"Ah… family support. You worry for nothing," Theresa said. "Look around this table. You and your family have family here that loves you and wants to come alongside you."

"Yes, they have taken me in as part of their community. I'm truly blessed by these people so much," Aisha sighed and shook her head. Suddenly she began to cry.

"Aisha, my love! Why are tears coming? What could be so wrong?" Abdul stuttered.

"Oh, Abdul! When I think about how much God has moved people to intervene in my life with such kindness and grace, it stirs something deep in my soul. I'm so grateful."

"We all love you, Aisha!" the whole table said in unison.

Epilogue

May — 2004

"Good morning, my dear. You had a long day working at Big Boys yesterday and then staying up with our son. But I'm so glad you had built up your resume and started training managers in a good company. You were never quite happy serving. I know you are getting ready to leave for breakfast with Sam, but could you help feed Elizabeth? She's already in her highchair! I need to go check on Aini, she's supposed to be getting ready. I'm taking her to the doctor today with Carmen. And where is Habib? He should be up by now."

Aisha looked down the hall toward his room.

"Relax, my love. Habib stayed up a little late with me. We played Mario Brothers on the new Wii system. Before I start feeding Elizabeth, I'll get him up. I reminded him last night he would be helping you with the girls. It was wise to schedule both girls with the doctor on the same day."

Abdul gently picked up his two-year-old and brushed his neatly trimmed beard against her cheeks. She giggled softly as they walked toward Habib's room.

It wasn't too long ago that a small rift simmered between Habib and me. Aisha seemed to pull all his affection, like a rock in the stream that draws the water to itself, subtly, without meaning to affect the flow.

I'd made a decision that I would make a better effort to show my love for my son. I know he needs more than the occasional moments I used to take with him. Habib deserves to share true mama and baba time, and I wanted him to know his baba loves him. And more importantly, he needs to know that, even if I fail him, the one true Baba--God, the triune God —never fails and always loves us.

After four years of walking with Jesus, I still am learning to walk humbly with God. He has taught me so much, but I hunger for more. This is why I haven't stopped going for monthly meetings with Sam. He, in his direct but graceful manner, keeps account of my continued progress in my faith. More than a mentor, I count him as a true friend. I wonder what new homework he might suggest for me. Earlier this year, he gave me a book called Pilgrim's Progress, *and we've been discussing the details of how the character, Christian, had to learn to completely give all his burdens to Jesus, the habits of sin that Christians still carry as they view their them and those of others. True relief is found when I learn to give them all back to Jesus.*

When Habib and I watched the movie from the church's library, we saw Christian walking on his path with the 'burden,' and it really struck me how the weight affected Christian. Habib noticed it and asked about it. We talked about the law that showed sin, and even how Islam had tenets of stringent codes to follow. Then we spoke of God's grace and mercy in the Christian faith. Habib's mind is sharp, and he asks pointed questions that I sometimes suggest we come back to. Then I search in the Bible and pray. Then I might call John from our church, or Pastor Pedro. Sometimes I'll email Sam because he's quick to notice my email and he has a passion for reasoning through a Bible question, though he doesn't just send me the answer. Sam will drop a string of clues, whereas I inevitably follow a trail of verses through the forest of ideas until the Holy Spirit speaks to me. In my head and heart, He speaks, "Abdul, see? Here is your answer."

"Hello Mario superstar, it's time to get up. Remember, your mom needs your help with the girls today?" Abdul bent over and kissed his son on the forehead. He whispered in his ear and gently fussed with Habib's hair while holding Elizabeth in his other arm.

"Good morning, Baba. Can we play Mario Brothers again tonight? I think I can beat you this time. What do you think?" Habib sat up and pushed sleep out of his eyes.

"Maybe for a little while. We'll see. I have to work early tomorrow and help train a morning crew. Perhaps we can show your mama how to play. She might like it also."

"Yeah, that's okay. But when she yells during the video game, I think it's really for my benefit," Habib said and smiled.

"Well, whatever the reason, she loves spending time with you, baba," Abdul said as he moved Elizabeth to his other arm.

"Baba... Baba." Elizabeth giggled as she spoke.

"Now, put on your jeans and a t-shirt, then go have a bowl of your favorite cereal while Mama gets herself and Aini ready to leave. I need to feed Elizabeth before she eats my ear."

"Well, they are big ears." Habib laughed.

"Very funny, baba. Let me hear you open the dresser and get those clothes on." Abdul strode from the room, quietly laughing to himself.

Once I finished feeding Aini her breakfast, I kissed Elizabeth and Aisha as they finished preparing to leave for the doctor. I gave a thumbs-up to Habib as he brushed his teeth and grabbed the keys to our used Honda. I still can't believe the people who were willing to sell us their used cars at such a low price. Aisha just kept smiling and thanking God for HIs blessings. The compact car gets much better gas than the SUV I drove around when working for Uncle Suhaib, but I appreciate that Sam continues to offer to find a restaurant for breakfast at about the halfway point for us.

We've stopped a few times in Detroit, and today he found Duly's Place. Apparently, it's been open for ninety-three years, and the community calls it a landmark. I just want a good breakfast with my friend on my day off.

Sam had explained how to take Vernor once I got off of I-75, but I still drove up and down a few streets until I found it.

"Abdul, you found it. Isn't this place just amazing? It's like we stepped back in time, and here we are in true Americana." Sam laughed as he met Abdul at the door. "See? This long white bar counter almost runs the length of the restaurant. People just jostle on up over a stool and talk and eat with the guy next to them. And the white peg letter menu board! Along the other wall are some booths, and we can sit at one of those. But this restaurant is what is called a diner, and many have survived the years. We Michiganders call them a variant on Coney Island now, but years ago, they were fashioned after a train car."

"Really? Well, I think I remember seeing one as a special exhibit at the Henry Ford Museum. In fact, Habib and I actually had a shake." Abdul laughed and sat down in the booth across from Sam. "This place is different from some of the other places we've eaten."

"Oh, I know, and I hope you don't mind. Last time we found a good I-Hop, and we've tried to stay away from Big Boy since you started working there. I didn't want some manager to recognize you and feel pressured to run around trying to fix everything while we try to eat."

"I suppose it comes with the job when I was promoted to Restaurant Field Trainer. Although I don't mind eating our breakfast buffet, I enjoyed comparing the menu at I-Hop." Abdul couldn't stop glancing around the restaurant and looking up at the menu. "Their menu here is simple but easy to read, as long as you can read the wall."

"I know, it's not like the four or five pages that Big Boy has. I can't believe you were a manager for a year and then they promoted you to trainer." Sam shook his head. "And you and Aisha balance the family so well, especially with the two-year-old, Elizabeth."

"Our newest baby girl still grips my heart. All of our children are special. But she is the one that seemed to bind us as family. She was born just a year or so after I committed my life completely to Jesus. Our family really started to come together once I understood I needed to lead my home in God's authority. We wanted a Bible name for this daughter, and Elizabeth fit since it denotes a dedication or oath to God. Our family now has all dedicated themselves to Christ, and we're so content."

"That, my friend, is the truest of blessings. When you can see God's work in you as a father and husband, leading and serving as Jesus has called his men to lead." Sam held up his hand in praise to God. "God is so good."

"All the time, God is good," Abdul answered.

"God is working in you, my friend."

"I think if you asked about my promotion a year ago, my answer might have been less about the blessing it brought me to learn to balance my family life. I might have even complained about how I deserved the promotion and should have been in a better position in management years before."

I looked down. I remember how I used to dwell so much on my work and recognition. It was really what I worked for.

"Perhaps I would have placed blame on my uncle or father. I thank God that I'm drawn in a relationship with Jesus now, abiding in Him. I can see how much He has grown me over the past two years. I keep wondering what else God has in store for me, and my family."

"Well, my friend. As we grow in Him, and He sees we are ready for more, He then gives another adventure. Remember the parable of the stewards, and the one who invested wisely was given more to handle? I'm sure God has more for you," Sam smiled at him.

"Hello guys, how are you this morning?" A taller red-headed waitress with a southern accent stopped at their table.

"We're doing fair to middlin'," Sam answered with a big smile.

"Oh, and might you be a southern boy? I used to hear that saying often when I was working in Texas," she asked.

"Not much," he said through a chuckle. "Although I did spend some time out west, my family hails from Tennessee. I think my father picked it up along the way."

"Well, good enough. Are you two ready to order or do y'all need a few more minutes?" She flicked her long curly hair back and looked up casually to see another table that had just sat themselves. She tapped her left foot, nonchalantly.

"I don't think we're quite ready. You can go on ahead to your next table while we talk and review your menu," Sam answered.

"Our two breakfast specials are a favorite and will fill ya up quick." She winked at them.

"Thanks," Sam said as he held the menu she was pointing at.

"She's a little different as a waitress." Abdul laughed. "At Big Boy we want the servers to be relaxed and friendly but focus on the needs of the guest."

"Yeah, but in diners like this they get the people in and out quickly. And they try to remain friendly," Sam added.

"I understand that. I just can't help watching her and the other servers, since I've stayed in the business as a manager and then trainer. I pay much closer attention to the dining room staff."

"That's fine, but while you watch the staff here, try to relax enough to think about what you want to eat. Also, I'm wondering if you've finished 'Pilgrim's Progress,' after we talked about it some."

"Yes, sir, I finished it. And it proved very thought-provoking. I used some of the comments you had emailed me as I completed the book. Now I'm wondering what you've brought me this month." Abdul pushed the book across the table and sighed.

"Excellent, Abdul. I'm glad you enjoyed it. I have three books that will really strike you. I know you like to analyze things, so here you are."

Sam pulled out the books and set them on the table.

"The top one is *A Case for Christ*, by Lee Strobel. It's a journalistic look that verifies Jesus' divinity based on numerous kinds of evidence. The second one is written by the same author, and is another in the series, *A Case for Faith*, and it looks at the tough questions in life and how our faith in Jesus is still validated. And the last one is by Josh McDowell, *More than a Carpenter*. It focuses also on the evidence that Jesus is who He says He is. I know you have grown in your faith in Jesus, and these books help affirm your faith in Him. But even more, they will help to prepare you in sharing the Gospel of Jesus to others."

"I remember," Abdul said. "We talked before how we are commanded by Jesus to spread the Good News to our local community, and further."

"You got it. It's called the Great Commission, as Jesus gave it at the end of Matthew 28:18-20 and then again in Acts when He tells them of the Holy Spirit's coming upon them. God put it on my heart last night to tell you something, Abdul."

"Really? God spoke to you, like He did with Moses and Paul on the trail to Damascus?"

"Not this time," he replied with a laugh. "But I have the thought enter my mind and resonate in me as I thought about the books in my library to give you. I've thought about how much you have grown in your faith. You've studied the Bible and been involved in your men's group at your new church. I'm rather proud of you, Abdul."

"I appreciate your friendship and how you have helped to guide me in my new faith."

"Others have mentored me, and God wants me to do the same. What I'd like you to do is think about the Great Commission, and how it applies to you. How are you speaking up to others about how Jesus has changed you and your family?"

"I know Jesus commanded us to love our neighbor, but you know I don't see my neighbors much. The people around our home don't talk a lot with us. That's a little different from Dearborn where we all seemed to know each of our neighbors."

"Do you remember the parable Jesus told when one man asked a similar question? Jesus told a story about how a man was robbed and left on the roadside. Two different religious men had seen the man but did nothing to help. The third man who passed by was a Samaritan of the hated country next to Israel, and he not only helped with the man's wounds but also took him to an inn. There he paid for the room and board and any other costs. That is what truly demonstrates love for a neighbor."

"Okay, so what's the point? Do you want me to go find homeless people on the street and help feed them on my day off, Sam?"

"Not necessarily. But if you are led to do that, then you should do as the Holy Spirit leads you. What I'm saying is that you should be ready for when the Holy Spirit puts people in your path. Be ready with an answer to give them about your faith, and the hope that's in you. 1 Peter 3:15 tells us this, but to do so with gentleness and respect. Caring for the homeless and feeding them is good, but we need to find ways to meet their spiritual needs too. Jesus is the bread of life, and He said He meets our needs."

∽

Aisha and Abdul

2017-September (Seven years later)

"Aisha and Abdul! You both came! I'm glad you drove all the way out from Waterford this morning. Thank you for coming," Sam walked from behind the eight-foot folding table and gave them both a hug.

"Well, we both were able to get the day off today from work, and then we just had to find a babysitter early in the morning. It's a blessing that Aisha has good friends who support us many times over," Abdul said as he stepped back from the hug and looked down the two connecting tables. He took another step back and appraised the banner taped to the front of the tables.

"So, we return to *Faith and Reason*. Do you really get a lot of discussion from this promotion?" Abdul asked.

"Well, we are on a college campus—Henry Ford College—and everyone tries to think and reason, though I'm not sure how much faith they have here," Aisha said, looking around at the students hurrying to the Liberal Arts building for class.

"Oh, you'd be surprised. Many have faith; it's just placed in themselves or technology, and many here are Muslim. That is why I'm so pleased you two are here. You both will be able to speak of a true relationship with the one true God of the Bible," Sam nodded at them.

"You called, but even better, the Holy Spirit led us here today. So, tell us how we can best serve?" Abdul asked.

"Let's finish unpacking these books on Jesus and Islam from a Christian perspective. You'll notice I've purchased a number of titles that are controversial, which in itself may provoke someone to want to get in a conversation. Remember, we always lead them back to the Bible and who Jesus is. But you certainly at any point could speak of your own testimony and what Jesus has done in your lives." Sam pointed at the various books on the table.

"Ahh, we've read some of these," Abdul said. "Here is Lee Strobel and Josh McDowell. But Abdu Murray and Nabael Qureshi... who are they?"

"Wow, you're quick," Sam replied. "I've been meaning to have you read one of them next on our list. They're both former Muslims who converted to Christianity. Their books are very well written, and I know you both would enjoy reading them." Sam picked up one called *Seeking Allah, Finding Jesus*. He showed Abdul the cover. "This one, he wrote in 2014. I bought it at full price, and it was worth it! I find it a very valuable resource."

"Do you have any female authors in your box to put out on the table, Sam?" Aisha asked as she sorted through the box.

"Oh, here is one of my favorites: Ann Graham Lotz. *My Jesus is Everything*. I wonder if it's good."

"I'm not sure if it's a good read or not," Sam said. "But the title grabs students, and it opens up great conversations when I put it on the table. Ann says Jesus is her everything. It strikes a chord with many people, and they ask how or why."

"Well, I read some of Ann Graham Lotz in my small group, so I know I like her," Aisha said.

"Another great book is *The Reason of Reason* by Scott Cherry. He is a new local author who writes about the intersection of faith and reason. His writing is quite thoughtful," Sam said.

"Sounds like you might have to add it to my list, Sam," Abdul quipped.

"Okay, great, but how about we get started in the moment?" Aisha nudged Abdul.

"You two look over more books and some of the tracts I have. Then think about how your conversations might flow. Remember, this is practice time for you. I'm so encouraged that you two have decided to return to Dearborn and involve yourselves in ministry. I know God has huge plans for both of you," Sam said as he looked up and stopped for a moment. "Thank you, Lord!"

Sam

November 2017—Local Dearborn church

It's amazing how God works. I remember the day Aisha was working the counter at the Java Blue Cafe like it was this morning. She and I talked a bit, and I could tell then the Holy Spirit was pricking her heart. It's even more incredible how God worked through Aisha and her choices to lead Abdul to question more of his faith in Islam.

Soon, he and I became friends. And now, years later, his mind won't stop probing, applying the scriptures to his life, and seeking God's wisdom. In those early years, I prayed for them that they might come to know Jesus. I never considered that years later the family would be led by God to come alongside me in spreading the Gospel in Dearborn. Their family has completely shunned them, but their home church in Waterford, and now my church, have become their family. This sense of community is the way God has intended the church body to function, and it's such a blessing to see God make it happen.

Once the pastor completes the sermon and his prayer, then he will introduce me.

"Hello, everyone. Pastor Jim asked me to spend some time talking about our new member candidates before he takes the formal vote to bring them into our church family. He is so excited to see another set of evangelists join our church. Many of you know that Pastor served in the Middle East with his family, and we know that Jerry and Jen did as well for a number of years. I've never personally had the opportunity to serve God in the Middle East, but instead He has called me to serve in Dearborn where I mostly interact with college students at U of M Dearborn, Henry Ford College, or Wayne State University. This couple has proposed to partner with me and our church to serve the Muslim community. Both have shared their heart's desire to find creative strategies, along with ones already in place, to share the Gospel here in Dearborn. I'm sure some of you have met them, since they have done a number of events with us. They've also attended a few Sundays here and have been out to lunch with a number of you.

"Before I ask them to stand up, I would like to point out their support group. If the whole first row could stand, please," Sam invited. "Let's see if I can get the names correct. We have Pastor Pedro and his wife on the end. To their right are some other Michigan evangelists who serve locally, John and Theresa. And to their right, Carmen and Roberto, some of Abdul and Aisha's good friends. On the other side of the aisle here, well I believe here this has been the real support group." As he nodded in their direction, all seven ladies of various ages started to laugh. "I understand this is the small group that Aisha and Carmen attend on a weekly basis, and these prayer warriors have lifted the whole family up to God over several years. Thanks to all of you for coming today. They not only came to support the family, but also to represent them as the sending church for this missionary family. I have the greatest pleasure of formally introducing the newest candidates to our church. Abul and Aisha, please stand up to my left. And their children, Habib, Aini, and Elizabeth."

The whole church stood and said, "Amen."

"Well, Pastor, I'm not sure how much more of an affirmation you'll need. I think we want to welcome them into our fellowship."

Acknowledgments

I would like to deeply thank Scott Cherry for his continuous and thoughtful suggestions in editing. He is a great friend who got caught up in my vision of the story of Aisha and Abdul.
Thanks to Jon and Jayne Frazier in reviewing the story and making recommendations.
Thanks also to Wissam Al-Aethawi and Adam Adam for their encouragement as beta readers.

I appreciate the efforts of Ron Epperson and Jim Stolt in assisting with the final edits of the manuscript.
Prayerful thanks to a few good men who have consistently been lifting this project up to God in heaven.
A heartfelt bit of gratitude to you the reader that's taken the time to read the story, as you journey on the road set before you.
Most importantly, I want to give thanks and glory to my Lord Jesus, that He may be glorified in what I have written.

About the Author

Wayne Stolt resides in Dearborn Heights, Michigan. He has over forty years of experience working in the food service industry, with the last twenty-two years in teaching Culinary Arts and Restaurant Management. Wayne has a bachelor's degree in Hospitality Management from Eastern Michigan and a Master's degree in teaching from Wayne State University. He is certified as a ProStart Educator with the National Restaurant Association Education Foundation and a Certified Hospitality Educator through the American Hotel and Lodging Educational

Institute. Wayne is married to Patricia, with two daughters. He enjoys working in local ministries with others in the area. Wayne appreciates good fiction to read, a bicycle ride in the park along the river, and dining in a well-organized dining room with good food. Wayne's website can be found at www.immigrantsdreams.com, where he has links to his books and blogs he has written.

If you have enjoyed this story of Abdul and Aisha, please leave a review on the author's page on Amazon. Consider reading Wayne's first novel that tells the story of Roberto.